Booty Bones

Center Point
Large Print

Also by Carolyn Haines and available from
Center Point Large Print:

Bones of a Feather
Bonefire of the Vanities
Smarty Bones

**This Large Print Book carries the
Seal of Approval of N.A.V.H.**

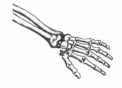

Booty Bones

Carolyn Haines

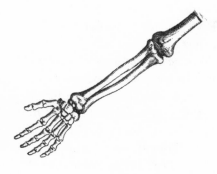

CENTER POINT LARGE PRINT
THORNDIKE, MAINE

The text of this Large Print edition is unabridged.
In other aspects, this book may vary
from the original edition.
Printed in the United States of America
on permanent paper.
Set in 16-point Times New Roman type.

ISBN: 978-1-62899-227-4

Library of Congress Cataloging-in-Publication Data

Haines, Carolyn.
Booty bones / Carolyn Haines. — Center Point Large Print edition.
pages ; cm
Summary: "Sarah Booth Delaney's vacation on Dauphin Island goes
disastrously awry when she's asked to solve the murder of a treasure-
hunter"—Provided by publisher.
ISBN 978-1-62899-227-4 (library binding : alk. paper)
1. Delaney, Sarah Booth (Fictitious character)—Fiction.
    2. Women private investigators—Mississippi—Fiction.
    3. Murder—Investigation—Fiction. 4. Mississippi—Fiction.
    5. Large type books. I. Title.
PS3558.A329B68 2014b
813′.54—dc23
                                                        2014019452

For Aleta Boudreaux—
for too many reasons to count

Acknowledgments

When I started writing *Booty Bones*, I knew only two things. The book would have something to do with pirates. And it would explore some of Jitty's secrets. Many other things happen in this book, some for which I was totally unprepared. Sarah Booth and I both had to accept events we couldn't foresee and I couldn't predict.

This is the fourteenth Bones book. I've spent many hours each day for the past fifteen years with these characters. When people tell me (and how I love this!) that the characters are real to them—"just like friends"—I'm not shocked. I've spent a large part of my life with Sarah Booth, Jitty, Tinkie, Cece, Millie, Madame Tomeeka, and the men of Zinnia. There have been times when I tried my hardest to stop Sarah Booth from some headstrong measure (just as I would my flesh and blood friends). Often I fail, and Sarah Booth and I learn the lessons generated together.

I want to thank my readers, who approach these books with such enthusiasm and joy. For those who "talk me up" to their friends and relatives, I thank you. For those who post reviews, I thank you. For those who buy my books and check them out of libraries, I thank you. For those who attend book signings and visit with me, I thank you.

There is a strange bond between writer/ characters/readers that develops, especially with series characters. My only regret is that when I do travel to a signing or conference, I never have enough time to visit with people. It is often a whirlwind of meetings without the "have a cup of coffee and visit for a spell" that I would enjoy. My chosen life as owner/operator of Good Fortune Farm Rescue is demanding of my time, and I yield to the needs of the animals.

I also want to thank my agent, Marian Young. We've been well-matched for longer than either of us wants to count. Onward!

My editors at St. Martin's, Kelley Ragland and Elizabeth Lacks, always make the book better. As do the copy editors. In my writing life I've been fortunate to work with editors who find a problem, offer suggestions, and yet never tamper with the concept of the book. That is a talent, and Kelley and Elizabeth have it in spades.

A big thank you to Suzann Ledbetter, who is always my first reader and the Darth Vader of wordiness. If we ever plotted a crime together we could become wealthy—if I didn't talk too much.

I love this cover. Many thanks to artist Hiro Kimura and jacket designer David Rotstein.

Join me on Facebook to keep up with my foolishness. And please sign up for my newsletter at www.carolynhaines.com. I really have a lot of mischief planned for the future. Don't miss out!

1

The setting sun casts gold upon the white beach, and the azure curl of surf takes on a lavender cast as it rushes the shore and spreads a mantle of foam. The waves crest inches from my bare feet, a rhythmic tidal pull that comforts me, promising that life continues. The end of an October day is nothing less than stunning on the small barrier island named for French royalty: Dauphin Island, Alabama.

Graf Milieu, my fiancé, is in the beach cottage I've rented for a week. My hope is that Graf will find walking in the sand good therapy for his gun-shot leg and the island's beauty healing to his injured spirit. Graf's wounds go much deeper than a shattered bone, and they are my fault. He was abducted, shot, and held prisoner without medical care because my private investigative work spilled over into his life.

But that is the past and cannot be changed, no matter how hard I wish it. What I'm planning with this Gulf Coast getaway is to protect the future.

Sweetie Pie, my loyal hound, roots her nose into the back of my armpit, letting me know she sympathizes with my worry. My dog and Pluto, the black cat who lives with us at Dahlia House, my ancestral Mississippi Delta home, are here

with me at the beach to aid in Graf's recupera-
tion. I need all the help I can get.

The wind is chilly off the water, and my butt is
damp from sitting in the sand. Pluto struggles
toward me, his dainty little paws sinking with
each step. With a kitty sigh, he plops into my lap.
He has only contempt for the surf and for anyone
who admires water—even the dazzling aqua
waves of the Gulf of Mexico. Water is necessary
for fish, and that's as far as Pluto is willing to go.

"Where's Graf?" I ask the critters, hoping he is
not far behind them.

They both look back toward the beach cottage.
Sweetie's long, delicate ears droop more than
usual. The critters are worried about Graf, too.
He's been in a terrible state since he was shot.
The surgery to repair the bone was successful,
but the recovery has been painful. The doctors
saved his leg, but there is a chance he will always
limp. Graf is an actor with a good chance of
becoming a movie star. Physical disabilities don't
fit into that equation. He's fighting hard against
the anger, fear, and depression that are normal
emotions accompanying such an injury.

And have I mentioned this is all my fault?

The wind whips off the water and sends a salty
spray into my face, and for a moment I remember
this same beach some twenty-five years earlier,
when I vacationed here with my parents. The
beach cottages were much plainer, less luxurious,

and no oil-drilling rigs dotted the horizon. The sand was pristine then and hadn't suffered the thousands of gallons of oil from BP's Deep Water Horizon well that blew and polluted the Gulf. My parents were alive, and I was safe, expecting only the best of a bright future. Life has certainly taken me down a peg or six.

Sweetie's cold nose against my armpit brings me back from those carefree childhood days. The sun has dropped below the horizon, and the sky-line to the east is swiftly changing from peacock-blue to indigo. Time to gird my loins and do battle against Graf's worries. I shall bring joy back to his life. I shall do it with my bare intention and will.

I stand up suddenly, just in time to catch the image of a woman clad in widow's weeds on the other side of the sand dune. She is there one moment and gone the next. Sweetie sees her, too, as does Pluto, who puts on his Halloween arch. Like most felines, Pluto disdains unexpected company.

"Who was that?" I asked, even as I loped over the sand in pursuit of the strange figure.

When I rounded the dune, the light was fleeing the sky, but I could make out the feminine sil-houette. Her antebellum dress grazed the sand and belled out behind her as the Gulf wind struck the skirt. A black veil floated like the banner of a dark empire. What the hell was going on?

Sweetie passed me and gave chase, but she

wasn't baying like she would if she was on a scent. Pluto, too, for all of his heft and waddling belly, outdistanced me. The phantom floated across the deep sand while I floundered.

"You! Wait up!" I called. No one—not dog, cat, or woman—slowed his pace. I notched it up to a full-fledged run. "Hey! Stop, dammit!"

The stranger slowed and confronted me. Her gown and veil popped in the gusting air, and I was reminded of Deborah Kerr in the *The Innocents*, the film adaptation of "The Turn of the Screw." Brilliant and terrifying.

The figure seemed to wait for me, and I thought of death. I'd always expected the Grim Reaper to be male, but this black-clad raven of gloom persuaded me otherwise.

"What do you want?" I slowed to a stop in the deep sand two dozen yards from her. She was slender with perfect posture, but her features were obscured by the mourning attire.

She said nothing.

Sweetie and Pluto were frozen in place only a few feet in front of me. They made not a sound.

If this was death come to lurk around the shadows of my life, she would not find hospitality. "You've taken too much from me. Get away from here. You have no business with me or the people and animals I love. Be gone!"

"I've lost, too," she said. "More than anyone should."

In the softness of her voice and the plaintive tone, I realized this was no threat, but someone who knew suffering. "What are you?"

"A friend."

"A widow from the distant past?" Judging from the dress style, I'd estimate the mid-1800s. It took me a moment, but then I knew. "Jitty?"

She lifted the veil, and I saw sorrow etched in her mocha skin.

"Funeral crepe? That's the best you could do for a beach costume? No polka-dot bikini? No tawdry flip-flops and big hat? Miss Fashion Plate, where is your style?" I vacillated between relief and annoyance. "You scared the life out of me."

"I'm a haint. That's what haints do—we frighten people."

"But you're *my* haint, and upsetting me is not allowed. You live by the rules of the Great Beyond, but I live by Delaney rules, and I just wrote that one."

Her chuckle seemed to hold the fading sunlight for a moment longer.

"Why are you here, Jitty, dressed like a mourner from the eighteen hundreds?" My momentary humor was gone, and worry returned.

"Life is a cycle, Sarah Booth. You know this."

"I do. I don't like it, but I know it. I'm in the summer of life, and so is Graf. There's no cycle crap happening here that needs widow's weeds."

13

"Perhaps not." She made no promises. It was against the rules of the Great Beyond for her to tell me anything about the future. "But remember the wheel of life turns again and again."

"If you're warning me Graf is in some new danger, just spit it out."

"The French call orgasm 'the little death.' " Her smile was luminous. And still sad. "At the peak of joy is always the descent into death."

Too bad there was only sand around. Had there been rocks, I would have picked one up and thrown it at her. "Say it plain."

She shook her head. "So much history has happened on this island beach. The French settled here and named it Massacre Island because their first discovery was a mound created from human bones. It was a Native American burial site." She looked out toward the water, and the last lingering bits of peachy light played across her face. "Not a bad place to meet an end."

"And not a good place either. Who are you mourning here? Coker died in the war, not on a barrier island."

"Very true. My husband died on a blood-soaked battlefield with Alice's husband, your great-great-great-grandfather. But there's history here on Dauphin Island, Sarah Booth. Important history. I suspect you'll find out soon enough."

She flickered in and out, as was her wont when she was ready to take a powder.

"Jitty, will Graf be okay?"

But there was only the sound of the surf and the wind whipping my shirt like a tattered flag. Sweetie, Pluto, and I turned toward the three-story cottage. A light bloomed in an upstairs window, a smudge of cheer against the star-spangled night.

It was time to make dinner for Graf. I had a plan to enliven his spirits. A secret plan. And it would work, because I had no other alternative.

I took the stairs to the second floor. All of the beach cottages were built on pilings, a precaution against a tidal surge, but it also gave us a primo view of the Gulf. I found Graf on the balcony, leaning on the railing and staring out at the wind-whipped water.

I poured glasses of red wine and took them outside. I handed him a glass and then snaked my arm around his waist. He'd lost weight, and he didn't need to.

"Thank you, Sarah Booth. You've been a perfect Florence Nightingale."

"Florence Nightingale died a single woman. Not going to be my fate, Graf Milieu. Just giving you a heads-up."

The long drive and then the lengthy walk on the beach had tired him. I traced the lines in his face with gentle fingertips as he spoke. "Once I'm healed, I promise, I'll make an honest woman of

15

you." He drew me close and kissed me with lingering tenderness. "I'm getting stronger each day. Walking on the beach and climbing the stairs at the cottage—exactly what the doctor ordered. Thank you for convincing me to come here."

"I am your Gale Storm with full attention to social and recreational activities, and never forget it." I tiptoed and kissed his chin. "I've booked a tour of the old fort for tomorrow. This place has a fascinating history. Native Americans, French, Spanish, British, Confederacy, and United States. This area has been ruled by a number of different nations."

"You take the fort tour and I'll work out on the beach." Graf sipped his wine and gazed at the crashing surf. The wind ruffled his dark hair. He needed a haircut and a shave. He'd come so close to dying, and he'd fought so bravely to regain the use of his leg. Sometimes, though, depression snuck up on him. Doc Sawyer had warned me to be on the lookout and to keep him distracted.

"Aarrgh! Disobey me and ye'll walk the gangplank!" I used my finger to poke him in the ribs like a sword.

"Am I going to have to endure pirate parodies for the whole week?" he said teasingly.

"Maybe. I discovered the Gulf waters were swarming with pirates and buccaneers. And the fort here, Fort Gaines, played a vital role in the

16

War Between the States. Also in the two world wars."

"I never realized you were such a history buff, Sarah Booth. I always viewed you as a girl of the moment. All flash and dazzle and heat. Some very interesting heat."

My heart surged with hope. Since the gunshot, Graf had avoided intimacy. I'd seen him staring at the nasty wound on his leg and now the glaring scar. He was no longer physical perfection. I didn't care, but he did. I had to play this cool. "Wars don't interest me a lot. But pirates—now that's another story. I love pirate tales. Especially stories involving treasures."

"Shiver me timbers." Graf swept me backward, bending me over his arm as he held me and rasped his beard along my cheek and neck.

I tried to push him away, but he was too strong. "What does that even mean? You've been watching bad pirate movies. Next thing I know, you'll have an eye patch."

"And maybe a parrot." He drew me to my feet with ease. "Actually, I know a little about sailing. The phrase comes from the ship pounding up and down in rough seas or battle. The concussion would rattle the mast, which was made of wood."

"I may have to reconsider my engagement." I held out my left hand with the beautiful diamond. "I'm not sure I want to marry a know-it-all."

"No danger of that. But I can read. Maybe you should give it a try."

I punched his arm lightly. "Oh, I brought some books for the beach. I intend to enjoy the surf and an adventure while you complete your physical therapy. I can watch and make sure you're doing it right."

Before I'd packed to come to Dauphin Island, I'd met Doc Sawyer, my friend and family doctor, at Millie's Café for a cup of coffee and a chat. I needed his professional advice on dealing with Graf's emotional and physical wounds.

"Graf has to find his way, Sarah Booth. It isn't just the shattered bone and the pain. This injury has changed how he sees himself. It's shaken loose everything he ever believed about his life and his future."

"I have to help him."

Doc took my hand and gave it a hard squeeze. "Be there. Be strong. Supportive. Caring. But don't make the mistake of pandering to him or trying to make this easier. He'll resent you, and he'll hate himself because you pity him. Don't coddle him and for God's sake don't let him act like a tyrant."

I clung to those words as I inhaled the salty air and gripped the railing of the balcony. "I brought some cards. Care for a few hands of poker?"

"In a little while. I'm happy here, listening to the surf. To be honest, I'm tired. I never thought learning to walk could be so exhausting. How do babies do it?"

"They don't know any better," I said, kissing him. "I'll put the salad together. We can eat when you're ready. No rush." I picked up his empty glass and left him in the night and wind.

"Sarah Booth?"

I turned slowly, trying to disguise the hope I felt. Would he suggest an appetizer before dinner? "Yes?"

"I love the way you help me. You don't have to, though. I don't blame you for what happened."

"I blame me."

"Stop it." He spoke gently. "I'm healing, and you have to do the same. If you continue to blame yourself, this will always be between us. No one could have predicted what Gertrude would do. It wasn't your fault."

"Right now, let's focus on getting you back one hundred percent. After that, I'll work on my guilt issues."

"It's a deal." He blew me a kiss. "Just remember, I love you."

I took that tiny grain of joy and savored it as I went to the kitchen and threw together a curried shrimp salad, one of his favorites.

Sunday dawned with a mantle of lavender and gold. October was closing out, and the beach—normally filled with tourists and surf lovers—was empty in the chill morning. Graf had fallen asleep on the sofa, and I had left him there. It hurt me that he hadn't come to share my bed, but Cece had given me a primer on the subject.

Cece Dee Falcon, my friend, knew more about body image than most psychologists. She'd once been Cecil. Only her strong will and intense self-knowledge had given her the strength to fight family and often her community in a quest to become the person she was meant to be.

"Graf feels diminished," Cece had warned me. "Don't push intimacy. He has to see himself as sexually desirable before he engages. Let him come to you, Sarah Booth. And don't take it personally. This isn't about you. It's all about him."

So I tiptoed past him with Sweetie and Pluto following, and we went out on the sand so I could smoke a cigarette. I didn't do it often—had in fact fought and beaten the demon tobacco for years. Now I was cutting myself a little slack. Graf and I would both recover our strength and put this behind us, including the smokes.

A child's laughter caught Sweetie's attention, and she bounded over the sand dunes and disappeared. She was a gentle dog, but I didn't want her size to intimidate a kid. I stood up and followed with a disgruntled Pluto at my side. The cat was not a fan of early mornings either. The tang of salt in the air only made it worse for the water-disdaining feline.

I stopped on top of the dune. Down the beach, Sweetie Pie ran circles around a child with flowing brown curls that hung to her waist. She looked to be eight or nine. When Sweetie paused, the child spun cartwheels in the sand. She was too far away for a clear view, but her delight in the beach and water was obvious.

I'd been happy at her age. Endless laughter and adventure. The joy of sun and sand and movement. Shading my eyes with my hand, I searched for an adult. The surf could be dangerous, and the girl was far too young to be outside alone.

A slender woman with long blondish curls waved a scarf, and the child skipped to her and took her hands for a swing. Mother and daughter, I thought. They knelt side by side and lavished affection on Sweetie. One day Graf and I would have a child that beautiful. Two. A girl and a boy. Or two girls. Or two boys. It really didn't matter, as long as they were healthy.

Fear had kept me from starting my own family. I lost everyone I loved, and I didn't believe I could recover if something happened to my child. So I'd run away from the possibility. I'd held Graf off, postponing wedding dates and potential children. My miscarriage hadn't helped. Now, though, I was done with fear and running. Graf and I would build a family. I was strong enough now.

Not to mention the thing Jitty kept a countdown on—my biological clock was ticking away. This week, while my fiancé and I were on the beautiful beach, I would commit to Graf and a bicoastal life that included children, movies, horses, travel, and a deep and abiding love for my husband. And Jitty, of course.

The mother and daughter raced down the beach, and Sweetie returned to me, ears flopping and tail wagging with delight. Pluto, on the other hand, stared at me with golden-green eyes that seemed to say, "Look at that stupid hound. There is nothing more pathetic than a dog."

"Let's make some coffee," I suggested. "Graf and I have a guided tour of Fort Gaines at ten. Time to roust him up and get him ready for the day."

Fort Gaines was built for people much shorter than my height, and poor Graf had to stoop to pass under some of the arched entrances. The group for the Sunday morning tour was small, a handful of fall beachcombers taking advantage of the October weather. In the summer, I could imagine the fort would be crowded with tourists.

Our tour guide, Angela Trotter, was a slender young woman with navy blue eyes and a love of the old fort and its checkered history. Originally used as a port and defense point by the French explorer Iberville, the barrier island, which has shifted and changed shapes and locations as a result of hurricanes, played a role in the development of the Gulf Coast rim. Military strategists had used Dauphin Island to defend the vulnerable —and valuable—inner waterways. The island had also been a waypoint for pirates, and Angela Trotter brought the past to life.

"One of the most colorful pirates to sail these waters was Jean Lafitte. A French nobleman by birth, he attracted the best sailors, some of them French nobility who were more in the model of anarchists than Black Beard pirates."

Angela outlined Lafitte's colorful career—the island stronghold he built off the coast of Louisiana on an island in Barataria Bay, and how he declared the island a free state, where slaves kidnapped from the cotton, rice, and sugarcane fields were given the full privilege of citizenship.

"One such highborn lieutenant of Lafitte's was a pirate named Armand Couteau," Angela said. "It's rumored he hid a treasure worth millions on Dauphin Island. Many have hunted for the lost gold using all types of equipment, but nothing has ever been found. Most believe the hiding place is now underwater. Savage storms have shifted the island's contours too many times to count."

Unfortunately, I couldn't give the tour my full attention, because I was worried about Graf. He'd gone for a long walk up and down the beach before we came to the fort, and now his face was pinched with exhaustion and fatigue. He was trying too hard, another thing the doctors had warned me about.

When the guide moved us along the barricades that gave a glorious view of the Gulf, Graf lagged behind. I dropped back to walk with him.

"Go with the group," he urged me. "My leg is hurting, and I'll take it slow for a little while. Make notes so you can tell me all the stories." His smile was more grimace.

"Let's head back to the cottage. I'm tired, too."

"Don't mollycoddle me." He ran his hand through his hair. "I'm sorry. I didn't mean to snap. I'm just spoiling it for you. Go listen to the tour. I'll catch up in a bit."

"I came to spend time with you," I said. "The tour isn't important. Look"—I pointed to the south—"This is the place where Union naval commander Admiral David Farragut tried to navigate the mine-salted Mobile Bay and declared, 'Damn the torpedoes, full speed ahead.' "

Movement across the fort's yard caught my eye. The blond woman from the beach disappeared into one of the old powder buildings. If she was on the tour, she'd dropped out to pursue her own interests. Maybe she was a local who already knew the history. I was about to ask Graf if he'd seen her when footsteps alerted me that someone approached.

The young tour guide joined us. "You guys

okay?" she asked. "I haven't bored you into a coma, have I?"

"We're just enjoying the view," I answered. "My fiancé is a little tired."

"We'll wait for you in the hold." She didn't give us a chance to decline. She hurried away to catch up to the group.

"Ready to rejoin?" I asked.

"Let's see this to the end. Then I'm going to need a hot soak in that lovely bathtub and a long nap."

"You've got it." I turned to follow him and saw the blond woman. She was half in shadow behind the powder house, and her attention was directed at Graf.

I wondered if she recognized him from one of his films, or if she was wondering what injury he'd sustained. With any luck, he'd heal perfectly before the Hollywood gossip machine found out he'd ever been hurt.

2

It was lunchtime when the tour concluded, and Graf and I headed to the parking lot.

"Want to grab something to eat in Mobile?" I asked. "You could nap while I drive."

"I'm more tired than hungry. Why don't you run into Mobile and look around a little. I'll clean up, have a rest on the sofa, and cook dinner for us when you return."

His limp was more pronounced—he'd really pushed himself. "Sounds like a plan. What shall I pick up to cook?"

"Excuse me!"

Angela Trotter's long, purposeful stride held a natural grace that made others stop and watch her. "I'm sorry, but I was just concerned. Is everything okay?"

"We're fine. My fiancé is recovering from an injury, and while walking is good for him, it's very tiring."

"I could arrange for a scooter if you'd like to come back. No charge."

"That's very generous." Graf looked uncomfortable. "I'm healing. Walking is exactly what the doctor ordered."

"You missed a lot of the tour."

In her quest to be kind, she was only pointing

out Graf's disability. "You're very thoughtful," I said. Pulling a business card from my pocket, I handed it to her. "I'd love to come back. When you set up another tour, could you give me a call?"

"Will do." She pushed the card into her jeans pocket. "Have a great stay on the island." And she was gone.

"Why does everyone feel they have to make special allowances for a cripple?" Graf asked.

"She's really proud of the history of the island. She just wants to share her enthusiasm."

"Sorry, didn't mean to sound ungrateful. It's just hard when all people see is my injury."

"At the rate you're improving, by the end of the week no one will even know you were hurt. You just have to build up your stamina again."

He nodded. "You're my private cheering squad. Thanks, Sarah Booth."

When I was pulling into the cottage, my cell phone rang with a number I didn't recognize. Angela Trotter was on the line. I signaled Graf to go on inside while I took the call.

"Your card says you're a private investigator. I googled you. You have a remarkable success rate," Angela said.

"Okay." I didn't know where this was headed.

"My father was murdered here on the island. I want to hire you to investigate his death."

I wasn't prepared for a job offer. "I'm on

vacation. My fiancé is recovering from an injury—"

"Sustained when he was kidnapped because of a case you were working. I know the timing is awful, but I'm desperate."

She'd done her homework, but that didn't change the facts. "I'm sorry. I can't help you." The one thing I didn't need to do was take on a case. Graf was my priority.

"An innocent man is serving a life sentence. He's been in jail for over a year. I need your help to free him. Larry Wofford didn't kill my father, but he'll rot in prison unless you help me find out who did."

Her tactics might not be fair, but they were effective. My father had been a lawyer in a rural Mississippi county. He'd stood up for the rights of the poor and those whose skin color set them up for mistreatment and injustice. He'd taken cases pro bono when he felt an innocent man was at risk of being railroaded. Unknowingly, Angela Trotter had pressed my hot button.

"Can we at least meet to talk about it?" she asked. "I'm parked on the road in front of your cottage."

I glanced toward the road—a little blue compact idled beside the drive. Since she was already there, I didn't see the harm in hearing her out. "Sure, the least I can do is listen."

In less then a minute she was parked and

standing beside me, the wind riffling her dark curls. "I realize you're here to be with your fiancé, not take on a new client. But I've tried to work with the sheriff here, and with some local private investigators. I haven't gotten anywhere." Tears shimmered in her eyes, but she managed to control them.

"I have to put Graf as my first priority. He needs me now."

"He's hurting. I understand." Her chin lifted half an inch. "But you could look into this in your off time. Just see what you can turn up while you're here. Do it when Mr. Milieu is resting. I wouldn't ask more than that."

How to explain that an investigation deserved a hundred percent of my efforts and so did Graf. "I'll be happy to find someone local who can help. I'll only be here a week. That's not enough time."

"I want Delaney Detective Agency. It's like fate brought you to me. I can't help but believe providence is at work. Will you just do what you can? At the end of the week, I won't ask more." And then she added the killer. "Larry Wofford has already lost a year of his life. Every day that passes is another cheat against him. My father was brutally murdered on his own boat because he claimed to have found a pirate's treasure. Someone killed him for a stupid legend that likely wasn't even true."

"Ms. Trotter—"

"Call me Angela. I'll pay your full fee. No matter what you do or don't find."

I hesitated, and she jumped on it.

"Thank you. Can we get together later today so I can give you the full story? I'll have a check ready for you, and I'll give you all the information I've gathered. Thank you, Ms. Delaney. Thank you so much."

She never allowed me a chance to say otherwise. She jumped in her car and drove away. I debated whether I should call her back and make it clear I wasn't taking the case. Then I reconsidered. Everyone urged me to allow Graf to find his own path. Perhaps this was providence, giving me a focus that kept me from mother-henning him to death.

When I left the beach house to meet Angela, Graf was asleep. I'd told him about Angela's request, and he'd encouraged me to at least explore the details of the case. We'd lunched on leftover curried shrimp salad, and Graf had taken a mild pain pill and conked out on the sofa. Because I was meeting Angela at the marina, I took Sweetie Pie and Pluto along with me. The marina might provide some interesting aromas for a bored kit-kat.

Angela was standing on the dock when I pulled up. Sweetie and Pluto brought up the rear as I walked down the wooden pier to a grand old sailboat, the *Miss Adventure.*

"She's a beauty," I said.

Angela bit her bottom lip. "I spent summers on this boat with my dad, helping him hunt for pirate's booty. He always believed he would hit the grand slam of treasures one day." The softness that had touched her face hardened. "He believed he could make up for neglecting my mother and me. Like he could undo time and rewind all the recitals and field hockey games he missed. All the nights my mother worked a second job to pay the mortgage." Her laugh was sad and bitter. "He never lost his dream. And the night he was killed, he called me to tell me he'd hit the mother lode. He'd figured out where Armand Couteau had hidden the great Esmeralda treasure."

"Did he find it?" The idea of a real pirate's gold excited me. What kid hadn't read adventure tales and dreamed of finding fabulous wealth?

"He was killed before he could claim it. If someone else found it, they sure kept it quiet." She shook her head. "One of the reasons I've stayed here, though, is to keep an eye out. The person who finds that treasure will be my father's real killer."

We stepped aboard the boat, Pluto with more grace than I'd ever attributed to him. For a porcine pussy, he could make an elegant leap when the mood struck.

"My father was shot in the chest in his cabin." Angela led the way down a steep, narrow stairway. She stopped outside a door, her hand on the worn wood.

The boat shifted in the water, and I realized I'd need practice to gain my sea legs. Technically, I wasn't a boat person. Given a choice between a boat and land, I would take mother earth every single time, but I needed to investigate the place where Mr. Trotter had died.

"Did you live on the boat with your father?" I asked.

"Only part time, when I was a kid. After my parents divorced, I spent the summers helping with Dad's treasure hunts. During the school year, I lived with my aunt Molly. My mom died when I was sixteen. After I graduated college, I came to Alabama and went to work for the newspaper in Mobile."

Angela had had a rough go of it, for sure. "Did you talk often with your dad?"

"At least once a week. Dad was independent. And he was obsessed with the Esmeralda treasure. He'd worked on it, off and on, for two decades. It was a puzzle he could never walk away from." She hesitated before adding, "Our relationship was a bit thorny."

"So tell me about the treasure."

She leaned against the closed door. "After the pirate Jean Lafitte moved down to the Texas coast, Armand Couteau became the most notorious pirate on these waters. He was a relative of Napoleon and, from all accounts, a handsome man with great charm. He'd attack the Spanish and French galleons headed into Mobile Bay or New Orleans, rob them of their riches, and send the shamed crews into port. Couteau wasn't a ruthless man, but he was a pirate. It was said he entertained the wives and daughters of the Mobile and New Orleans ruling class right under the noses of their husbands and fathers."

I could only imagine the appeal of such a man. "There's something about a scoundrel that heats the blood."

She laughed. "How true. At any rate, Couteau and his crew of pirates intercepted a Spanish ship that was bringing a young girl of noble birth to Dauphin Island. She was set to marry one of the fort's commanders. With her was a huge dowry of gold and jewels."

I saw how this story would go. "Couteau intercepted the ship and took the dowry and the girl."

"Well, he was a man of honor. He declared a cease-fire and escorted Esmeralda to shore and into the arms of her betrothed. While he was onshore, the Spanish ship was burned. Some say the fort's commander ordered the ship burned. Others blamed the pirates. But the treasure either sank or was taken by the pirates. My father believed Couteau brought the treasure ashore and hid it."

"Is there any evidence the story is true?" I had to bring a little skepticism to the high-seas tale of romance and gold.

"My father searched the records, and one Jean-Jacques Baton, the fort's second in command, was married to an Esmeralda Cortez about the time this would have occurred."

So far, so good. "And what did your father tell you about the treasure."

"He was so excited the night he called. I'd never heard him so over the moon. He apologized to me about the neglect. He told me he'd never loved anyone but my mother and that he would make up all I'd lost out on. He wanted me to finish my graduate degree. He intended to retire the *Miss Adventure* and buy a house, and he said he would be home every night, should I ever want to see him." Her voice cracked, but she held it together. "He never got a chance to make any of it happen."

The last little vestige of guilt at taking the case evaporated. Angela needed my help, and Graf was fine with it.

"Tell me exactly what he said," I asked.

"Dad said he'd found the key. I asked him what he meant, and he said he knew how to find the treasure. He had a list of things he had to accomplish, and the first was to buy back a spyglass he'd sold. Once that happened, he said he'd have the treasure within a week. He was so *positive* he'd figured it out."

"Your father was a treasure hunter. He spent his life chasing a dream. Is it possible this was all just wishful thinking?" I had to ask, and I was as gentle as I could be.

Angela slid the door open to a spotless bedroom/ office. Every trace of the murder had been removed, but it didn't take much imagination to understand what had happened. The space was small but tastefully decorated with what looked like original artwork in a modern style. Shades of blue, green, and teal painted on a translucent sheet rather than canvas reminded me of the crystal water on the south side of the island. A blank spot on the wall indicated someone had removed one of the paintings.

"Dad dabbled in painting," Angela said. She went to the blank spot. "He gave a lot of paintings away, but the one that was here—it was his last. I tried to find who he gave it to, but no luck." She was lost in memory for a moment. "He was like that. Just giving things away."

I continued my examination of the state-room. A bunk took up the wall to the left, and a large desk was centered in the remainder of the space. Built in filing cabinets and storage lined the wall to the right. The only space for a body was on the floor behind or in front of the desk. "You believe he found the treasure?"

"Dad was a dreamer, that's true. This was different, though. He was excited, but also grounded. Whatever it was he'd found, it was something solid."

"What do you think he meant by the key?"

"The way he said it, it had to be a physical thing. Maybe even a real key. It wasn't just an idea or a mental thing. He'd found something physical."

"And you searched the boat looking for it afterwards?"

"I can only assume the killer took it."

"But the killer hasn't used it to retrieve the treasure?"

"Not to my knowledge."

"Which leads me to believe the killer doesn't understand the value of this key or hasn't figured out how to use it."

Angela's hand brushed across the teak desk. The gesture spoke more eloquently of her loss than words. "My conclusion exactly."

"Do you have any idea who killed your father?"

"I wish I did. I'd confront him. I'd make him confess."

Not the smartest move. Someone who had killed once would do so again. "How long since your father died?"

"Eighteen months. Larry was convicted a year ago. I haven't found a damn thing to help apprehend my father's murderer."

"And yet you haven't given up." She was as hardheaded as I was.

"I can't bring my dad back, but Larry Wofford was falsely convicted. He said he didn't do it, and I believe him. I won't give up trying to help him, and I need to find something before his appeal date." She sat on the edge of her father's desk. "So you'll help me?"

"As much as I can without neglecting Graf. And only for this week. I'm headed to New Orleans on Saturday, and I won't be back this way."

"Deal." She reached out her hand and I shook it. She pulled a check from her pocket. "Is five thousand enough?"

I pushed the check back at her. "Let's see how much time I have to work on it. It won't be a lot." I really didn't feel I could accomplish much, but I'd try. She carried a lonely burden, and some-times just a friend on the road was a big help.

"What's your first step?" she asked.

"I'll call the sheriff's office in Mobile. I need to talk to the officers who investigated and check with the court clerk to see the trial transcript."

"Sheriff Benson is a complete ass," she warned me. "When I was a reporter, I did some stories that teed him off. He won't go out of his way to help."

"He doesn't have to help; all he has to do is not obstruct." Besides, I had my own secret weapon. Coleman Peters, the sheriff of Sunflower County, where I lived, would call the Mobile County sheriff and ask him to cooperate with me. Most lawmen offered courtesy to their fellow officers. Maybe Coleman could work a little magic.

"When will you start?" she asked.

I checked my watch. It was after three on a Sunday afternoon. "The courthouse is closed, so I'll try in the morning. I'll let you know what happens."

"Thank you," Angela said.

"Don't thank me until I get some results."

3

Graf was ready for an outing and interested in the sparse details of Angela's case when I got back to the cottage. The day was sunny, and the wind brought the tantalizing smell of salt and faraway places as we strolled along the abandoned beach. I chose a path near the surf line, where the sand was firmer and easier for Graf to navigate. We both rolled up our pants and walked barefoot in the edge of the foam.

I caught Graf's fingers in mine and was gratified when he squeezed my hand and held it, his thumb kindling a fire as it circled my sensitive palm. I was relieved to see the sensual, loving Graf emerging.

This was what I wanted my future to be: Graf and me, hand in hand in the surf with Pluto and Sweetie Pie frolicking beside us. Well, frolicking was a bit too enthusiastic for Pluto. The cat was not at all thrilled with our afternoon activity.

"Graf, I have a special surprise planned for you." I wanted to ease him toward the idea of a beach wedding. We'd planned on marrying in Ireland in April, but I didn't want to wait. I'd checked into the marriage-license application. Easy-peasy. I only needed to fulfill the three-day residency requirement and apply for the license.

Graf's injury had taught me one thing—the future was not mine to plan. All I had was the here and now. And I meant to make hay while the sun shone.

"A surprise?"

"A good one. Just for us."

"What we have right now is enough for me, Sarah Booth. I'm trying to adjust to a new . . . idea of myself. I don't know if I can maintain my balance with surprises thrown at me."

Why not just stab me in the heart? Wouldn't that be kinder? And quicker? "Of course," I said, forcing a casual tone. I was pushing too hard, too quickly. "Nothing you can't handle. I promise."

"Good. I feel like I'm on the edge of a cliff, Sarah Booth. A strong wind might topple me. I'll get my footing back. I will. Just give me some time."

"Of course." I squeezed his fingers and was stunned when he withdrew his hand and shoved it in the pocket of his jeans.

"I think we should turn around," he said. "I'm tired. I want to take a nap."

"You did great today." My enthusiasm wasn't manufactured. He was working hard. "We've walked for several miles, at least."

"Four months ago, I could have run a marathon," he said, stepping out ahead of me in the journey back to the cottage.

The remark was directed not at me but at

how far he had to go to get back to the peak of his abilities. Even knowing that, I felt the cut deeply.

True to his word, Graf napped when we got back to the cottage. I went outside and sat on the stairs and called Coleman.

"How's my favorite girl detective?" he asked.

"Needing a favor."

"Is everything okay, Sarah Booth? You sound lower than a well digger's ass."

The temptation to blurt out my heartache was almost too great, but my love for Graf kept me in check. Whining to Coleman about Graf's recovery and my fears would accomplish nothing. While Coleman had settled into the role of solid friend, there was a time, not so long ago, when we'd almost been romantically involved. He'd been married at the time, and that wasn't a line he'd been willing to cross. "I'm fine. I met a woman here who wants me to investigate her father's murder. She says the wrong man is in prison. She claims the sheriff over here in Mobile County is uncooperative. Could you make a call for me? I want to see the trial transcripts and evidence. The case is on appeal."

"You can ask. Trial transcripts are public record. The evidence may be another matter."

"True, but you know how long an uncooperative law enforcement official can tie things up.

I'm here until Saturday. I don't have a lot of time to waste."

"I see your point. Sure. I'll make a call. Maybe I can soften the ground for you."

"Thank you, Coleman."

"I don't mean to pry into your business, Sarah Booth, but should you be taking on a case right now?"

He asked the question any friend would put forth. "Graf sleeps a lot. He has to work through some stuff by himself, and, in a way, it's good for me to be out of his hair. I've been told the worst thing I can do is treat him like a baby. And he encouraged me to do this."

The silence on the other end of the phone told me my argument was not totally successful. "Is the water too cold to swim?"

"I've seen a few surfers in wet suits, but I'm not interested in a polar dip. We're focusing on beach walks and rehabilitation."

"I see. I'll make that call."

"Sheriff Osage Benson. It's the John Trotter case. Larry Wofford is serving a life sentence. Happened on a boat in the Dauphin Island marina."

"I'll let you know what he says."

It was time to hang up, but talking to Coleman gave me a sense of balance that was missing with the emotional turmoil in my life. "Have you talked to Tinkie lately?"

"She's in New Orleans helping Cece with the preparation for the Black and Orange Ball. I hear it'll be the gala event of the year. Cece has lined up a dozen film and music celebrities to attend. All proceeds for charity. And I hear she has a special surprise for you."

"A surprise?" I perked up. Cece's surprises were always fun. "What is it?"

"Then it wouldn't be a surprise if I told, would it?"

"Dammit, Coleman, that should be illegal."

"Didn't your aunt Loulane tell you that patience is a virtue?"

"She told me a lot of things, and that might have been one of them. She wasn't always right, though."

His chuckle was warm and reminded me of long ago days picking plums from the wild trees along an abandoned fencerow. "Pester your cohorts in crime. I'm not telling anything. I'll get back with you once I've talked to Benson." I expected to hear the click of the receiver. Instead, I heard his breath exhale. "Sarah Booth, Graf is a good man. I can only tell you that if I were in his shoes, I'd be acting like a total jackass. An injury of that kind, one that is so public and puts the future in jeopardy—it's easy for a man to lose his way. Keep that in mind. He'll recover. His love for you is the beacon he needs to find his way."

I'd never been a crier, but I felt tears threaten. "Thanks. You're a good friend to Graf and to me."

I hung up. Words of wisdom from Coleman. Everyone told me the same thing, and I knew they were all right. The week of my beach vacation stretched out like a long, treacherous road. At times I had the sense I walked on eggshells. No one could try harder than Graf—he pushed his body to exhaustion. I had to learn not to over-react to each shift in his attitude. Every time he sighed or looked down, I couldn't interpret it as a crisis. I couldn't control Graf's emotions, but I could my own.

I was shifting to my feet to return inside when I heard Sweetie's soft harrumph of greeting.

No vehicle was visible on the road in front of the cottage, so I glanced behind to the sand dunes. Standing amid the sea oats was a slender woman in a pillbox hat with a thick veil and a classy skirt and short jacket. The black fabric contrasted starkly with the blues and whites of the beach.

Her dark hair blew in the wind, but I didn't need to see her face. I would recognize Jackie Kennedy anywhere—but why had Jitty brought Jackie's persona to Dauphin Island?

She approached with an elegant grace I could only envy.

"Why Jackie?" I asked.

"Iconic."

"No doubt, but on what level?" There was

always a message in Jitty's appearances, but seldom was I able to discern it.

"Widowed twice, she never bowed her head to tragedy."

Something heavy and unpleasant settled in the pit of my stomach. "What's with the widows' outfits, Jitty? You're starting to make me a little paranoid."

"Whatever fear or disappointment Jackie faced, she never let on in public."

I considered her words. "She lost a lot. Thank God she didn't live to suffer the loss of her son. That would be too much to bear."

Jitty lifted the heavy veil that had concealed her face. "We bear what we must, Sarah Booth. Hold on to that."

"Stop being so damn enigmatic. If you have something to say, spit it out."

Jitty gazed past me. "You can't cling to things. Not love or power or success. Time marches past us all, Sarah Booth. Best to let things go when the struggle is too hard."

Panic swelled my arteries to the point I thought my blood had ceased to flow. "You're not the Jitty I know and love." Jitty never gave up. Never. "What's wrong with you? You're a fighter, like Alice. Like me. We've always fought."

"I'm rethinking my position on the never-say-die situation."

Coleman thought I was low when he spoke to

me on the phone. Jitty was so far down I didn't know if she'd sink out of sight. "What's wrong? Maybe I can help."

"Coming here was a mistake for me, Sarah Booth. I should have stayed at Dahlia House. The past here is a stain."

She wasn't making a lick of sense. "Are you talking about my case?"

She frowned. "What case? I turn my back for one minute, and you're involved in a case? What kind of case?"

"It's more of an inquiry. I'm only here for a few more days, and my client knows it."

"Client? You been paid?" She still looked like Jackie, but she sounded more like a wet hen. "What kinda fool brings her man, her man who was shot bad, to a beach paradise and then gets involved in a *case?*" The depression was gone at least, burned away in the fury of her anger.

"No, I haven't been paid. This is more a favor. An innocent man may be in prison for a murder he didn't commit."

"Save me from my lunatic charge," Jitty whispered. "Girl, has somebody bonged the soft spot on the top of your head? Does Graf know about this?"

"He knows I'm looking into something for Angela."

She clucked her tongue in disgust. "If I had me a switch, I'd make the backs of your legs sting."

"Stop it." I found my own anger. "I love Graf and I'll do anything to help him, except stop living my own life. Graf is struggling. He's scared. I know this, Jitty. I know it because I am, too. I did this to Graf, but I can't give up who I am. It won't fix anything."

Jitty pondered my words. "You need to talk to Graf. Get rid of all the guilt and anger."

"You're right, Jitty. I'll speak to Graf."

"Girl, if you're sayin' I'm right, I'm really worried. Be quick about it."

"I promise." But I spoke only to the wind and my pets. Jitty was gone. Graf descended the stairs.

"Who were you talking to?" he asked.

"I was having a long, serious talk with myself," I told him.

He sat down beside me. The wind ruffled my hair, blowing it into my eyes and mouth. Sweetie joined us, and he absently stroked her long, silky ears. "I'm glad you've found a new client. Even a part-time one. Your job doesn't define you, but you're a great PI."

I leaned into him, glad for the warmth of his body in the brisk wind. "I care more about you than any career. I'm rethinking my life, Graf. I can let go of some things. I want to spend more time with you."

He pulled me against him and kissed the top of my head. "Once I'm back on my feet, literally, let's have a talk about the future. Our future. I can't go there until I'm positive I'm the man I want to be for you. Give me a little more time."

I pushed thoughts of my surprise wedding aside. Coleman was right. Patience was a virtue. "You've got it, *ma puce*."

Graf gripped my hair and tilted my head so he could kiss the sensitive spot below at the side of my neck. "Call me a flea again, and I'll have to resort to force."

"Gotta love the French. They sure know how to create terms of endearment." We were both laughing as we went inside the cottage.

I found myself in a dense woods, a place where light couldn't penetrate the canopy of trees. I had no idea if it was night or day. My feet sank into a layer of dead leaves, soundless. I knew I dreamed, but I had no idea how to wake myself.

Someone watched me from the trees. Someone bad. Someone who meant me harm. I tried to run, but the darkness and the thickness of the underbrush held me in place. The harder I struggled, the deeper I sank into the damp, rotting leaves. The detritus closed around my ankles, my knees, my hips.

I wanted to call out for help, and I tried, but it seemed the woods drank my pleas. The silence sucked all noise into it, so that my battle caused no ripple of sound.

The leaves closed around my waist, and then my armpits. My neck. Only my head managed to stay above the suffocating leaves.

When they covered my mouth and nose and eyes, I let go. I accepted the darkness and felt it swallow me like a tasty morsel. It was over. At last I could rest.

I woke up with Graf's hand shaking my shoulder. "Sarah Booth! You've got a phone call." He gave me the cell phone.

Before I spoke, I checked caller ID. Angela Trotter. It was 3:00 a.m.

"I'm sorry," she said. "Someone shot out the front window of my house. I called the sheriff's office. They're sending a deputy."

She was frightened. "Calm down. I'll come over," I said.

"Do you think someone meant to hurt me?"

"It's possible." I didn't know the crime statistics on the island. Was gunplay par for the course? I doubted it, but I'd know in the morning. It was a curious coincidence that she'd hired a private investigator and, the very same day, someone shot out her window. "Lock your doors. Let me get my clothes on, and I'll be over." I wrote down the address she gave me.

When I hung up, I sat beside Graf. "Someone shot out one of Angela's windows. It could be an accident or a stray bullet, but she was upset."

He didn't say anything.

"I told her I'd come over. Are you okay with that?"

"I'm not particularly fond of the idea that you're going to a place where gunshots have been fired."

I picked up his hand and laced my fingers through his. "Angela called the sheriff's department. Officers will be on the scene. I don't think it's dangerous for me to go, but I'll cancel if that's what you want."

He dropped my hand and stood. "I told you I want you to continue your career. I meant it, but I can't help but worry. You have to let me heal, and I have to let you work. Check on her. Just be careful. And take the dog and cat. Sweetie is a far better judge of character than either of us."

"I will." I kissed him good-bye and set out for Angela's with Sweetie and Pluto at my side.

4

Angela sat glumly on the steps of her cottage, the surf only a murmur because of her distance from the shore. The interior light illuminated several missing panes in the front window. Two bullet holes, small caliber, marred her living room wall.

"Where were you when the shots were fired?" I asked.

"In my bedroom."

"Was the living room dark?"

"There was a lamp on. I should have closed the blinds, but there's never any traffic on this street. Just the folks who live here."

"I think the shots were a warning of some type. If they'd been trying to kill you, they would have shot through the bedroom window. This was a down-and-dirty drive-by to give you a heads-up." I sat beside her.

"Warning for what? How did anyone know I was talking to you about Dad's murder?" she asked.

"It's a bit of a jump to take it as fact that this" —I waved at the destruction visible in the porch light—"is because you hired me."

"It's connected." Angela was adamant. "I just have to figure out how."

51

We halted the discussion because the patrol car stopped in front of the cottage and two uniformed deputies walked toward us.

"Looks like you made more enemies, Miss Trotter. Or rousted up some old ones." The deputy who spoke had a swagger and a name tag that read Randy Chavis. "You got a way of pissing people off."

My shock at the deputy's unprofessional behavior gave way to anger. "You must have passed the course on Blame the Victim. You need to rethink your attitude."

He swung around to face me, and clear blue eyes raked me as harshly as if he'd touched me. "And who are you, little lady?"

"A friend." Angela stepped between us. "You don't have to like me, Chavis, but you do have to do your job."

So there was bad blood between the two. Likely because of Angela's persistence in helping Larry Wofford and because she was a journalist. Cops and reporters were often at odds and viewed each other with suspicion.

"Maybe if you weren't always trying to tell people how to do their jobs, you'd get better cooperation."

"Maybe if you officers did your jobs I wouldn't have to point out the problems in the newspaper."

Now I stepped between them. "Enough. Ms.

Trotter's house was shot. She could have been injured or killed. What can you do?"

He almost snapped at me, but instead he turned to his partner. "Check for shell casings. Talk to the neighbors; see if they heard or saw anything. I'll take some photos." He pointed at Angela. "Can you describe the people who did this?"

"I was asleep. It was over by the time I got dressed."

"Any suspects? Anybody want to harm you?"

"I'm not a reporter any longer, Randy. I give tours of Fort Gaines. No, I can't think why someone would want to hurt me."

"You can't help yourself, Angela. You're making trouble wherever you turn. You haven't been stirring the pot on Larry Wofford again, have you?" Chavis asked.

"No," she said, and I could almost hear her teeth gritting.

The second deputy returned. "Neighbors across the street were up. They noticed a dark car driving down the street real slow. It took off right after the gunshots."

"Good job, Teddy. I'll get after the photos." He spoke to Angela. "If we come up with anything, we'll let you know." Chavis walked away.

"And I won't hold my breath," Angela said. "That man hates me."

"Why?"

"He was up for detective, and I wrote a story

that put him in a bad light. The story was true, but Chavis holds it against me. He feels like I ruined his chances for promotion."

For the first time, it occurred to me that Angela might be taking the lid off a box of snakes. It was always true in crime investigation: if an innocent man was in jail, then a guilty one was on the loose. A guilty man had a lot to lose if I solved the case. Intimidating Angela was a tactic a lot of guilty people might use.

"You look worried," Angela said.

"If the person who killed your father is free and is still around here, you could be in danger."

"And you too."

"I have to really discuss this with Graf. I can't put him in a place where he could be hurt again."

"I understand."

"In the meantime, write down everyone who might be linked to your father's death. And a list of everyone you talked to since you met me. Maybe a list of the people who took the fort tour." The strange behavior of the slender woman wearing the hat and sunglasses came back to me. "There was a woman. Tall and blond. Attractive. Maybe my age. Hat and sunglasses. Do you recall her?"

"Yes." Angela considered. "She wasn't on the tour, but I saw her several times, trailing behind us. It's odd, but I didn't think much of it at the time."

"Nor did I. I saw her on the beach earlier. She's here with a child, presumably her daughter. Probably just tourists." Still, if I saw them on the beach again, I'd initiate a conversation and see if I could find out more about them. Strangers were always worth a glance in an investigation.

"Someone has something to hide, Sarah Booth." Angela lowered her head.

"If someone intends to hurt you, Angela, this may be a blessing in disguise. At least now we're on the alert. Forewarned is forearmed, as my aunt Loulane would say."

"She must have been a mighty wise woman."

Truer words were never spoken.

When I returned to the beach cottage, Graf was gone. For a few heart-pounding minutes, I suffered under the delusion he'd been kidnapped yet again—until I found the note he'd left on the kitchen counter saying he couldn't sleep and was taking a walk on the beach.

Dawn was not far away, and I was too keyed up to sleep. The deputy, Chavis, had a huge chip on his shoulder where Angela was concerned. I understood why law officers were suspicious of the press. Whenever a lawman messed up, it was generally the media who pointed it out. And journalists had written more than a few stories of lawmen taking justice into their own hands.

From the officers' side, they felt journalists rushed to print and jeopardized cases, even lives.

Lucky for me, my experience with Coleman gave me a new perspective. He told the truth to Cece and other reporters. He didn't always tell all the facts, because he had an investigation to run and protect. But he offered what he could, and Cece trusted him. Things worked out very well. But that was a rare arrangement.

When I got the chance, I wanted to read the stories Angela had written when she worked for the local newspaper. That might explain Chavis's antagonistic attitude. The other possibility involved guilt—and wanting to stop her from finding the real killer. Fifty-fifty either way.

Hitting the beach, I headed west. At one time the island extended farther west, but storms had eroded the beaches. Numerous cottages had been washed away or destroyed by the fury of the Gulf hurricanes. As I looked down the beach, no lights were visible. For all practical purposes, I was alone.

The wind off the water was cold, and there was a sense that something big and powerful lurked just beyond the horizon, out on the water. Pulling up what I remembered about the Gulf Coast history, I knew there were Native American tribes that lived along the coastal rim. None built permanent homes on the barrier islands. They knew better than to trust the weather gods.

Hurricane season extends from June 1 through November 30. Late-season storms are often less powerful, more drenchers than blowers, but could still do millions in damage because the coast had become the haven for the wealthy who could afford to build on the water's edge. The Indians were smarter. They lived on the beach for short stints but moved inland when foul weather threatened.

The worst storms come in late July, August, and September. The names of the hurricanes that had strewn disaster along the Alabama-Mississippi coasts were legendary: Camille, Ivan, Katrina. The effects of the last big hurricane were evident all around me.

My mind on the power of nature, I was startled to see lights in the distance. They were near the water, and they moved back and forth. My imagination had been teased by Angela Trotter's stories of pirates, and my first thought was smugglers sneaking booty onshore.

In this day and age, it wouldn't be gold and jewelry. More likely drugs. And drug smugglers were far more dangerous than pirates any day of the week.

A low growl slipped from Sweetie's throat.

"Easy girl, let's take cover behind the dunes."

Using the drifts of sand to block us from the view of those on the shore, we made our way toward the lights. Before we could see anything clearly, I heard voices.

"That's one! Look, it's headed straight into the water. It'll make it." The male speaker couldn't contain his excitement.

"Will they be okay if a storm comes up?" a young woman asked.

"A storm won't be good. Not for those in the water and especially not for the ones still hatching here on shore."

Instead of pirates or smugglers, I'd stumbled into a nest of biologists working with turtles. Abandoning the dunes, I walked toward them.

"Hold up!" A tall, athletic woman in an insulated jacket held up a hand to stop me in my tracks. "Don't come any closer. You'll crush them."

Sweetie and I froze. The woman's tone of voice made me feel as if I'd committed a capital crime. "What am I about to crush?"

"Loggerhead turtles. The species is fighting extinction. We don't need a big foot smashing them."

After my last case with a wacked-out academic who wore banana boats for shoes, I was a little sensitive about the size of my feet. "Now hold on. No cause for insults. I was merely out for a walk."

"If I had my way, you tourists would be shipped off this island, along with most of the residents. This place could be the finest habitat for aquatic reptiles along the Gulf Coast. But no, it's just one more beach for people who have too much time and too much money."

A tall man approached and gripped her arm. "Dr. Norris! You can't accost people. The city council will ban you from working with the turtles."

I could almost feel the heat of her anger, but she checked herself. Even in the dim starlight I could see her efforts to relax her shoulders and straighten her posture. "I apologize. These turtles struggle against so many predators, and man is the worst. Thoughtlessness kills eighty percent of the hatchlings. This is a very late nest, and the babies are finally trying to make it to the water."

"You're obviously passionate about the creatures." I could appreciate a person who defended the helpless. "It's okay. I'm not offended. But, really, my feet aren't that big."

She laughed, and it was a transformation. "I do apologize. My behavior was awful. I'm Phyllis Norris." She reached out and took my hand. "Let me show you."

I followed her to an indentation in the sand. In the beam of a flashlight, the tiniest baby turtles crawled out of the nest and scurried down the beach. Several volunteers made a wedge-shaped human barrier to keep humans and other predators away and to give the hatchlings a chance to gain the water.

"How many will make it?" I asked.

"Not enough. This particular turtle is in danger of extinction. Climate change has impacted the nesting times. Late October is unheard of for hatchlings. That's why we're out here. I mostly believe in letting nature take its course, but the oil spill hit the turtles hard. Not to mention relentless development of the Gulf beaches."

She didn't bother to hide her bitterness. Development on the beachfront was an ecological and insurance disaster. Yet the developers returned as soon as a hurricane knocked them down.

"The Gulf Coast has been lucky this year," I said. "No serious hurricanes, and the season is almost done."

"Don't speak too soon. There's a tropical storm off the coast of Jamaica. Good chance it'll go into the Yucátan Peninsula, but if it veers into the Gulf and heads this way, it'll be terrible for these nesting turtles. The beach erosion is devastating."

"A storm? I checked the weather Saturday, and there wasn't a mention." The beach cottage had a television and radio, but neither Graf nor I had turned them on. I was way out of touch with what was happening outside of my tiny world.

"Tropical Storm Margene. It may not develop into a hurricane, and it may not come this way.

Welcome to the watch-and-wait lifestyle of the Gulf Coast."

"Sometimes the remnants of the storms make it up to the Mississippi Delta." And brought floods, relentless rain, and wind gusts, not the full-bore effect. Even the last vestiges of a big storm could prove destructive, though.

"What brings you to Dauphin Island?" Dr. Norris asked.

"My fiancé and I are vacationing for a week."

She tried to hide the distaste she felt for more tourists, but in the glare of a coworker's flashlight, I caught the fleeting expression before she covered it. "The island is at its best in the fall. Most of the tourists are gone. The beer swillers, sun worshippers, and litterbugs have returned indoors."

I understood her frustration, so I let it go. "We toured the old fort yesterday. An interesting history."

"Then you met Angela Trotter?"

"I did."

"I wish she'd accept what happened to her father and move on. She'll end up spending her entire life championing a man who doesn't deserve it."

In small towns, everyone knew the business of everyone else, so I wasn't surprised at Dr. Norris's knowledge of Angela's situation. I was a little shocked at her blunt assessment made to a stranger.

"You believe Larry Wofford is guilty?"

"I see she's filled you in on all the details. Poor Angela. She tells every new person she meets about the injustice served on Wofford. She wants to believe her father died because of a treasure. It's hard for a daughter to accept that two drunks got into an argument and one killed the other."

"Simple as that?" I asked.

She checked on the progress of the turtles before she answered, and she motioned me away from the group. "Angela was a top-notch reporter. She dug into things and held people accountable. She could have gone on to national prominence. Then her father was killed. Her whole life contracted, and she gave up reporting and moved to the island. She's spent the last year asking questions. It's a waste of talent."

"You know a lot about Angela." More than a casual acquaintance should.

"I do." She hesitated. "I dated John Trotter for two years. When I couldn't take his drinking any longer, we broke it off."

"I see."

"Angela and her father were estranged. I was trying to repair their relationship, and making progress. They'd begun to talk a bit, and Angela even visited him on the boat. She felt abandoned by his pursuit of the everlasting treasure. John was a dreamer. An extraordinary man who could weave a tale and captivate any audience. Even me." She gave a sad shake of her head. "I didn't care that he talked foolishness. I just loved his heart and his undying hope."

"And you think Larry Wofford killed him?"

"Beyond a reasonable doubt. I attended the trial. John and Larry drank together. A lot in the latter months of John's life. Two old sea dogs hitting the bottle, sharing yarns and tales of treasure. Both had given up their families."

The picture she painted was all too familiar. Lonely men drinking, an argument, a gun. It happened all the time. "Why do you think Angela is so determined to believe Wofford is innocent?"

"I'm no psychologist, but she can cling to the belief her father was about to find the treasure of his dreams. He can be a near success instead of an alcoholic failure. Wouldn't you rather believe that about your father?"

"So it's more about her father than Wofford?"

Phyllis Norris shrugged. "That I can't determine. Wofford is a handsome guy. Charming as all get-out. Angela has a thing for him. That'd make it doubly sad, wouldn't it?" She shifted so she could monitor the turtles. "I have to get back to my students and volunteers. Enjoy your stay on the island."

"I will. Thank you. And good luck with the turtles."

5

I entered the cottage on the QT, but my efforts not to wake Graf were pointless. He hadn't returned from his walk. I tried his cell phone, only to hear it ringing on the kitchen counter. He hadn't taken it with him.

I dropped my clothes on the floor and climbed into bed. I'd opened a window, and the pounding surf seemed to match the rhythm of my heart, an echo of loneliness in that empty chamber.

"Having lost much, I know how you feel." The soft, Southern drawl came from a woman no more than five feet tall, plump and dressed in a gown of black brocade. A thick veil covered her face.

Sweetie raised her head and gave a low, bluesy moan, then returned to sleep. Walks on the beach were wearing her out—and besides, we both knew the apparition was merely Jitty, in the guise of Mary Todd Lincoln.

"What sadness does your getup bode?" I pulled the covers over my head.

"Why do we suffer so much in this lifetime?" she asked.

Peeping out from the covers, I watched her as she lifted the veil to reveal a round face ravaged with sorrow. "I can't answer that, Jitty. Just tell me, is something bad hanging over Graf?"

"I don't know," she said. "Mary Todd Lincoln lost her sons, her husband. Her family never forgave her for marrying a Unionist. They were wealthy Kentuckians and supported the South. After Lincoln was shot, poor Mary Todd ended up with nothin'. One remainin' son, who put her in a mental asylum. And you feel like you're alone, Sarah Booth. At least you got your posse."

"Thanks for that, Jitty." Because my last case involved Lincoln's extracurricular love life—or at least the supposition of one—I had to ask. "Was Mrs. Lincoln insane?"

Jitty sat down on the edge of my bed. "She had no friends in Washington. She had no family because of her political beliefs and marriage to Lincoln. The man she loved was gunned down in front of her. Was she insane or simply too sad to care?"

Jitty never gave a simple answer. It was almost as if she took pleasure in enigmatic responses. I'd learned badgering did no good. Whatever she intended to reveal would come in its own time.

"What should I do to help Graf?" Maybe that was a question she'd answer. In the past, she was all about micromanaging my love life. Now, when I needed her help, she was mute.

"Might be time to bring in reinforcements."

Her words were a twist of the knife in my heart. Jitty was worried. "Tinkie?"

Jitty's frown told another story. "I was thinkin' more along the lines of Coleman. Maybe a little competition would turn Graf around. Nothing like another dog wantin' your bone to get a man interested in gnawin' again."

"Gee, thanks. I love the comparison to a bone."

"Maybe you need some silk and satin? Stop by one of those shops that specialize in lace and spandex. Something a little naughty might do the trick."

The words juxtaposed with her attire were enough to make me question *my* sanity. A sex lecture from a historical figure was too bizarre.

"Stop it. Coleman has a county to protect. He can't come running to the beach to make Graf jealous. I wouldn't ask him to."

"Tinkie would. That gal has spunk. Call her down here. Maybe she can wake him up."

"I can snap him out of this." She was making a federal case out of it. So he hadn't slept with me in a couple of months. "He's just getting his strength back. Give it a rest."

"Be careful, Sarah Booth. In his mind, he's drawn a dividin' line. There's the hale and hearty Graf before the gunshot. That's the Graf you fell in love with and agreed to marry. On the other side of that line is crippled Graf, the man who may or may not have a movie career. You've got to figure a way to jump that line and get him to see you're right there beside him now. Tinkie may be able to help."

"I'll give her a call in the morning."

"Look out yonder window." Jitty's warm chuckle escaped and the short and plump body of Mary Todd Lincoln shifted to the more familiar figure of my taller, slender haint.

"Please! Don't bastardize Shakespeare." Outside the window, sunrise marked another day. A new opportunity. I would seek advice from Tinkie, and I would refocus Graf and save the day.

"Thanks, Jitty. Sometimes you do come through for me, though never without abundant torment." But she was gone.

When I roused myself to make the coffee, I found Graf asleep on the sofa in the den. The television was on, but the sound was muted. I made coffee and took a cup to him, nudging him gently awake.

"This is a remarkable place, Sarah Booth. An island paradise. Is everything good with Angela?"

"The sheriff's department isn't taking the gunshots too seriously. Maybe it *was* kids driving by." I didn't believe it, and neither would Graf.

"Kids with loaded guns. Perfect." He rose and poured us both more coffee. "I'm getting stronger every day." He handed me a cup and returned to the sofa.

"I'm sorry about your leg. I've never been more sorry about anything in my life. And I know saying it doesn't change a thing."

"I don't blame you." He stroked my hair back from my face, and I leaned into the warmth of his hand. "Where are you off to so early?"

"I have errands to run in Mobile. There's a wine shop I want to visit. I thought maybe we'd celebrate tonight."

"Celebrate what?"

"A surprise." I wasn't giving up. I couldn't. I could take the disappointment and the rejection, but I couldn't quit. I would pick up our license today and propose the beach wedding to him. I would finish the arrangements with a preacher or judge to meet us on the beach Saturday morning to have a wedding ceremony. It would all come about—because I was hardheaded and stubborn and had all the traits that made me successful and such a pain in the ass.

"I'll be back by lunch. Shall I pick up some sushi or something?"

"Sure." The smile he wore was hard won and marred by tension around his eyes.

Dauphin Island is connected to the mainland by the huge hump of the three-mile-long Gordon Persons Bridge, known informally as the Dauphin Island bridge. It is a great vantage point with a tragic past. Even in Zinnia I'd followed

68

the news story of the four young children thrown from the bridge to their deaths by a deranged father.

The world was full of wounded and crazed people who wrecked the lives of others without a second thought. Was a killer still at large in Angela Trotter's life? Or was she simply incapable of accepting her father as he had really been, as Phyllis Norris contended, a charming yarn-spinner prone to alcohol and violent arguments with his drinking mates?

Angela wouldn't be the first daughter who couldn't accept family as they were. And she wouldn't be the last. I owed Tinkie a call with an update of what I'd gotten Delaney Detective Agency involved in. I also wondered if she had any suggestions for wooing Graf. She knew every trick in the trade, and I was desperate enough to sign on for massive manipulation per the Daddy's Girl Rulebook for pleasing (and controlling) your man.

I dialed her cell phone as I drove past the bay and canals flanking both sides of State Route 193. I'd barely gotten hello out before she pounced. "What's wrong, Sarah Booth?"

"How do you know anything is wrong?"

"Oh, please. Your tone of voice is all screwy. You should be filled with sexual languor or at least mischief. You sound like you're attending a funeral."

"Well, no wonder Graf doesn't care to spend time with me."

Silence was her response as she evaluated my last statement. "Who is he spending time with?"

"Himself. The beach. The dark moon. He slept on the sofa and walked the beach all night last night."

"What about the beach wedding?" I'd shared my plans with only Tinkie, who'd supported them one hundred percent.

"I haven't told him. The timing hasn't been right. He's trying hard, Tinkie, but something isn't right."

"I can come today. Be there in under three hours."

Tinkie was ready to rush to my assistance, and I loved her for that. "I'm not calling for you to come. Not yet. Tell me how to seduce him." My cheeks flamed at my ineptitude. Never in my life had I ever needed to ask such a question. "Everything I try—he's very tender and loving, but just . . . not interested."

"He hasn't wanted to be intimate since the gunshot, right?"

"Yes."

"Then you have to get past that event. It's like it's built up in his brain. He's like a horse that's been hurt jumping. Just get him over the hurdle, and things should be terrific."

I wasn't certain Graf would appreciate the

comparison, but it worked for me. "Are you sure?"

She laughed, and the sound of her tinkling merriment cheered me more than anything had in weeks. "There are no guarantees where a man is involved, but it sure can't hurt anything, right?"

"I suppose not."

"Sarah Booth Delaney, quit acting like an eighth-grade girl with a crush. He's your fiancé. Entice him, tease him, please him—you know how this is done. Want me to draw some pictures and text them to you?"

"Absolutely not!" The idea of what Tinkie might come up with generated a potent combo of embarrassment and curiosity. I could imagine stick figures in compromising positions.

"I might find a new talent. Just think, this time next year I could be exhibiting at galleries around the country. I could lecture on how my artistic renditions of sexual seduction saved your relationship."

She was making me laugh, which was her purpose. "Right. Just what I dream about. Having the country caught up in my personal business."

"It couldn't hurt." Tinkie was on a roll. "We could maybe do webisodes. Post them to YouTube. I'm sure Cece could run the camera. Sort of a nice combination of acting and therapy for you and Graf."

"Stop!" I couldn't take much more.

"No, you stop! Quit skulking around acting like a timid schoolgirl. Take action. Get that man in your bed and put a smile on his face."

"Aye, aye, captain."

With Tinkie's encouraging words ringing in my ears, I drove straight to the clerk's office and completed the paperwork for a marriage license. I also contacted the officiant who'd agreed to perform the beach ceremony and supply the witnesses. She wasn't a county official and she wasn't a minister, but she was licensed by the state and that was good enough for me.

Then I drove to what had once been Mobile's daily newspaper. The digital age had hit *The Mobile Chronicle* hard, kicking a daily with a large circulation back to a publication schedule of three days a week. Cece would be mortified. *The Zinnia Dispatch*, with a miniscule circulation compared to the *Chronicle*, still printed daily. But the Zinnia paper was owned and operated by a local family, the way most newspapers used to be. It wasn't part of a corporate conglomerate.

I pulled into the parking lot and within a few minutes was inside, talking my way into viewing the newspaper morgue. It took a bit of sweet talk, but Angela Trotter was still highly regarded as a journalist there, and I soon had a thick file of her stories.

Angela had been a thorn in the side of the sheriff's department, the county commission, the city councilmen and mayor, the school system, and just about every other public body or elected official. She knew how to keep a fire lit under those paid to work for the citizenry.

I scanned story after story of ineptitude, outright incompetence, and political wrangling, where the sheriff sided with powerful allies to the point of thwarting justice. Sheriff Osage Benson buttered his bread on both sides. And he'd been in office for at least twenty years.

I wondered how a man with such heavy—and traceable—baggage kept getting elected, especially with Angela's stories painting him as either stupid or corrupt.

As I read, I made notes of people who might possibly want to harm or annoy Angela. When I finished, I had filled three pages of my notebook with names of people powerful or wealthy enough to cause Angela grief.

And a few of them might have been motivated to kill her father. Deputy Randy Chavis was at the top of the list. Angela had caught the deputy in several instances where a routine case took a wrong turn because of an oversight or action the deputy had taken, and yet he was still in law enforcement. The sheriff obviously condoned the deputy's activities.

The second suspect was a county commissioner who'd been implicated in taking kickbacks from land developers on Dauphin Island.

Angela's stories had busted up a high-scale condo development on the shifting sand beaches of the barrier island. Rick Roundtree lost a lot of money and his reputation. No jail time, and he kept his elected office—an amazing feat given the facts.

And third on the list was former Governor Jameson Barr. He'd paid a hit man to kill his wife and was doing time in prison. But that didn't mean he couldn't reach out and harm Angela. She nailed him to the wall by tracking payments from the former governor to a hired gun.

While I hadn't discovered evidence connecting any of these men to John Trotter's murder, I had provided motive. Angela had mucked around in each man's reputation. Barr had gone to prison. Roundtree had lost money. And Chavis had been painted as a fool.

When I finished with my suspect list, I read the account of Larry Wofford's arrest and trial. It appeared to be pretty basic and by the book. The murder weapon was never found, probably because it had been dropped far out in the Gulf waters.

The testimony against Wofford centered on an eyewitness account given by the marina owner, Arley McCain. Wofford was seen leaving the *Miss Adventure* near the time of death for Trotter as established by the medical examiner. McCain testified that Wofford was the only person he saw coming or going on the dock that evening. The truly damning part was how Wofford was covered in blood and blind-stumbling drunk.

As his defense, Wofford insisted he'd almost collided with "someone in a yellow rain slicker" who'd rushed down the dock and into the night as he was returning to the marina. He'd seen the lights on in Trotter's cabin and gone by for a nightcap, only to discover Trotter was dying. He'd attempted assistance to no avail. Trotter died and Wofford panicked, rushing off the boat and down the dock, where he was seen by McCain.

Wofford's fingerprints were found all over Trotter's desk and bedroom, where the murder occurred. Wofford conceded his prints were everywhere because he and John often had a drink together in the evenings. The sheriff's office turned up no evidence of "the rain-slickered stranger." No one near the marina had seen or heard anything.

Chavis was the lead officer investigating the murder. His testimony was heavily weighted against Wofford.

Coty McGowan was the defense lawyer, another person I needed to pay a call on. He made a case that Wofford found Trotter as he was dying and tried to help him, but the jury didn't buy it. Reading the trial coverage, I had my doubts about Wofford's innocence.

More than likely I was spinning my wheels, but

I put in a call to the sheriff's office, hoping Coleman had kept his promise to soften Sheriff Benson up. If Coleman had reached out to the sheriff, it was only partially effective. The high sheriff stalled, forcing me to wait until after lunch for an appointment. So I called McGowan, the defense attorney, and booked an interview with him.

McGowan worked out of an old Victorian building on Church Street surrounded by oak trees dripping Spanish moss. Mobile had a charm not unlike New Orleans without the big-city feel. And it was far more buttoned-up.

Though the law office was busy, the attorney saw me right away. He was a lean man in a three-piece suit with an impressive amount of gray hair that curled. Before I was even seated, he started.

"Larry Wofford is innocent. I have no doubt. His case is on appeal, but who knows what that means."

"How was it that the marina owner saw Wofford stumbling, covered in blood, off Trotter's boat but failed to see anyone else leaving?"

He leaned on the back of his chair. "That's the whole basis for the appeal. That and the fact that the security cameras at the marina were on the blink that night."

"On the blink?"

"They worked the night before and the night after, but not that night."

"Did someone tamper with them?"

"We can't prove it, but it does lend itself to reasonable doubt." He stacked a pile of papers. "That video could have proven my client innocent."

"What were the facts against Wofford?"

"The prosecution insisted Wofford rushed onto the boat, shot John, and was stumbling down the dock, all within three minutes. That's not how it happened. Larry was on the boat at least fifteen minutes. He stayed with John, holding him as he died. He was shaken up. And drunk. So he made a bad decision not to call the police or report the crime. That's a bad decision, not the basis for a life sentence."

McGowan's passionate defense moved me. "How do you intend to prove this?"

"Larry was too drunk to drive home. One of his lady friends drove him to the marina and let him out. It was twenty minutes later that McCain saw him stumbling down the dock. Larry spent that time trying to save his friend's life."

"Why didn't this witness testify at the trial?"

"Larry wouldn't give me her name, and, to be honest, I didn't feel that her testimony as to the time she dropped him off would make a difference."

"Why wouldn't he name her?"

"She's married. There's nothing between them, but Larry said it would end her marriage. He feared her husband would hurt her. The jealous type who likes to reason with his fists. Larry didn't even tell me this until he was convicted."

"Chivalrous if stupid."

"Yeah, that's Larry Wofford through and through."

"Her name?"

"Lydia Clampett. I haven't had any luck getting her to return my calls."

I took down her name. The appeal might well be the ticket to Wofford's freedom, but I'd check with Mrs. Clampett just to cover all the bases. "Did you ever investigate to find out who might have killed John Trotter if your client didn't?"

McGowan shook his head. "Larry barely had the money to cover legal fees. He sold his boat, and after that money ran out, I took the case pro bono. There wasn't money to hire an investigator. The good news for Larry is the case has generated some media interest. Once I get the national media down here, that'll keep the prosecution from pulling any funny business."

"What was the other evidence against Wofford?"

McGowan slapped the arms of his leather chair with a resounding smack. "Very little. He had a history of drinking and brawling. Witnesses had heard him argue with Trotter in the past." He held up his hands, palms toward the ceiling. "The prosecution had no real evidence, but public sentiment was high. Trotter was a character almost everyone knew. Wofford radiated trouble. And he swaggered and refused to show concern. He was out drinking the night before the trial. He *looked* guilty."

"Surely you have some theories about who might have killed Mr. Trotter." It would be interesting to hear whom McGowan came up with.

"Trotter's daughter, Angela, pissed off a lot of people. Powerful people. I'd heard rumors Jameson Barr vowed to get even with her about the stories she did on him. He would have skated on hiring a hit man to kill his wife if Angela hadn't bird-dogged the story."

Check! His name was on my list, too. "Anyone else?"

"The sheriff hasn't lost any love in her direction, but Benson's a smart man. Why risk everything to kill a harmless old dreamer like Trotter just to settle a vendetta with Angela?"

I saw his point. "What about Rick Roundtree? I hear there was bad blood there."

He shrugged. "My money would be on Barr. The thing with Roundtree—Angela rode his ass about development on the island. You know building contracts are where a lot of money slides in the back door. Angela opposed development on the island, so she made it her life's goal to keep those contracts honest. It killed a bunch of deals. But Roundtree wouldn't have harmed the old man. If Trotter had actually found the Esmeralda treasure, it would have opened the door to tourism on a big level. Theme park, diving adventures, you name it. The discovery of pirate's booty on Dauphin Island would have created the biggest boom in development possible. Roundtree might have hired someone to kill Angela, but not her dad."

6

Only a few blocks uptown from the lawyer's office was the sheriff's office, a far cry from the low-tech, charming old courthouse domain of Coleman Peters. Sheriff Benson's suite of offices was housed in a new brick complex. When I was shown in, he rose from behind a desk that must have been six-by-eight, a vast expanse of mahogany. Behind him were flags, awards, and grip-and-grin photos celebrating official ceremonies.

"Sheriff Peters called," he said without preamble, "and asked that I extend every courtesy to you. He also assured me you were licensed and ethical. Such isn't always the case with private detectives."

"Sheriff Peters and I have worked together numerous times."

"So he says." He motioned me into a leather wing chair that faced his desk. "Here in Mobile County, law enforcement is done by professionals, not private investigators."

"Sheriff Peters believes we can all work together in the pursuit of justice, but I've handled cases in other counties where the prevalent attitude was similar to yours." I paused. "And I've worked in places where law enforcement was

81

corrupt. For obvious reasons, I wasn't welcome there."

His lips compressed, and I wondered if I'd pushed it just a smidgen too hard. But I'd done nothing to warrant such a high-handed attitude. Pushback followed on the heels of nasty arrogance.

"What do you want, Ms. Delaney?"

"To examine the physical evidence in the Larry Wofford case and permission to speak with law enforcement officials who were involved in the investigation."

"You don't mind asking for the moon, do you?"

"That's what I need. Provide them, and I won't trouble you again."

"You do know that Ms. Trotter has tried to prove Wofford's innocence before. Unsuccessfully."

"She told me."

"I understand you're on vacation. You'll be gone in what, five days tops? Why take on this thankless case? Wofford killed John Trotter. He may regret it. Hell, he may not remember it— the man spent half his time pickled in alcohol. But he did it. I have no doubt. None." He patted the top pocket of his shirt, and I realized he had once been a smoker.

I eased the pack out of my purse and held it up. "Is there a place we can smoke without being arrested?"

He gave an unwilling chuckle and hit the intercom on his desk. "Wanda, please bring two coffees to the ... portico."

"Yes, sir."

He rose and motioned for me to precede him out the door. He led me through a maze of corridors until we came to a glass door opening on an outside covered drive-through. Cigarette butts filled an ashtray. I gave him the pack of Native American cigarettes made from organic tobacco and no chemicals. He shook one out and offered it to me. We both exhaled, just as his secretary delivered two black coffees and a disapproving glare.

"Thanks," he said. "Smoking is the one vice I can't shake."

"I quit for a long time."

"Don't make it a habit," he said with a wry grin. Sheriff Benson had a certain amount of charm when he wasn't being an ass. "Why have you taken on Angela Trotter's ghosts? This is a waste of your time."

The question was truly none of his business, but we'd established a truce and I didn't want to fire the first cannonball. "She believes Larry Wofford is innocent. She wants the person who killed her father to pay. I understand her emotions, on a lot of different levels."

"Wofford is in jail, where he belongs. All you're doing is encouraging Ms. Trotter in false hope."

83

I shrugged one shoulder. "You know, I've been guilty of a whole lot worse."

He laughed. "Haven't we both? Here's my deal. You can see all the trial evidence. Whatever you want. If you promise one thing. Once you've gone through it, you do your best to convince Ms. Trotter justice has been served. If I thought Wofford was innocent, I'd be working right beside you. The truth is, he and John Trotter were drinking buddies. They got toasted on a regular basis. When that happens, sometimes two men disagree. In this instance, Wofford and Trotter got into some kind of argument, and Wofford shot him in the chest. It's just that simple. No conspiracy to hide the truth, no ulterior motive to frame Wofford. He's a damn good carpenter who happens to be a violent drunk."

"I heard there was a problem with the security cameras at the marina."

"That's a question better put to Arley McCain, who owns the marina. We collected the recordings, just as we would in any other case. When we tried to look at them, the CDs were blank. Faulty wiring, wet night, someone failed to turn the system on—it could be any of the above. Bottom line is there was no evidence to prove Wofford's statement that someone else was on the dock but also no evidence to show him running away from John's boat covered in blood. It sort of balanced out, if you ask me."

"Were there any other suspects?"

Impatience tightened Benson's expression. "Feel free to interview the investigating officer. I'll tell Randy to find the time to speak with you."

I had a question about Chavis. "He's a patrol officer, not a detective. A story Angela wrote about him kept him from being promoted to detective."

"Chavis is one of my best officers. He displayed poor judgment a time or two in a high-profile case, and Angela rode his ass for it. That's all true. But Chavis has closed cases no one else could. He was first on the scene at Trotter's murder, and he led the investigation. He's lived on the island his entire life. Some of those islanders can be clannish. It was better to have one of their own work the case."

"Thank you. Where will I find the trial evidence?"

He motioned me back inside and left me with the secretary, who delivered me to the court clerk in charge of trial records. It was going to be a long search.

Mobile County kept trial evidence in a storage facility, and after doing a little legwork, the property clerk helped me locate the Larry Wofford file. The sad thing was, there was little to go on. No murder weapon. No evidence of a motive. The physical evidence was a box with fingerprint files, blood samples, photos—the usual.

A private investigator shouldn't be upset by crime scene photos, but I was. John Trotter was shot in the chest in front of his desk. He fell backward and died on the floor. It was a violent and gruesome scene. A man was dead, and his daughter was left with a sense of injustice and loss.

I'd get a trial transcript from the court records for reference, but the attorney McGowan had filled me in on the broad strokes. As much as I liked conspiracy theories, it didn't seem probable Sheriff Benson had gone out of his way to frame Larry Wofford. Or I hadn't found the connection to take me down that path. Not yet, at least.

From the evidence, which included Chavis's investigation notes, Wofford's conviction rested on the fact he was on scene, which he never denied. No motive except drunkenness had ever been tendered or proved. Alcohol, guns, and tempers could be a lethal mix, but these men were known to be friends. Benson believed they'd caught and convicted the right man, but I wasn't so certain.

On the drive back to the island, I listened to a local radio station, surprised to hear that the tropical storm in the Caribbean has been upgraded to a Category One hurricane. According to the excited DJ, the storm was headed into the Gulf, where it was expected she would slow forward movement and gain intensity.

It was hard to take such things seriously when the weather was picture-perfect. When I got back to the cottage, I needed to see if the television had access to a twenty-four-hour weather channel. While there was no sense of urgency or worry, I also knew enough about gulf storms to realize I had to pay attention. Hurricane Margene might be the biggest bitch I'd ever confronted.

I stopped at a specialty grocer and picked up organic vegetables for dinner and then hit a local seafood shop on the way back to the island. Nothing like fresh red snapper for a perfect meal. And a sushi snack for Graf while he was waiting for dinner.

Tonight, I would propose the wedding to Graf. I simply couldn't allow his distance to thwart me. I had to bring our relationship back on track, and I couldn't let my tender feelings get in the way of achieving the goal. Graf loved me and I loved him. Nothing else mattered.

When I got to the cottage, Graf was watching television. "It could get bad, Sarah Booth. Maybe we should pack it in and go home to Zinnia."

According to the news coverage, the storm was compact—nothing like Katrina. That didn't mean it wasn't dangerous, but it wouldn't overwhelm the Gulf Coast. Everything depended on which steering currents took hold of it. On east and west extremes were Tampa and Brownsville. In other words, Hurricane Margene had the entire Gulf Coast as her playground. Only time would tell where she would strike.

"It's still too early to throw in the towel," I said.

"I don't want to be here if Margene comes dead at us."

"Me either." I moved behind his chair and rubbed his shoulders. They were tight. Graf might appear relaxed, but the opposite was true. He was like a high-intensity spring—coiled and ready to unleash.

"Let's have an early dinner. Spend some time together."

"Do you have something on your mind, Sarah Booth?" There was almost a suspicious tone to his voice, as if I were plotting some nefarious deed.

"Being with you. Putting the past behind us. We can play cards, talk, drink ourselves silly. What does it matter as long as we're doing it together? I miss you, Graf. You're right here in front of me, but you're not really with me. It feels like a part of me has been amputated."

He caught my hands in his and squeezed them. "You deserve so much better than me."

I felt my heart crack at his words. "Oh, no, Graf. You're the best thing that ever happened to me. You are. I'm sorry you were hurt, but I've learned something so important. There is nothing in my life that even comes close to you."

He inhaled and his shoulders sagged. "I'm not worthy of your love."

I would not badger or argue. I would only love. I kissed him, slow and tender. "I missed lunch, but I picked up some sushi to snack on until I grill the snapper, asparagus, and sweet potatoes."

"Sounds delicious."

Pluto jumped in Graf's lap and rubbed his whiskers on Graf's chin. I went to the kitchen. Pluto could do more to lift Graf's spirits than I could. And I had work to do.

After the grilled snapper, we took a stroll on the beach. Graf improved each hour, it seemed. He was walking and jogging in the sand, tackling the rehab with all he was worth. I wanted to praise his hard work, but I wisely kept my mouth shut.

Instead, I held his hand and let the wind blow the cobwebs of strife out of our lives. A more perfect day could not have been invented.

Back at the cottage, we talked about the Black and Orange Ball and what surprise Tinkie and Cece had in store for me. They'd promised something special, but I had no idea what it might be. Graf had purchased a gown for me on Rodeo Drive, and it was a creation to behold. He had a tux that would have made James Bond howl with envy. We were ready for the big event, which would also mark the celebration for our wedding, though Graf didn't know it yet.

As we talked, my dream of marital bliss seemed within my grasp. We'd gone through the dark land of shadows and doubt and come out on the other side. "Let's go back." I tugged at his hand as I whistled for Sweetie Pie. Pluto had refused to leave the cottage.

"Sarah Booth . . ." His voice faded.

"Yes."

"I love you."

"I love you, too." I closed the distance and wrapped my arms around his neck. "What is it, Graf?" Lingering doubt kept him from sweeping me into his arms, as he would have done before he was shot. "I don't care if you act again or not. I've made some decisions about my life. I'll find someone to care for the horses, and I'll stay in Hollywood with you. I want a solid marriage. I want that more than a career."

He untangled my arms and held me at arm's length. His expression was . . . disturbed. "I won't allow you to do that. I won't."

"I'm doing it because I love you and want to be with you. In Los Angeles, while you're making your films. We can return to Dahlia House in between. This is the right thing, Graf. I want to be your wife, the mother of your children. I want to champion your films and be with you to share your successes."

"That's not who you are, Sarah Booth. I won't allow you to turn yourself inside out for me. I don't deserve it. You won't give up your life for me." He strode away from me, and for a long moment I stood on the beach and watched him disappear into the distance, walking away from the cottage rather than toward it.

7

The cottage came with two bicycles—the wonderful old cruiser kind with fat tires and upright handlebars. Although it was windy, the sun was bright and the day warm enough for jeans and a short-sleeve shirt. I decided to ride into the town of Dauphin Island and see what I could discover.

Graf's reaction had unbalanced me. Instead of dwelling on why he'd reacted so strongly to my offer to support his career, I decided to work. Time and distance might generate the wisdom I needed to figure out what was going on with him.

Because Sweetie Pie was the best-behaved dog in the universe, she went with me. A constant breeze blew the tang of salt as we set out. For the most part, the pedaling was easy, except where sand covered the road. That required a bit more effort and better balance, but as we left the west end of the island, the road cleared and our ride took us beneath palms and oak trees that had weathered many a storm.

As I rode along, I tried to imagine what the island was like when the first European explorers came on the scene. It was long a destination of the Native American tribes that populated the Gulf Coast. Pascagoulas, Biloxis, Chickasaws,

Creeks, Choctaws—there were many different tribes and allegiances. It must have been a paradise with the white sand beaches and the beautiful aqua surf.

When I came to the T where the main road ended, I chose town. Sweetie trotted at my side, barely panting while I huffed and puffed. The coastline of the island was spectacular, but the interior held a different kind of beauty—pines, oaks, palm trees, and older residences that had withstood many a hard storm.

The island was home to a number of families who'd settled there in the late 1800s and early 1900s. Whatever their heritage, they all had a huge helping of tough. When the hurricanes came barreling out of the Gulf, these people hunkered down, rode it out, and managed to survive, often cut off from the mainland and all power supplies.

They were the shop owners, the men and women who earned their living from the water. Boat repair, beach rentals, grocery providers. It was a tightknit community much like Zinnia.

I passed the marina, where the *Miss Adventure* was moored. She was a beautiful boat, and well cared for. In fact, cleaning and paint supplies were on the deck. I wondered if Angela maintained the boat herself. It hurt my heart to think she kept the boat so well preserved as an homage to her father. I'd always been told the two most labor-intensive hobbies were boats and horses.

I couldn't speak to boats, but horses required time and sweat. And were worth every minute of it.

Looking at the lines of the sailboat, I could appreciate the high adventure of treasure hunting and the life of a vagabond sailor. John Trotter had been a romantic, a dreamer, and the boat reflected those things in her graceful lines and teak fittings. She was the epitome of a treasure-hunting boat with her high mast and crisp black, red, and dark green trim. If I were the type of person to indulge in fantasies, I might imagine Jack Sparrow or even Captain Hook striding across the deck to the bow.

The figurehead was incredible—a woman in flowing robes, one arm pointed toward the sea. Whoever had carved her had been a master. I'd read that the figurehead was used to ward off bad luck. A woman, snakes, unicorns, or other animal forms supposedly protected sailors from the many disasters that could arise on a voyage.

The lovely lady on John Trotter's boat hadn't been able to protect him. His quest had ended in a tragic death, and one that had marked his daughter in a cruel way.

I pushed off in a northerly direction. Exploring the small town on bicycle took me back to my youth, when I'd cruised around Zinnia, finding shortcuts through people's yards and playing cops and robbers with my classmates who lived in town. Zinnia had seemed so big then. Now it was a small town whose city limits could be cleared in less than ten minutes. Perspective.

An antique shop sign caught my eye, and I parked on the side of an alley and asked Sweetie to guard the bicycle. I wasn't too worried anyone would steal it. The city center was empty, and Dauphin Island didn't seem like a place where a bicycle thief would lurk.

As I pushed open the door to Terrance Snill's Antiques, a brass bell jangled. A slender man with a crop of sandy curls stood up from behind a counter with an old-fashioned cash register. He held a beautiful silver platter he'd been polishing, but he put it aside and came out to greet me.

"May I help you?"

The scent of lemony furniture polish filled the shop, and I glanced around at highly waxed and burnished antiques, some of them exquisite. Cece and Tinkie would have a field day in this store. A china cabinet with a curved glass door and an intricate beveled mirror would look fabulous in the dining room of Dahlia House. The lovely library table would be the perfect touch in the Delaney Detective Agency office. I had to shut off the consumer streak that had suddenly opened up before I had to hire a furniture truck to get home.

"I'm renting a cottage this week on the beach," I said, extending my hand and giving my name.

"Terrance Snill, proprietor and recently retired postmaster."

"You have some lovely pieces."

"Thank you. A lot of the best old family pieces were lost during Katrina, but I've picked up a few nice ones over the past years." His hand brushed lovingly across the surface of the oak library table I'd admired. "Antiques are a sad business. These were pieces once loved by families who have either died out or been left to those who don't care about old things."

I'd never thought of antiques in that way, but it was sad. Dahlia House had so many wonderful pieces that were part of my ancestry and personal history. The old horsehair sofa—as uncomfortable as it was—I couldn't imagine parting with. The sideboard in the dining room had held breakfast buffets for the Delaney family since before the Civil War. I knew the stories for each chair or table or dresser. The family tales about each scar that marred a wooden surface were part of me.

"I guess some people just want new things," I said.

"So true. Philistines who think nothing should last longer than five years. Not furniture, not a car. Not even a marriage. But on occasion good families fall on hard times. That's the worst. I pay top dollar, but money doesn't mitigate the awfulness of watching a woman cry as my movers haul out her great-grandmother's pie safe." He shook off the melancholy that had settled over both of us. "But what can I help you with today?"

"I'm not a serious shopper. I just saw your store and came in to nose around. I have a house in the Mississippi Delta. Growing up around so many antiques, I can't resist admiring them."

"Help yourself." He stepped back, and my gaze followed him to a painting on the wall. In the oil portrait, a dark-haired man wore a ruffled white shirt with a rich wine-colored coat. He stared boldly down at me. My knowledge of historical styles was limited, and while I couldn't pinpoint his decade, I was familiar with the mischievous glint in the man's eyes. He was a rascal and likely a lawbreaker. Even with the long curly dark hair and formal heavy velvet coat, he was a bad boy.

The artist had done a remarkable job. The man posed before a globe showing a ship sailing across the blue Atlantic. His right hand held a spyglass and his left a map.

Terrance Snill tsked. "Ah, so you're taken with Armand Couteau. He's quite a popular local figure. French nobility, blackguard, buccaneer, and savior of young slave women. A romantic figure. Not a single woman comes into this store who doesn't fall in love with him, at least a little bit."

"I've heard of him." I recalled Angela's

comments. "He's a very handsome man. A real swashbuckler."

"And lived life by his own rules. He threw over an inheritance as a relative of Napoleon Bonaparte and threw in with famous French pirate Jean Lafitte. They were the terrors of New Orleans for a number of years. Stories have it that the mayor of New Orleans put a price on Lafitte's head and had flyers printed and posted all around New Orleans. Lafitte printed handbills of the mayor, doubling the ransom offer. Guess who was worried? Not Lafitte."

I laughed out loud, and realized how long it had been since I'd done so. Snill was a fine storyteller. "There's a story about a treasure Couteau buried here. I can't recall the details," I prompted.

"Treasure, stolen slave girl who became his wife, and so much more."

"Do you have time to refresh my memory?" I asked.

"Since I've retired, I have nothing but time. This is the slow season here on the island. In fact, I frequently lock the doors on weekdays and only open on Saturday. But have a seat. Perhaps a cup of tea or cocoa?"

"Cocoa would be lovely."

He went in the back of the shop and returned in a few moments with two steaming cups of cocoa. Tiny marshmallows floated on top of the chocolaty beverage. I would need the warmth for the bicycle ride back to the cottage. October wasn't cold, but it was brisk, and the afternoon was fading.

"My dog is outside. May I bring her in?"

"Of course. I love dogs," Snill said. "My best friend, Maybelline, died last year. I'll go to the shelter and get another dog, but my heart needs time to heal."

I understood his need to recover, but I also knew I could never be without my four-legged friends, and so many wonderful dogs needed a home. When Sweetie was resting at my feet, I settled back to hear the tale of a Mobile Bay pirate.

"Pirates like Couteau and Lafitte were very bold. They robbed the ships right off the coast, and within a matter of weeks, they'd smuggle the stolen goods ashore and sell them on the streets of New Orleans. Often they'd sell them to the very people who'd already paid to have them brought over from Europe."

It was indeed an audacious scheme. The ruling class would be furious, yet the pirate's actions appealed to me. Not exactly a Robin Hood angle, but close.

"Couteau took the loot and spared the lives of the sailors. In fact, a lot of sailors changed allegiance and went to sail with the pirates. Like Lafitte, Couteau had an island garrison off the

Louisiana coast. He declared his island a free state and imposed his own rules, which followed the tenets of socialism. The wealth the pirates stole was divided among all of the residents, and women were given an equal share."

"Fascinating." I hung on Snill's every word.

"Couteau was a notorious thief of slaves, both male and female. He snatched them from the streets of New Orleans or Mobile or even off slave ships. Once they were safe on his island, he gave them their freedom. They could leave or stay. The majority stayed. If they'd gone back to the mainland and been captured, chances are they would have been sold back into slavery."

"Couteau treated them as people, not property." I took the last swallow of the delicious cocoa.

"The part most of my female audience enjoys is the story of Armand's masterful theft of a beautiful young slave girl, a princess snatched from the coast of Benin and brought to America in chains."

"What could be more romantic than a pirate and a slave girl?" I asked. Sweetie agreed with a soft hound-dog yodel.

"LuAnn is an interesting figure," Snill said. "My research proves she did exist. And she was a princess. She was fluent in French as well as her native language and she was apparently an acclaimed musician. She played a type of wood-wind instrument."

"How did she come to be taken as a slave?"

Snill shook his head. "There are no accounts. She first entered the history I know in New Orleans. She'd been brought from Benin to Louisiana and sold to a wealthy sugarcane planter in Louisiana to work the cane fields, but he heard her playing the flute and brought her into his home as a house servant."

A lucky break for her. The cane fields were hard labor. "How did she meet Armand?" Snill had swept me up in the story.

"The pirates had a warehouse near the French Quarter in New Orleans. As I said, Couteau was brassy. He strolled the streets of New Orleans, almost daring the authorities to take action against him. Of course they didn't, because they feared retribution from the pirates. Couteau was selling their stolen wares right under their noses."

It was a damned clever scheme, and one that required guts as well as brains.

"LuAnn had been sent to the French market for fresh fruit and vegetables. She was shopping when Armand saw her. It's said he fell in love instantly and followed her back to the Thomason home, where she lived."

I could picture it. This beautiful woman moving sensually between the tomatoes and peppers, the long strings of garlic. She gathered the provisions she needed in a basket, unaware she'd caught the eye of the handsome pirate.

"Armand shadowed her for several weeks. One day he approached her in the market. She was very shy, but few women could resist the pirate's dark charm. He brought her presents. The best gift of all, though, was her freedom. That's what he offered her."

That would be the ultimate gift. "And so she left with him?"

"Indeed. They were married on his island, and for a while they lived a wonderful life."

Until it ended. This part wasn't something I was ready to hear. I stood and handed Snill my empty cocoa cup. "I think the conclusion is going to make me very sad."

"It doesn't turn out well. Shipwreck, Couteau dies in prison here on Dauphin Island. LuAnn, who was on board the pirate ship, was rescued and sold back into slavery. They held the slave auction right on the beach, just about where your rental cottage might be. They wanted to make an example of LuAnn to the other pirates. From a life of relative luxury, she was sent to Alabama to work in the cotton fields."

"A harsh sentence."

"Runaway slaves were treated like murderers. In some areas, they were killed. LuAnn wasn't executed because it was widely believed Couteau stole her against her will. And after the shipwreck, she was thought to be a little insane. She kept insisting that she could find a great treasure if only they would free her. She said she knew where to find Couteau's map revealing the location of the treasure he'd been trying to claim when a storm smashed his ship against a reef."

"Do you believe there's such a treasure?" I wondered how the local populace assessed the old legend.

"It's Couteau's treasure one of our local residents said he'd found. But he died before he could retrieve it."

Here was more than just folklore. This was pertinent to my investigation.

"Do you believe John Trotter really found Couteau's treasure?"

"I do, and I see you've heard the tragic story. John was a dedicated hunter. He worked on Couteau's missing booty for more than a decade, and it cost him his life."

"You know a lot about Trotter's business." I tried to soften the words with a curious tone.

"I was the postmaster. Letters coming in and going out. John wrote hundreds of organizations, other treasure hunters, historians, and even a few kooks who claimed to have information about the pirate. He also wrote the Thomason family— the people who bought LuAnn. John believed LuAnn did know how to locate the treasure, and he was hoping the Thomasons had some record of her claims. I think he found what he was after. Of course, I don't know what the letters said, but I do know he worked at it hard."

"And you really think he found it?"

"John stopped by the shop late on the afternoon he was killed. He was on top of the world. He said he'd found the key to bringing up Couteau's gold. Said he'd have it in his hands within the week. He just had to get back something he'd sold."

"What was it?" I couldn't believe my good luck.

"He didn't say, exactly." Snill rubbed long, thin fingers on his chin. "But he went to stand in front of Couteau's portrait. And he laughed and said, "What a clever devil Couteau was. The key has been right in front of us.""

Opinions didn't carry much weight, but I figured I'd ask while I was there. "Do you believe Larry Wofford killed John Trotter?"

He laughed heartily. "That's ludicrous. They were friends. Sure, they sometimes drank too hard and got sloshed, but neither of them had a violent temper. Larry is harmless. He adored John. And Angela. He thought that girl walked on water. The way I see it, Larry was easy to convict, and the sheriff's department needed a resolution to a murder. They'd had a rough year with a number of unsolved crimes, and I have to say, Angela had given them the dickens when she was a reporter. She kept things stirred up about the incompetence of the sheriff and his department. Larry

Wofford was an easy target. No money, no family to fight for him."

"That's what Angela says."

"So you've met our island princess?"

I nodded. "I'm working for her. Just for this week while I'm vacationing on the island. I'm a private detective."

Instead of being taken aback, Snill was thrilled. "I hope you can find evidence to overturn Larry's conviction. He's a good guy. You'd be righting a terrible wrong." He hesitated. "Just be careful."

Goose bumps danced along my skin. "Why do you say that?"

"John was a dreamer, but he wasn't superstitious. The day he was killed, he told me that he was worried. Something in a letter he received."

"You were the postmaster, can you remember who John corresponded with?"

Snill snapped his fingers. "There was a flurry of letters from a man named Remy Renault. Another treasure hunter. He has a private dock off an inlet in Heron Bay not too far from here. Word was he dredged and put it in before the EPA stopped such things. Anyway, John hinted that Remy might attempt to jump his claim on the Esmeralda treasure."

"Did the sheriff pursue this line of investigation before arresting Wofford?"

Snill slowly shook his head. "I don't think so.

To be honest, I can't recall mentioning this to the sheriff. I never considered Remy a real treasure hunter. He never did the work, but he might try to jump someone else's claim." His eyebrows drew together in consternation. "Do you think I've been sitting on important information and didn't have the good sense to know it?"

I could only hope that was true. "I'll check it out." I took down the directions to the private dock.

"Be careful. Remy is known to have a hair-trigger temper. And he's not much for manners. He moored here a while, but several of the regulars complained because he said rude things to them. There were incidents where boats were damaged. Maybe not by accident."

I didn't say it, but Remy Renault sounded far more like a candidate to commit murder than Larry Wofford. I had one more name to check. "What do you know about Lydia Clampett?"

He tilted his head. "Can't say I've ever heard of her. How does she fit in?"

"I'm not sure. I heard she was a friend of Wofford's."

"She's not local. And whoever she is, she sure didn't stick around when Larry was charged. Larry had a reputation as a rounder, which worked against him as far as John was concerned. He was protective of Angela. This Clampett could be some woman from Florida.

Larry did a lot of carpentry work for the ladies, if you get my drift."

"I do." Wofford made questionable life decisions. As Cece would put it, he wasn't always thinking with his big head. But if that was a jailing offense, a respectable percentage of the population would be in the slammer.

8

Darkness had fallen over the island like a star-spangled blanket. Sweetie and I paused in front of Snill's shop, taking in the scent of the ocean and the beauty of a sky unclouded with pollution. I pedaled hard toward the cottage and Sweetie galloped at my side. Like most hounds, she was well put together and aerodynamic. She made running at twenty miles an hour seem like a piece of cake. My legs were about to come off at the hips, but Sweetie bounded along without effort.

When we got to the cottage, it was full-on dark. The night and the cottage. Where was Graf? Pluto was gone, too, so perhaps he and the cat had taken a stroll. I would get a flashlight and track them. Better yet, put Sweetie on the scent, and I would have Graf in my sights in no time. Why mess around with flashlights and sandy tracks? We hurried to the beach and Sweetie turned east, toward the long row of mostly empty cottages.

I loved the wind whipping my hair and clothes and the sound of the surf. The magic of the island was almost overpowering. When Sweetie struck a trail and took off, I shifted into a jog to catch up with her.

Down the beach, a child's squeal of delight was answered with Sweetie's happy bark. Movement ahead alerted me that I wasn't alone. Graf stood at the edge of the water looking south, toward the Caribbean and the waters that Armand Couteau had once used as his hunting grounds. I couldn't wait to tell him the romantic story of the pirate and the slave girl.

But then another person appeared against the white sand. Two more, in fact. The slender blonde and the child, sharing a flashlight, walked away from Graf, heading down the beach. The child raced into the foaming surf as Sweetie Pie barked and played at her side. The woman's laughter rippled on the gusting wind.

Something about the scene stopped me dead in my tracks. I wanted to rush to Graf and ask who the woman was and whether he knew her. I couldn't. Dread held me motionless. Had Graf come down to the beach to meet this woman? Or was it just coincidence?

The woman and child disappeared into the darkness, and I still couldn't move. In a moment, Graf approached me, and I forced myself to call his name. I didn't want him to find me standing in the dark as if I was spying on him. When he drew abreast, I waited for him to greet me with a hug, but he didn't.

"I'm glad to see you're making new friends," I said, hoping my tone was not accusatory.

"The lifeguards had red flags warning against swimming. I just wanted to be sure they knew."

He bent to pet Sweetie, who was dancing around him. "What's for dinner?" he asked.

My sleep that night was restless and filled with images of jagged glass, knives, saws, scissors, and a fleeting blonde who moved through the shadows like a ghost. Graf and I had watched a movie, and he'd fallen asleep on the sofa. I left him there.

When I finally got up, dawn was breaking. I made coffee, and Sweetie and Pluto followed me outside, where I sat on the steps to smoke a cigarette.

I crushed the butt beneath my heel and sipped the hot black coffee. The gulf breeze rattled the sea oats growing on the dunes. As much as I loved the Delta, the sea spoke to me. The rush of the waves against the shore, the wind, the dazzle of the white sand in the sun, or the shifting clouds massing on the horizon—each held its own allure.

The water's vista stretching to the edge of the earth was similar to the Delta, but the Gulf had suffered some hard environmental blows in the past decade. Years of fertilizers and pollutants washing down the Mississippi had been dumped into what was once the most bountiful marine incubator.

My thoughts turned to Dr. Phyllis Norris and her desperate attempts to save the turtles. What once had been so natural and easy was becoming a life-and-death fight. Thank goodness for people like her, working to save species. I sure didn't have any answers. Not personal ones or the bigger ones for the planet.

"Are there any real answers? I've asked Clark again and again, but he doesn't tell me anything."

The question came from my right, and the speaker was a pregnant woman in a black designer suit à la 1960, wearing a thick veil that hung to her waist. I knew the image. It was part of every film buff's lexicon. Jitty had come a-calling as another young widow. "Kay Gable?" My heart fluttered at the implications.

"I will never understand why Clark had to die before the baby was born," she said. "Knowing his son would have given him such joy. He was a good man. He should've watched his son grow up."

And my parents should have known me as a grown-up. Orphaned at twelve was a cruel fate. But I didn't say it. I merely took in the apparition Jitty had created. The wind buffeted her dress and the veil, emphasizing her evident pregnancy.

"You never remarried." I wasn't an authority on Hollywood history, but I recalled Mrs. Gable had often attended functions with handsome escorts, but she'd died Clark Gable's widow.

"I was married several times before Clark. Of course, he was, too. It took us a while to find each other, but we were really in love. I didn't think I could love anyone that way again." She lifted the veil and revealed her neat blond hair and clear eyes. She was a lovely woman, serene.

"Do you have a message for me?" I dreaded to ask, but I had to know. This widows' parade held significance, even if Jitty wouldn't come right out and say it. I felt surrounded by loss.

Her features transformed into those of my most beautiful haint. "Life continues, Sarah Booth. If you don't die, you survive. You can choose to survive and have a life of joy, or you can survive and have a half of a life, one foot in the grave. I was young when Coker died. Same for Miss Alice. We had children to raise. There wasn't really a choice for us. Not much choice for Kay Gable either. She had a baby to tend, and she had to keep herself healthy to do it."

"Jitty, why are you coming to me as widows? I know you'll say you can't tell me, but you have to. If there's danger around Graf, I deserve to know."

"I don't know, Sarah Booth. Just because I'm dead doesn't mean I can summon information whenever I snap my fingers. I don't know. That's the answer to both your questions."

"Can you change what you're doing, then? As much as I hated the cartoon characters, they're better than these black-clad mourners. I'm worried enough. What about famous cancan dancers? Or maybe famous strippers? Or famous female outlaws? Anything other than famous widows."

She chuckled softly and sat beside me on the steps.

"Can you talk to the dead, Jitty? Can you ask Mrs. Gable or Jackie Kennedy questions?"

"Messages have a way of gettin' relayed in the Great Beyond. No guarantees, though. I put it out there, and sometimes it gets through. Like with your mama and daddy. They know you're in a hard spot right now. They're aware, but there's not much they can do. They did all they could for you while they were alive. Got something you want to say?"

I considered. "Maybe just thank you."

She sighed. "You're lower than a snake's belly."

"There's a woman on the beach. I've seen her with Graf."

"When a man's self-image is damaged, he wants to see a new reflection of himself. Another woman can sometimes supply that. The gunshot made you realize exactly what you want. For Graf, it's just the opposite. He knew. He had the future all lined up in his head. Now those plans don't fit him anymore because he sees himself as damaged goods. You got to give him back another reflection of himself."

"How do I do that?" I would try anything.

"Call Tinkie. Don't just talk to her; get her over

113

here. She's the smartest woman I know at showing a man the reflection he wants to see. If that don't work, she'll kick his butt." She arched an eyebrow. "Or you could pull on your big-girl panties and confront him about the woman on the beach. Don't let him dodge the issue."

For all of Jitty's advice, I got a second cup of coffee and another cigarette. Graf was still sound asleep, and there was no chance of relaxing for me. I left him a note and told Sweetie and Pluto to watch out for him. I could be at the inlet off Heron Bay in no time—and back before Graf was ready for breakfast.

The tricky part was the location of Remy Renault's boat. I drove down the barely paved road where the wild foliage brushed against the sides of the car. Isolated didn't do the place justice. If Remy Renault was as bad-tempered as Snill indicated, I could be making a mistake coming alone. And unarmed.

The house was a surprise—a fine brick structure, but obviously a summer home for someone wealthy, because the shutters were closed and the place locked down tight. When I got out of the car and walked toward the back, I saw the dock and a boat the same size as the *Miss Adventure*, but in a sad state of repair. Tied off to the dock was a Cobalt ski boat with a 300HP outboard. The ski boat was in a lot better condition than the sailboat. A middle-aged man wearing jeans, a white T-shirt, and suspenders came out of a small rental cottage.

"This is private property. Get!" He couldn't bother with even a shred of courtesy.

"Remy Renault?"

"What's it to ya?"

"I'm interested in the Esmeralda treasure. I heard you might know something about it."

If I was reading him correctly, he was torn between ego and annoyance. Ego apparently won. "I know something about it. What's it worth to you?"

"Maybe an interview in a start-up magazine called *Secrets of the Deep*. Sarah Booth Delaney," I held out my hand, which he ignored.

"I don't talk for free."

"And I don't pay for an interview unless the person actually knows something of value."

Heat jumped into his cheeks. He was a drinker with a temper. "Are you calling me a liar?"

"I'm not calling you anything. You appear to be a blunt man. I thought you'd appreciate a direct answer. Tell me what you know and if it's worth my while, I'll set up for a full interview. We can offer up to three hundred dollars."

"Pah!" He turned to leave.

"Which could lead to more interviews."

That caught him, and he pivoted to face me. "I want the money first."

"No deal. I've got a lead on another treasure hunter who was murdered. That may be the more interesting story anyway."

"Hard to interview a dead man." He grinned.

"I'll bet there are plenty of living people who can remember John Trotter. Seems he was well liked. Which can't be said about you, Mr. Renault."

His hands clenched into fists, and I thought for a minute I'd overplayed my cards. "Get out of here." He shook a fist at me.

"Okay. I just thought you might want a chance. Trotter is dead and you're alive. But I'm easy." I made it twenty paces across the lawn before he called out to stop me.

"What is it you want to know?"

"Did Trotter find the key to the Esmeralda treasure? And if he did, was that the reason he was murdered?"

He looked to the right and down as he thought. "John Trotter was a lying thief. We were partners. He was supposed to share his findings with me, and he didn't."

"Was there a contract between the two of you?"

"Gentleman's agreement. There was a time when a man's word was good enough. We shook on it."

"So he must have shared his findings with you." I didn't believe a thing he said. Remy

Renault was all about bravado, braggadocio, and plain old bullshit.

"I don't like your tone." He'd grown quiet. And far more dangerous.

"I'll need to verify your claims, Mr. Renault." I had slipped my cell phone from my pocket and used the camera to snap some photos. It might be interesting to see if Renault had been around Trotter's boat the day he was murdered.

"Get off this property, and if you show up again, you'll regret it."

"Are you threatening me?" I asked. He did have a wicked temper and a wild look in his eyes.

"I don't make threats. I just fulfill promises." He spun around and headed back into the rental unit.

"Where were you the night John Trotter was killed?"

"I've got an airtight alibi. Check it out. I was in jail in Mobile. Got into a bar fight at the Dog River Marina. Took my sister three days to bond me out."

That was easy enough to check. "Thanks for your cooperation." I couldn't resist having the last word—a trait that had gotten me into trouble more than once.

When I got back to the beach cottage, Graf was still sleeping. I wanted to wake him, to snuggle with him, to find the safe place in his arms that

117

now seemed unavailable to me. Instead, I called Sheriff Benson. Perhaps I yielded to my cowardly nature, but I couldn't force myself to confront Graf. I didn't want to be that insecure woman who flew to conclusions because I saw my man speak to another woman. Graf had never given me a reason to be so . . . suspicious. He worked with beautiful women every day in the movies. My reaction was nuts, and it was only because I felt guilty about the gunshot.

I had to gain control of my reactions to everything before I tried to make it Graf's problem. With that in mind, I focused on Angela and her case.

Larry Wofford's innocence—or guilt—that's what I had to prove. So I called Sheriff Benson and asked him to arrange a visit for me at the state prison in Atmore. Benson wasn't pleased, but I explained Angela wouldn't rest until I spoke to Wofford face-to-face.

Ten minutes later, he called me back. "Come by here. Deputy Chavis will drive you to Atmore. He can give you the details of the investigation before you allow Wofford to fill your head with stories about how he was framed."

I didn't relish hours in a car with Chavis, but I couldn't easily refuse. "I'll be there as quickly as I can. By the way, can you verify that Remy Renault was a guest in your jail the night John Trotter was killed?"

"Without a doubt. He was there for assault charges. Ms. Delaney, we did investigate this murder, though you seem to think we didn't."

"Thanks, Sheriff."

When I went back inside, Graf had made fresh coffee. "Thought you might need a jolt of caffeine," he said as he handed me the cup.

"I do. Thanks. Graf, should I be worried about us?" I stared deep into his eyes and he didn't blink.

"I love you, Sarah Booth."

It wasn't the sentiment I was expecting. I had a harder question for him, but he beat me to the punch. "Headed to the prison to see the convicted killer?"

"If you don't want me to go, I won't."

"Sarah Booth, I don't blame you for the gunshot. Gertrude was mentally off. If you'd been a newspaper reporter or a painter, she might have zeroed in on you and blamed you for her problems. It wasn't you or your job. Visit Larry Wofford and see if he can tell you anything useful."

"I know you're going through a lot. I came to Dauphin Island to be with you, to share this and help."

Instead of looking at me, his gaze centered on the beach visible through the window. "See what you can do for Angela. I love you, Sarah Booth. There are things I need to figure out. I always knew you were haunted by the past. Now I understand. I'm not being dishonest or dishonorable. I promise you that. And I'll tell you everything as soon as I can. For right now, work on Angela's case. That's the best thing for both of us." At last he faced me. "I love you so much. I only want to do right by you. I have to figure out what that is."

Before my heart broke and fell at his feet, I hurried to the car for the drive to Mobile. If space was what he wanted, I would oblige. What other option did I have?

Chavis insisted that I ride in his patrol car. I was surprised he didn't put me in the backseat. We'd barely gained the interstate before he speared me with an icy glance. "Larry Wofford killed John Trotter. You're wasting your time, and if you're taking Angela Trotter's money, it's highway robbery."

"I'll be sure and pass on the information. Angela will be impressed you're concerned about her finances. And I appreciate *you're* convinced Wofford is guilty. Still, there're some troubling irregularities." I tried to walk a fine line.

"Such as the fact I'm not a detective and worked the case?"

"It's a point of curiosity. In most large departments, there's a distinction between the two divisions. Is it common practice in Mobile County to allow patrol officers to handle homicides?"

"No, it's not. Occasionally advantages override duty assignments. I grew up on the island. Believe it or not, I liked Mr. Trotter. He was a character. Some evenings, when he had a drink or two in the Mermaid's Cellar, I'd join him after work. He could spin a yarn. More than a couple of times I drove him back to his boat when he got too tipsy to walk home safely."

I was surprised at the genuine warmth in his voice. Up until that moment, I'd wondered if Randy Chavis had a human side. "You certainly don't care much for his daughter, Angela."

The deputy sighed. "I'm aggravated at her. She's thrown away the last year of her life trying to save the man who murdered her father. I have no idea why she persists in believing Wofford is innocent. He's a damn fine carpenter, but he's a drunk. In case you haven't had the pleasure of knowing one, alcoholics do whatever is necessary to ruin their lives and often the lives of those who love them. Angela can't see that."

I didn't doubt she knew Wofford drank too much, but it was a far cry from being a murderer. "The case against Wofford was circumstantial."

"A lot of cases are."

He was correct, but those instances always left me with reasonable doubt. The burden of proof was on the state, and I wasn't certain the prosecution had met it. "Did Wofford have an adequate defense attorney?"

"As far as I could tell. McGowan got records, interviewed witnesses, the whole nine yards. Wofford had every benefit, including the victim's daughter testifying on his behalf. And he was still convicted. That should tell you something."

"But the most incriminating evidence was Arley McCain's testimony, right?"

"Without a doubt." He took an exit off the interstate, and in a moment we were driving through flat, clear fields where hay and other crops were grown. In the distance the road cut through what had once been a grove of pecan trees. We were almost at the prison.

"What's your take on McCain?"

"Arley's salt of the earth. Angela is like a daughter to him. And he looked out for John as best he could."

"And Wofford?"

"There were times Wofford didn't pay his slip fees for six months. Arley carried him. Folks at the marina look out for each other like a family. It killed Arley to testify against Larry, but he told the truth. Angela can't accept it because she's sweet on Larry. Those are the facts, Ms. Delaney. I did my job. I put a killer behind bars. You can investigate all you want, but it won't change the truth."

"What are your feelings for Angela?"

The skin beneath his left eye twitched, and I couldn't tell if it was guilt or surprise. "My feelings have nothing to do with Larry Wofford's guilt."

"That right?" I'd hit a nerve. His attitude toward Angela had always been too extreme. Because he had romantic feelings for her? Or was something else at work? "Who shot up her house?"

"We didn't find much to go on. No witnesses to speak of. A neighbor saw a black sedan slow down just before the shots were fired. We searched, but there wasn't any physical evidence. Believe me, I'd like to catch the bastards, whether it was someone intending harm to Angela or juvenile delinquents, who fired off guns in a residential area."

"So you dropped the investigation?"

He shot an angry glare at me. "We did not drop it. I can't manufacture evidence, though you seem to think I do it all the time. We recovered the two bullets from her wall: .22 longs. It could have been kids acting out. Or it could have been a warning. Since Angela quit the newspaper, there's little reason for people to want to intimidate her. She's minding her own affairs and leaving the politicians alone."

"Except for hiring me to reinvestigate her father's murder."

His grip tightened on the steering wheel, but he didn't respond.

"Don't you find it coincidental that Angela hires me and someone shoots her house?"

"I haven't quit looking into it."

A crack in the denial. "Thank you."

"It's a waste of your time and Angela's money, but do what you want. Talk to Arley. Once you do, you'll realize Wofford wasn't railroaded. Maybe he was too intoxicated to remember what he did, but he shot John Trotter. Take it to the bank. He came off that boat covered in John Trotter's blood and Arley saw him. No one else was on that boat."

He slowed the patrol car as we entered a speed zone. Fields stretched on either side of the road, reminding me of the Delta. We closed the distance to the prison, a series of long, flat buildings with guard towers and concertina wire all around the chain-link enclosures. A dozen inmates wearing the traditional prison ring-arounds played basket-ball in a fenced yard.

"Did you ever look into Remy Renault?" I asked when he'd parked.

"I know who he is. He never came into the case."

"He told me he and Trotter were partners on the Esmeralda treasure. A gentleman's agreement. He feels cheated."

I could tell my news surprised him. "Stay away from Renault. He's been arrested for assault several times. He's got a hair-trigger temper, and

124

based on past actions, he doesn't care if it's aimed at a woman or a man. The night John was killed, Renault was arrested for fighting. Not the first time, either. A week before, he hit a woman. He's trouble."

"A woman?" He was a piece of work. "Do you remember her name?"

"Something from a TV show." He thought for a moment. "Clampett, like the *Beverly Hillbillies*. The first name escapes me."

I was careful to show no reaction. "Thanks for the warning about Renault." I had one more question. "Why do you think the security cameras at the marina failed to work that one night?"

Chavis got out of the car. When I stood beside him, he looked down at me. "You've got half an hour with Wofford. That's it. This is a waste of my time."

9

I walked into the visitor's room, where Larry Wofford was sitting behind a metal table bolted to the floor. I'd been told, repeatedly, that Wofford was a charmer. He was an appealing blend of Elvis Presley, Johnny Depp, and a dash of the rebel James Dean.

He nodded a greeting, waiting for me to state my business. It was clear he had no expectations of this meeting. He was neither beaten down nor tough-guy prison con. While his bad-boy grin should have been on the movie screen, he couldn't hide the fatigue and lack of hope in his gray eyes.

"What are you? Journalist, writer, film director, curiosity seeker?"

"What do you want me to be?" I asked.

"I'd like for you to be the head of Project Innocence who's here to tell me you've found new evidence to free me."

So his hope wasn't dead yet. Badly damaged but not dead. "Angela sent me."

His soft-spoken reply lazed with a Southern drawl. "She should drop it. She's wasting her time and her money. I'm in for twenty-five to life. Maybe a chance of parole for good behavior if I don't annoy the warden and the guards. I can't say that for certain, but it's something to work toward."

"What happened that night, Larry?"

"I'm not telling it again. I've told it to a thousand people, and the result is the same. I've been convicted. I have to accept this and endure the sentence. I can't keep getting my hopes up and then crashing down. I won't do it again. Please tell Angela to stop. She should sell her dad's boat, take the money, and build a life for herself somewhere far away from Dauphin Island. There's nothing there for her but reminders of all she's lost."

"That's a smart attitude. I don't know that I can do anything to make Angela adopt it. She's a stubborn woman, and she believes you're innocent. She believes the person who killed her father remains unpunished. That's tough to put behind you."

His hands flattened on top of the table, his fingertips gently gripping the metal. "She needs to let this go. Let me go. There's no justice for her, but the bigger injustice would be to continue to spend her life chasing something she'll never catch. Guard! Please take me back to my cell."

I agreed with him. In principle. But not in fact. Justice wasn't something that could be left behind. It was a basic human need. "I told Angela I'd talk to you. She believes in you enough to foot my bill. Whether you talk to me or not, she'll pursue this. I might be able to help."

I wasn't trying to badger him into talking to me, but he had a right to know Angela was spending her money on his behalf.

"Tell her not to waste her savings. The only thing I did wrong was happen into the wrong place at the wrong time. And then try to help John. They framed me good and proper. I'm caught like a rabbit in a snare. I can't keep hoping new evidence is suddenly going to appear and clear me."

"Your case is on appeal. Your lawyer believes in you too."

He shrugged. "That and a dollar will buy you a cup of coffee."

He wasn't cynical; he was trying not to snap under the weight of his circumstances. "Will you answer some questions? If not, Sergeant Chavis is waiting for me. He's not a patient man."

"Randy Chavis brought you here? To see me?"

His interest was piqued, as I intended. "Sheriff Benson suggested he bring me. It was the kind of suggestion I couldn't ignore, if you get my drift."

"Oh, I get it. Chavis is a righteous bastard. He set me up. The security cameras didn't work that night. Right. I don't know how he convinced Arley to testify against me, but he did. Arley knows me better than that. He knows I wouldn't hurt anyone, and especially not John Trotter. Sure, we'd argue when we were both drunk and make wild threats. It was all part of the show."

Wofford might not want to talk about his situation, but he couldn't stop himself. "Just tell me what happened. One more time couldn't hurt." I tapped my watch. "I don't have long."

His shoulders slumped, and he leaned forward with his forearms on the edge of the table. "I met John the first day he docked at the marina. We hit it off, and we met most afternoons for a drink or two when I wasn't out of town on a job. He'd spin some yarns about this treasure hunting. He'd been all over the world. He had tales that would curl your toes. Adventure, brushes with celebrities and rulers of places I'd never heard of. The man was a walking encyclopedia."

"Did he confide in you about the Couteau treasure?"

"Hell, he talked to everyone on the island about it. That was John's big flaw. He couldn't keep his mouth shut. Especially not when he thought he'd actually found the key to the treasure. He blabbed about it in the post office, the grocery store, the barbershop. I'm surprised he didn't book himself on a radio talk show. I kept telling him to shut up, but he wouldn't. He was that excited."

"The last day, did he mention anything specific about the treasure?"

"You mean the key?"

I nodded.

"Oh, he was drinking and carrying on. I'd never seen him that worked up."

"What was the key?"

"Damned if I know." He compressed his lips as if he was done, but then added, "He was reading old journals, always digging around in the library and archives, visiting families who'd been on the island for generations. He and Terrance Snill were thick as thieves." He was smiling when he said it, letting me know it was a phrase, not a character assassination of his friend.

"Do you believe he threw in with Remy Renault? Remy is claiming he and Trotter had an agreement."

"I don't know. Remy had been hanging around the boat. Arley threw him out of the marina. I can't see John working with him. There were times John was lonely, though. To be honest, I didn't believe in the treasure. It was a pipe dream. Or at least that's what I thought. You know, John needed something to hang on to. Some magic to put his life in perspective. I thought the treasure was a fantasy, the pot of gold, the big lotto win, the dream that dreamers cling to even when reality proves otherwise." His gaze intensified, and I felt a chill race up my arms. "Until that last day. I saw him that morning when I was leaving for work. He was on the deck of his boat with a cup of coffee, and he looked sober."

I was curious about his line of thinking. "What did he say?"

"John said, 'I found the key. I can find the treasure now.' Those were his exact words, to the best of my recollection. And he wasn't full of alcohol or bluster. He was dead serious, and calm. Before, he'd get all excited and make grandiose plans. This time, he was different."

"But he gave no details?"

"No. John was very precise. It's one of those crazy things. We both drank way too much. We'd get sloppy with it. But he was a real spit-and-polish guy when it came to his work. Made me think he had a military background the way he kept his boat. Everything put away, neat and all. He was like that when he talked that last day. Careful to say what he meant, but secretive."

This was exactly the detail I needed. "So did he call you to visit him on the boat, or did you happen by for the traditional evening happy hour?"

Larry frowned. "I was drinking pretty heavily then. I'd finished a job over in the Destin area, and I'd been paid very well." He took a deep breath. "That was my pattern. I would get a check and then drink it away. When I didn't have another dime, I'd get another job. It was a vicious cycle. The one thing about being here in jail is that I haven't had a drink in eighteen months. Maybe I've learned to control the addiction. Maybe I've licked it." He chuckled. "Like getting clean will do me any real good."

"So you don't remember if John called?"

"I do remember. Vividly. John had hired me to do something for him."

"Which was?" I had eight minutes left. I needed to get Wofford to the nut of the matter.

"He'd sold an old telescope to the Mobile Maritime Museum back when he was down on his luck. It was antique and a nice piece but not really valuable. John wanted it back. Said it was his good luck charm, and he didn't want to go after the treasure without it. Sailors are superstitious, in case you haven't been around a lot of them."

"I've heard stories. Isn't it bad luck to have a woman on board a boat?"

He cocked an eyebrow, the bad boy coming through. "Only if it's the wrong woman." The spark of mischief danced in his eyes before it died.

"So Trotter wanted you to get the telescope from the museum?"

"He tried to buy it, but the curator, that pantywaist Dr. Lionel Prevatt, wouldn't sell it. Not even when John offered triple what he'd been paid."

The little hairs on my arms quivered. "Why

was John so interested in this telescope? If he was that desperate to get it back, surely he viewed it as more than just a good luck piece."

"I don't know. John was a curious man. He had things he loved. Old things. Mostly about sailing. He polished them and cared for them. It was almost as if he had a romance with the sea, the old ways. The spyglass was personal to him, and he wanted it bad. When he couldn't buy it back, he hired me to steal it."

This was an unexpected twist, and one I hadn't heard from Angela. "And did you?"

"I tried. I went to the museum, and there it was in the case just like John told me it would be. I couldn't get Prevatt distracted long enough to get the damn thing. I used to be a pretty good thief. It should have been simple. But Prevatt watched me like he knew my intentions were dishonorable. He followed me around pretending to tell me about the different pieces and so forth. He acted like he couldn't trust me to even look at his precious artifacts."

And with good reason, but I kept my lip zipped. "What was it about the spyglass?"

"John never said. It was special to him and he wanted it back and now he could afford to buy it. He said once he found the treasure, the value of everything connected to him would go up and he'd never be able to get his hands on it. He was right. Prevatt would never part with it, no matter how much John offered. That's why he decided to steal it instead."

"How'd it go down?"

"I put on my best suit and went in pretending to be a collector, but Prevatt wouldn't even take it out of the case so I could hold it. Said it was too valuable. Lying cheat. He only gave John a hundred dollars for it when John was desperate for cash. Anyway, nothing I did could pry Prevatt away from the telescope. So that's why I stopped by to see John. To tell him I'd failed in my mission. Unfortunately, I'd stopped by a few clubs on my way home. Like five or six. Had I gone back right away, I could have saved him from his killer."

He stared at the table until he composed himself. "And that's when I found him dying. I tried to help him. I put pressure on the wound in his chest and tried to stem the blood, but it was useless. I'd lost my cell phone, and John's was nowhere to be found. I had to make a choice. Try to help him or run for help. He died only minutes after I arrived. You know the rest."

"Why didn't you call the cops and report it?"

"He died so quickly. Then I panicked. I knew how it would look, so I ran out, intending to go to my boat. That's when Arley must have seen me. I got to my boat and drank everything I could put my hands on. I passed out. John was dead, and I wasn't thinking rationally."

"Did you ever tell anyone about the telescope?"

"Why paint John to be a thief? Didn't seem to be a point in hurting Angela."

The way he said her name told me a lot. He cared for her. In the romantic way. And I had no doubt she returned the emotion. My heart went out to Angela Trotter. She was caught between the devil and the deep blue sea. She was in love with the man convicted of killing her father. "Were you dating Angela?" I posed the question as gently as I could.

"Absolutely not. She doesn't need someone like me in her life. She's a good person. She deserves more than a man who drinks his life away."

I wasn't sure that was the proper characterization of Larry Wofford. While he was certainly handsome and obviously had a problem with alcohol, there was more to him than I'd expected.

A tap on the door told me my time was up. "One more thing about Remy. Did you know he'd assaulted a woman?"

He couldn't follow where I was headed. "He was always a jackass. Beating up on a woman sounds just like him."

"The woman was Lydia Clampett."

His reaction was shock. "Lydia? She said her husband hit her. Was she hurt?"

"Not enough to press charges. It just occurred to me, Larry, that the two of them may have played you. Remy kills John and Lydia delivers you into the trap. Think about it."

"Shit!" The color had drained from his face. "I just met Lydia. She drove me from the bar because I was so drunk. She said she was married and made me promise I wouldn't tell anyone. I wasn't involved with her or anything, but she made it clear her husband would hurt her." He looked like he wanted to cry. "Shit."

I took pity on him. "Don't get your hopes up, but I'm doing what I can."

"I'm going to take a risk and trust you, Ms. Delaney. So far, my judgment hasn't been too good." He signaled me to lean closer to him, and his voice dropped to a whisper. "John found something at Fort Gaines. I have no idea what, but it pertained to the treasure. I'm sure of it."

"Did he hint at anything?" This might be helpful.

"Believe me, I'd tell Angela if I knew anything. He never gave specifics, but it was the way he acted. The fort plays a role in this."

Staring into Wofford's gray eyes, I believed him. "Thanks. You'll be hearing from me."

"Don't waste your time, Ms. Delaney. I won't be out until I'm in my sixties. That's a bitter pill, but best to swallow it and move on. In here, one thing is for certain. I won't fall off the wagon anytime soon." His grin, while devil-may-care, couldn't hide the pain.

When I got outside the room where Wofford was still held, I couldn't find Chavis. The corridor was empty. Only a moment before, he'd been knocking at the door, urging me to finish.

Footsteps alerted me to someone coming and I turned, expecting the deputy. Instead, a large man in an orange jumpsuit barreled toward me. He clipped me hard with an elbow as he passed. "Watch yourself," he said.

I couldn't be certain if it was meant to be a warning or a random accident. But a good PI knows there is no such thing as a coincidence.

10

The ride from the prison back to Mobile was one long silence. Chavis seemed lost in his own thoughts, and I had plenty to chew on. If Chavis had sent the inmate to intimidate me, I wasn't going to let him know I'd been affected, so that topic was off limits. I did have a few questions about the murder scene.

"Did you find any evidence of a burglary on Trotter's boat the night he was killed?" I broke the silence.

Chavis chewed his bottom lip for a moment. "No. We looked, but nothing obvious was missing. Of course, no one really knew what John had on the boat, other than the essentials. There wasn't an inventory of possessions, and John did have a few valuable nautical antiques. Those were untouched."

The killer could have stolen from the boat and it wouldn't have been obvious. "Angela wouldn't have known?" I asked.

"Relations between Angela and John were strained. He loved her, but guilt kept him from acting on it. I know she loved him, but she was angry and hurt. Still, she moved to Mobile and took the job at the *Chronicle* to be closer to him.

Given more time, they would have come to an understanding and put the past aside."

Chavis wasn't the cynic I'd painted him. "How do you know this?"

He hooked a finger in the collar of his shirt. "John talked to me. His big plan was to find the Esmeralda treasure and make up to Angela the years he hadn't been a real father to her."

"The picture I'm getting is of a man who talked too much about everything."

Chavis cast me a sidelong glance. "John talked too much and bragged too much, but he knew where to draw the line. I never heard him give up any specific details of his hunts. Just big generalities wrapped around a good yarn." He exited the interstate and looped around toward the sheriff's office, where I'd parked. We were almost done.

"Have you ever had any doubts about Wofford's guilt?" I asked.

"Do you really think if I'd put an innocent man in prison and then realized I'd made a mistake that I wouldn't try to rectify it?" He halted the car in a parking slot.

"Some officers wouldn't." It was an ugly fact. Careers could be broken with a bad arrest and conviction, even when the officer had done everything in his power to apprehend the right criminal.

"You obviously have a low opinion of law

enforcement officials, Ms. Delaney. Despite what you think, we want justice as badly as anyone else."

"I know plenty of good officers, Sergeant Chavis. Unfortunately, I also know some really bad ones."

"And you've got me pegged as one of the bad ones?" He opened his car door, got out, slammed it, and started toward the building.

"I don't know yet," I called at his back.

On the drive back to the island, I stopped at a couple of specialty shops for wine, cheese, seafood, and fresh produce. A few Sand Mountain tomatoes were still available, though the season was long past. I picked up two bunches of turnips to cook later. And sweet potatoes. The local fall crops had come in, and I was eager for the fresh produce. Or at least the idea of it. My appetite was nil.

When my errands were done, I called Tinkie and updated her on all I'd learned about John Trotter's murder—and Chavis's human side. I also asked her if she could get Cece to check on the whereabouts of one Lydia Clampett. As a journalist, Cece had access to databases that I didn't. And the newspaper business was like a secret society of nosey people with good sources.

"I'll get her on it. But think about this. If Wofford was framed, there has to be someone on the inside of the sheriff's office, too. And the threat from the inmate confirms that. Someone had to put that brute up to intimidating you."

She was right. And clearly Randy Chavis, the man on the scene, was the obvious choice.

"I'm not saying Chavis is playing you, but it wouldn't be the first time a wolf donned sheep's clothing." Tinkie was ultimately logical, which was why she was the perfect partner for me. "Be careful, Sarah Booth. You're a long way from home, and you don't have me watching your back. How's Graf doing?"

Loneliness washed over me. "He's working through some things. How are plans for the Black and Orange Ball?" I didn't want to talk about me or my problems.

"Cece has outdone herself. I believe she'll top out at close to a hundred and fifty grand for charity. And just to lift your spirits, the surprise she's concocted for you will blow you away."

"Great." I forced enthusiasm into my voice. "Any hints?"

"Can't do it. Prepare to be shocked, though. In a good way. You have your dress, right?"

"Of course." It hung in the closet beside Graf's tux.

"Just FYI, Mattie Carlisle has set her cap for Harold. She asked Cece if Harold was bringing a date. When she found out he wasn't, she made it clear she's going in for the kill."

Mattie Carlisle owned a Delta plantation and a New Orleans townhouse. She'd married well—and become a well-off widow—and inherited from her daddy. From a financial point, she'd make an excellent wife. I'd be willing to bet, though, when she doesn't get her way, her hair turns into snakes. "Did you warn Harold?"

"I will. After a bit of fun."

"Tinkie! Harold is our good friend."

"And nobody's fool. He can handle Mattie with both hands tied behind his back. I'm curious to watch her frontal assault. I'm thinking playbook of Attila the Hun."

She did make me laugh, and I felt immensely better. I needed a good dose of Tinkie. Jitty was correct about that much. "Could Cece spare you for a day?"

"She has minions galore. Millie is here. I can't believe she left the café, but she did. And Madame Tomeeka. She's giving readings at the bar, but she has plenty of time to help Cece. And there's a host of New Orleans society ladies Cece loves to boss around. Sure. How about tomorrow? I'll run over and we can work on the case."

"Excellent."

By the time I got back to the cottage, it was the shank of the afternoon. The slanting sunlight was incredible, and I unloaded the groceries. Graf was freshly showered and going over a page of figures. "How was the trip to the prison?"

"Wofford wasn't what I expected." The case was our neutral ground. We could discuss that without treading on boundaries.

"Do you think he's a murderer?"

"Hard to say. If he did shoot John Trotter, he may not recall it. Alcohol blackout is a real possibility. Or he could be innocent."

"What's your next step?"

"I want to revisit the fort. Wofford suggested there might be a clue to the Esmeralda treasure. If I can prove the pirate's booty was the motive for John's murder, I think I can bring new evidence for Wofford's appeal. Want to go with me? The light is stupendous."

"You go ahead." Graf tapped the notepad. "I've neglected my bills and a number of other matters. I tell you what, I'll put the turnips on to cook while you're gone." His cell phone buzzed the alert to a text message, but he didn't reach for it.

"Aren't you answering your phone?"

He shook his head. "My agent keeps aggravating me about two scripts he sent. I haven't read them, and I don't want to deal with it right now."

Graf had worked too hard for each opportunity that came his way. Ignoring potential roles wasn't his style. Still, I knew better than to question him about it. "I'll be back in an hour or so."

He blew me a kiss and returned to his calculations.

Sweetie wanted to go with me, but I asked her to stay behind with Graf. He needed her company. Besides, it was almost five o'clock and the fort would be closing. I might need to slip around a bit. While Sweetie could be appropriately sneaky, she was also a big red tic hound that weighed seventy pounds. Hard to miss.

I managed to get into the fort before it closed, and I made my way to the older section. From Civil War garrison to World War II post, Fort Gaines had been renovated and expanded. It was the older section that intrigued me. Wofford had said there was something at the fort that John Trotter had been very excited about. I wanted time to search. Alone.

An hour passed as I investigated the fort. Five lookout points gave views of the opening of Mobile Bay and also the Gulf of Mexico. Within the walls of the fort, soldiers had lived and trained. Atop a parapet, I stopped to watch the sun hang on the horizon at the level of the water, sinking second by second. How brave the men and women were who sailed to this country across miles of ocean and months of being trapped on a boat. My own Delaney relatives had emigrated from Ireland in the 1800s. I wasn't certain I would have been able to find the grit and resilience to make such a journey.

Shadows in the fort were lengthening—time to get about my business. I was looking for something that couldn't be moved. So what was it? A cannon, a building, a hiding place for the treasure? If such a treasure even existed.

Moving down a dark and empty hallway, my footsteps echoing on the stone floors and against the passageway walls, I felt a chill trace along my back. I turned, expecting to see Jitty. Instead, I heard footsteps that stopped only an instant after mine.

When I looked, there was no one behind me.

The rush of adrenaline sent my heart rate into overdrive. Taking slow, deliberate steps, I slipped down a corridor I hoped would give me an exit to the courtyard. There were outbuildings with better vantage points—and hiding places.

The footfalls imitated my own. Same pace, same speed. Someone stalked me, and didn't care that I knew it. I thought about the big felon at Atmore. The look in his eyes, the way his elbow had jammed hard into my ribs meaning to hurt me. I could be in a very bad place.

I couldn't stop moving for fear the stalker would come upon me, so I kept walking. Pulling my cell phone from my pocket, I dialed 911. Nothing. The walls of the fort were thick. Reception on the island was iffy at best. Here, at Fort Gaines, there was nothing. I shoved the phone into my pocket so the telltale light wouldn't give me away.

The corridor was blindingly dark. It seemed to stretch forever as I groped forward as quietly as I could. The footsteps drew closer. Unhurried, but gaining ground. My pursuer had longer legs than mine, which led me to believe he was a man. And he wasn't stumbling as I was. He knew the terrain.

At last I came to a window and caught the glint of moonlight on the Gulf water. The waves crested in the silver light, and I looked out and down for an escape route. Below, waves crashed against boulders put there to stop erosion. No freedom there.

I had two choices. I could continue down the corridor at a cautious pace, or I could run. Both had inherent dangers. One suited my nature better than the other. I sprinted into the darkness, one hand in front of me to stop a head-on crash into a wall.

It took a moment for my stalker to realize I was in a dead-out run. Then I heard him after me, footsteps ringing on the stone floor.

I ducked through openings with barely an inch to spare, and at one point I heard a curse. I didn't recognize the voice, but it bought me a bit of extra lead time.

When I came to a small alcove, really nothing more than an indentation in the brick wall, I pressed myself inside it and crouched, doing my best to suppress my harsh breathing. My pursuer slowed also. His footsteps drew slowly closer, step-by-step. At times he paused, and I could only guess he was listening for some sign of my whereabouts.

In my youth, I'd played hide-and-seek with my school friends. It was chilling fun on a hot summer night when we burrowed among heritage camellias and shrubs. I remembered the excitement and tension of waiting to be found, trying hard to remain quiet and still. I'd never been much good at it, but this night I had no choice but to perfect the skills. Knees hugged to my chest, I pressed my face into my jeans and sought perfect calm.

He drew close—the footfalls sounded heavier, male. The leading edge of a flashlight beam climbed along the stone floor in front of my hiding place. I held my breath and pressed against the cold stone, wishing to merge with it. The light scampered along the hallway cobbles, seeking a clue to which direction I'd gone.

My breath sounded like a train roaring in my ears, but I knew it wasn't loud. Still, I did my best to draw in oxygen, shallow and soft, squeezing my eyes tight in the foolish notion that if I couldn't see him, he couldn't see me.

Unbelievably, the footsteps drew abreast of me, and I peeked out. The flashlight illuminated black pants and black spit-shined shoes, about a size ten. His right hand hung down at his side, a .38 gripped loosely in his fingers.

I had no time to ascertain other details. He moved down the hallway, the light flicking here and there, searching. And then he was gone.

I waited as long as I could and removed my shoes. In my socks I hurried down the hallway the way I'd come until I came to a narrow opening that appeared to lead out of the fort. Ignoring the gravel and debris, I raced across an open area toward the parking lot.

When I finally got to my car, I took a deep breath. Shifting behind the wheel, I glanced in the rearview mirror. A flashlight beam signaled from one of the parapets on the fort wall. The light shone and blinked. Then winked back to life. Five times. A signal. I thought of the old pirate tales where islanders lured ships onto a reef, deliberately causing a wreck.

The villagers then rushed out into the shallows to pillage the remains of the boat. A similar thing had happened to Armand Couteau's ship. When he'd returned to Dauphin Island with his beautiful bride to reclaim the treasure of Esmeralda Cortez that he'd hidden, he'd ventured too close to the island's changing coastline. A sudden storm had blown the ship onto a reef, and she'd grounded and broken apart.

Couteau and LuAnn had washed ashore. They'd both been taken prisoner, and he'd died of his wounds. LuAnn was returned to slavery and sold. A bitter ending to a fairy-tale romance.

But I couldn't waste time romanticizing the past and pirates and treasures. I put the SUV in drive and blasted out of the parking lot, spinning rocks everywhere. I considered the dangers of going home, but there was no evidence of anyone following me, so I returned to the cottage.

When I was parked beneath the beautiful beach house, I sat for a moment, allowing my breathing and heart rate to calm. There was a possibility that the person pursuing me had been a night watchman, someone paid to make sure teenagers and vandals didn't get into the fort and damage things.

Or, it could have been someone snooping around, the same as I had been. Someone hunting for clues to a long-lost treasure.

The possibility that concerned me was that it was someone who'd been watching me and saw an opportunity to catch me alone and scare or harm me. My gut told me it was this third option.

By the time I'd run through the various scenarios, I could enter the cottage with perfect composure. Graf had left the sliding glass doors to the beach balcony open, and the drapes billowed in the sea gusts. I could almost taste the salt on the air. The surf surged, a sound both gentle and wild.

"Graf?" There were no lights on, and I wondered where he was. Both bicycles were in their places beneath the cottage. I'd had the car.

If he left, he was on foot. Dauphin Island didn't have a taxi service that I knew of.

"Graf?"

A low whine carried from the bedroom, and I hurried to release Sweetie Pie and Pluto. When I stood in the doorway of the darkened room, I realized the sliding glass door here, too, had been left open.

And yet there was no sign of Graf.

Fear paralyzed me for several seconds. The notion that someone had come and taken Graf—maybe hurt him—was an emotional sledge-hammer into my brain. Perhaps not rational, but neither was Gertrude's attack on my fiancé.

A low-pitched whine brought me back to my senses. Sweetie grasped the hem of my shirt and tugged me downstairs. With my dog in the lead, I crossed the living room to the balcony. Passing through the kitchen, I caught the scent of food cooking. Graf was sitting on the balcony in the dark, a glass of wine in his hand.

Relief was sweet, but it also brought a tide of anger. "You scared me. Are you okay?"

He remained in the dark, the moonlight glinting on the glass, but his features were obscured. "Yes, I'm sorry. I didn't hear you come in. Everything is ready except the fish. I'll put it on whenever you're hungry."

We left the wild night and worked together in the kitchen to put the finishing touches on the meal. "Did you talk with your agent?" I asked. I'd been eager to tell him about the encounter at the old fort, but now I held back. Something was wrong with him, and I'd halfway convinced myself the man at the fort had been a night watchman, not someone hunting for me.

"I did. The roles are both good. I should take one."

"When would you start shooting?"

"You know Hollywood. Lots of hurry up and wait."

I heated the skillet while Graf cut up cucumbers for the salad. "Tell me about the parts." I loved hearing the details of his work, and I needed the talk of work and career. Graf's latest cowboy movie had opened doors, and now he was getting offers for roles as the tough guy as well as romantic leads. The movie we'd planned to film together was still a possibility, too. Whatever he wanted—I'd made peace with the idea that for the next few years, I would follow my man. It was only temporary. If this was what he needed to get his career back on track, it would happen.

"In one I'd play the father in a coming-of-age story set in the nineteen sixties. It's a great role. The other is an action movie."

The scripts were on a table beside the lamp and chair. I wiped my hands on a dishcloth and picked them up. *Season of Innocents* was an adaptation of a novel. Marion Silber was the screenwriter. I glanced through the first pages. The opening was compelling. "Sounds great."

Graf snapped on the television. "Dauphin Island is under a hurricane watch. It's too soon to tell which track the storm will take, or the strength at which it'll come in, but we need to keep alert."

"We can always pack up and head home."

"Is that what you'd like?" he asked.

"No." He'd asked for space, but I had to be honest. "Graf, I picked up a marriage license in Mobile. I've arranged for an officiant to perform the ceremony on the beach Saturday morning. My plan was to get married, then meet up with our friends in New Orleans to celebrate at the Black and Orange Ball. I wanted to surprise you, to show you how much I love you. I don't want to risk the storm, but I'd like to seal our marriage, if you—"

"It's impossible to make plans with a storm out there."

"I know. We may have to abandon the plan, but you're so close to a full recovery. You've worked hard, and the limp is gone." I had to believe in the future, in our future. I'd been too tentative in accepting Graf's marriage attempts. It was my turn to push.

I retrieved the velvet box with two Irish wedding rings I'd purchased. He started at the rings, running his finger lightly over them. "They're beautiful. The perfect rings."

Yet he didn't sweep me into his arms. He didn't kiss me. The joy I'd imagined was missing. "I'm sorry. You asked for some space." I threw the dishtowel on the counter and fled.

His hand caught my wrist. "This is everything I ever wanted, Sarah Booth. Everything. A future with you—I couldn't ask for more."

"Before the accident, this was all you wanted."

"Things have changed."

"What's changed so drastically that you don't want to marry me?"

"I'm not certain that path is open to me." He picked up his jacket. "I'm going out. I'm sorry."

"No, you are not going to walk out on me. What's going on with you? I deserve to know."

"How can I tell you what I don't know myself?"

"I understand that the gunshot changed things. Changed you. But every day that passes, you withdraw a little more. You have to talk to me."

He put a hand on my jaw, caressing my cheek. "I make you a solemn promise, Sarah Booth. When I come to terms with things, I will tell you. I simply can't right now. I'm going for a walk."

11

I awoke with Sweetie Pie licking my face, a damp warmth that made my stomach churn. Reaching for my cell phone to check the time, my stumbling fingers encountered an empty wine bottle. The momentary bliss of amnesia the wine had given vaporized as events of the night rushed back. Graf had rejected my marriage proposal. My brilliant response was to drink myself silly.

Now it was midnight, and Sweetie was licking me like a Dreamsicle and whining in my ear. Had I even remembered to let my loyal hound out for a bathroom break?

"Shit." I sat up and felt the first throb of a bodacious headache. My stomach sloshed dangerously and pain slammed into my fore-head. Wine hangovers are the worst.

Sweetie's dash to the door reminded me of obligations I had to tend to no matter how bad I felt. "I'm coming," I said, struggling to my feet and tripping over a second dead soldier. With a hangover, I should at least have some respite from hurt feelings, but such was not the case.

The night had turned chill, and there wasn't a glimmer of moonlight from the overcast sky. Throwing on a jacket, I opened the front door and followed Sweetie into the night. The hound bounded over a dune and toward the beach.

"Sweetie," I called, struggling through the cold sand to catch up with her. My feet felt too big and clumsy.

When I crested the rise, I saw my hound on the beach, nose to the ground. She'd hit a scent. But of what? The memory of the man in the old fort hit me like a physical blow, dissipating the brain-fog effect of the hangover. That quickly, my mind sharpened and my senses focused.

Sweetie's long, bloodcurdling howl reminded me of the nemesis of the Baskervilles. And then my pup was off, down the beach like a streak. I thought fleetingly of the gun in the trunk of my old roadster, back at Dahlia House. I hadn't brought a weapon on vacation. I'd never anticipated working while at Dauphin Island. Fate had simply handed me a puzzle to solve. There'd been no way to anticipate that asking a few questions would result in danger.

Gun or not, I wasn't about to let Sweetie Pie track down a potential stalker without backup. I took off at a sprint.

Each step in the sand was answered with a pounding pressure in my forehead. Running with a hangover headache wasn't my smartest move, but I had no choice.

Sweetie streaked to the east, toward the more populated area of the beach. I increased my speed, barely able to match my fleet hound, who was nothing more than a dark, fast-moving blot against the white sand.

When I was about to give up hope that I'd catch her, Sweetie stopped. Nose in the air, she sniffed the wind.

"Criminy, Sweetie, do you want to give me a heart attack?" I grabbed her collar. "What is it?"

Sweetie's low whine sent a chill over me. The dog obviously sensed danger. But from where? I scanned the beach. The white sand stretched in both directions, empty of all save the crashing surf.

There was no sign of anyone.

Ready to turn back to the cottage and seek out water and a bottle of aspirin, I urged Sweetie toward home. Instead of her normally docile reaction, she braced her legs and stood her ground. With a quick twist, she was free and racing down the beach.

"Dammit!" I jogged after her. "Sweetie!" My command was lost in the wind. The dog completely ignored me and kept going. My only option was to give chase.

Sweetie ambled up a dune, and I followed, cursing under my breath. When I accessed the top, I almost tripped over my dog, who'd stopped dead in her tracks. Her body was rigid, her tail pointed straight behind her.

"Dadgummit, Sweetie." Movement at the bottom of the dune caught my eye.

A man and a woman were locked in intense

conversation. The woman's beautiful blond hair blew behind her. The man, dark and lean, reached out a hand and touched her face. It was a touch so intimate, so melancholy, that I swallowed a lump in my throat.

In a startling move, the woman rushed to him, pulling him into an embrace and a kiss. It was the stuff of every romantic song I'd ever danced to. Sand, surf, wind, lovers separated by other obligations and finally yielding to the temptations of the flesh.

The gut kick to my heart told me the truth my eyes couldn't discern. Graf was kissing another woman. A blonde. *The* slender blonde who shared the beach with us this last week of October.

In the dim light of a bleak night sky, I couldn't see details, but my body's reaction told me everything I needed to know. That and the sharp cry of betrayal that came from Sweetie Pie.

Unable to move or look away, I watched as Graf eased back from the woman, shaking his head. She reached for him, but he stepped to the side. The woman pointed up at the cottage not far away, where lights offered a warm glow against the brisk wind. Again, Graf shook his head.

Every molecule in my body told me to turn away and go back down the beach, but I was paralyzed. I couldn't move. The second I stopped looking, I'd have to deal with the emotional jack-hammer. Now, as I watched, it was almost as if a theatrical production played out in front of me.

Sweetie made the decision for me. With a low growl, the dog started down the dune. No doubt to tear a hole in the woman. I caught her just in time.

"No," I said, pulling the dog back down the beach side of the dune. "No." I sat down in the sand and cradled my dog in my arms. "No. No. No." I repeated the word over and over, as if denying it could make it disappear.

Graf's strange behavior, his reluctance to hold me or kiss me, his withdrawal—everything suddenly made sense. I'd assumed it was because of his injury, that he'd felt somehow diminished. That his ego and identity were all wound together regarding his physical perfection.

What a joke. He'd found someone else.

For a moment I thought I might vomit, but I held myself in check. After a few steadying breathes, I stood up and returned down the beach the way I'd come. My first instinct was to confront Graf. Now. In front of his new girl. But what would that resolve? This was definitely not the time to rush into an emotional action.

The first thing I had to decide was what I wanted to happen. Acting out of hurt and betrayal wasn't smart.

I reached in my pocket for my cell phone and

texted Tinkie. "Call me immediately. Betrayal."

I'd barely put the phone back in my pocket when it rang.

"What's happening?" Tinkie asked. "Who betrayed whom?"

"What are you doing up at midnight?" I asked, unable to tell Tinkie that Graf had found a new love. I had to form the words and have them ready.

"We were partying on Bourbon Street. Is something wrong? You sound sick."

"Graf is on the beach kissing another woman. A really beautiful blonde." I paced toward the rental cottage as the silence on the other end grew.

"You saw this with your own eyes?" Tinkie cut to the heart of my possible delusions, bad dreams, or simple misunderstandings that an eyewitness might have screwed up.

The tears came from nowhere. I cried so hard I couldn't see to walk. I sank to the chill sand, and I had the strangest memory of the little turtles, climbing from their safe nest and rushing to the sea. Braving predators and the natural elements, barely able to crawl, they rushed toward their destiny. I had no such courage. I wanted to curl up and hide.

"Sarah Booth, answer me. You're scaring me."

"I just came from watching him. I proposed to him tonight, and he turned me down. He said things had changed. And then I got drunk, and when Sweetie woke me, she raced down the beach. I followed to get her, and she led me to them. She wanted me to know he had betrayed me."

"I'll be there tomorrow, Sarah Booth. Don't do anything until I get there. Promise me?" No sympathy, no promises that everything would be okay. Tinkie didn't deal in deception. She believed in revenge.

"Okay." It turned out not to be a hard promise to make. What other options did I have? Order him out of the cottage? Pack the car and leave him there? Not hardly.

"Find someplace to be tomorrow morning about nine thirty. When I get there, I want to talk to Graf alone. And don't tell him I'm coming."

"Okay," I agreed. "Thank you, Tinkie."

Graf showed up at the cottage only twenty minutes or so after I did. He turned the television on. Storm reports pierced the shroud of my tormented sleep. Like Graf, Hurricane Margene was proving to be treacherous. She swept into the Gulf and gained a notch in her belt to a Category Two storm.

Now that she was in the warm, warm Gulf waters, all bets were off. She could double back and catch the west Florida coast, angle over to Mexico or Texas, or move north-northwest and target Dauphin Island or the Mississippi Gulf Coast.

No one wanted the storm, but it appeared that someone would have to host her.

When I woke up, Graf was sound asleep, the television still tuned to the weather station. I checked the storm's progress. The forecaster indicated it would be the weekend before the storm's course would be clear. And her strength. The longer she hovered in the Gulf waters, the stronger she could become. Or a wind sheer could knock the top out of her and reduce her growth.

So all told, anything could happen concerning the weather. Could the same be said for my relationship?

Graf twitched in his sleep, and the dark stubble of his beard matched the circles beneath his eyes. His appearance didn't lie. Whatever he was up to, it was taking a toll on him, too.

So why didn't he just say that he'd fallen for someone else? Why not put an end to this misery and move on to the woman he wanted?

And who the hell was she, anyway?

Where had he met her? Hollywood, no doubt. She had that look about her. The camera would love her. But I didn't recognize her from any film roles. Of course, I'd hardly had a good look at her. I could only remember a classic profile, that incredible cascading hair, the way she carried herself with such confidence.

I slammed the heel of my hand into my fore-head to stop the thoughts. Erosion of my self-confidence wouldn't do a whit of good. Torturing myself with all the qualities she had and I didn't was stupid. The smart move would be to find out about her. And as soon as Tinkie got here, we'd do exactly that.

Picking up my shoes, I waved Sweetie and Pluto out the door and down to the car. We'd take a little drive on the island. Maybe go for breakfast. It was closing in on nine o'clock. Tinkie would be here any minute, and I had explicit orders to be out of the house.

I didn't feel bad at all taking the car and leaving Graf without transportation. He could just trot down the beach and ride in his honey's red Jaguar parked beneath her beachhouse if he needed to go somewhere.

On that thought, I spun sand and headed to town. I'd seen a diner that might be open for breakfast. Instead, I ended up with a sack of "to go" breakfast biscuits and parked in the library lot. Sweetie wolfed down her biscuit and most of mine, and Pluto nibbled at the rasher of bacon I'd purchased for him. It wasn't really up to his standards, but beggars couldn't be choosers.

The day was overcast and blustery, and I left the windows down while I ducked in to do a little research. Sweetie and Pluto might explore around the library, but they wouldn't go far. My brain could hardly focus because I was waiting for Tinkie to call, but I did what I could.

At one time, Dauphin Island had a small tabloid newspaper, and I found an interesting article about John Trotter written by a female reporter he'd apparently charmed. The longish story recounted several of his seafaring adventures with great white sharks, sunken galleons, treasures that insurance companies stole from him—tales of high adventure and near misses of great wealth.

John Trotter told his stories with flare and gusto. I could see where a woman might find him very appealing.

Beside the article on Trotter, another featuring Dr. Phyllis Norris and her work to protect the loggerhead turtles of Dauphin Island shared the page. She made a point that the real wealth of the island was natural resources, not development. I happened to share her view.

The library archives held some interesting historical documents. I had time to kill, so I spooled through microfiche, wishing it had all been converted to digital.

A document caught my eye. SLAVE AUCTION in big letters topped the sheet. YOUNG FEMALE. CERTIFIED HEALTHY. GOOD FOR FIELD LABOR. SPEAKS FRENCH. LUANN. The location was on the beach right about where my rental cottage sat, just as Terrance Snill had advised.

I had no doubt this was Armand Couteau's widow, the African princess who'd found her freedom only to be sold into slavery for a second time. A hard ending to her brief years of love and freedom.

My cell phone buzzed, and I left the past behind and confronted my future. Tinkie had texted me to return to the cottage.

When I arrived, I found Tinkie and Graf sitting across from each other in the living room of the cottage. The chill in the air told me things had not gone well, but I hadn't a clue what doors Tinkie had opened. I looked from one to the other. Graf stood. "I should go to Mobile and do some shopping. Or else we should pack to leave. That storm is moving closer, but no one can say where it will hit."

"New Orleans is in a tear," Tinkie said. "Cece is beside herself. The storm might ruin the Black and Orange Ball. People are calling to cancel their reservations. They tell her to keep the money because it's for charity, but she'll be destroyed if no one comes to enjoy the party she's planned."

Such an ordinary, everyday concern prompted a million solutions. "We can bring people from shelters to enjoy the food and music. We can bus in people from other places. High school students—"

Tinkie's look was as effective as a slap.

"Sorry. I just wanted to solve a problem. Any problem." I looked at Graf. "Since I can't solve my own."

He picked up the car keys from where I'd put

them on the counter and walked out without another word.

"Did you ask him about the blonde?" I asked Tinkie.

She shook her head. "We didn't get that far. He shut me down the minute I tried to talk to him. Told me he respected our friendship and my loyalty, but this wasn't a topic where I should trespass."

"And you let that stop you?" Tinkie was not easily deterred.

"Only because I love you, and I don't want to push Graf into doing something he'll regret. Men have to be handled carefully, Sarah Booth. There's pride and the male desire to be seen as strong and in control. Graf isn't in control of his life or his future, and he doesn't need me to point that out. He'd never forgive me. Or you. Because I'm your friend, my actions would reflect back on you."

She was right, dammit. While my gut instinct told me to pin Graf in a corner and demand answers, I knew it was the wrong way to proceed. What if the blonde was an old friend? What if she was a colleague? What if—screw that line of rationalization. If those were the facts, why wouldn't he invite her around for a drink with me?

The answer didn't have to be written in ten-foot letters painted on the wall. My heart knew it.

Tinkie's fingers snapping in front of my face brought me back to the moment. "Shit."

She frowned. "What happened to your creative cursing? You know, all that saint foolishness and biblical references?"

"I don't have time to curse creatively. I just don't have the heart for it." I slumped onto the sofa. "He's leaving me, Tinkie. And I feel like it's my fault, though I've done nothing."

She examined the floor.

"Do you think my work as a private investigator justifies Graf betraying me?"

Her eyes filled with tears. "I most assuredly do not. This isn't your fault, Sarah Booth. You're innocent. But so is Graf. Don't you see—he's been irrevocably changed. The man he was before that bitch Gertrude Strom got hold of him is not the man he is today."

"He can go back. He can." Sorrow laced my voice because I didn't even believe my own words.

Tinkie's bejeweled fingers clutched mine. "No, he can't. And neither can you."

"I'm not different." I'd made certain to maintain my normal behavior. "I've been so careful not to tromp on his feelings or push him. I've been chipper and charming and the best support on the planet."

She gave a crooked smile and wiped the tears from her eyes. "Exactly my point. You're like a bulldozer. The *real* Sarah Booth would have kicked his ass from here to next March."

"Are you saying I'm wrong to try to support him?"

She sat down beside me, still holding tight to my hands. "What I'm trying to say, and doing a poor job of it, is that there is no right or wrong. You are *both* doing the best you can. But this is a life-changing event. For me as well as for the two of you. And for Oscar. And Cece."

"If we're all so right and correct, why is he kissing another woman on the beach?" Anger fueled my words, and I snatched my hands away from her.

"None of that matters, Sarah Booth. It's a reaction to a set of circumstances that are fact. The only thing that matters is that you find your way back to each other."

Her logic squelched my anger. "And how do I do that?"

She bit her lip, and in a moment it popped out of her mouth, and I remembered the way I'd viewed her when I first returned to Zinnia. She'd been the ultimate sorority girl at Ole Miss, the rich princess who had every fantasy met—either by her father or by the numerous men in thrall to her. I'd viewed her as a shallow fool. I'd never underestimate her again. Not as a friend or as a smart woman.

"I don't know that," she said. "I wish I did.

But I'm here with you to help you figure it out."

I pulled her into a hug and held on. She was a constant in my life, and there were so very few of those. For everyone. I could only cherish her and thank her for being the friend she was.

"Why don't we go visit that maritime museum?" I asked. "You can distract the owner while I scope out the old telescope there." Her frown told me she wasn't following my thought processes. "I'll explain on the way. It involves the pirate treasure John Trotter claimed he'd found a key to."

"So you aren't dropping this case?" she asked.

"No, I'm not." I kissed Sweetie and Pluto good-bye and followed her down the stairs to her car. "I think the worst thing I can do is give up my life and become dependent on Graf. That would feel like a trap in no time."

"Smart girl," she said as we both slammed our doors and headed to Mobile and the local university.

Dr. Lionel Prevatt was a slender man in a starched blue shirt and khaki pants. Though he was in his fifties, an air of youthfulness surrounded him. He walked with a boyish bounce, and he greeted me and Tinkie with a firm handshake and a smile.

"Welcome to the Mobile Maritime Museum. We've documented the history of the first ships of the explorers to the present day." He waved a hand around the two-story building. "Is there a particular aspect of history you're interested in?"

The museum held only four other tourists, so perhaps it wasn't so unusual for the curator to welcome us so enthusiastically. But Lionel Prevatt's fawning was a little disconcerting. At least to me. Tinkie was eating it with a spoon.

"Pirates are our interest," she said. She was a perfect example of a simpering female. It worked on Prevatt like Viagra. He was swollen with manly gallantry.

"Right this way, ladies."

Tinkie took his arm, and I followed behind them to the back reaches of the museum. "Why is the pirate collection so . . . discreetly displayed?" I asked.

"My dear, some of Mobile's most prominent families can trace their lineage back to the pirates that raided ships off the Alabama, Mississippi, and Louisiana coasts. Fortunes were made in these illegal pursuits. Land was purchased, and in the space of a generation or two, the families gained respectability. They prefer their past remain . . . in the back of the museum, if you would." He laughed, and Tinkie charmed him with a twitter of merriment.

"You have a way with words, Dr. Prevatt," she said, hanging on his arm and looking up at him with her big blue eyes.

"Are any families related to Armand Couteau?" At last I'd found a possible motive for the murder of John Trotter that would make the puzzle pieces I held fit neatly together. The scenario that assembled in my mind went like this—Trotter finds location of hidden treasure. Prominent Mobilian who has something to hide finds out Trotter is about to reveal sordid family past, kills Trotter to shut him up. Treasure is taken or possibly never found.

"Why do you ask?" Prevatt's loquacious manner dimmed considerably.

"I saw a portrait of him at an antique store on Dauphin Island. I'm vacationing there," I said as sweetly as I could muster. "He's a handsome devil. I just wondered if his good looks had passed down through the generations." I tried to look dreamy eyed and romantic.

When Prevatt wasn't looking, Tinkie stomped my foot and drew a hand across her throat to tell me to cut out the theatrics.

"He was a handsome man and quite the rogue," Prevatt said. "I have several artifacts from his shipwreck on the reef near Dauphin Island."

"We'd love to see them." Tinkie stuck to him like a burr as he maneuvered toward a glass cabinet on the far back wall.

I followed along like the good first mate, admiring Tinkie's handiwork. No matter how

170

many times I saw her tie a man in a knot, I was always impressed. What a useful skill. One day I hoped it would rub off on me.

Prevatt opened the case with a combination, using his body to block us from seeing. When the heavy, shatterproof glass door swung wide, he extracted a sextant and demonstrated the use to Tinkie. My eye was on the telescope, a work of brass and what appeared to be teak. My hand itched to reach for it, but I knew better. If Prevatt sensed my interest, he'd be on to us.

Tinkie oohed and aahed appropriately and asked questions that surprised even me. "How do you know so much about sailing?" I asked.

"While you were busy with greasepaint and Sam Shepard plays, I took a class in sailing." She laughed at my expression. "You were so dedicated to the theater, Sarah Booth, you missed out on a lot of other stuff."

"You're an actress, Miss . . . ?" He finally really looked at me.

"No," I said. "I was in college. My fiancé"— I must have looked stricken because Tinkie picked up flawlessly.

"Her fiancé is Graf Milieu, an actor."

"I know his work," Prevatt said with a return of his original enthusiasm. "The prereviews for his western are terrific. Even though the movie hasn't been released, Entertainment Buzz is comparing him to Brando."

I said nothing. The ache in my heart made me think I might need an ambulance.

"He's staying at Dauphin Island," Tinkie said without missing a beat. "He's preparing for his next movie."

"I'd love to meet him. Will he visit the museum?"

"Perhaps," Tinkie said. "We'll put a bug in his ear. What is that?" She reached in and picked up the telescope and put it to her eye. "My goodness, a magnifying glass! How clever. I believe I saw Errol Flynn use one of these in a pirate movie. Or was it Lionel Barrymore? Now were you named for Mr. Barrymore, Lionel?"

She was smooth. By the time she'd finished the discussion of Barrymore's great films, I'd recovered enough to take the spyglass from her and glance out the front of the museum. It was an effective magnifying glass, bringing distant vistas into sharp focus. But using only one eye, it lacked depth perception, and there was a scratch on the glass.

"How was the lens scratched?" I asked.

"It was like that when we received it." Prevatt was annoyed by my question.

"How did you come to own these items?" I asked.

Prevatt studied me. "They were purchased."

"From John Trotter?"

He took the spyglass from me and returned it

to the case, careful to lock it. "Who are you and why are you here?"

He was nobody's fool. "We're private investigators, and we're working for—"

"Get out! That relentless bitch Angela Trotter sent you here to snoop. Her father sold the artifact. He took the money and sold the piece. It's a done deal. She can't have it back, no matter how much she harasses me or offers to pay for it. Tell her those exact words. Now leave."

Tinkie's eyebrows met, and I could almost swear lightning forked on the back of her retinas. "Listen here, you pompous ass. You can answer our questions now or find yourself before a grand jury for attempting to thwart an investigation."

Doubt flitted across Prevatt's face. Tinkie was a damned genius. She'd been around him ten minutes and knew perfectly how to play him.

"I'm not obstructing anything, but I don't have to tolerate being harassed by Angela Trotter just because she wants her daddy's artifact."

I wanted to ask him if he'd ever lost anyone he loved. But I didn't. An appeal to his emotions wouldn't work. A threat of legal action did. Tinkie's tactic was what I went with. "Asking a few questions hardly qualifies as harassment," I said calmly. "Why do you think John Trotter valued the spyglass so much?"

"It belonged to Couteau. There's no doubt

about it." He unlocked the cabinet and brought the item out again. Pointing to the burnished brass plating, he said, "See the writing?"

And I did. A. C. in ornate script was etched into the metal. Below that, a symbol I didn't recognize. It looked like a sun with an arrow and a number I couldn't read clearly. "What is that?"

"We aren't sure. I personally think it may have been his mark. The sign he left behind after he'd robbed a ship or one of the New Orleans town-houses he was wont to burglarize. Pirates did that to prove their success."

"I haven't heard of his land activities. He robbed houses?"

"Oh, he was supposedly quite the cat burglar. Jewels, silver, artwork. He would charm his way into the household, get the lay of the land, and then strike while the owner was away. Except for the slave girl he stole. He took her from the French Market in broad daylight."

"The beautiful LuAnn," I said.

"So you know the story."

"I am, after all, a detective," I said wryly.

"And a good one." Tinkie took my arm. "I think we've discovered all we need here. Thank you, Lionel. I'm sure we'll return for another visit before we finish our case."

He rolled his eyes and drilled our backs with his gaze as we took off.

12

The trip to the maritime museum had been a wonderful diversion from my romantic worries, but as we crossed the big hump of the Dauphin Island bridge, I was dumped back into the reality of my wayward fiancé.

"I'll show you the beach," I offered. Anything to keep from finding myself at the cottage confronting Graf.

We parked at the public beach, intending a walk all the way down to the cottage. We could ride the bicycles back to fetch Tinkie's car. The day was overcast but still warm. At times the sun peaked through the clouds. I hoped Hurricane Margene had turned to the west. I didn't wish her on Texas or Mexico, but I didn't want her either.

Tinkie and I had only gone a short distance down the beach when I saw Dr. Phyllis Norris and her turtle crew digging in the sand. I started to skirt by her, not wanting to interrupt her work, when she called out to me.

Once Tinkie was introduced, Phyllis signaled us off to the side so her coworkers couldn't hear. "Angela told me she'd hired you as a PI to investigate her father's murder. I'm worried about Angela," she said. "I saw her yesterday, and she seemed a little . . . irrational."

"How so?"

She frowned. "She asked me about her father. Had he said anything about the treasure. She thought he *might* have shared information with me that I *might* have forgotten to mention."

A polite way of saying Angela had accused her of lying. I waited for her to go on.

"Of course, I told her I didn't know anything else. I've wracked my brain for any scrap of conversation or gesture or hint that might help Larry Wofford's case. Nothing."

"Why are you concerned about Angela?" I asked.

She looked past me at the researchers working with a nesting turtle. "Angela has put so much hope into freeing Larry. Failure will be like another death to her. Once she realizes Larry won't be out for a long time, she'll have to face the fact she's all alone. That concerns me. John told me—" She broke off, looking slightly stricken.

"Told you what?" Tinkie asked.

"I shouldn't reveal his confidences," she said. "It's wrong."

"If it could help Angela, maybe it isn't wrong," I said.

"He just said she was an idealist. That she expected the best of herself and everyone she came into contact with. That kind of idealism often results in disillusionment and cynicism.

He didn't want that for her. John felt he'd failed her as a father. By following the treasure hunts, he left her alone too much. He wasn't the dad he should have been." She exhaled. "He beat himself up for all the things he didn't do exactly right and never gave credit for all the things he did."

"The sorry state of human nature," Tinkie said, giving me the stink eye. "Sarah Booth has a tendency to do the same thing."

I wasn't about to argue my character traits in front of a biologist, so I ignored Tinkie. "Angela is convinced Wofford will prove his innocence."

"Sometimes not even the truth is enough. I just don't want to see her heart broken again. Please don't give her false hope." She smiled to take the sting out of her words. "By the way, I saw your handsome fiancé down the beach. He was walking with his friend. Everyone in town is buzzing how we have a movie star visiting."

"His friend?" Tinkie asked. "What friend?"

"The woman who rented the Ocean Breeze. That's the best cottage on the beach. Full Jacuzzi on the balcony. Every luxury you could desire. Now that's the place to take a vacation."

"Thanks," I said. "How are the turtles faring?"

"This nest is almost gone. A few more along the beach and the season is over. We're racing the approach of the storm." She looked out to sea. "This could be paradise. The barrier islands of the Gulf are the most fragile and significant parts of a delicate environment. When they fail, it is the beginning of the end. If I had my way, not another person would be allowed on this island for any reason. Humans destroy everything they touch." With a forced laugh, she pulled herself back. "My, how I do carry on. You ladies have a nice walk on the beach."

Grasping Tinkie's elbow, I aimed west, toward the cottage and Graf. While I'd been dreading a confrontation, I was now ready for it. If Graf felt no shame about strutting down the beach with his new friend, I intended to find out who she was and why he was spending time with her. Enough kicking myself. I had another target.

13

"Calm down, Sarah Booth," Tinkie said, trying to use her weight to slow my churn toward Graf. I was too agitated to even go back for Tinkie's car.

"I won't calm down. I've pussyfooted around this for the entire week."

"A mild exaggeration." She pulled me around to face her. "Stop it. Rash action could prove fatal. Or at least lethal to your future relationship. Let's think this through."

"What's to think?" Instead of crying, I was furious.

"Oh, a little thing like let's find out who this woman is. Maybe there's a legitimate reason. Maybe he hired a coach or rehab specialist. Maybe this is a relative he's never told you about. Maybe—"

"She's a hooker who's doling out physical therapy of a very special kind." Even as I said it, I didn't believe it. The woman was elegant in a way that spoke of self-confidence, assurance, intelligence. Not that a hooker couldn't have those traits. But generally she didn't haul a young child along.

"Hey!" Tinkie put her hand to my cheek. "Calm down."

The tears in her eyes got to me when reason wouldn't. "Don't you dare cry. I'll take drastic action if you do."

"I'm not going to cry," she said, "and neither are you. Salt water isn't the solution here. If it were, there's an ocean to draw on."

"What is he doing?" I asked.

"Let's do what we do best, Sarah Booth. Let's investigate. We need to get photos of this woman and figure out who she is."

Logical, common-sense approach to the problem. That was Tinkie's strength.

"Okay."

"Come on." We moved down the beach again, this time with Tinkie in the lead. She had her cell phone out, and I wondered whom she might call.

When we were close to the beach house the blonde had rented, Tinkie scanned the area until she found a suitable dune. "See, we can tuck in here and wait."

"You think he's in the house with her?" That seemed a million times worse than walking on the beach.

"I do," she said. "And he'll have to come out eventually. Let's just hope she comes out with him."

"How long do you think it'll take?" I realized I sounded exactly like a spoiled rotten child on a car trip—are we there yet?

"As long as it takes. From here, I can get a fair shot if she comes onto the sand."

"Thank you, Tinkie. I know you should be in New Orleans helping Cece."

"Cece has the whole Black and Orange Ball committee. She doesn't need me. But you do."

"Yeah, I do."

"You love hard and strong and you are truly, deeply in love with Graf."

"One hundred percent committed. No holding back." I managed not to cry.

"Then we have no choice but to straighten him up."

Her confidence raised my hopes, and just in time. Graf stepped out of the house, and the woman followed. Up close, she was even more beautiful than I'd suspected. Her flawless skin, startling blue eyes, and a countenance that bespoke serenity and also passion. Not to mention hair that would make Rapunzel jealous. My gut dropped to my toes.

"Who the hell is she?" Tinkie whispered as she snapped photo after photo. "She isn't from the Delta."

The woman reached for Graf's hand and clung to it, bringing it to her lips and pressing a kiss onto his palm. The way she looked at him made me want to claw her eyes out. But I didn't budge.

"No, she's a city gal. Look at her clothes." The flowing linen shirt and red leggings were casual but fashionable. "California." I could identify the look even if I couldn't imitate it.

"I agree. Los Angeles. Diamond Rolex, gold necklace, very understated. She looks like a walk on the beach, but she's wearing forty grand in jewelry."

"Who the hell is she?" I repeated Tinkie's question.

"We will find out."

"How?" Taking photos was one thing. Figuring out who this person was would be another.

"I have my sources," Tinkie said with the hint of a smile. "Coleman."

"He won't be happy."

She laughed softly. "To help you, Sarah Booth, he would wade through a lot of annoyance with me."

She selected a few of the best photos of the woman and sent them to the Sunflower County Sheriff's Department with a note—"This woman is stalking Sarah Booth. Can you ID her?"

"Not exactly truthful," I noted.

"But effective. You'd do exactly the same for a client."

No point denying it; she was right.

"Let's get out of here before they catch us," she said. "You can confront Graf once you know the score."

She was right. Jumping the gun and rushing over the sand dune like an invading army would only put Graf on the defensive. I followed her down the beach side of the dune, and in a quarter of an hour we were back at the rental. Graf had left the keys to the SUV, so I drove Tinkie to pick up her car.

"I know you need to get back to New Orleans," I told her, though I desperately wanted her to stay. "Call me when you hear from Coleman."

"I'm not going anywhere." Tinkie lifted my chin with one finger. "Cece doesn't need me. Oscar has golfing dates back-to-back for the next two days. He'll understand."

Our tactic was normalcy. Tinkie and I agreed to strive for routine. I put together a seafood salad and served it on crisp lettuce and the last of the season's fresh tomatoes. I'd just put the finishing touches on when Graf returned, wind-whipped and smelling of the sea.

"Have a nice walk?" I asked, earning a hard look from Tinkie.

"I did."

"You're looking much better." Tinkie said. "I can't detect any signs of your injury, Graf. Sarah Booth was a genius to bring you here. You're a lucky man to have someone who loves you as much as she does."

"I am indeed." He walked through the room and out onto the balcony, closing the door after him.

I swallowed hard and poured a large glass of wine. Alcohol wouldn't fix this problem, but it might anesthetize me enough to get through the evening while we waited for Coleman's response.

Tinkie took the glass from my hand. "Let's get out of here."

The day had slipped away from us, and the sun vanished beneath a bowl of clouds that picked up the reflected light and turned the sky into a Cecil B. DeMille production.

We walked toward town. The shops were mostly closed. Instead of slowing, we continued up the hump of the big bridge.

"This place has a sad history." I relayed the tragic story of the father who threw his four children off the bridge, allegedly because of a fight with his wife.

"I can't believe that." Tinkie's horror turned into denial. "No one could be angry enough to throw their children off a bridge."

But even as she spoke, I heard the faint echo of children crying. It wasn't real, just a bit of geographic resonance. "I think sometimes people lose their minds." It took effort to speak clearly and walk up the bridge at the same time. And I'd thought I was in pretty good shape.

Tinkie pointed to the crest. "We'll talk there."

She, too, was having a hard time making the climb and talking. I didn't feel so bad about myself.

Huffing and puffing like the hungry wolf in the Three Little Pigs, we finally made it to the top and stopped short at the stuffed teddy bear and a bouquet of black-eyed Susans someone had left to mark the spot of tragedy.

"Time to go home," Tinkie said instantly. She hadn't brought me on a walk to make me think of even sadder situations than my life.

"Look out to the southwest."

Night invaded the sky from the east, and lights on Dauphin Island blinked on. It reminded me of an old soap opera that my aunt Loulane adored. *The Edge of Night.* As I watched, darkness moved across the sky. We both stood and watched the magnificence of nature until the lights on the bridge blinked on with the orange cast of mercury vapor. It was a sickly contrast to the natural beauty of the sky.

"We should—" I stopped as Tinkie's cell phone rang.

I tried, without success, not to eavesdrop and focused on a car headed toward us. In our long walk, we'd seen only a handful of cars headed in either direction. With the approach of night, the day-trippers had gone home. The island residents were settling in for a brisk fall evening.

Tinkie arched one eyebrow at me. "Yes, Coleman. It's a legitimate case—I assure you. Who is the woman?"

As hard as she tried, she couldn't hide her

reaction. She lowered her eyes and bit her lip. "I see. You're positive?"

She thanked him and hung up.

"Who is she?"

Tinkie prepared her answer. "Her name is Marion Silber. She's a screenwriter and director."

"I know that name. He has her script." Relief. Sweet relief. This wasn't so bad. Their talks were work related. But that wasn't the complete truth. If it was work, why hadn't Graf introduced her to me?

Tinkie shivered. "Let's go."

There was something she didn't want to tell me.

"And?" I prompted.

"And she and Graf had a two-year affair back long before he came south and found you again."

Marion Silber was an old lover. Someone he'd been close to. I wanted to sit down near the bridge railing, but I didn't. I'd tasted defeat before, but never this bitter. "Why did they break up?"

"Coleman didn't have any details. He was just shocked we were asking about a Hollywood type. He's not stupid, Sarah Booth. If he hasn't figured out what's at the bottom of this, he will. He could see the beach in the background of the photos I took."

"It doesn't matter." And it didn't. If Graf was two-timing me with an old love, all of my friends would know sooner rather than later. My wounded pride was the least of my concerns. "I don't want to go back to the cottage."

"Where do you want to go?" Tinkie asked.

"Maybe we could pack up and head to New Orleans." I didn't want to go there, either, but I couldn't very well take Graf's SUV and leave him stranded, though it would serve him right.

"Okay." Tinkie didn't voice her doubt, but I heard it in her tone.

"Let's move." I started down the bridge's hump, aware of a car speeding toward us. Out of habit, I grasped Tinkie's upper arm and shifted her closer to the rail. The vehicle hit warp speed, and the driver seemed inebriated or worse.

"What's wrong with that driver?" Tinkie asked, alarmed.

"Hell if I know." We inched even closer to the rail. I took one long look down at the water. The steep drop would kill us.

"Sarah Booth, he's headed straight at us."

She wasn't exaggerating. Grabbing her jacket sleeve, I yanked her to the other side of the road just as a sleek black sedan hit the curb and jumped toward the bridge railing. Just in time, the driver managed to regain control and aim the car toward the center of the lane.

Red taillights gleaming in the dark, it disappeared over the crest.

"He meant to hit us," Tinkie said.

I couldn't dispute her deduction. I ran to the top of the bridge and watched the car disappear, the driver now completely in control. He hadn't been drunk or distracted. He'd been intent on murder.

Slightly out of breath, Tinkie stopped at my elbow. "What the hell have you gotten yourself into, Sarah Booth?"

"I wasn't certain Larry Wofford was innocent of the murder of John Trotter, but now I am. I'm trying to free an innocent man from prison."

14

Tinkie spent the night in the bedroom with me. Graf had, once again, selected the sofa. Now I realized his sleeping arrangement wasn't a choice of protecting his injured leg from an accidental jostle. He was on the sofa because he was guilty. He was two-timing me with an old flame. Maybe I should be grateful he had enough ethics not to sleep with me while wooing another woman, but I wasn't.

The intimacy Graf and I had shared was sacred to me. From the very beginning, we'd enjoyed our physicality, and the sex was great. No working at it as some couples reported. Now it was gone—evaporated in the betrayal. I found myself trapped in that strange limbo of physical desire but emotional fury. Disgusting and unhealthy.

My partner was still asleep when I left the bedroom and headed to the kitchen to brew coffee and let Sweetie and Pluto out. From the second-floor window, I watched feline and canine cavort.

For the cat, the beach was an exotic world of small crabs, lizards, and birds that raced on foot along the edge of the surf, taking flight only as a last resort. To my keen eye, Pluto had lost at least three pounds. A good thing for such a hefty kitty. Sweetie simply enjoyed the wind flapping her long hound ears and bringing the seafaring smells to her nose.

With a cup of java in hand, I stopped by the sofa to watch Graf sleep. It occurred to me that I might pour the hot coffee on him, but I didn't. That wouldn't make him love me. In fact, I couldn't think of a single thing I could do—good or bad—that might reverse the choices of his heart.

Who knew what emotions had played into his decision to spend time with Marion Silber, but he owed me answers. Had he planned on meeting his old lover at the beach? How had she managed to show up at the same time we were there? Had the relationship begun as a business meeting over a script and evolved?

Even more important, why couldn't he talk to me? Tell me what he was feeling or needing. Give me a chance to meet him halfway. In this last week, I'd surrendered my heart to him completely, and I feared I would pay a terrible price. Letting my guard down would result in pain and anguish. Yet it was done now, and there was no undoing it. I loved him completely.

He stirred in his sleep, restless, as if ready to awaken and get away from me as fast as he could. I saved him the trouble and hurried down to the beach with my coffee and my four-legged family.

Pluto had cornered a hermit crab and was trying to bat the poor creature into a game of chase. I saved the crab and earned a scowl from my cat. "Tormenting helpless creatures isn't for us," I scolded him.

Sweetie played chase with the surf, and far down the beach I thought I recognized the turtle protectors, a group of five or six dedicated biologists and students who seemed never to sleep.

I had a question for Phyllis Norris about her relationship with John Trotter. It would eat up some of the morning until Tinkie awoke, so I sauntered down the beach toward the group. It wasn't until I was almost upon them that I realized Phyllis wasn't with them.

"Will Dr. Norris be here soon?" I asked a thin young man with a sunburned face.

He shrugged. "She was here and she left." He put aside the buckets of water he was hauling and wiped perspiration from his forehead. Temps on the beach would register under seventy degrees, but with a warm wind blowing and the sun reflected off the water and sand, it was hot.

"She sure seems devoted to the turtles."

He rolled his eyes. "A little too devoted, if you get my drift. This is her life, and she expects us to feel the same way. Hell, I haven't had a date in two months. We're here every night and all day. This late clutch of turtles is like a mission for her. She's more protective than a mother eagle, and she's just as likely to attack anyone who threatens them."

"If you weren't here, would the turtles survive?"

"It's a losing battle." He squatted down in the sand. "We can save these, but then what? Pollution, fishing nets, oil spills—look at the rigs out there. We can't stop that. People are stupid. They want cheap oil and gas, and they don't care that the backend payment will be the souls of their grandkids."

I heard what he was saying loud and clear, but I had no solutions. My next car would be electric. Maybe too little too late, but at least it was an effort. And maybe some solar panels on Dahlia House. That would be nice. Graf would like—but Graf wouldn't be there.

I jerked my thoughts back to the present. "Did you happen to know John Trotter?"

"The treasure hunter? Heck, everyone on the island knew him. He was a great guy. Always had these crazy stories." His smile erased another five years from his features. He could easily be a high schooler. "Phyllis—Dr. Norris—spent a lot of time with him. She wasn't all that keen on the treasure hunting, but I think she really liked him. He'd come along to help us with the turtles. I think they would have married if he hadn't . . ."

"Been murdered," I finished for him.

"Yeah, that. Phyllis said she really regretted the

last time they were together they got into an argument about the treasure stuff."

I hid my keen interest. "Folks argue. It's part of a relationship."

"Yeah, not the good part." He stood up again. "I have to get back to it. If she pulls up and I'm jawboning and not working, she'll jump my case. She can be tough. Really tough."

"People on a mission often are. Hard on themselves and others."

He picked up his pails of water and set off. Before he got out of earshot, I called after him. "Any idea where Phyllis went?"

He turned but kept walking backward. "She was with that deputy. The asshole. I don't know where they went, though."

Still chewing on that tidbit, I rounded up the critters and headed back to the cottage. While I had no appetite, Sweetie and Pluto bounded down the beach, knowing breakfast was just around the corner.

The critters disappeared in the dunes, but I heard Sweetie barking. She made enough racket to wake the dead. Hurrying after her, I caught sight of a woman in a full-skirted black dress that swept the sand but left her creamy white shoulders bare. She stood among the dunes, hair parted in the center and pulled back to reveal an oval face. I knew it was Jitty, but in what guise?

"You've suffered," I said, taking in her solemn countenance.

"There is no substitute for a mother's love," she said in a perfectly modulated tone. Very Victorian and proper.

"Who are we today, Jitty?"

" 'Nothing is so painful to the human mind as a great and sudden change.' How true that is," she said. "We have both suffered a change."

"Give me another hint, please." I'd pinpointed the historical era, but I couldn't identify the young beauty.

"If I cannot inspire love, then I shall inspire fear." She waited.

I knew her then. Creator of *Frankenstein*. I had read the book as a young girl and had wept in sympathy for the monster who wanted only to be loved.

"I don't want to inspire fear," I told her. " And what is this great change?" I didn't like the sound of that. Losing Graf would be a great change, a terrible one. "Is that what I should expect? To be alone again?"

Already, I could feel the emptiness of Dahlia House without Graf. If he was truly in love with Marion Silber, he would leave me and Mississippi and live in Los Angeles, where his work was. "Is Graf leaving me?"

"I don't know," she said. "Perhaps it's best that way. If Mary Shelley had known what her future held, would she have remained with her father and spurned the advances of a poet?"

"Shelley was a bastard to her." Sort of the understatement of the century. "She denied her talent and gave up so much, and it didn't do a lick of good."

Jitty faced the water, still in the guise of the long-dead writer. "I wanted him dead, you know. There are times I prayed he would die. I was nineteen when I eloped with him. I lost everything familiar to me. My father disowned me. I gave up everything for Percy, and it never mattered to him."

If tragic love was the lesson Jitty meant to teach, she'd made her point. I'd been depressed before she showed up. Now I was scraping the bottom of the bucket. "You aren't helping me, Jitty."

"*Frankenstein* came out of my personal grief and betrayal. I created a monster who sought love. A reflection of how I saw myself."

"You created a masterpiece and launched a genre of work. Science fiction grew out of your novel." I found myself arguing her case. "Besides, there are those who would debate who was the monster. Both Dr. Frankenstein and his creature were flawed and sad."

"Much like me."

"Not to mention Shelley. If you want to talk about flawed, let's tweak the wart on the witch's nose." I'd read enough to know Percy Bysshe

Shelley followed his pleasures and desires far more often than a code of honor.

"I thought I could build a home, a family, and love would follow. It isn't true. Like my creation, I was cursed from the beginning. But you, Sarah Booth, you have known the love of both parents. Of a community."

"Knock it off, Jitty. You're about to send me into a spiraling depression that has no bottom."

Her creamy skin began to take on the mocha tones of the haint I loved. "Why is it that the need to bond with another takes precedence over everything else?" she asked. The hint of a Southern drawl had crept back into her voice.

"I don't know." The truth was, Graf's sudden actions had left me with no solid ground under my feet. I could psychoanalyze his actions and put them into cause and effect. The bigger question, though, was, Could I forgive him? Or perhaps the better question would be whether there was anything to forgive aside from his not telling me that an old flame, Marion Silber, had rented a cottage on the same island that we vacationed on. Much would depend on whether this was design or happenstance.

"Don't you have any questions for me about the Great Beyond?" Jitty asked.

"No." I didn't want answers. Not yet. I was afraid of what they might be. "I need to work through this myself."

"You have Tinkie and the rest of your friends."

"Yes." I hesitated to think what Cece would do to Graf if he cheated on me. Or Millie. The idea of it made me dread the Black and Orange Ball.

"What you got planned?" Jitty asked. Though she still wore the Victorian dress, she was her regular self.

"I don't know yet."

"Don't let it get to the point you wish him dead."

And I saw the wisdom of her widowhood as Mary Shelley. Love and hate were sides of the same blade. I couldn't imagine that, but betrayal and grief had the potential to warp a person's spirit. Jitty's words were wise.

"I won't."

"I wish I could help you."

"Me too." For once, I accepted that she couldn't. Jitty could prod and push to manipulate me along a certain path, but I stood at a crossroads now. The choice was clear—life with Graf or life without him. And I had no clue which path my foot would take. And for once, I didn't want to know the future. I feared it.

"No man chooses evil because it is evil; he only mistakes it for happiness, the good he seeks." Jitty had begun to fade.

I wondered if this last line was a plea to forgive Graf, or perhaps to forgive myself.

"What should I do?" I asked. Jitty was little

more than a shimmer against the beauty of the isolated beach. "Answer me as Jitty, the haint of Dahlia House, as the spirit of my departed relatives, as the embodiment of those who loved me."

"Give it some time, baby girl," Jitty said in the rich drawl of the Mississippi Delta. "Seek out the facts, Sarah Booth. That's the ticket. Find out what Graf is up to before you accuse him of messin' around. Remember, he has a past just like you do. Coleman Peters could be a constant source of jealousy, but Graf don't let that happen to him. Maybe this Silber woman is his past, too."

Jitty was dead-on right. Though she'd come to me in the guise of a woman married to a terrible philanderer, she'd suggested logic and a rational approach to my romantic problem.

I crested the last dune and saw Tinkie on the steps drinking coffee. Graf's SUV was gone.

"He went to buy groceries," she said. "Anything to get away from me."

"Did he say anything about . . . the woman?"

"He said, 'Good morning. I'm headed to buy groceries,' and he was out the door before I could even respond."

I hated it that Graf was acting like such a coward. Instead of commenting, I filled Tinkie in on my conversation with Dr. Norris's student worker.

"It must be hard for someone who loves nature

198

to see those oil rigs out there. Especially after the BP Horizon blowout." Tinkie stood and we walked inside, the pets at our heels. I would make some breakfast and something for Sweetie and Pluto, too.

"I think we should report the attempted hit-and-run to the sheriff," Tinkie said. "I know you don't want to because of Graf and all, but someone tried to kill us."

I shook my head. "We can't prove a thing. It's pointless. I didn't get a tag number, and neither did you. All we can say is a dark car almost ran us down. The deputies will say it was probably a drunk driver."

"Not like working with Coleman, is it?" Tinkie said. "By the way, he called."

I plunked myself glumly at the counter in the kitchen. "Did you tell him?"

"No. That's up to you. He just wanted to be sure you were okay. He's worried."

"Funny how that seems to be the refrain of my life."

"Just be glad you have those who love you enough to worry." She slapped me on the back none too gently. "Now what's the game plan for today?"

"We talked to everyone involved in Larry Wofford's conviction except the marina owner, Arley McCain. Let's go there."

15

The *Miss Adventure* bobbed on a choppy sea, straining her tie-lines. The marina was in great shape, rebuilt after the 2005 hurricane. New planking, fresh paint. An abundance of booger lights would discourage vandalism of or theft off the unattended boats. Three video cameras, if they were working, would record the comings and goings of those with business, legitimate or otherwise, at the marina.

A burley man with a captain's hat stood on one of the piers arguing with Dr. Phyllis Norris. I motioned for Tinkie to be quiet as we eased closer. The lapping of the water against the pilings disguised the sound of our approach.

"Angela pays the docking fee every month, and though it's none of your business, I give her a break." The burly man, who I pegged as Arley McCain, marina owner, was in Dr. Norris's face. "Why should she sell the boat?"

"She isn't healing, Arley. She's had the deck and interior of the boat repainted. She's spending money she doesn't have to maintain the *Miss Adventure*, all as some sad homage to her dead father. That boat is a tragic reminder of her father's brutal murder. She needs to put all of that behind her."

"And why is that your business?" Arley demanded.

"Because I care about her. You know I was close with John. He loved his daughter. I'm just trying to help. If you force her to move the boat, she'll begin to let go of it and everything associated with it. She hasn't taken the damn thing out a single time since her father was killed."

"That's not your business, Phyllis. You're meddling in things you shouldn't."

I had to agree with Arley, though I was touched Phyllis cared enough about Angela to try to manipulate her affairs. And I feared she was right. The *Miss Adventure* was a symbol of everything Angela had lost. Her father, Larry Wofford, a treasure, her childhood. But it wasn't up to Phyllis to try to force Angela to let go of the boat.

Phyllis wasn't about to relent, though. "Angela Trotter views that boat as representative of her father. As long as she keeps it spic-and-span, she's honoring his memory. That's expensive and sick. Can't you see that?"

Arley put his hands on his hips. His shoulders were so broad, he blocked the entire walkway. "I *see* you're nosing into things that don't concern you."

Phyllis matched his stance, though she was a mere shadow of his bulk. "*I* see you don't want to lose a permanent boat-slip fee."

"That's a nasty accusation." He almost growled in her face.

Beside me, Tinkie tensed. She was ready to spring into action to defend Phyllis from what appeared to be an imminent attack. I remembered what Larry Wofford had said—that he'd seen a man with large shoulders rushing away from the marina as he headed onto the dock. A man Arley McCain hadn't noticed. A man who might have a reason to give false testimony.

A new and very viable suspect had lumbered onto the scene. Tinkie's thoughts reflected mine, if I was any judge of her alert expression.

"That monthly berth rental is more important to you than a young woman's emotional health." Phyllis had pulled out all the stops. "Can't you see how detrimental this is for Angela?"

"I see a busybody woman manipulating another person's life. That's what I see. I wouldn't like it, and I'll bet Angela Trotter will be angry when I tell her."

That pulled Phyllis Norris up short. "Don't do that, Arley. She will be angry. I'm only trying to help her."

He took his hat off and wiped his forehead with the sleeve of his shirt. "I don't doubt that, but you're going about it the wrong way. If the boat is a part of her dad, you can't rip it away from her. She'll grow tired of the responsibility, especially if that hurricane comes in here. Let her grow out of it naturally. Boats are too expensive and time-consuming to keep as a monument, unless you're loaded, which she ain't. But the timing of letting the boat go, that's Angela's to figure out."

Phyllis's shoulders slumped. "You're right. Dammit. It's been over a year, and she can't seem to move on. She needs to find a man and start her own life instead of living in the dregs of her father's. Every spare penny she has goes toward upkeep on that." She pointed at the bobbing sailboat.

"Tell you what. I've had a couple of people asking about the *Miss Adventure*. She's a handsome sailboat. I'll get some offers and take them to Angela. She may not heed them at first, but it'll plant the idea she could be free of the upkeep, earn a little nest egg, and maybe start anew."

Phyllis put her hand on Arley's arm. The potential for a bad argument had blown away with the wind. "Thanks, Arley. We both have her best interest at heart. I just got offtrack a little."

They turned and saw us standing there. Phyllis had the courtesy to show a sheepish grin, but Arley McCain was all bluster.

"What're you eavesdroppin' on us for?" he demanded. "Who are you?"

"Angela hired the tall one. She's a private investigator," Phyllis explained. "Angela is still trying to prove Larry is innocent."

"And this is my partner, Tinkie Bellcase Richmond." I made the introductions. "Mr. McCain, if you have a moment, I'd like to speak with you."

"Do it now, Arley, or they'll dog you to your grave." Phyllis took the sting out with a pat on my shoulder. "They're good folks. Help them if you can."

"The murder case that would never die." He shot a look at Phyllis. "If I sell the boat, maybe all of this will finally stop."

"Maybe," she called over her shoulder. "But we need to sell the boat for Angela's sake. Nothing else."

Arley made a growling sound and waved her away, but he was smiling. He was obviously fond of the biologist even if they didn't see eye to eye.

"Ladies, come into my office." He whipped around and headed for a low wooden building not far from the marina. Tinkie and I followed. She cast a lingering look at the *Miss Adventure* and whispered to me, "She's a real beauty. I know some people who might be interested in buying her, too."

"That's a discussion to have with Angela. She has to want to sell the boat."

There was no time for more conversation as Arley held the door open and waved us into an office whose décor surprised me. I'd expected a seafaring theme, but Arley was apparently an

204

avid golfer. All things Tiger Woods. There was even a putting game taking up half the floor space. Boys and their toys, as the old saying went. I did recognize one of John Trotter's unusual paintings on his wall.

"There's not much I can tell you about John's murder," Arley said before we'd sat down in the wooden chairs he indicated. "When I saw Larry Wofford coming off John's boat, covered in blood, I called the cops. They came, took Larry, and the next thing I knew, Larry was charged. End of story. That's what I testified to at the trial."

"What about the security cameras?" I indicated the recorder in a corner of a bookcase. "I see it goes straight to CD."

"Yeah, that's a strange one. The CDs were blank. I checked the cameras and the equipment. They worked fine. Might have been a loose wire, or maybe someone turned them off. The stranger Wofford said he saw."

"Did you check the CDs yourself?"

"Randy did. He's the one called and told me."

"Did you hear a gunshot?"

"I didn't," Arley said. He blustered a bit. "It was a stormy night. The gunshot could have been covered by thunder."

"Or it could have been the killer used a silencer." I let that sink in. "Which would mean John's death was premeditated. Which rules out Wofford killed John Trotter in a drunken rage."

"What sent you out on the dock so late at night?" Tinkie followed up before Arley could regain his equilibrium. Tinkie and I often made an effective tag team in questioning.

Arley tipped his hat back and scratched his head. "I heard a sound. Not a gunshot. I can't put my finger on it. But I heard something that made me decide to check the boats."

Tinkie tranced him with her big blue eyes. "What would be out of the ordinary?"

"I never said it was out of the ordinary." He grumped. "A sound caught my attention, and I went out to check. Only John and Larry were living on their boats. I gave them a break on the rental because I enjoyed having them around. Cut down on a lot of teenage mischief."

"Had you been troubled by mischief?" I asked.

"I'd sent another boater packing. Troublemaker. Always stirring up shit with everyone who came to the marina."

"Who?" I had my pencil poised.

"Remy Renault."

"Wait a minute. He was docked here."

"For a month or so. He and John stayed at each other's throats. John thought Remy was following him whenever he took his sailboat out. There was a bit of a scuffle over Phyllis Norris, too. She was John's girl, but Remy pursued her. Bad blood."

"So Remy knew his way around the marina?"

I tried to keep the excitement out of my voice. "He did."

"Would he have known how to disable the camera?"

"Maybe."

"Did you ever hear him talk about Lydia Clampett?"

Arley shook his head. "He had a few girlfriends who'd go sailing with him. Nobody stayed around too long. Bad-tempered ass."

Tinkie put a question to him. "Did you ever think Renault might have slipped back to the marina to settle a disagreement permanently with John?"

"I wouldn't put it past him," Arley said. "But I didn't see him that night."

"You also didn't hear the gunshot." Tinkie bit her lip, and Arley watched her with fascination. When her lip popped out, he slapped his leg.

"I remember what I thought I heard—a boat motor. Nobody would have taken a sailboat out in that weather with lightning popping. It had to be an outboard. But that didn't make sense, so I went to check. When I looked around, I didn't see anything. I thought I'd imagined it."

"Could you have missed the boat?" A clear memory of the powerboat tied to the dock beside Remy Renault's sailboat came to mind. I'd share this tidbit with Tinkie later.

He considered. "*If* someone was leaving. *If* he'd

parked behind some of the bigger ships. *If* he was running without any lights. Yeah, I might have missed it. The rain was coming down hard, hitting the dock and water. Bad visibility and lots of noise."

"Thank you, Arley. One more thing. Larry insists he saw someone in a yellow slicker. What were you wearing that evening?" Like it or not, Arley had been on the scene of the murder, and he fit Wofford's description of broadshouldered.

"I had on a slicker. A blue one. I don't own a yellow one. And I don't like what you're gettin' at."

"Chavis never asked you these questions?" Tinkie used a gentle voice.

"Asked and answered. I was apologizing to my wife at the time John was shot. The law checked the phone records. Told her I was on my way home. Then I heard the noise and went to check. When I saw Wofford looking like he'd been in a blood bath, I called the law. That's how it happened."

"Why were you working so late?"

He looked a bit uncomfortable. "The wife and I had a disagreement. I'd come up here to simmer down." He shrugged. "It happens in a marriage."

"Do you think Wofford killed John Trotter?" Tinkie asked.

"Larry isn't the violent type, but he was

drinking pretty hard." He tilted his head. "I don't know. I didn't want to believe it, but who else could it be? I've known Randy Chavis most of his life. He's got a chip on his shoulder, but he's a good cop. Why would he go along with framing Larry?"

"Maybe Wofford served a purpose as a scapegoat."

Arley's heavy brow wrinkled. "That's a vile accusation, Ms. Delaney."

"Murder is a vile act, Mr. McCain. Framing an innocent man is even worse in some respects. If Wofford is innocent, he's lost more than a year of his life being punished for something he didn't do."

"Do you have evidence that supports this claim?"

"Not yet," I admitted.

"It doesn't make sense to pin this on Larry. He never did a lick of harm to anyone but himself."

"To protect the real killer," Tinkie said.

"They never found the murder weapon," I pointed out. "Just suppose that Larry Wofford told you the truth—that he went to see John and found him dying. That he tried to staunch the flow of blood and that's how he got John's blood all over him."

Arley was clearly worried by the train of thought I'd given him. "Randy wouldn't change evidence or lie."

"Not even for a king's ransom in treasure?" Tinkie asked.

Arley got up and paced the room. He went from his trophy case that displayed golfing figures to the back wall, where maritime charts had been hung and framed. "Randy's had to deal with the locals and drunks here for his entire life. They view him as a traitor because he's a law officer. His patience is a little short, but he wouldn't do anything illegal."

"Then who would?" I asked.

Arley took his time answering. "I've never had a lot of respect for the sheriff. He's a politician. John's murder was a big case. National news. Benson was running for reelection, and he had a strong rival. He needed to solve the murder and quickly. If anyone threw Wofford under the bus, it would be him."

"Did John tell you about the treasure?"

"Hell, he might as well have taken out an ad. I told him to hush. If he really did know where it was, he should have shut up until he had it in his possession. Lots of folks will jump a claim. The thing is, though, about three times a year, John would get all wound up about claiming the treasure, and it never came to anything. Folks just got to the point they didn't pay a lot of attention anymore."

"Angela says this time was different. That John really had hold of a clue."

"He was wound tight about the treasure, that's for sure. He might have drawn some interest from folks who thought he'd hit on something solid. I know Remy had plenty to say about what he called John's 'fantasy treasure.' Remy was jealous of John."

"Anyone else come to mind?" Tinkie asked.

His eyes widened. "Yeah. A guy by the name of Prevatt. He runs a museum. John told me that Prevatt tried to force John into taking him as a partner in the treasure hunt. John didn't like the man and would have no part of it. Prevatt insisted. It got nasty. That's all I know, and that's gossip. John and that museum fellow had a feud going over other things."

"Did you mention this to anyone when they were investigating John's murder?"

"I did. Told Randy Chavis. He made a note and said he'd follow it up."

"Thanks, Arley." We'd gotten what we came for and more.

"If you see Angela, tell her to come and talk to me about the approaching storm. The time to make preparations is now."

"Will do," I assured him.

16

My reluctance to return to the cottage led us to a bird sanctuary on the island. A large wooden plaque showed several nature trails and informed visitors that Dr. Phyllis Norris had marked the trails with the names of trees and plants and donated a substantial amount of money to create the preserve. Phyllis not only talked the talk, she walked the walk.

The oak trees created an intimate space, the sun blasting like shotgun pellets through the wind-whipped leaves. Once we were out of the car and leaning against the hood, we were surrounded by birdcalls and the gentle sounds of nature. Clouds scudded across the sky, a typical day. No evidence of the storm building far to our south. The wind blew the oak limbs, scattering shadow and light, an ever-changing pattern that mimicked my emotions.

"I have reasonable doubt that Larry Wofford killed John Trotter, but I don't see a clear path toward proving his innocence," Tinkie said.

"I know. Arley was the most convincing witness against Larry. He told what he saw, nothing more. But it was damning. I'm not sure how to counteract that testimony. We've uncovered some interesting connections, but nothing that would overturn a conviction. I know someone else was on the boat, whether it was Remy or a paid killer. I just can't prove it."

"The murder weapon was never found," Tinkie mused. "Is there a chance we could find it?"

"I doubt we'll unearth it. Even if the killer kept it, we don't know where to look. Sheriff Benson's not going to help us."

"Maybe we can turn up another witness. Someone who hasn't come forward. If there was a motorboat, maybe someone else heard it." Tinkie pushed off the car and wandered down a trail. "Let's walk. I think better when I'm moving."

"Unless we can come up with a suspect with a dynamite motive for killing John Trotter, I don't see a way to help Wofford." I sighed. "This is a next-to-perfect frame-up."

"So our potential motives are to punish Angela for nosing into things, or to steal the Esmeralda treasure from John, or some unknown reason we have yet to discover."

"Money and sex are the most common motives for murder."

"Don't discount revenge. A lot of people are driven by the desire to get even."

She was correct. "If this hurricane blows in, the physical changes to the island could be catastrophic. If there's any evidence—and that's a big if—laying around, we need to find it before it's blown away."

"Talk about putting pressure on a person. Let's just hope Margene cuts east or west and all we get is a bit of rain. Poor Cece is going nuts with worry. Whoever dreamed we'd be facing a hurricane on Halloween."

As if speaking her name had conjured her up, Tinkie's cell phone rang and Cece was on the line. I could hear her agitation from ten feet away.

"Calm down," Tinkie suggested. "Sarah Booth is here with me. Now tell us both what's the trouble." She switched the phone to speaker.

"You will not believe this. You simply will not! It's an outrage."

"What's wrong?" Tinkie and I asked in unison. It was one of our trademarks—to say the same thing at the same moment.

"Cornelia Holsteadler, she's the problem."

"Because?" It wouldn't take much to prompt Cece into a full-blown hissy fit, so I tried to speak objectively—and calmly.

"She copied my ball gown! And she swears she's going to wear the imitation to the Black and Orange Ball."

"The bitch!" Tinkie was ready to do battle. "She can't. We'll stop her."

"How?" It was kerosene on a fire, but someone had to ask.

"We'll catch her and strip it off her." Tinkie's words weren't empty threats.

"Ladies, calm down." I had to be pragmatic. A copycat dress wasn't a catastrophe to me, but Cece had spent months finding the perfect dress, having it fitted, making sure that she would be belle of the ball. And she'd earned the right to shine. I knew Cornelia Holsteadler by reputation, which was that she'd never had an original thought in her brain but that she had a fat checking account and often bought the creativity of others. She'd been jealous of Cece and her work with the Black and Orange Ball and fundraiser for charity for the past several years. Now she'd struck like a viper.

"I can't calm down," Cece said. "I've spent eleven months working on this ball. She's going to ruin it for me."

"No, she won't."

"And just because you ask her pretty please, you think she'll cave?" Cece asked. "I need a wooden stake and some silver. That unoriginal hussy needs to be staked and put in the ground. I'll have to make sure she doesn't dig her way out."

"Colorful, Cece, but not necessary."

"Okay, Miss Smarty-Pants. How would you handle it?" she asked.

"Covert action. Pretend to be a maid, slip into her room, do what's necessary."

After a long moment of silence, Tinkie spoke. "That's good, Sarah Booth. Cece can so pull that off."

"If reason won't work, take an action that ends it. Once the dress is . . . dispatched, she won't have time to whip up another imitation."

"Perfect. Thank you, Sarah Booth. Now here's the information you asked for. This Clampett woman has quite a rap sheet. She did some time here in New Orleans for theft. Worked as a bartender here and along the Mississippi Gulf Coast. No serious crimes, mostly shoplifting, that kind of thing."

"Did you get an address on her?" I asked.

"Last address on file was from a year ago. She was living with her brother off Heron Bay Road."

"Her brother? Would his name be Remy Renault?"

"Bingo, dah-link!"

Tinkie and I exchanged excited looks. "Thanks, Cece. That helps a lot."

"Glad to be of service. So when are you coming to New Orleans? Tinkie, I need you back here."

"Soon," we said together. "Very soon."

The conversation done, I angled back to the car. "So easy for me to solve Cece's wardrobe problems, but I can't decide what to do about Graf."

"My best advice is to get through the Black and Orange Ball. Once you're home at Dahlia House, have a long conversation."

"Can I wait?" I asked myself as much as her.

"Can you afford not to? You've made a bunch of assumptions"—she held up a hand to forestall my immediate defense. "Logical assumptions, I agree. It looks bad, especially with their past romantic involvement. But give the man a chance to tell you the facts. She's a screenwriter. This could be business."

As soon as we reached the cottage, I telephoned Angela. I needed more information on the maritime museum director, Lionel Prevatt, and Angela was the place to start. When she didn't answer, I left a message and walked by Graf's phone. Where had he gone that he'd left his cell phone? Maybe just down to the water.

Opening the sliding glass door, I eased through and stepped onto the balcony. Tinkie had snapped on the TV, and a meteorologist was giving new coordinates on Hurricane Margene. Not much had changed. She still moved north-northwest but hadn't picked up a strong steering current. Her barometric pressure had dropped another couple of bars, indicating she was gaining strength.

Arley had mentioned how Angela would be ready to sell the *Miss Adventure* if a hurricane blew in. I hoped we wouldn't have to find out if he was correct.

At the edge of the surf, movement caught my eye. To my surprise, Graf was alone on the beach, sitting in the sand where the surf stopped at his toes. A big wave would soak him, but judging from his posture, he didn't care. Strange that he hadn't brought the critters with him. Instead, he'd left them shut up in the cottage.

I could read a lot into that if I let myself. Instead, I closed the door and went to his phone. Only a fool would pass up such an opportunity. There were no voice messages, but there were texts from Marion Silber. I wrote down her number and read the messages that consisted of times to meet and *the usual place.*

No sexting. No romantic messages. Just business-sounding meetings. Except Graf had failed to tell me anything about the woman or the reason he kept meeting her.

My cell phone rang, and my heart almost stopped. Guilt. It wasn't a comfortable fit. I'd stooped to snooping on my man. How tawdry. And while I'd lost a chunk of my pride, I'd learned nothing of significance. Hardly a fair transaction.

I answered Angela's call and put the question to her about Prevatt.

"Lionel is officious and dangerous. He figured out that my father really wanted that telescope back."

"Were you aware Prevatt attempted to force a partnership on your father?"

"Dad never told me, but it makes sense. Prevatt knew how badly Dad wanted that telescope, so I'm not surprised he tried to blackmail his way into being Dad's partner." Angela was slightly breathless. "Prevatt isn't the kind of man who would kill, but he would certainly rob a grave."

"Did your dad ever say he was worried about Prevatt, or concerned?"

"Dad treated Prevatt like a joke, until he couldn't get the telescope back. My father hid too much from me, all in an effort to protect me. Deception is deception, no matter what label you put on it."

Truer words, etcetera etcetera. "Did your father have any other business dealings with Prevatt?"

"None I know of," Angela answered cautiously. "I wish he'd told me how the spyglass plays into the treasure. It's old and a pretty piece, but he was obsessed with getting it back."

"I looked at the spyglass. It's an antique, but the lens has a scratch. I wouldn't think it would be that valuable."

"To my father it was."

"The question to ask is, why?"

"Hard to do when Lionel wouldn't even let me touch the damn thing."

"He won't let me near it again, either. Can we appeal to someone at the university?"

"I seriously doubt it, but I'll ask around. Have you learned anything else?"

"Angela, what do you know about your father's relationship with Remy Renault?"

She didn't hesitate. "I think he may have killed Dad. I didn't want to say anything or influence you, but you've dug him up all on your own. He was so jealous of my father. At first, he hung around trying to be friendly and weasel his way into helping in the hunt for the Esmeralda treasure. But when he realized Dad would never include him, he became angry and vindictive. He'd damage the boats in the marina and try to make it look like my father did it. He's a snake."

Renault was getting hotter and hotter as a potential suspect. "Did you ever meet his sister?"

"He has a sister?"

That was answer enough. "Thanks. That helps."

"Be careful, Sarah Booth. He had a girlfriend, Lydia something. They were always scheming and conniving. I think they'd kill for a profit without blinking an eye."

So Lydia was a girl for all seasons—sister, girl-friend, she apparently assumed whatever role she needed to play. "I'll look into this Lydia, too." I didn't want to frighten Angela, but I filled her in about the reckless driver on the bridge.

"Sarah Booth, you should let this case go." She was upset. "I'm serious. You came here to help your fiancé heal, and now someone is trying to hurt you. And someone did shoot out my windows. They're armed and willing to discharge a weapon. None of this is good. In fact, it could be awful. I think this has gone far enough. I'll pay you for your time."

"I'm not ready to call it quits. I want to do some checking on Prevatt. Just background stuff. Nothing dangerous."

Her hesitation alerted me. "What's wrong?" I asked.

"Everything we do seems to upset someone. I was having dinner at the Crab Shed and Randy Chavis came in. He told me Prevatt had filed a complaint against you and your partner. Said you'd tried to steal something. He made a scene at the sheriff's office, but there weren't grounds to press charges. Chavis also accused me of trying to ruin his name. He vowed he'd fight back with everything he had."

Chavis was involved in this up to his eyeteeth. I just couldn't put together how. "Do you think he was threatening you? Like with physical harm?"

"No, he wouldn't beat me or shoot me. At least I didn't think so until you told me about the car trying to hit you on the bridge. Hey! What kind of car was it?"

I wished I had a better description. I'd been blinded by the headlights when it came at me, and then it had disappeared over the hump of

221

the bridge. "Black or dark blue. Something like a Crown Vic. You know, a heavier sedan. Sounds suspiciously like the dark car driving down your street when your windows were shot out."

"Maybe like a police car that's been painted?"

"Exactly like that. Why?"

"Randy bought one of the unmarked police cars at an auction. He had it painted black. The joke around town was that he was on the clock even when he wasn't. Folks around here give him a hard time about his job. It isn't undeserved. He thinks his badge puts him above the law."

So I'd heard. But that wasn't what interested me. The fact that Randy Chavis could have been the driver who tried to run me down was what held my attention.

"I'll check on Chavis's car and then find out what I can about Prevatt."

"He was hired by the university about ten years ago, when they opened the museum. He appears to be a knowledgeable curator."

"Just not a very nice person," I added.

"Please be careful, Sarah Booth. I can't take it if one more person gets hurt."

"Angela, have you considered selling your dad's boat? I saw where you'd had it painted."

I couldn't tell if the silence on the other end of the phone was resignation or maybe a little annoyance that I was butting into private territory. "It's odd how life changes you. In the past I resented every moment of polish and paint, every dollar my father put into the *Miss Adventure*. She was my competition for his time and love. I'd watch him polish the brass in the wheelhouse and think that not one time had he ever brushed my hair or tied my shoes. He was always gone. And I hated the *Miss Adventure*."

"And now?"

"When I work on her or make sure she's in tip-top shape, I feel closer to my dad. She's the link that holds him near me."

I wanted to tell her that such slavery to a boat was foolishness. That she should sell the boat and free herself from such a big expense. But how could I, the girl who refused a movie career to stay in the ancestral home, give that advice to anyone? "I understand."

"Has Phyllis been chewing on your ear about it?"

I laughed out loud. "How did you know?"

"It's her favorite refrain. She thinks she's saving me from myself. In her eyes, my attachment to the boat is sick. She thinks I should sell it and move away from the island. Find a new life, one where I can fall in love and start a family and just live the whole picket-fence dream."

Angela wasn't the picket-fence type, even I could see that. "It's nice someone is looking out for you, even if it isn't the way you need."

"Story of my life. The folks who care about me often hurt me the worst."

Graf popped unbidden into my mind. "Story of everyone's life, Angela. I'll let you know what I find out about Prevatt and about Chavis's car."

When I hung up, I pulled out the laptop and researched Lionel Prevatt's past. My first Google search turned up his bio page. While not exactly dark, it was more interesting than I'd ever anticipated. He got his PhD in museum management from Brentledge University, a place I wasn't familiar with. Then again, I hadn't spent a lot of time learning about doctorates in museum management.

He was originally from Oklahoma, but he'd left after high school and done a stint in the navy. He won a medal for rescuing a fellow sailor who fell overboard. In 1990 he finished graduate school. And then there was a gap from 1990 until 2000, when he moved to Mobile to run the maritime museum on the university campus.

If anyone searched my online résumé, there would be gaps of years when I was trying to act on Broadway and working here and there as a waitress or whatever fill-in job I could find. But a ten-year gap was a bit perplexing for Prevatt, who would certainly have been employed in some federal or state job. Interesting but not criminal. He may have worked overseas or in a private situation.

The car registration was a little trickier, and I had to ask Deputy DeWayne Dattilo in Sunflower County to lend a hand. Turned out, Randy Chavis owned a black Crown Vic, model 2011. The vehicle was similar to the one that tried to run over me and Tinkie.

Chavis was definitely a man to watch. With that in mind, I put in a call to my favorite sheriff.

"How's the beach vacation, Sarah Booth? Are you coming home all tan and rested?"

His question caught me off guard. It was the antithesis of my vacation. "Sun isn't good for skin," I managed, trying not to outright lie or, even worse, let him hear my concerns in my voice.

"Since when has the notion of something being bad for you stopped you?"

He was teasing, and I spurred myself to answer in kind. "I turned over a new leaf. Don't you know? I'm only doing things good for me."

"How much did your nose grow?"

He made me laugh. "Okay, so maybe a few things bad. Like Officer Randy Chavis. Can you check him out?"

"You want me to run a background on a fellow law officer?"

Until he said it, I hadn't realized how much I was asking. "Never mind. Bad question. I wasn't thinking."

"What do you suspect Chavis of doing?"

So I told him about the bridge and the car.

"Give me an hour or two. I'll make some calls." Coleman, like other good law officers, wanted to weed the bad ones out of the profession. Trying to run down two women—if that had indeed been Chavis—would put him way on the wrong side of the law.

Tinkie offered to drive back to New Orleans and give Graf space, but I asked her to stay. I opened a bottle of wine and poured two glasses. Tinkie plopped in front of the television.

"Hurricane Margene has reached Category Three status and as predicted has taken a sharp northerly turn." The weatherman stood before a map of the Gulf Coast. The red cone of probable landfall for the hurricane had been narrowed. Mobile Bay was still dead center.

The meteorologist went into lengthy descriptions of millibars and longitude and latitude and other things I didn't understand. My mind had frozen at the image of the red cone and the little multicolored spaghetti lines that showed landfall of Margene from Bay St. Louis, Mississippi, to the Florida panhandle.

"We anticipate the storm will stall and lose power, probably reaching landfall over the weekend as a Cat One. This will be a rain-maker. While the winds will be down, the chance of tornadoes increases as the warm wall of the hurricane collides with a cold front sweeping down from the north."

Farming was important in Zinnia, and I often listened to the weather. While I didn't farm, I did lease farmland and had horses that required a good supply of winter hay. Lightning, too, was a worry. Tornadoes were rare, but always possible when a storm cell passed through. Ice storms were the big threat in the Delta. Heavy ice brought down power lines and left folks freezing and without lights or heat for days.

The rotating wall of wind and water that was a hurricane, though, was a totally different kind of storm. Sitting in a cottage on stilts not fifty yards from the Gulf, I had a new respect for the power of hurricanes.

"This puts the finish on it," Tinkie said. "Start packing."

I stood mutely watching the TV screen. It was almost Halloween. Such a late-season hurricane was rare, yet it was happening. My week at the beach had proved a disaster on every front possible.

"Are we leaving?"

We both turned to see Graf standing in the doorway. He'd been for a jog, and he was windswept and breathing hard.

"The storm could be dangerous," I said.

"Do you really think it'll come here?"

"It's still several days out. The forecasters say it could turn or dissipate."

"What's the time frame?"

"Landfall over the weekend."

"Let's grill some shrimp for dinner and decide in the morning," he said. "We'll have plenty of time to leave."

Before I answered, a loud knock at the door made me jump. I opened it to find Randy Chavis wearing his brown deputy uniform staring at me.

"Ms. Delaney." He looked beyond me. "Mrs. Richmond, I need to ask you both some questions. We can do it here, or I can take you downtown."

"Questions about?"

"A valuable artifact has been stolen from the Mobile Maritime Museum, and the last people to show any interest in it was you two."

So, someone had stolen the spyglass. A coincidence? Not likely. But it begged the question as to who else would be interested in the artifact that John Trotter had set his heart to reclaim.

"And you want to question us because you think we took something?" Tinkie asked, hot under the collar at the mere suggestion she was a thief. "What are we supposed to have stolen?"

"A telescope." Chavis watched Tinkie for any indication of guilt.

"Why would we steal a piece of junk like that?" Tinkie asked. "We looked at it, and frankly I didn't see any value in it."

Chavis tilted his head in an obvious assessment of Tinkie. "The curator at the museum seems to believe you might have taken it. He said you displayed unusual interest in that one item. Funny you were there and now it's missing."

"Funny how it was in the locked case when we left the museum." I started to close the door, but Chavis stopped me with his hand.

"Do you mind if I search the premises?"

"Do you have a search warrant?" Tinkie asked.

He didn't answer, but he stepped back from the door. "It would go easier if you cooperated," he warned. "I can come back with a search warrant, but if you don't have the telescope, why not let me search? Don't make it hard on yourself."

"Since we did nothing wrong, there's nothing to go hard on us about," Tinkie answered. She could buy and sell the entire museum if she wanted.

"What's so valuable about that telescope?" I asked. "It's antique, but it's just an old spyglass."

"Historical value. Armand Couteau is a local legend, and it's reputedly his."

Graf came to stand behind me. "Officer, unless you have a search warrant, I think you should leave. These ladies resent being called thieves."

"And who are you?" Chavis asked.

"I'm their friend. Unless you have proof that these women have broken the law, you need to leave."

"Don't leave Mobile County," he said as he backed up.

"There's a storm coming." Tinkie put her hands on her hips. "Surely you don't expect us to sit here and wait for a tidal surge to sweep us out to sea."

"Don't leave Mobile County," Chavis said with a grin that told me he viewed himself as the victor in this round. "If you don't want to stay on the island, there are hotels inland."

Graf's jaw was clenched. He was angry, but I couldn't tell if it was directed at the deputy or me. As soon as Chavis drove away, Graf walked down the stairs without another word. Tinkie and I remained at the open door, looking out. Neither of us had to point out that Graf identified himself as our friend, not as my fiancé.

"Tinkie, I was wrong to ask you to stay here in this mess. You should pack and head to New Orleans," I said.

"Not a chance." She slammed the door. "Let's pay a visit to the hussy down the beach."

My smile was wan, but it was there. "I think we should focus on finding out who stole that spyglass. And I think maybe I know who did."

She arched her eyebrows. "Who?"

"There are two possibilities, the way I see it. One is Angela Trotter. She knew her father's attachment, and she's been angry for several years that Prevatt wouldn't return it to John."

"And the other?"

"John's killer. Who else? Do you really think the telescope has any value as an antique?"

Tinkie shrugged. "Things are worth whatever people will pay. So if we can't go intimidate Marion Silber, what should we do?"

"Find Angela. If I'm going to help her, I need to do it now. I won't be here much longer, and I seriously doubt I'll come back. My life is too unsettled."

"If that storm comes ashore here, there may not be anything to come back to." Tinkie hit the last word hard. "I think you should load up the animals and go home to Zinnia. If Graf wants to stay, that's his decision."

My partner was well and truly over the conduct of my fiancé—a fiancé in name only. "I can't leave him. Not just pack up and take the SUV and leave him behind with a hurricane coming. I can't do it."

Her anger evaporated, replaced with empathy. "I know." She crossed her arms. "If we're going to stay, let's look into those politicians Angela made life miserable for. Remember our motives. Greed, revenge. Maybe not sex, but the first two. Framing another person for murder takes money or smarts or both. If they aren't involved, we need to rule them out."

Tinkie understood the trappings of power far better than I did. She and Oscar wielded clout. In the Delta, the bank was the source of the greatest influence. Oscar could stop a loan and destroy a farmer. Farming vast tracts of land required access to fluid cash for equipment, fertilizers, and labor. To his credit, Oscar operated with ethics and not personal gain. Tinkie had learned this at her father's knee. Avery Bellcase owned the bank in Zinnia and ran it before Oscar married into the family and took over the daily management.

I refreshed her memory about the county commissioner, Rick Roundtree, and his development schemes on Dauphin Island, foiled by Angela. And about the former governor Jameson Barr, who'd left a sloppy paper trail when he hired a hit man to kill his wife. He was in prison, along with the paid gunman. But that didn't mean he hadn't struck back at Angela by hiring someone to kill her father. He obviously had no problem paying someone else to do his dirty work.

"And it could be someone in the prosecutor's office," Tinkie said, tapping her chin with a finger. "Let's start with island development, and I know just who to ask."

17

Cece Dee Falcon had taught me two approaches to politicians. If one had the evidence in hand, then a frontal assault was the best option, bulldozing them into either a confession or a dead-out run. Since we had only supposition, we were left with the second approach—deception.

With a few phone calls, Tinkie found the county commissioner hard at work drinking coffee at a small diner not too far from the island. I parked outside, and for ten minutes we watched him through the plate-glass window. He was a hail-fellow-well-met kind of guy, waving his hand and yukking it up with all the locals. But it was impossible to miss the shrewdness in his eyes or the way he laughed and assessed his audience simultaneously.

I took a seat at the counter and ordered coffee and a slice of fresh coconut pie. Tinkie slid into the booth across from Richard Roundtree. "Would you gentlemen give a lady a moment alone with the county commissioner?" she said to the men who'd surrounded Roundtree, hoping no doubt for some scraps to fall from the tax-payer trough. If she'd batted her eyelashes any harder, she would have taken flight.

Chairs scraped, and a few men chuckled as they

moved to another table, leaving Tinkie a clear field. We didn't have any of the recording equipment we sometimes used, but Tinkie's cell phone was set to document the conversation. It wouldn't be high-quality, but it might save our bacon at a later date.

"I won't waste your time trying to pretty up my story," Tinkie said, blinking back tears. "I'm Tinkie Bellcase Richmond of the banking Bellcases of Zinnia, Mississippi, and my husband is cheating on me, lowlife bastard that he is. While my pride has taken a beating, I won't let my net worth be diminished." She blotted a few tears with a paper napkin from the table. "My daddy controls the bank and all of our money. When I told Daddy what Oscar was up to, we had a nice long chat, and he told me to look into some investment properties. I want to invest in coastal development and tie up every liquid dollar we have, which I figure is close to ten million. My daddy, Avery Bellcase, told me to see *you*. He said you were the man for Dauphin Island development."

I doubted the name Avery Bellcase meant much to Roundtree, but it was the way Tinkie said it, leaving no doubt her daddy was a man of means and one to take seriously. It was a thing of beauty to watch my partner work.

"And what, exactly, can I do for you, Mrs. Richmond?"

"I want to build a resort. Something with permanent condos and also luxury hotel rooms. I want to thwart my soon-to-be-ex husband from getting a penny, but at the same time, I want to grow my investment. No reason I can't do both. So what's the political climate on the island for a development like that?"

"You are a blunt woman," he said. The smile never made it from his lips to his eyes. His brain was feverishly at work, calculating the money he could make. Dollar signs reflected in his pale blue gaze. "I presume you have the full financial backing of your . . . daddy?"

"Of course. We just need to move forward quickly, before my husband catches wind of this and puts a stop to it. Once the deal is struck and the money tied up, Oscar will be history. He won't get one red cent of my daddy's fortune."

"I like a woman with brains and beauty." Roundtree signaled the waitress for fresh coffee for himself and a cup for Tinkie. "What's my role?"

"You'd be the liaison between the contractors, the landowners, and me. Project manager. I can't be down here watching over the building of the resort, so that would be your job. And you would be handsomely paid. Maybe even a partial interest if we can find a satisfactory meeting of the minds. There's one little thing we need to settle. I understand there's a newspaper reporter on the island who successfully stopped your last bid to develop this little paradise. Will she be a problem now?"

He brushed it aside with a flick of his fingers. "She made some trouble. Then she got involved in her own world of sh . . . I mean issues. I think she's retired from the news business."

"You *think* or you *know?*"

"Before we proceed, I'll know. She left the local paper, but I'll make sure she hasn't been picked up by an Internet news organization. I'll have every risk assessed." He smiled his sharky grin. He never stopped swimming forward, gobbling everything in his path.

"Is there anyone else who might give us trouble?"

"The majority of the island residents would like development. The right kind. They don't want to see Gulf Shores revisited here. Too much high-rise and not enough community, if you get my drift. The mayor and council will have to be brought on board in the right way. And I won't lie to you: there are a handful of biologists and environmentalists who will fight this tooth and nail. There's a citizens committee headed by Tom Brennan. They're opposed to development. Nothing new, I assure you. It's always a fight to bring progress. But there are ways to deal with them."

"And you can manage them, right? I mean that's where I see your *real* value."

"I can."

"And you will be richly rewarded for doing so."

I shifted uncomfortably. He was such a cold-blooded predator I was afraid he might bite off Tinkie's arm in a moment of unfettered greed.

"But of course."

"And you will take whatever steps are necessary to hold up your end of the bargain?" The hard look in Tinkie's eyes made me do a double-take. Had I not known her true heart, I would have thought her capable of anything.

He looked troubled. "What do you mean? I don't mind greasing the skids with some bribery, but what are you implying?"

"I heard you were a man who took prompt action. When that reporter woman got in the way, bad things happened to her."

Roundtree's jovial demeanor evaporated. There was nothing left but the sleek outline of the shark. "I'm afraid I don't catch your drift. Are you accusing me of something?"

"Absolutely not. I'm just hoping I've found the man I need." Tinkie stood up. She dropped a hundred-dollar bill on the table. "Make sure the waitress knows I appreciate her service. I do like to reward the people who serve me well."

Every pair of eyes in the place watched her as

she walked out with a swing to her hips that practically screamed hot sex.

I finished my coffee and pie and chatted with the waitress for a few minutes about the approaching storm. Some of the locals might already know me and my connection to Angela, so I didn't want to taint Tinkie. As hard as it was to sit still, I did.

Diner chitchat gave the local opinion that Margene would blow through with drenching rains, some wind, but no serious damage. I could only hope they were correct.

Ducking out of the café, I walked to Snill's antique shop. Tinkie was already there, in the midst of a rapture over the library table I knew she'd have to have. Snill put a SOLD sticker on it just as I jangled the doorbell.

"And thank you for the reference to the shop, Sarah Booth," he said. "Your friend has excellent taste."

"And a well-funded checking account." I noticed three other SOLD stickers on various items. Tinkie had been a busy, busy girl.

"Sarah Booth, Mr. Snill is fascinating. He knows the personal history of each of these pieces. It's so beautiful to connect with the people who loved them before. He's shipping these pieces to Zinnia tomorrow before the storm comes in."

"As interesting as furniture might be, I wonder

what our retired postal employee can tell us about Jameson Barr."

Snill's eyebrows almost hit his hairline. "Oh, do sit down. I'll put on the kettle for some cocoa. This will take a while."

Exactly what I wanted to hear.

When we had our hot chocolate and Snill had pulled the old-fashioned shades down on the windows and doors and hung the closed sign, we settled in for a good gossip fest.

"Jameson Barr was the fair-haired child of the state of Alabama, heir apparent to a conservative Senate seat. His father was a televangelist from New Orleans who retired to Gulf Shores. Jameson was a late-in-life child, an only child. He grew up with all the advantages." Snill had told this story more than once if his delivery was a clue.

"Was he handsome?" Tinkie asked.

"He was a sun god," Snill said. "Bronzed skin, blond hair, he was the perfect beach boy. And he could charm the pants off any woman he set his cap for. And let me just add right here that he had a fondness for the women."

I laughed out loud at Snill's delightful entertainment.

"His big mistake was his marriage," Snill said. "He could have had his pick of any woman on the planet, but as sometimes happens in life, karma took a swing at him."

"Who did he marry?" Tinkie was enthralled.

"Lorraine Copeland was the descendant of a famous outlaw in these parts. She was a beautiful woman, as dark as he was light. She had these cascading waves of black hair and pale skin with hazel eyes. When she walked in a room, she could truly silence a crowd. And best of all, she had no use for Jameson."

"That drives a man wild," Tinkie said, nodding sagely. "If you don't want them, it makes them nuts."

"Lorraine had her own reputation in the area of *amore*. She lured men in and then tossed them aside. She liked the hunt, but she had no use for the prey once she caught it. And Jameson had never had the tables turned on him. He didn't even realize he was the prey until she had the ring on her finger and his . . . well, private parts in the palm of her hand."

"Oh, my!" Tinkie put a hand over her mouth, feigning shock.

"It was a fiasco. The biggest wedding in the Southeast, and they couldn't get through the after-ceremony photos without a fight. It was a scandal. And in this state, Jameson couldn't divorce if he had any political aspirations. He was stuck."

"In some very conservative states, even today a divorce is hard for a politician to overcome," I agreed.

"Lorraine worked hard for his campaigns, and

in her own way she was even more ambitious than Jameson." Snill sipped his chocolate and sighed. "The two of them could have made it to the White House. If they'd pulled together, they could have had anything they wanted. The combination of brains, physical beauty, and charm . . . . deadly."

"How did he kill her?" I asked.

"It was a fall down the stairs at the governor's mansion. Very dramatic. Very much designed to garner public sympathy. And it worked perfectly, until it was revealed she was pushed."

It was a bold thing to do—to push his wife down the stairs in the state's most famous home. Falls weren't always fatal.

"How did they catch him?" Tinkie asked.

"Angela Trotter dogged that story. You would have thought she and Lorraine were best friends, but I know for a fact Angela hated her guts."

Now this was interesting. "Why did they hate each other?"

"Angela is her own woman. She makes her mistakes and pays the consequences. Lorraine never took the blame for anything she did. She left wreckage behind her left and right and was shocked that anyone would try to hold her accountable."

That kind of personality would grate on my last nerve, too. "So how did Angela figure it out?"

"Jameson had an airtight alibi. He was at the Shakespeare Festival in Montgomery at a performance. He took his parents and half a dozen of their friends. They had drinks at the Golden Chalice and then went to the play. He was in the public eye at the time his wife slipped and fell to her death down a winding flight of stairs."

Jameson had hired someone to kill his wife, but how had Angela gotten the goods on him? "So he had an alibi. How did Angela put it together?"

"The man hired to kill Lorraine didn't take into account Lorraine might have a lover. Jameson was so arrogant, it never crossed his mind Lorraine would step out on *him*. Had he simply paid attention, he could have divorced her for adultery and kept the public sympathy. Down here in Alabama, a cheating man can be forgiven, but never a cheating wife. The double standard is firmly in place. He could have legally dumped her and kept the governor's mansion and his daddy's money."

"What an interesting world," Tinkie said. "It's sad to say, but you're right, Mr. Snill. Men can be forgiven for cheating, but women often aren't."

"At any rate, Angela dug around until she found Lorraine's lover. He was terrified, because he knew if Jameson became aware of him, he

242

would run into an accident, too. Angela found him, but he refused to talk."

"How did Angela convince him?"

"He was between a rock and a hard place. She made him see that putting Jameson behind bars was his safest alternative. He told a grand jury that on the night Lorraine fell, he was sneaking into the mansion at the same moment the killer pushed Lorraine."

"Lorraine had an assignation, not a headache." Tinkie nudged me in the ribs.

"That's correct," Snill said. "Lorraine refused to go to the play so she could stay home and play with her boyfriend. At any rate, the lover gave Angela a good description of the man coming out. Angela did the background check, found out this guy was a gun for hire. That's all it took."

"Did Angela testify against the governor?"

"She didn't have to. Her stories burned up the pages of the paper. And burned down Jameson Barr's career. Not even all his daddy's money could buy an innocent vote by the jury." Snill took great satisfaction in the turn of events. "And Angela earned herself some powerful enemies. The Barr family hates her and swore they'd sue her for libel. They tried, but there wasn't a case, which only made them hate her more. I often wondered if they hired another hit man to kill her father. Just to show her she would suffer for messing with Jameson."

A chill raced over my skin, and I looked behind me to see if Jitty had put in an appearance. No Jitty, but I knew the source of my discomfort. A premonition. The Barrs were dangerous people. They acted with impunity because they were insulated from consequences by money. Killing the father of a woman who annoyed them—to punish her—would be right up their alley. That kind of arrogance was very dangerous.

"You okay?" Tinkie asked.

"Someone just walked over my grave," I said, repeating an old superstition Aunt Loulane used to say.

"Now we'll have none of that," Snill said. "Another round of cocoa?"

"If I stay, I'll just buy more antiques," Tinkie said.

"Exactly my plan."

I couldn't help but like Snill. He wasn't devious, and he'd been a great help to me. "Do you remember the name of the hit man Jameson Barr hired?"

"You should love this. His last name is Chavis. Zeke Chavis, cousin to our island lawman."

"Where is Zeke Chavis?"

"He's in the same prison as Larry Wofford. Up at Atmore. He got life with no parole. Barr got twenty-five, but he managed to pull some strings and was transferred to another prison."

"That's hardly fair," Tinkie said.

"Not fair, but that's the way life unwinds."

"When was Lorraine Barr killed?" I had to see if the time frame worked. And I remembered the big convict who'd given me a warning at the prison. I'd put the blame on Randy Chavis, and it well might remain there. But Zeke Chavis was an equally intriguing suspect.

"About four months before John Trotter was killed. Angela broke the story about a week before John's death. And Zeke was out on bail at the time John was shot."

"What does Zeke Chavis look like?"

"A great deal like his cousin. Broad shoulders, big man." Snill all but rubbed his hands together. "Strangely enough, a lot like the man Larry said he saw leaving the marina when he arrived."

When we went back outside, a gust of wind nearly snatched Tinkie's perky little sailor blouse right off her.

"Sarah Booth, we need to get an update on the storm." Tinkie grabbed her shirt and held on.

She was right. "Chavis said we aren't allowed to leave the island." I couldn't help the worry. If Margene blew in, did Chavis have the authority to put me, Graf, and Tinkie at risk?

"Under what law?" Tinkie asked. "I'll call Coleman. I think he was bluffing."

I put my hand over her phone before she could speed-dial. "Don't."

"Because you're afraid of what he'll ask."

I nodded. "Coleman is nobody's fool. He knows something is wrong in my world, and he knows Marion Silber and Graf are at the root of it."

She sighed and put her phone away. "As long as the storm hasn't picked up speed, I'll spend the night, but in the morning, we're all leaving. Chavis can come to New Orleans and arrest us if he has probable cause, which he doesn't because we didn't take anything from the museum."

"Let's crank up the computer and see what we can find about the pirate Armand Couteau and his spyglass."

When we arrived at the beach cottage, I was relieved to see Graf on the sand dunes with Sweetie and Pluto. He dodged and played, and the critters were eating it up.

"He's looking better, Sarah Booth. Won't be long before the whole incident is just a bump in the road."

I couldn't love her more for trying to put the best spin on a vacation shifted out of control. "Doc said exercise would bring him around."

"And he was right." She put an arm around my waist as we watched the antics of man and beasts.

"It won't ever be the way it was before he was shot."

"His leg?"

I hesitated, because I had been talking about his leg, but I realized my simple statement was more profound. "Nothing will. Not his leg, not our relationship."

She squeezed me tight. "Everything changes. That's a fact. Up and down, better and worse. We age. His leg will always bear a scar, but if he can run and play and pursue his career, what more can he ask?"

He saw us and waved. When he came trotting over, I thought my heart would break. The wind rumpled his dark hair, and his smile could have been featured on any Hollywood billboard. I had loved him so much in New York, and he'd broken my heart. I'd come home and healed and allowed myself to love him again. And I did love him. More than I'd ever thought possible.

"Where have you girls been?" It was the old Graf. The pre-gunshot Graf.

"I've been buying antiques," Tinkie said. "And you?"

"Groceries are in the kitchen. I got some ice chests and ice in case the storm hits and the power goes out. That's what all the locals told me to do. Water, ice, flashlights, and batteries." There was a hint of excitement in his tone. "I want to get in one more jog through the sand." He scooped Pluto up and handed him to me. "He can't keep up, but he's been giving it valiant effort."

"You're looking good," Tinkie said after him as he sprinted toward the beach.

He waved a hand at us as he disappeared over the dune with Sweetie Pie hot on his heels. Pluto, exhausted from slogging through the deep sand, leaped from my arms and flopped on the bottom step.

We entered the cottage, and Tinkie began stowing away the groceries. Graf had stocked up on peanut butter, tuna, beans, and ice—the hurricane essentials for survival if the power went out for several days.

"Sarah Booth, you're out of coffee. How about I run to the store and buy some?"

"Sure, coffee is good. Maybe some ice cream, too. Jamaican almond fudge or espresso with chocolate-almond nuggets. We can eat the whole thing before the power goes out."

She gave me a hug. "I'll be back with ice cream in a flash."

The strains of a sweet violin drifted to me, almost as if the breeze had captured it from some conservatory and bore it straight to me. I remained at the window, listening, as the music teased my heart.

"Who now?" I asked, because I knew when I turned around, Jitty would be with me in the guise of my violinist.

"Someone who lost much to violence, too."

I faced her. She was young and black and

beautiful, gracefully sawing the bow across the strings of a violin. It was a piece I recognized but couldn't name, hauntingly sad in a minor key. "A vision from the past," I said.

"Not so many people remember that I was trained in music."

"You made your mark in social activism and courage." I spoke to Coretta Scott King, or at least Jitty's personification of her.

"When I first met my husband, I saw only happiness and the joy of working together for justice. We shared that ambition. And lord, we shared a belief that we could accomplish miracles. Had I known the true cost, I might have taken another path."

I closed my eyes. It seemed the individual cells in my body responded to her violin music with a terrible yearning. "If we knew the price we'd pay for loving another person, I think all of us would head for the hills."

She stopped playing. The black silk dress rustled as she came toward me. "Is love always painful?"

"So it would seem." But there had been weeks and months of joy. "But *not* loving—what is the cost of that?"

Her laughter was silky and vibrant. "You ask the right questions, Sarah Booth."

"And I have none of the right answers."

"We're guaranteed only this moment. Live it completely, without holding back."

"Even knowing how much it will hurt when things come crashing down?"

"In the end, we all walk to our destiny alone. In between birth and death, there's time for love. Take advantage of it. Individual love and love of a cause."

She was a wise woman, but my heart had been weakened by loss. "Tell me how not to be afraid?"

"Ah, but that's the exquisite part of it. You love even while you are terrified."

She thinned, her substance gradually fading away.

"Jitty, don't go!" I really wanted her to stay. In all of the hard places I'd found myself since returning to Dahlia House, Jitty was always a presence I could count on.

She flickered back into a more corporeal form, and this time her features were those of my haint. "I bring you all kinds of wisdom, and you still want to linger in that window and feel sad. Gird your loins, Sarah Booth. Take the battle to him."

I had to laugh. The contrast between Mrs. King's gentle encouragement and Jitty's drill-sergeant kick in the pants was striking. Between the two, I couldn't find a single place to feel sorry for myself.

Jitty swished up to me, rustling the silk of her dress. "Graf ain't dead. Yet. Better get him while he's still breathin'. Once Cece and Harold and

Coleman get a hold of him, he's gonna be hurtin' too bad to even think about plowin' your fields. They won't put up with someone who mistreats you, Sarah Booth."

"So he is cheating on me?" I'd suspected, but confirmation was a bitter pill.

"I didn't say that." Jitty sashayed around me. "You actin' like he died. All you know is he's talkin' with a woman in his own profession. Don't mean nothin' 'til you make it mean something."

She was right. I could mope and moan and wail and whine all day long, but nothing was real until Graf and I talked about it. While I'd taken Jitty's appearance as the widow of Martin Luther King Jr. as a sign for permanent loss and great sacrifice, perhaps it was about listening to others without jumping to conclusions.

I remembered a famous quote from Dr. King that I'd heard my parents repeat often. "I have decided to stick with love. Hate is too great a burden to bear."

Jitty's face was luminous. "Good girl. When you put hate and fear behind you, you'll finally be free to grow into the person you're destined to be." And then she was gone. Simply there one minute and gone the next.

As good as her word, Tinkie turned into the driveway and was soon at the door, coffee and ice cream in hand.

"Put the ice cream in the freezer. Let's brew a cup of coffee and decide how to proceed," I suggested. But I took a moment to text Graf's cell phone. "We must talk. Soon."

Tinkie's smile said it all. "Welcome back from the land of the emotionally battered, pardner."

18

I'd just poured coffee for Tinkie and me when there was a loud bang on the door of the cottage.

"Mobile County Sheriff's Department, open up."

"Better hurry or you'll have to replace a door," Tinkie advised. She continued to pour cream into her coffee.

My feet hit the floor at a run, and I flung the front door open just as a deputy lifted a foot to kick it in. "What now?" I asked Randy Chavis. He'd brought three other deputies as backup.

He thrust some folded papers in my hand. "Search warrant."

I opened the door wide. "Be my guest."

The search was more aggravation than any real attempt to find stolen goods. And while the deputies threw things around, especially our clothes, they did no real damage to the furniture. It was over in half an hour.

"I hope you enjoy the words 'I told you so,' because I told you so. Tinkie and I aren't thieves."

"I've got men searching your vehicles." He was a sore loser.

"Fine by me as long as you don't damage them." I gave a one-shouldered shrug. "We have nothing to hide because we didn't steal anything."

"Yet you made me get a search warrant."

"Because you have such an officious and shitty attitude," Tinkie said. "And if you put one single scratch in my Caddy, I'll make sure your department pays for it. And just so you know, if we had stolen a stupid telescope, we wouldn't be so dumb as to hide it in our cars or where we're staying."

Red flushed Chavis's cheeks, but the skin around his eyes whitened. Never a good sign. "You think you're smarter than I am because you grew up with money and privileges. But you aren't. I'll catch you yet, and you'll get to sample the hospitality of an Alabama prison."

"Then we could visit with your cousin." I watched him closely as I spoke. Lightning forked in his pale eyes. "You might have told me Angela Trotter was instrumental in putting your cousin in prison."

"Zeke put himself in prison. He chose to be a gun for hire. I'm not sore at Angela for figuring out he was on Barr's payroll. The ex-governor paid Zeke to push his wife down a flight of stairs. They both got what they deserved."

Chavis's words were heated, but I couldn't tell if his anger was at his brother for being a stupid killer or at me for bringing it up. Before I could pursue the matter further, he stomped out and slammed the door.

"Does he have a chip on his shoulder or what?"

Tinkie asked, but she was a little shaken by his behavior.

"He's pissed because he's wrong about us being thieves. He's not a stupid man, and he knew he was wrong before he searched. He *wanted* us to be guilty. And I rubbed a little salt in an old wound."

"He was really weird about Angela. He actually sounded like he didn't blame her."

"He had a crush on her." Chavis had too many personal feelings involved. He never should have been allowed to handle John Trotter's murder case. His ties to Angela were a conflict of interest.

"Speaking of Angela: if Chavis has a search warrant for our place, don't you think he'll hit Angela's place, too?"

Tinkie was correct. And it would be interesting to see how Chavis handled our client. "I bet they'll search the boat first."

I wrote a quick note to Graf, then loaded Sweetie, Pluto, and me into Tinkie's Caddy. In no time at all, we zoomed toward the marina. On the way, I called Angela to alert her. She agreed to meet us. Her voice was strained, but I didn't have time to guess why. I'd ask her face-to-face.

Angela pulled up just as I got out of the car. Chavis and the deputies were arguing with Arley McCain on the dock. It was clear the marina proprietor took exception to the search warrant and the way Chavis was proceeding.

"Your daddy would be ashamed of the way you're acting," Arley said quietly, his broad-shouldered bulk blocking the deputy's passage. "I let you ramrod me into giving testimony that helped put Larry behind bars, and now I'm not so sure I wasn't played."

"Don't be a fool, Arley." Chavis held his temper by the hardest. "Those private investigators have turned you inside out. You testified to what you knew. Don't go rewriting history."

"The only rewriting I do will be at Larry's appeal. Maybe those lady PIs are right and Wofford was a patsy. Maybe someone snuck onto John's boat, shot him, and escaped before Larry even showed up. Maybe that someone knew how to turn off the security cameras. The more I think about it, the more I think that doesn't make sense. I won't be part of an innocent man being railroaded."

Chavis took a deep breath. "You do whatever you feel is right regarding Wofford's appeal, but right now I intend to search this boat for stolen goods. Step back. I don't want to arrest you, Arley."

"I don't think you should try. I whipped your ass when you were a teenage punk stealing hubcaps with that lowlife cousin of yours. And I can whip it again."

Chavis went beet red with fury. Beside me, Angela was rigid and Tinkie pulled out her cell phone to call 911. The law was already here, but maybe we needed the state police or the highway patrol. Blood was about to be spilled.

"I grew up, Arley, and you know it. I did what Zeke couldn't do and put my juvenile delinquency behind me. I don't want to hurt you, and I sure don't want to arrest you, but I'll do both if I have to."

"You surely didn't get over holding a grudge against people. You never forgave John Trotter because he told you he didn't want Angela dating a punk."

So here it was. The gristle on the bone that Chavis so enjoyed chewing. Before I could stop her, Angela ran toward the dock as the two officers with Chavis prepared for a brawl.

My hound bounded into the fray. "Sweetie!" But it was too late to call her back.

She got between Chavis and Angela and growled at both of them. Never one to rush when a saunter would work as effectively, Pluto followed my hound. He gave the water a look of disdain and sat down to clean his paws, but his wary green gaze locked onto Chavis with clear intent.

"Well, I'll be," Arley said, laughing. "That dog means to stop anyone from taking a swing."

The tension collapsed, and I found I'd been holding my breath. "Let Chavis execute his search warrant. There's nothing for him to find."

I shifted toward the boat with Tinkie at my side.

The deputies boarded the *Miss Adventure* while Angela, Arley, Tinkie, and I stood on the dock. Sweetie was having a sniff fest as she wandered from boat to boat, but Pluto remained seated on the dock. He didn't have to be able to talk to let us all know he was over the adventure at the marina and ready for a nap.

Half an hour later, Chavis came off the boat, empty-handed, as I knew he would be.

"I don't know where you've stowed the spyglass, but I'll find it eventually." He spoke to me instead of Angela. When he felt her gaze on him, his cheeks colored again. So Arley was right. He'd been sweet on Angela, and might still be. Whatever had happened between John Trotter and the deputy regarding Angela, it was still a source of shame for Chavis.

He started to leave, but Angela called his name. He stopped, and she joined him as he went down the dock toward the patrol cars. The deputies hung back, giving the two a bit of privacy. Whatever she was saying, he was listening to her.

"So Chavis had a crush on Angela?" I asked Arley. "It might have been nice to know this sooner."

He shrugged. "Angela could have told you too. John pretty much said Randy wasn't good enough for his girl. That's a hard thing for a man to hear."

"And great motivation for a man to act out of passion instead of reason," I pointed out.

"I think we need to have a word with our client," Tinkie said, and her tone could have frozen ice cubes in hell.

"Good idea."

After the deputies were gone, Arley returned to his office and we had a chance to speak privately with Angela.

"You might have told us Chavis had a thing for you," Tinkie said with some heat.

"It was a long time ago." Angela pulled her Windbreaker closed. "Dad was hard on him. Chavis and his cousin got into a little trouble when they were young. Like Dad hadn't had his share of brushes with the law." She blew out her breath in exasperation. "It wasn't fair, and it pissed me off that my father would suddenly decide to assume a parental role by trying to dictate who I should and shouldn't date. I'm not a child."

I could see her point. Absentee father suddenly becomes overprotective bear. Still, she should have told us. "It's good motivation for Chavis to hurt your father and pin the blame on Wofford."

Angela motioned us onto the boat. Sweetie made the leap to the deck with grace. Pluto assumed the gargoyle pose on the dock. No way was he boarding a boat.

The deputies had done a remarkably neat job

of searching, and she adjusted a few throw pillows and closed the galley doors before she poured us each a glass of juice and motioned us onto the deck, where we settled into comfortable chairs.

"I felt bad for Randy. He's been an ass, I know. But part of it was because my father scalded him with that 'you're not good enough' speech. I didn't want to bring it up. It shouldn't have happened. I had no interest in dating Randy. If Dad had let me handle it, a lot of hurt feelings could have been spared."

"You have to be honest with us," Tinkie said. "We can't work for you if you lie to us or hide facts."

Angela got up and walked to the rail. "Then I have a confession."

I didn't like the sound of that. "Which is?"

"I stole the telescope from the museum. I have it hidden."

"Why?" Tinkie and I said in unison.

"Because it meant something to my father. And because Prevatt is an arrogant man who thinks he can bully and blackmail people. I wanted to take it right after Dad died, but I knew that would point the finger at me. With the storm coming and all, I just did it."

"That's not a good reason to commit larceny. Or is it grand larceny?" Tinkie asked. "How much is that thing worth?"

"He paid Dad a hundred dollars for it. It's probably worth five times that. But it isn't the monetary value I care about. It was my father's, and he sold it in desperation. Prevatt should have willingly sold it back to him. A gentleman would have. Instead, he tried to horn in on Dad's treasure hunt."

"You could have reported that to the police," Tinkie said.

"Right. I had no evidence. I did put Prevatt forth as a suspect in the murder, but the sheriff didn't take any action. From the very beginning, Sheriff Benson and Randy Chavis were determined to make Larry Wofford the killer. So I saw an opportunity and took the telescope. It's justice in my book."

"Stealing is wrong." Tinkie looked at me as if I would have an answer. Not going to happen. I couldn't condone stealing, but in this instance, I also couldn't condemn it. If Prevatt had been a decent human being, he would have sold the artifact to Angela and let it go at that.

"Maybe we can put it somewhere the law will find it." That was my suggestion. "If it's returned, maybe they'll give up hunting for the person who stole it."

"Forget it. I'm keeping it." Angela crossed her arms.

There was no profit in arguing. Angela was as hardheaded as Tinkie or I ever dared to be.

"There's something else I need to tell you," Angela said. She swung around to face us. "Someone called me last night. A man. He said if I didn't back off trying to prove Larry innocent, he would hurt me and 'my nosey investigators.' He said the shot into my windows was to let me know he could strike anytime, anywhere. With the storm out there, maybe you should leave the island. We're making someone very uncomfortable, so I know we're making progress. I'm willing to double your fee if you come back after the hurricane passes."

"We're not leaving yet. Who called?" Tinkie asked.

"I tried to trace the number back, but I wasn't able."

"Did it sound like anyone you know?" I asked. My first thought was Remy Renault. He struck me as the kind who'd use anonymous threats.

"The voice was muffled, like they were talking through a cloth or something. It was male."

"Angela, we should all evacuate. Until we do, though, I'm not quitting as long as I'm on the island."

"Unless the storm gains speed, I can stay until Saturday morning." Tinkie was no quitter, either. "Then I have to get back, and so do you, Sarah Booth. Cece is probably ready to skin me as it is."

Footsteps on the dock drew our attention. Arley

McCain stampeded toward us like a linebacker rushing for a tackle.

"Latest weather alert has the storm coming up the Gulf in this direction. It's too early to call it, but we'd better batten down the hatches. Angela, I'd set sail if I were you. Either head up Fowl River to safer waters or move down the coastline. Maybe west toward New Orleans based on the current predictions. Stay to the west side of the storm, and you should be fine."

Angela's eyes expressed her doubt, even if she didn't voice it.

"What's wrong?"

"I haven't sailed since Dad died."

I didn't know enough about hurricanes and sailboats like the *Miss Adventure* to offer an opinion. She wasn't like a motorboat that could be loaded on a trailer and pulled behind a car. She was too big. "Maybe you should take her inland?"

"She'll need a crew." Arley's brow looked like plowed Delta soil. "I'm taking another client's boat up the river. After Katrina, we're all a bit skittish about the tropical storms. Once I'm done with that, I'll help you, Angela."

"I could try—" I didn't get a chance to finish.

"She needs experienced sailors." Arley put a hand on my shoulder. "Good effort isn't enough. The river's tricky, and Angela isn't a captain. The waters prove challenging for even experienced sailors."

"Let me make some calls," Angela said. "Maybe I can pull some sailors up for a short jaunt. The problem is, I've lost contact with the sailing world."

"In another hour, this place will be crawling with boat owners. When they finish with their own craft, they'll likely help you out."

The sound of a motorboat drowned out Angela's reply, and Dr. Phyllis Norris cut her engine and drifted up to the dock in a sleek powerboat. "Getting all tied down for the storm?" she asked.

"Angela wants to take her dad's boat upriver. She needs a crew."

"Let me make certain everything at the lab is shipshape, and I'll give you a hand motoring up the river." Phyllis jumped onto the dock and looped the painter over a bollard. "I used to sail with your father, so I know the ship and how she handles. I'll be happy to give you a hand."

"Thanks." Angela's demeanor lightened. "Can I help you with anything, Phyllis?"

"I'm gassing up, getting a few provisions. We've got a secure dock back at the lab, so I'll leave my boat there. I don't see this as a major storm, at least not based on the latest reports. Of course, everything can change in an hour. I'm focusing on a few loose odds and ends to pick up and store."

"How bad do you think it'll get?" Tinkie asked.

"This is a tight storm. Small eye but a lot of banding extending out for over a hundred miles. Predictions aren't for fierce winds, but on-and-off deluges, so that could mean a lot of flash flooding. If it's a direct hit, the thing to worry about is the tide. I doubt the wind will stay at a Cat Three. She'll likely come in as a One. Still, if you're in the wrong place at the wrong time, it can kill you. You folks heading back upstate?"

"New Orleans," Tinkie said.

She nodded. "Looks like the Crescent City dodged this one. New Orleans will be fine, and the partying never stops." She laughed. "Even if Margene pays us a visit, it won't be like Katrina. My worry involves the impact on the turtles and other wildlife. We were just recovering from Katrina and the oil spill." She indicated the oil rigs out in the Gulf. "If those haven't been maintained properly, if the storm pushes a boat or something else into one of them." She shook her head. "I don't even want to think about it."

"I'd be happy to help you with the turtles," Angela said again.

"Not necessary. My staff is on top of it, and then they're going to head to Mobile. I'll run my errands and be back to help you move the boat. Maybe you should secure your cottage while I'm tending to the lab."

"Good idea." Angela held out a hand to Arley. "Thanks for calling me about the search."

We all three angled toward the parking lot. At Angela's car, I stopped her. "You have to report the telephone threat. This isn't optional. If something should happen to you, we need to show it was premeditated."

"That'll be a comfort for me while I'm decomposing."

Tinkie laughed first, and then I joined. Angela had a dry wit when she chose to use it. "Okay, so I could have phrased it better, but you know what I meant."

"I think it's a waste of my breath to call the sheriff's office."

I didn't disagree, but I wondered if she had specific reasons. "Why?"

"I thought of it when I was talking to Randy. The person who called said I would be hurt and so would those nosey private investigators. Who really knows that I hired you—Chavis, the sheriff, Prevatt. We've rubbed their noses in it, so to speak. I think it had to be one of them. So why call the law if they're the ones who did it?"

She had a point, but others knew we'd been hired, too. "Snill knows, and by now probably everyone on the island. Still, we need to document the threat. At a certain point, this could become a lawsuit." I wasn't litigious, but sometimes only threat of legal action forced people to do the right thing.

"I'll think about it. But first I need to take care

of my cottage. There are a few sentimental items I want to stow in a safe place."

"Where's the spyglass?" Tinkie asked.

"Oh, you can bet it's well protected," Angela answered. "I won't involve you, though."

She wasn't about to budge. I had one more topic to discuss. "I did some checking." Sometimes it was hard for a client to accept her history could prove fertile ground for trouble. This required delicacy. "Jameson Barr has a real reason to hate you. And he has connections. Do you think—"

"That he killed my father to get even for newspaper stories?"

I hadn't intended to be that blunt. "Yes."

"I haven't ruled it out completely. Don't you think I've tried talking to Zeke? He hates my guts. As unreasonable as it is, he feels like I caught him. Like he would have gotten away with killing Mrs. Barr if I hadn't poked around in it. He'd rather stay in jail than help me. Even if I could convince the DA to offer some kind of incentive for him to tell the truth, he would hold it back just to spite me."

"We've tried to link the murder to the treasure and your father's actions. What if we've been on the wrong trail?"

"Barr is capable of anything. He's an old-school politician who controlled Alabama for a long time because he rewarded those who were loyal to him and punished those who dared to challenge him. I have thought about this. But I believe Dad's murder goes back to the treasure. That's what my gut tells me."

"We need to figure out the identity of the man Wofford saw on the wharf." Tinkie came full circle.

"The problem is that as far as the authorities are concerned, that man is a figment of Larry's imagination." Angela held no illusions about what we were up against.

She was right. Without evidence to back it up, Wofford's claim was viewed as a desperate attempt to throw suspicion on someone else.

"Maybe we should talk to Zeke," Tinkie suggested. "What if Barr used the same hit man to kill his wife and Angela's dad? Why don't we head up to Atmore? It's only a couple of hours. We can be back before it gets dark and still have plenty of time to pack up."

"I'd feel a lot more comfortable if you'd head on to New Orleans, Sarah Booth." Angela's slumped shoulders told me she carried a heavy weight. "I have a bad feeling trouble is headed our way and it's packing a wallop."

"Maybe she's right." Tinkie faced the southern horizon, where storm clouds massed, a dark presence. There was no doubt bad weather was moving in, but it seemed far away. "We can come back, Sarah Booth. After the storm passes. Let

Angela take care of her house and the boat. We'll take care of ourselves and wait for this to blow over."

At my feet, Sweetie Pie moaned as if it were the best idea she'd heard in a while.

"I agree with your partner," Angela said. "See to your safety, then come back. You've made more progress than anyone else, and for the first time in months, I feel that we may be able to figure out what really happened to my father."

Tinkie's small hand grasped mine. "Let's go to the cottage." She tugged me behind her. "This isn't over, Angela. We aren't quitting, I promise."

19

The cottage was empty when we got back. The SUV hunkered beneath the first-floor rafters, along with both bicycles. Graf was on foot. The day was winding down, and my life felt totally out of control. I checked my cell phone twice to see if he'd responded to my last text. Nada.

I stepped into the bedroom and went out on the balcony and dialed his number. His phone rang and finally went to voice mail. "Graf, we need to talk. We can't keep avoiding this." I almost said please, but I stopped myself. "Whatever is going on, ignoring it isn't working." I hung up, hoping he'd call me right back. When he didn't, I rejoined Tinkie in the kitchen.

"Let's call Arley and see if he kept slip rentals at the time John Trotter was shot." Tinkie knew work was the best medicine for me. "We can interview the people we run down, maybe jog a memory. If we could get our hands on one other person to corroborate Wofford's story of the yellow-rain-slickered person on the pier the night Trotter was shot, it could help Wofford."

"Or even someone who saw or heard a motorboat. Good idea."

While I brewed coffee, she took down names and phone numbers as Arley searched his records. "He gave me three names. It's a long shot," she said. "A lot of boats were docked, but no one lived on them. The night Trotter was killed, it was also raining. The people who were around were likely snugged into the apartments they were renting, but I'll ask if they heard or saw anything that night. I don't feel good about trusting the sheriff's department to do a thorough job."

My cell phone rang, and for a second I hoped it was Graf, but Cece's number popped up.

"Hello, dah-link!" she said. "Are you ready for the latest gossip from the City that Care Forgot?"

"Slap me upside the head with it." I wasn't in a gossiping mood, but my friends were rallying to keep my spirits up, and I intended to meet them halfway.

"You remember Samantha Hebert, don't you?"

"The striking filmmaker from Seclusiville Plantation?" I remembered her vividly. She could walk in a room and stop conversation. She was only in her twenties, but she'd directed an independent film that swept the Sundance competition. Graf had labeled her film brilliant.

"That's her. She has a lot of grit and gumption."

Cece would get to the story at her own speed, but I prodded her with a question. "Wasn't she engaged to that stockbroker from Virginia? Handsome but stodgy."

"Tim Kelso."

"Yes. I recall. The young set thought he was the best-looking man they'd ever seen."

"Fresh face on the scene. Always creates a stir."

"Where's this going, Cece?" I checked my watch. I was primed for action, not conversation.

"She broke off the engagement this afternoon in the hotel lobby. It was something of a scene."

"Why?" She'd hooked me despite my best attempts not to be sucked in.

"Do you want the long story or short version?"

What I really wanted was to choke the details out of her. "Nutshell."

"He went behind her back and mucked up the distribution deal she was working on for her film."

"Why?" No reasonable explanation came to my mind.

"He was afraid she'd go to Hollywood and leave him behind. He was fine with her being a big fish in a little pond in Mississippi. He feared if she went to Los Angeles, he would lose her."

"And so now he has." I wasn't sorry for him, but the situation was sad. Maybe he didn't care about her in the right way, but he did care.

"The scene in the hotel lobby was exquisite. She pulled out all the stops. She brought in the Louisiana State University cheering squad. They spelled out B-A-S-T-A-R-D and then shook their pom-poms. I personally felt she went a little over the top with the Elvis impersonator singing

'Jailhouse Rock,' but it's her breakup scene. Let's just say folks will be talking about this for a long time to come."

"What did he do?"

"She caught him completely unprepared. It was a beautiful thing in a terrible way. I suspect he'll move and start over."

"Men have to learn they can't suffocate a woman into a secondary existence. Samantha would never have left him behind, no matter how successful she became."

"I agree, but there's no healing this wound. She tore into him publicly. The entire lobby of the hotel ground to a halt. Humiliating for him to the extreme."

"I'm glad I wasn't there." I had my own kettle of fish to tend. I didn't need to watch another person's romantic conflagration.

"So when are you girls leaving the beach?"

Here was the real reason for Cece's call. She was worried and wanted us on the road. "Probably tomorrow morning. The storm is all but stalled. We still have some time to work on the case."

"And Graf?"

"I honestly don't know, Cece. He's asked for space. I'm doing my best."

"I think I'd like to be involved with someone, but then I witness Samantha's breakup and hear the pain in your voice. Maybe being single isn't so bad."

"Maybe it isn't. I'll give you a call when we get on the road."

Tink and I played several hands of poker while we waited for Graf. We'd turned the television off by mutual consent. The storm inched toward us. Watching was worse than a dental appointment. Night fell, and still no sign of my fiancé. I'd talked myself into the whole "giving space," but the approach of the storm and Graf's continued absence was unraveling my resolve. And my temper.

"I'm going to look for Graf." I grabbed a Windbreaker. The air was cooler, and the pending storm had also brought in an element of chill. Or maybe it was purely emotional.

Tinkie put her hands on my shoulders and pressed me into a chair at the kitchen counter. "Don't, Sarah Booth."

"But—"

"Don't go sniffing after him."

Tinkie was always the one to urge love and romance and never say quit. "Do you know something I don't?"

She slowly shook her head. "Not about Graf. But I do know that if you follow him and find him with that woman, the end result will be you ending it forever. You have too much pride to see that and not take action. You and Samantha Hebert aren't women to sit around and take misconduct." I'd relayed Cece's gossip to her.

Tinkie knew me inside and out. "I can't just wait here, hoping he drags back in after he's done with her. It makes me feel like an old shoe."

Her tinkling laughter was the one ray of hope in the cottage. "You are certainly not an old shoe. Look, when he comes back, let's ask him about leaving. We don't want to pack and push him into a corner. We'll take this one step at a time. I just checked the weather online, and the storm is crawling toward Mobile Bay. It hasn't veered course, it hasn't strengthened, and it hasn't picked up speed. "

Sitting at home in Zinnia, I'd watched more than a few hurricanes roar toward the Gulf Coast. I'd been mesmerized by the potential for destruction, and often for the horrible aftermath. But it wasn't personal. Not like it was now. My admiration for those hearty enough to live with this impending doom rose to new heights.

"Tomorrow the roads will be jammed with people smarter than we've been. We should have left yesterday."

Tinkie patted my back. "Shoulda, woulda, coulda. That's a fool's game. You weren't ready to go, and neither was I. We can leave in the morning, in the daylight, and make New Orleans. The interstate may be crowded, but I know a few back roads. We'll be fine. We can be in New

Orleans before lunch. We'll have time for a nap and a little beauty parlor pampering before touring the French Quarter. We just need a good night's rest so we can look magnificent for the ball. Settle back. Let's see what we can find on the Internet about Jameson Barr's hit man. That Zeke person."

"Good idea. I think you should call Roundtree again. Keep his feet to the fire about all the money he can make from your development plan."

"I agree." She put her Bluetooth earpiece in. "Stand back and watch me work this guy. Greedy men are like taffy. A little pull here, a tug there, and soon they're way overextended."

At the last minute, she pulled out the earpiece. "Speakerphone might be more in order."

She must have known my mind had wandered to Graf and where he was and, more important, what he was doing. My thoughts refocused on the job at hand.

"Well, Mrs. Richmond, it's good to hear from you." Roundtree was smooth as an oiled hinge.

"You had me checked out, didn't you? Talk to Oscar at the bank? I hope you didn't let on about our little deal. If he gets wind of it, he'll shut me down."

"I was very discreet, but let's just say your credentials were verified."

I'd wondered at the time if it was wise for

Tinkie to use her real name and background. She was not only right, but brilliant.

"I'm going to enjoy doing business with you, Richard. Or should I call you Rick? I like a man who uses precautions." Her laughter chimed lightly. "So this storm is headed right up our posteriors. This will be a good test. Maybe see how bad erosion is on the beach side."

"We can possibly bulwark or create barriers to the storm surge. It's been done other places."

"But wouldn't that interfere with the waves and surf?" Tinkie knew a lot more than she let on.

"We'll cross that bridge when we come to it." Roundtree soothed her doubts.

"You said there were environmentalists opposed to development. How much influence do they have?"

"Dr. Norris with the turtle research is the most outspoken, but they don't have the money to be a real bother. Then there's Tom Brennan. I believe I mentioned him. Now he might be a thorn. He's smart, and he isn't afraid to speak out and rally support. We'd need to slide this past him. Get to the stage where it's gone too far to stop. So with that in mind, I presume you will refrain from talking about our partnership."

"And who would I talk to but you?" Tinkie cooed.

I made gagging motions and rolled my eyes.

She completely ignored me. Her mama had trained her well.

"You're as smart as you are pretty," Roundtree said. "Why don't we seal our little bargain with a drink this evening? I'm moving my yacht inland. We could sail upriver. Drink some champagne."

"I'm still married, Commissioner Roundtree." Tinkie played it coy.

"I won't tell a soul."

"I believe there's a private investigator following me. Let's just say I can't risk photos taken with a man as attractive as you are. It might give Oscar grounds in the divorce, and God knows I'm not giving him a penny I don't have to."

Roundtree laughed. "If I had any illusions about marrying you, Mrs. Richmond, they are shattered. You're too smart. But I'll look forward to a more intimate relationship once you're divorced."

"Let me call my lawyer and get that ball rolling," Tinkie said.

Her enthusiasm elicited more gagging motions from me.

"You do that, darlin'. After the storm blows through, we'll take a survey of the island. There's a piece of property that will make you salivate."

"I can't wait." Tinkie clicked off the phone and rounded on me. "I should beat you up," she said, holding back laughter. "You almost threw me off my game."

"Tinkie, you're the best I've ever seen."

"Men are simple, Sarah Booth. Unless you really love them. Love complicates everything."

"Do you think maybe Phyllis Norris or Tom Brennan might have been involved in hurting John Trotter? I mean, if he found the treasure, it would mean development. There's no way around that."

"Norris was dating him, and she seems really fond of Angela. Let's pull up Brennan and also the hit man."

For the next hour, we surfed the Web. Tom Brennan was a firebrand and activist. He practiced civil disobedience by staging nonviolent sit-ins. Dr. Norris was an outspoken advocate for keeping Dauphin Island pristine, but her tactics revolved around giving papers at academic conferences, testifying before Congress, and taking the news media on tours of the island paradise.

"Neither of them seems dangerous or likely to kill." I simply couldn't find anything that led me to believe either environmentalist would be a killer.

"So we're left with Chavis, Barr, Renault, Prevatt, and Roundtree as our primary suspects." Tinkie tapped her fingernail on the table. "Frankly, I don't think Roundtree is our man.

He's greedy, and it isn't that he wouldn't kill someone. I think he fears getting caught too much to actually do it."

She could be right, but I still wasn't ready to rule him out. Greed was always a good motive for murder in my book, though revenge was better. "I wonder if Coleman might be able to check out Zeke Chavis in the Atmore prison."

Interest sparked in Tinkie's eyes. "Damn good idea. They'll talk to a lawman where they won't give us the time of day."

"Will you call him, Tinkie?"

She considered my question. "Yes. I will. I love you, Sarah Booth, and I don't want to see you do anything you'll regret in a week or two."

"I don't want to be that woman."

"Then I won't let you." She dialed the Sunflower County Sheriff's Office, and, in no time at all, Coleman had agreed to find out what he could about Zeke Chavis and his conviction for murder.

"He'll call us back when he has something," Tinkie said, clicking her phone off. "He did check on Randy. He said the deputy came back clean. The deputies Coleman interviewed seemed to think Randy was a good guy who deserved a promotion to detective. They said he'd been implicated in some events in the sheriff's office as a scapegoat."

"Coleman's a good friend to ask around for us."

"Indeed." She took her time, but at last she held my gaze. "Look, I have to say this. Coleman is our friend. We both know he carries a torch for you. Don't use him, Sarah Booth. Don't rush into his arms because you're angry and hurt with Graf."

I held my temper because she spoke out of love. "I don't want to do that."

"Then be sure you don't. If you end up with Coleman, it has to be because you're in love with him, not on the rebound or trying to strike back at Graf." She put a finger on my lips. "It happens. Remember when we first met? My obsession with Hamilton Garret V? I felt neglected and hurt. Had it not been for you, I might have hopped in bed with Hamilton and ruined my marriage. Friends stop each other from rash action."

"I agree." She had me dead to rights. Instead of her, I'd been the one who ended up in bed with Hamilton.

"You would never hurt Coleman deliberately, but it's up to you to control the situation."

"I want to point out I haven't done a thing to deserve this lecture."

She rushed to me and hugged me. "Not a single thing. I just don't want to see you hurt more or Coleman pulled into this in a way that harms his heart or his integrity."

I nodded. "We're on the same page." I kept my voice light, but deep in my heart, I felt a horrid ache. Tinkie expected me to rush to Coleman to assuage my pain. Which meant she expected to see me hurt.

I grilled some grouper marinated in a balsamic vinegar glaze and sweet potatoes with corn on the cob. It took almost no time, and when it was ready, Graf magically appeared.

"Been out stargazing?" Tinkie asked innocently.

"Trying to get a last workout in on the beach." Graf was sweaty, and the night was chill.

For four hours? "Bless your heart." It was the best I could come up with, and every true Southerner knew exactly what that phrase meant. Rough translation: "Kiss my ass."

Graf was oblivious to my subtleties. He continued speaking. "I've given it some thought, and I think we should get up at daybreak and head to New Orleans. I think we have a ball to attend."

Tinkie and I exchanged surprised looks, but neither of us commented. What had occurred in his absence to send him back to my orbit? I wanted to ask, but I would gain nothing from a direct assault in front of Tinkie. Before the night was over, I'd have some answers, though.

We settled around the table, and Graf ate his food with his former relish. Tinkie sipped wine, and the two of them engaged in friendly sparring about the best beach attire. The deep freeze around my heart began to thaw of its own accord. Maybe Graf had worked through whatever had been eating on him. It could have been a thorny script discussion with the writer. Still, he should have told me about Marion Silber.

I reached across the table and took his hand. He squeezed mine in return and warmed me with a smile. It was a small thing, just a touch of intimacy from the man I loved. It was enough to kindle the fire of expectation. But not for long.

My short-lived hope that the old Graf had suddenly returned was dashed when we finished dinner and Graf retreated to the sofa, saying he felt more comfortable there. Tinkie wisely said nothing as she went to the guest room.

"Graf." I sat down across from him. "Did you get my text? And my voice mail?"

He met my gaze. "I did. I've spent the whole afternoon trying to come to terms with some things."

"What things?" How I kept my voice steady was a miracle.

"I need time."

"To decide what? That you're leaving me? What happened? Is there someone else?"

"There is no one else. You have to give me some time, Sarah Booth. I'm struggling."

"And I'm not? We came down here, and we were in love. Now you sleep on the sofa and disappear for hours at a time. You avoid intimacy.

What conclusion should I draw except that your feelings for me have changed?"

"They haven't. I love you. Other things have changed." He leaned and grasped my hand. "Give me some time. I promise I'll explain everything and you'll understand."

I could have confronted him about Marion Silber, but what was the point? I got up and went to the bedroom and closed the door.

I slept fitfully, dreaming of waves that towered over me and the cottage on the beach. But I could swim underwater. As I watched my possessions float past, I angled for the sunlight on the surface of the beautiful aqua water. No longer churning with mud and silt, the water suffused me with beautiful blue light. And yet when I surfaced, I found myself in the dead of night surrounded by black water and no idea where land might be.

I awoke sweating and miserable. Tinkie slept on, as did Sweetie, Pluto, and, in the den, Graf. I dressed and went outside, wondering if sunrise would show the storm had moved inexorably toward the mouth of Mobile Bay.

The radio in the car would give me an update, so I found the keys and slid into the driver's seat. Local stations had given up music for full-on storm reporting. Margene had slowed and lost some momentum, falling back to a Cat One. She packed constant winds of seventy-five miles an hour with more powerful gusts. Predictions for rainfall went as high as eight inches in a very short time.

She was slated to make landfall at Dauphin Island Saturday afternoon—unless she hit a strong steering current. She could roar to shore in a matter of hours.

Agitation took me in its teeth and shook me hard. For a moment, panic ruled. I needed to wake up the household and get packed. After a few deep breaths, I forced myself to calm. It would take no more than half an hour to load the car. We could be on our way by 7 a.m. There was no need to shake people out of bed before dawn. We had at least twenty-four hours to evacuate, and the storm was not that severe.

I refocused on the DJ's voice. Reports from Alabama elected officials made it clear that no one expected the savage destruction of Katrina. The real danger was in floods across roads and the tornadoes a hurricane could spawn and send in any direction. There could be millions of dollars lost in timber, physical buildings, road damage, and flooding. But for humans who practiced a degree of safety and did not live in flood zones, it would be a minimal event except for the loss of power that always came with a storm. I could not comprehend for the life of me why power lines weren't buried in areas where the soil was easy to dig. Every year they blew down or trees fell on them. In the Delta, ice took them down every winter. It made no sense to me.

Because I didn't want to go back inside and wait for folks to wake up, I drove to the old fort. I found my way to the battlements and watched the surf as it battered the bulkhead of cement riprap. The sound almost deafened me.

Spray spewed in flumes that left me wet and tacky with salt. John Trotter's watercolors came to mind. The water had the same clarity and hue. Using a translucent background was a stroke of genius on his part. Maybe one day, the paintings would be worth a lot.

Thoughts of art left my head as an angry wave smashed at my feet. While dangerous, the power in the water and wind was also exhilarating. Jitty had recently appeared to me as Mary Shelley, the creator of Frankenstein, reminding me that her monster was created by the power of a strong electrical storm.

Perhaps it was my gothic musings or my last chance encounter with a stalker that made the hair on my neck stand at attention. Whatever, I knew I was under observation.

"You should see the Irish Sea crashing against the cliffs. Now there's a sight to stir a literary imagination."

The Irish accent, complete with such proper articulation, clued me in to Jitty's presence. Yet again she wore the full weeds of Victorian

286

widowhood. To be sure, I couldn't identify her this time. "Who are you portraying?" I asked.

"To be courted by two literary giants was never my dream."

I searched my memory and still couldn't place the phantom. She carried herself with great pride, and she was a beauty. Dark hair, pale skin, eyes that caught the last of the starlight and sparkled.

"Another clue, Jitty."

"My husband created a literary masterpiece on a par with Shelley's *Frankenstein*."

"Mrs. Stoker, the honor is mine." I gave a low bow. I didn't care that she'd scared me a little. I was desperately glad for the company. "What brings you to the battlements of Fort Gaines?"

"I'm contemplating my legacy. Did you know I was courted by Oscar Wilde?"

My knowledge of history was slim. "Didn't he go to prison for—"

"He did." She cut me off. "Ridiculous. He was a genius. Like Bram. And he was a gentle man."

"Which was the better conversationalist?" I had to ask. I loved the plays of Oscar Wilde, but *Dracula* had imprinted me with all the secret joy of the vampire world.

"Oscar was funnier. Bram the better story-teller."

"And you're here to lament your love life?"

She laughed. "No, that's your role. I'm here to tell you that love can't be rationed." She sighed.

"I outlived my husband by a quarter century. I survived on memories. That's what it comes down to. Make some good ones, because they will sustain you."

"Jitty, what is with the widows? Spit it out!"

She came closer. "Bram danced with the darkness of death. Out of it, he made great literature."

"I don't want to live death or write about it. I want to be happy. I want to go home to Dahlia House with Graf and my critters and have a wedding and start a family. I finally accept this is what I want. And before you point it out, yes, I do want it all. Husband, family, heritage, careers. And why shouldn't I?"

"Awareness sometimes comes too late. The art to living is learning to fight on and yet surrender."

"That's the stupidest thing I've ever heard. I'm serious. That's a crock of shit! It's unacceptable."

Jitty's low chuckle came again. "At least I got your Irish up. Now you're ready to fight. Crawl out of that hole of doubt and self-pity and show me your mama's girl."

And then she was gone.

A wave hit the riprap so hard the water almost knocked me off the wall. I backed away. In the east the sun rose, highlighting the massive storm clouds to the south. They boiled at the horizon's edge. It was time to leave.

I slipped into the fort. Walking the empty

corridors, my footsteps swallowed by the pounding surf, I felt more like a shade than a flesh-and-blood person. This must be how Jitty felt. Disconnected from the physical world. There, yet not there.

I found myself in what had once been used as a dungeon. Because the fort was built on the shifting sand of a barrier island, prisoners were at ground level, not the traditional dank dungeons of books such as *The Count of Monte Cristo*. I wondered if Armand and LuAnn had been held here.

Life was indeed cruel. And unpredictable.

Sunlight crept into the room, almost as if nature offered a bit of solace. The wall of the cell, a dun color, caught the sunlight and turned into a golden shade so beautiful I stopped to examine it. As the light intensified, a drawing began to come through. I froze.

Someone had drawn a coastline and words written in French. Had the image been there all along, hiding in the shadows of the cell? Surely if that were true, someone would have found it before now. But even as I watched, the sun rose higher and the quality of light changed. The drawing began to disappear.

I whipped out my cell phone and snapped a dozen photos, hoping to capture the details of the drawing even as the light changed and the wall became, once again, a dunnish blank. If I brought in floodlights and angled them just so, could I make the image reappear? I couldn't say. The genius of the disappearing drawing had to do with sunlight. Armand Couteau, who I believed from the bottom of my soul had scrawled the message on the wall, could never have predicted electric light.

But there was no need for artificial illumination. I checked my phone. I'd captured the map. Now all I had to do was figure out what it meant.

Was it possible John Trotter had found this? Was this part of the legend that would lead us to the pirate's booty that had eluded discovery for almost two hundred years?

I left the old fort at a trot. I could only hope the storm wouldn't damage the historic place, but Fort Gaines had survived far worse than Hurricane Margene.

Sunshine angled over the parking lot when I hurried out of the fort, but even before I could reach the car a cloud passed in front of the sun. We had to hurry. As Florence/Jitty had warned me, sometimes awareness came too late.

As I opened the car door, a gust of wind almost took it off its hinges. No time to waste now. I sped toward the cottage.

The voice of a radio newscaster, almost breathless with the rush of a breaking story, caught my attention. "Evacuation for Dauphin Island, Gulf Shores, and low-lying areas south of I-10 are advised by Alabama officials. Residents in flood zones are asked to begin the process of moving into shelters. The governor is considering a mandatory evacuation, but so far has taken no action in that direction."

Mandatory evacuation. Now this was something I'd never faced before. In my head, I was mentally packing and preparing for flight from the storm. Before I returned to the cottage, I detoured the short distance to the marina. The *Miss Adventure*'s berth would be empty, but I hoped to see Arley on the wharf. I needed confirmation that Angela and the ship had safely made the passage upriver.

When I turned into the marina, fear touched my gut. The *Miss Adventure* tossed on the rough water. She hadn't moved an inch.

And there was no sign of Angela.

20

I returned to the cottage to pack up. If Graf had already finished, he could drive the SUV to New Orleans with the pets while Tinkie and I tracked down Angela. If he wanted distance, he was going to get it.

I called Angela several times, but she never picked up. A gust of wind pushed sand over the roadway, a tiny reminder that I was in terrain I didn't know well. Beach scenes were fun and sand and sun—a bad storm was another matter.

Doing my best to stay calm, I ran up the stairs and into the cottage. "Where have you been?" Tinkie asked. "Is Graf with you?"

"What?" I glanced about the room. "Where is he?"

"When I woke up, both of you were gone. I assumed you were together." Worry knotted her forehead. "Where the hell did you get off to?"

I told her and showed her the photos I'd taken in the fort—while it didn't stop her worry, it did slow her complaints about my abrupt morning departure.

"This is a clue, Sarah Booth." Tinkie couldn't suppress her excitement, even though it was off-set with worry about the storm. "Our Internet connection is going in and out, but when we get to New Orleans or someplace where we have a reliable connection, we can research what this says. It's French. Something about sunrise and a cross. I don't know. I should have paid more attention in class back at Ole Miss."

"We'll figure it out."

"*Le Soleil Levant intersecte avec l'ombre d'un mur. Là se trouve le croisement du destin et de la fortune.*" Tinkie mouthed the words with a certain flair, but they had no meaning whatsoever to me. "Dammit. I just can't get hold of it."

"Translating the French will be easy enough once we find someone who speaks the language. I'm more concerned about Angela. She never moved her boat."

"That young woman needs to get her priorities straight." She paced the room. "I'm curious. What made you go to the fort?"

"I didn't sleep well. I was ready to pack at four a.m., but you and Graf were sound asleep. I didn't want to disturb you."

"Maybe you should get a shock collar for Graf. One with a physical limit, so if he goes beyond the boundaries, he gets toasted."

It wasn't a bad idea, though I would never do such a thing to Sweetie Pie. Graf was a different situation.

Tinkie's next statement echoed my thoughts. "If he's helping his honey pack up while we're

293

here loading our crap by ourselves, I say we drive off and leave him." My partner was highly agitato.

"Let's check on Angela." I tried to call her from the landline. There was no answer at her cottage or on her cell. Her cell phone, like mine and the Internet service, could be suffering intermittent transmission.

"Put the stuff in the SUV and let's drive over to the marina. Maybe she's there by now, though I wonder if it isn't too late to try to sail out of here." Tinkie could be counted on for practical solutions.

We hustled our suitcases down the stairs. The weather still held, but we had to fight an occasional stiff wind. Nothing an experienced sailor couldn't handle, but would Angela be able to round up a crew at this late date?

We hefted our bags into the back of the SUV. Even Sweetie trotted up and down the steps carrying her dog bed and supplies.

"This weather is ominous," Tinkie said. "Due south it looks like the sky might fall at any minute. The hard thing is, we know it's coming our way and we can't stop it."

"Feeder bands will arrive first. They can extend hundreds of miles from the eye."

"That makes me feel oodles better." Tinkie didn't bother to sound less than snippy. "The weather station says New Orleans is overcast, but not so much wind. The ball will go on as planned."

"Margene is tight. She'll only impact the place she lands and to the east. The Mississippi Gulf Coast and New Orleans are safe this time around."

"Then let's beat a path for the Crescent City."

When we had everything packed, we left the loaded SUV and took Pluto and Sweetie in Tinkie's Caddy to swing by Angela's cottage on the east end of the island. Overnight, the look of the small neighborhood had changed. Plywood shuttered windows, and many carports and garages were empty. People had evacuated. Stranded on an island without power or access to emergency help was no one's dream of the good life.

Angela's cottage was the exception. The front door swung open ominously as the wind gusted. The carport was empty. Not a window was boarded up, and lawn furniture and gardening tools, which should have been stowed inside, were scattered about the yard. Almost as if she'd been whisked away by goblins.

"This doesn't look good," Tinkie said.

"Maybe I should go in first." I couldn't take putting anyone else I loved in danger.

"Fat chance that'll happen. Sweetie, Pluto, and I are on you like glue."

We abandoned the car and halted at the front door.

"Angela!" I called into the house. My voiced reverberated, like yelling into a well. "Angela! Are you in here?"

"Turn on a light," Tinkie advised. "Don't you just hate those forensic shows where they go into a house and search by flashlight when all they have to do is flip a switch?"

I did. Light flooded the interior. The place was wrecked. Chairs and sofas had been toppled and the stuffing cut out of them.

"We'd better call nine-one-one," Tinkie said.

I pulled out my cell phone—still no signal—and then thought better of alerting the authorities. I wasn't sure they were uninvolved in ransacking Angela's house.

"Let's see what we find before we get the law involved." I continued forward to the bedroom and bath. Both were empty, and both had been torn apart. The only room left was the kitchen. A bad feeling made me hesitate.

"Let's get it over with." Tinkie talked big, but she waited for me to push through the door.

Sweetie's bark cinched it. She'd found something in the kitchen.

When I entered the room, I saw the blood. It was splashed across the counter and sink.

"It's not enough for someone to be dead," Tinkie said. "Hurt, but not dead."

She didn't say it, but we both thought it. That someone was likely our client.

• • •

Arley McCain didn't answer at the marina. Tinkie and I didn't know if it was because the lines were down or the towers out or because the destruction at Angela's house had spread to the *Miss Adventure* and therefore Arley.

"Should we call the sheriff?" Tinkie asked.

I could tell by her tone she had more negative feelings about such a call than positive.

"If Chavis is behind this, it'll tip them off to the fact we're on to them."

"Why abduct Angela?" Tinkie asked.

"The telescope." It was the only thing I could come up with. "Somehow, everyone knows how crucial it is to finding the treasure. If you and I didn't have it, stands to reason Angela would."

"So they were here searching and Angela walked in on them?"

"Either that or they waited here for her and intend to force her to talk."

Tinkie shivered. "We need to find her and evacuate. I know this isn't a big storm, but we could die. A piece of tin could fly through the air and slice us in half."

She was exaggerating, but only a bit. While the hands on the clock had spun around toward nine o'clock, the day was growing progressively gloomier, the weather more and more blustery.

I tried Graf's cell phone—no answer. But I did reach his voice mail and left a message telling him we were en route to the marina. No details. I didn't want Graf coming to find us if things were dicey.

Before we could get to the marina, though, a sheriff's patrol car pulled us over. The rain had stopped for a moment, and when the officer approached, I rolled down my window.

"We're evacuating the island of all tourists, ma'am. You need to head north or west. Evacuation routes are marked."

"My friend is back at our cottage," I said. "I have to check on him, and then we're leaving. Is this a mandatory evacuation?"

"Not mandatory, but highly recommended. Storm watching isn't worth risking your life. Be quick about checking on your friend, and then please leave. We don't want any injuries or casualties."

I didn't recognize the officer, so I took a chance. "I'm trying to find Deputy Chavis. Do you know if he's on the island this morning?"

He lowered the brim of his hat against a gust of wind. "Randy was called in by the sheriff last night. Haven't seen him. I can radio a message to him if you want."

I shook my head. "Is he on the island?"

"Couldn't say." He nodded and headed back to his car. In a moment, he pulled away.

"What do you suppose Chavis is up to?" Tinkie asked.

"The same thing you're thinking. I think he was involved in Angela's abduction, and he's probably holding her hostage."

"Or disposing of the body."

I punched Tinkie's arm lightly. "You're just the cheeriest little optimist I've ever met."

"We are about to be in the middle of a hurricane. Our client is missing, and there's blood in her kitchen. Since Angela doesn't strike me as a voodoo queen who might be sacrificing chickens, I wouldn't say this is looking like a case with a happy outcome.

"I should call Cece and let her know we're delayed," Tinkie said. "She's worried sick, no doubt."

She tried the call, and to my amazement it went through. Cece answered immediately, and Tinkie put the phone on speaker.

"Where are you, dah-links? Oscar is beside himself. He said you called earlier, but he hasn't been able to get through since then."

We summed up our situation, keeping it as positive as possible.

"The ball starts at ten Saturday evening. We'll be dancing at midnight on Halloween." Cece's voice held only a little panic. "You'll be here, won't you?"

"Wild horses couldn't keep us away."

"No, but a case might. Or a storm. I know it's only Friday, but you say you're coming, and then you never leave the island." Cece was nobody's fool.

"We have to find Angela. Our cell phones don't work all the time, and the landlines are down or something has gone wrong."

"What can I do?" Cece asked.

In the midst of the most lavish ball of the New Orleans season, Cece had time to help her friends.

"I snapped a photo of a drawing on a wall of the old stockade at Fort Gaines. If I can message it to you via the phone, could you research what it might be? There's something written in French, and we need the translation, too." It was a big request with everything else Cece had going on.

"Dah-link! I always have time for a riddle. Send away."

"We'll be on the way to New Orleans as soon as we can," Tinkie said. "Tell Oscar not to worry. We're fine. Once we locate our missing client, we'll leave."

"I'll tell him," Cece said. "Be careful, ladies. Folks go a little crazy when a storm is coming in. Something about a drop in the barometric pressure."

"No, that's supposed to bring on labor in humans and colic in horses," I corrected her. "Nothing about crazy. You're thinking of a full moon."

"You've never been on the coast during a hurricane," Cece said. "Drop in barometric pressure or fear-induced insanity, I can't say for sure. But I'm telling you, people start to act like there's no consequence to their behavior. The crazies come out of the woodwork. So watch yourselves."

"Will do," Tinkie assured her. She pinched me until I yelped an agreement.

"If you aren't here by five o'clock, I'm calling out the National Guard."

It wasn't an empty threat. Cece would do it. "We'll be there. And we'll be safe."

It was a big promise, but one I intended to keep.

The marina held an air of abandonment. Most of the boat slips were empty. Wise sailors had set sail away from the storm. Only a few boat owners worked frantically to lash their crafts to the wharf with extra ropes. I understood the concept of tying the boat so it couldn't bang into the dock or other boats, but the way the water was already rolling, I wondered if any of the beautiful vessels would survive. This was just the precursor of the storm. Unless Margene weakened drastically or changed directions, the worst was yet to come.

A car pulled in right beside us, and, to my surprise, Phyllis Norris got out and ducked into the backseat of the Cadillac. "Have you seen Angela? I've called and called. I'm worried sick. I thought she was moving her dad's boat, and I kept a crew at the sea lab shifting valuables to safer areas. But they finished, and I had to let them leave the island. I never heard from her, and I haven't been able to raise her with a phone call. She was supposed to move the boat yesterday."

"We're looking for her, too," I said. The *Miss Adventure* bobbed and tugged at her tie-lines. "Where have you searched?"

"She doesn't answer her door or her phone. I hope she didn't fall overboard."

I didn't want to tell her what we'd discovered in Angela's kitchen. There was no point worrying her more than she already was. And she'd added another layer of anxiety—I hadn't even considered a boating accident. "We thought we'd talk to Arley. Maybe he's heard from her, though earlier he was surprised she didn't move the boat upriver like she'd planned."

"I just don't know about Angela." Phyllis was frustrated. "She's so headstrong. She could be anywhere. Maybe on the way to Atmore to visit Larry."

"I don't think she'd abandon the boat."

"In some ways, it would be better for Angela if the boat sank. She'd be free of the cost and the past. And I believe John has a handsome insurance policy on it."

"Which wouldn't pay out at all if it was discovered Angela made no effort to secure the boat with a hurricane coming," Tinkie said. My partner knew more about business than most people. "And fat lot of good an insurance payment will do Angela if she's hurt."

"Good point." Phyllis sighed. "I just want Angela to live a little. She should give up hunting for the treasure and simply build a solid life with a husband and children. She's a fabulous writer. She could hire on at a bigger paper or maybe write a book. This quest for the Esmeralda treasure is stealing her life from her."

Everyone thought Angela was motivated by finding the treasure, even Phyllis. "Angela's quest isn't about the treasure. It's about justice."

Phyllis laughed. "*She* believes that. She does. I get it. When I talk to her, she's dedicated to saving Larry Wofford. I'll give you that. But even though she won't admit it to herself, Angela wants that treasure. She believes it's her due."

I'd never seen that in Angela. "I believe she's in love with Wofford."

"She has all the classic symptoms," Tinkie said.

"Oh, she is. But she's still after the treasure. Someone stole Couteau's spyglass, the one thing her father desperately wanted back when he claimed he'd figured out the key to Couteau's treasure. That spyglass has nothing to do with freeing Wofford. But it could be involved in finding the treasure. Ladies, I love Angela. I do. And I loved her father. But this treasure quest has become an obsession. It took over John's life, and now I see the same thing happening to Angela. She's been here on the island over a year, and she has no steady job, no steady income, and not one single person in her life. Tell me how that's healthy or a good life." She brushed an angry tear from her cheek.

"Angela can be obsessive." A point I had no choice but to concede. "But I don't think it's about money."

Phyllis laughed. "It isn't money. Never money. It's winning. It's doing the impossible, finding the thing that's eluded so many others, proving her father right for the years he spent doing the same thing." She sighed, her anger spent. "We could have had a wonderful life together. I loved him so much. But he loved the idea of the treasure more than me or his daughter. When I finally accepted that, I had no choice but to walk away."

She grabbed my shoulder in a tight grip. "If you find Angela, please call me and let me know she's safe."

"Our cell phones are iffy." I didn't want to make a promise I couldn't keep.

"I'll be at the lab." She opened the door, but a gust of wind snapped it closed again. "I'm behaving selfishly. You should leave the island.

Maybe Angela had sense enough to seek refuge in Mobile."

None of us spoke, but we were all thinking the same thing. Angela was too damned hardheaded to leave Dauphin Island and the boat. Voluntarily, at any rate.

"We will let you know."

"And I will do the same." Phyllis slipped out of the car. In a moment, the headlights of her car burned dimly in the gloomy morning and then disappeared.

21

Sitting in the car with Tinkie, I felt trapped by a force of nature, held against my will in the grip of the approaching hurricane. I couldn't leave until I found Angela and Graf, and I didn't want to stay. It felt as if the heavy sky was sinking down on top of me, pressing me into the earth.

Tinkie gripped the steering wheel and stared out at where the *Miss Adventure* lurched and struggled in the active seas. "Let me run in and see if Arley has heard from her. If not, we have to call the sheriff, Sarah Booth. There was blood in her house. We can't ignore the idea she's been hurt."

She was right. We should have called immediately when we found the blood. But we hadn't. Because I didn't trust Randy Chavis to really search for her or try to help her. Suspicions be damned, we had to notify the authorities that we suspected foul play.

"While you grill Arley, I'll take a look in the boat. Maybe she's below deck." I didn't add that if she was, she was probably hurt. Or dead.

"It's too dangerous. The way the boats are bobbing around on the wind and waves, you might fall into the water trying to board. Then the boat could crush you between the hull and the pilings."

"Wow, you're just Worst-Case-Scenario Wanda today. I'll be fine. Just ask Arley what he knows." We looked at each other, and I said, "One, two, three—" We threw our doors open and dashed in different directions as a warm rain began to fall.

Once I hit the slick boards of the pier, I almost fell. A gust of treacherous wind slammed into my body like a physical punch. The blast stopped as quickly as it started, which made me stumble forward. Rain stung my face and made it impossible to see. I used my arm to shield my eyes.

At last I gained the boat, and what had been a simple job of stepping from the dock to the deck was now a feat of agility, balance, and courage. The boat's deck rose and fell on the swells, and the vessel strained against the tie-lines.

"Angela! Angela!" I called, but the wind tore her name from my lips and sent it inland. She couldn't hear me.

The wind slacked off, and I saw my opportunity and jumped to the deck and managed to keep my feet. Stumbling forward, I went belowdecks to search for her. I entered the dark interior of the boat with a great deal of trepidation.

"Angela!" Her name echoed off the burnished teak walls. The boat, now steady and calm, made me think the storm had finally blown over. But that couldn't be true. Margene's eye was still miles offshore and wouldn't make landfall for another twenty-four hours.

"Angela!" I pushed forward past the galley, the head, and toward the master bedroom, where John Trotter had been murdered, moving forward by feeling in front of me. I didn't have a flashlight, and visibility was almost nonexistent. Slowly, I slid the bedroom door open and looked into the gloomy room. It took a moment for my eyes to adjust. Curtains had been drawn, and the light seeping in was muddy.

The room was empty. I checked the storage areas, the head, and the small kitchen. Angela wasn't aboard. I exhaled. I'd been holding my breath, expecting the worst.

I climbed back to the deck and made the jump to the dock before the wind picked up again. Tinkie returned, and we sought shelter in the car. The days had been crisp and autumnal, but now the humidity was like a soggy blanket. Unseasonably warm and sticky. Not a good omen.

"Angela hasn't been seen since yesterday, when she left the marina to call friends to help her move the boat," Tinkie said as she walked up. Her normally perfect hairdo was beaten down by rain. Water dripped from the ends of her curls. If she looked bad, I knew I looked even worse.

"She's not on the boat, either. Not a sign she was ever there."

"Then where the hell is she?" Tinkie was

aggravated. "Arley has been trying to call her all morning, too. He can't move the boat without her, and he says this is no place for a boat that size to be moored with a storm coming in. He's frantic."

"She wouldn't voluntarily act like this, Tinkie. She's a responsible person. She's either injured or someone is holding her captive."

She'd just finished speaking when my cell phone rang. I answered it, praying it would be Angela.

"I just had a fascinating talk with Zeke Chavis," Coleman said in his baritone drawl.

I clicked the phone to speaker. "Tinkie's with me. Go ahead."

"You've stepped in a hornet's nest, Sarah Booth. I'm worried that someone is in danger of being seriously hurt."

"That may have already happened," I replied.

He was suddenly all business. "What's wrong?"

Tinkie filled him in on Angela's disappearance but assured him we were unharmed. "Except for Angela, everything is fine, so far. We're just worried about the storm and all the complications it brings."

"Everything fine with you, Sarah Booth?" he asked.

"Tinkie's correct. Our client is missing. The hurricane is breathing down our necks, and I don't trust the local law enough to call them in to help search for Angela."

"Come back to Sunflower County. You can't do anything else there until the storm passes. Come home."

If only I were Dorothy and could click my heels three times and go back to childhood. The ultimate fantasy. "I'll be in Zinnia soon enough. So tell me about Zeke."

"I was shocked when he agreed to speak with me. He doesn't admit to anything except his low opinion of the former Alabama governor. Barr apparently reneged on half the agreed-upon payment."

Tinkie's snort was her answer.

"Why am I not surprised?" I said. Criminals. If a man would murder his wife, why would he pay a debt? Especially one accrued in the commission of a murder. What was Zeke's option? Report him to the law for failure to pay?

"Intelligent people don't go into a life of crime," Coleman said. "Zeke is smart enough to be wary of Barr, though. He said the governor had a very long reach. He likened him to a rabid dog and said he would bite anyone who got close enough."

"Did he know anything about John Trotter? Would Barr have killed John Trotter to settle a score against Angela for the newspaper stories she wrote?"

"Zeke insisted he had nothing to do with Trotter's murder, but he did say Barr was capable of such an act of revenge. Apparently, the ex-governor has no boundaries."

The matter-of-fact tone in Coleman's voice alerted me. "You believe Zeke, don't you?"

"It's impossible to tell, Sarah Booth, but my gut reaction was that he was telling the truth. He had an alibi for the time of Trotter's murder. I followed up and called his alibi witnesses. Three men corroborated his statement. He spent the evening in Shazam's Bar in Tillman's Corner, a community on the outskirts of Mobile."

"They remembered from over a year ago?" Tinkie asked the question before I could.

"As you would expect, they remembered drinking with Zeke on numerous occasions, but the night John Trotter was killed there was an incident."

"What kind of incident?" I asked.

"Zeke tried to do a male-stripper routine, and his friends duct-taped him in a chair. They all got drunk and forgot to untape him. The thing is, when they remembered, they were all afraid to cut him loose. So he stayed in that chair all night."

I took a deep breath. A night no one was likely to forget. "Okay, but did he know anyone else Barr might hire for wet work?"

"He's not a professional hit man, just a good ole boy willing to kill for two grand. Barr might have gotten away with killing his wife if he'd paid for a real pro."

"That's a comforting thought," Tinkie said.

Coleman chuckled. "I hear you, Tinkie. But Zeke said something else you might be interested in."

"Which was?"

"He said his cousin is a good guy and a dedicated cop."

"A great recommendation from a murderer." I spoke before I thought.

Coleman sighed. "You've been hanging around DeWayne too much. He said the same thing."

Coleman's number-one deputy, DeWayne Dattilo, and I shared a bit of cynicism when it came to the word of a murderer. "You honestly believe Zeke?" I asked. "You're as big a skeptic as I am, but you believe Zeke's story. And his assessment of his cousin."

"On the first count, his alibi is sound. On the second part, I do believe him. He said Randy had taken a lot of grief because of him. They were close at one time, and he said he didn't want his cousin tarred with his dirty brush. Apparently, Randy had a moment when he realized the path he was on would lead to a jail cell. He changed."

"They were both juvenile delinquents." I clarified the issue. "I don't think Zeke's word is good for much."

"I did some checking on Randy. I know a few deputies on the Mobile County force."

"And?" Tinkie had been watching the *Miss*

Adventure lurch and roll. She signaled we were leaving the marina. She'd obviously come up with a lead to follow, and who was I to stand in her way?

Coleman's answer was a surprise. "Randy is well thought of. As I mentioned earlier, several of his fellow officers feel he should have made detective. They say Randy aced the test for promotion but someone changed answers on his test. My sources believe he was set up by an enemy within the department."

"And did they opine why a patrolman who was passed over for promotion was allowed to act as lead investigator on a homicide?"

"They did. Actually. And the consensus of opinion was that Randy was singled out to fail. No one expected Larry Wofford would be convicted. The common belief among the deputies I spoke with is that John Trotter's murder was meant to remain unsolved. Randy would be left holding a high-profile case with no killer apprehended. He would be labeled an ineffectual investigator."

Tinkie gave me a quick frown. "That makes a certain kind of crazy logic."

"No, it doesn't make any sense." My stubborn streak jumped into play. "Randy is the sheriff's right-hand man. Why would Benson want to hang Randy out to dry?"

"That's exactly the question I asked—and got a resounding silence," Coleman said. "Maybe there's another person involved in this you haven't sniffed out. Someone willing to sacrifice Chavis and Wofford."

I considered for a moment, but I couldn't take that bit of information and make it fit. "What do you make of it, Coleman?"

"Come home, Sarah Booth, and we'll talk it through and I'll try to help. Or drive over to New Orleans for the ball. Just get off that spit of sand in the middle of dangerous water. Next week, when the weather has settled down, I'll drive with you and Tinkie to the prison. You can talk to Zeke yourselves."

It was a mighty generous offer. "Thank you, Coleman. You're right. Cece and Oscar are chomping at the bit to see us. We'll call it a day before too much longer."

"That's the best news I've had all morning," Coleman said. "We'll take care of this once the storm has blown through."

I didn't know if he was referring to Margene or my personal tsunami of emotional distress. Whichever or both, he was right. Once I had a line on Angela and knew she was safe, it was time to leave. "Coleman, you're a good friend."

"Someone has to keep an eye on you, Sarah Booth. It could be a full-time job."

Tinkie pulled onto the main road and took a right toward the cottage. Sweetie and Pluto needed food and a bathroom break. I took them for a beach run—accomplished quickly in a moment of calm—and then upstairs for chow.

"When Graf comes home, keep him here," I told Sweetie. "No excuses." Tinkie was waiting in the Caddy. She pulled back on the road. I didn't know what she was up to, but I trusted her instincts.

The clouds continued to gang up on the horizon, slowly moving toward us as we drove to Fort Gaines. My entire life I'd watched hurricane coverage—the weather-center employees clinging to signs and clutching their slickers and micro-phones. I understood the concept of rain coming in sheets and letting up, then blasting again. Soon, I would be living it. I knew what to expect in the future: one minute the deluge would blind us, and the next, the rain would stop for half an hour or more. As the storm drew closer, the feeder bands would become a solid onslaught of bad weather.

There was no sign of Angela's little compact at Fort Gaines—or any other vehicle. The fort looked dreary and abandoned. For one brief moment, I thought I saw a woman in a black dress on the wall, but if it wasn't Jitty, it was surely my imagination. Like the rain, she was there one minute and gone the next.

We left the fort and went by Angela's house. It looked as empty as the fort. This was our last effort to find her.

Tinkie turned into the driveway and stopped. "She could be in danger. Call the sheriff's office. We should have done it an hour ago."

I nodded and pulled out my cell phone. A burst of wind hit so hard it made me flinch. Tinkie gave a nervous laugh. "The idea of driving over that bridge in this weather is a little intimidating."

I hadn't given it a thought, but now that she said it, I felt a flutter of nerves. The wind was strong enough at ground level. On that high arch, it would be more forceful. "Maybe our timing will be good and we'll get over the bridge in a lull. Once we make it to I-10 it'll be a piece of cake."

The ringing of the phone startled me, and I jumped and dropped it. Tinkie laughed so hard I wanted to swat her. By the time I recovered it from the floorboard, Angela's number showed up on the ID.

"Where the hell have you been?" I asked with no small amount of irritation.

"Can you pick me up?"

Her voice was strange, but it could have been the storm making her sound like she was in a tin can.

"Where are you, Angela?" Tinkie had turned around and was driving toward town.

"I'm at the bridge. I've been walking back, but I'm not feeling so great."

I remembered the blood at her cottage. "Walking back from where?" It didn't make sense that she'd left the island. "Should I call the sheriff?"

"No!" Panic bloomed in her voice. "Don't call the sheriff's department. Just pick me up, please. I'll keep walking until I see you."

"We're in Tinkie's Caddy, but stay off the bridge. The wind is too high."

"Okay. I'll be sitting on the side of the road."

"We're on the way." I hung up. "Hurry, Tinkie. She sounds bad. I think she's hurt."

"We'll be there in less than five minutes."

Gusts of wind rocked the heavy Cadillac, but we made it over the bridge with no problems. Angela was easy to spot, sitting at the edge of the marsh grass. Behind her was a canal. My first thought, of course, was alligators. It looked like a great habitat for the reptiles. Ones that could run sixty miles an hour on six-inch legs.

There was no traffic in either direction, and Tinkie did a U-turn and stopped beside Angela. I rushed to her side.

"Are you hurt?" She had her hand over one eye, and when she looked at me, she appeared dazed. I helped her into the passenger seat and jumped in the back as Tinkie sped up the bridge. "Angela, are you hurt?" I shook her shoulder gently.

"I don't know what happened. I was in my cottage packing some photos and things. I heard what I thought was the wind at the back door. All

317

of a sudden, it burst open and Randy Chavis barreled into the kitchen. He started to say something, and that's the last I remember. I think I was struck on the head. Or maybe I was injected with a drug. I can't say. I just remember being very dizzy and falling into blackness."

I didn't see any obvious wounds or blood on her. Where had the blood in her cottage come from? "Are you bleeding?"

"I don't know." She felt her head and face. She pulled her hair back and revealed a gash in her skull. "I don't know how this happened."

Once we were at the beach cottage, I'd examine her more closely. "Was anyone else hurt at your cottage?"

She put a hand over her mouth. "I don't know. I can't remember anything."

"How did you get off the island?"

"I don't know that either. I woke up in this rancid little cottage on Heron Bay. It took a little while to figure out where I was, and when I did, I started walking toward the island."

"Was there a sailboat docked there?"

"Yeah, a rundown one. And a motorboat. A big house that was locked tight. I tried to get in to use the phone, but it was like Fort Knox."

"Did you see anyone?"

She shook her head. "But someone lives there. I saw men's and women's clothing. The place was a pigsty."

"I think you were held at Remy Renault's."

"Why?" She still was a bit dazed. "Why would he do this?"

I didn't have an answer, but I'd get one. As soon as I could.

"Why didn't you call us on your cell?" Tinkie asked.

"My phone was dead. I thought the storm might have taken a tower out, but then the service would come back on. I'd try to call, and the phone would be dead. I couldn't make sense of any of it."

She wasn't the only one suffering erratic-phone syndrome. "Well, you didn't drive in that condition, I hope, but your car is missing. And your house has been ransacked. I figured it was Chavis looking for that spyglass."

"The house was fine before I was taken." Angela tapped her forehead as if trying to clear cobwebs. "I have to remember."

"Angela, where is the telescope?" Tinkie asked. "Was that what they were after?"

"Maybe." She leaned back. "They'll never find it, though. It's well hidden."

It was possible Remy had taken Angela and stashed her at his house thinking he would go back and question her when she returned to consciousness. Only she'd regained her senses and gotten away. Or else someone had taken Angela there to frame Remy. They'd never anticipated that Angela would wake up. Either way, very sloppy work.

"Angela, if they knocked you on the head and took you, what makes you think they wouldn't hurt you enough to convince you to talk?" Tinkie had been held prisoner more than once and knew what she was talking about.

"I wouldn't tell them squat."

"Until they hurt you badly enough. Then you'd squeal like a pig." Tinkie was angry, and I didn't blame her. "We need to collect the damn telescope and leave Dauphin Island. That storm won't wait, and I for one don't intend to drown."

Silence filled the car as Tinkie pulled into the cottage, where Graf's SUV remained just as we'd left it.

"I'm sorry," Angela said. "You're right. I'll follow you off the island. It might be smart for me to book a room in New Orleans, just to be away from here."

"What about your boat?" I asked.

"I'll tie her off as best I can. It's too late to do anything else for her."

"Where's your car?" Tinkie asked.

"Behind my house. There's a place that's hidden from view. I was afraid the house was being watched, and I was right. Could you take me to retrieve it? I need to grab a few photos and things, and then we can meet at the marina and leave the island together."

I didn't say it aloud, but I knew I'd rest easier if I was certain Angela was off the island. Leaving together sounded like a plan. "You're welcome to ride with us, Angela."

"It will be smarter to take my car. If the worst happens, I don't want to leave it behind. I'll just snatch a few personal items and be ready to evacuate."

"Are you sure you're okay?"

"The fuzziness is fading." She reached to her neck and rubbed. "I remember something stinging my neck."

"Like an insect?" Tinkie asked.

"More like an injection." She grimaced. "Maybe it's just an overactive imagination. All I know is that one minute I was standing in my house confronting Chavis, and the next thing I knew, I was in that horrid apartment trying to remember what happened to me. But I'm fine now. And we can debate what happened in between once we're inland."

When we pulled up to Angela's house, she got out and ran to the door. She waved to us before we turned around and went back to the cottage. "I hope Graf is ready to depart," Tinkie said.

Something about the darkness of the rental cottage made me think otherwise. Graf wasn't there.

"Get Sweetie and Pluto. I know they're sick of the car, but let's hustle. We'll put them in the

Caddy. Leave the keys to the SUV for Graf, and we're on the road. You can leave a note." Tinkie was more outdone with Graf than I was.

"Okay." I didn't have any argument left in me. Graf was making it painfully clear where his priorities lay. It wasn't me, or the dog and cat. He'd abandoned Sweetie and Pluto, too. That added fuel to my fire.

I looked around the cabin. I'd loaded everything into the SUV already. There was nothing to do but walk out. Yet I hesitated. Stepping through the door would be saying good-bye to my dreams, and my feet dragged. I had to call and cancel the marriage officiator, but I could do that while we were on the road. In all likelihood, she would realize a beach wedding was a fantasy in a hurricane. Still, I made sure her number was in my cell phone.

I went to check the third-floor balcony one last time. Tinkie was busy downstairs throwing everything out of the refrigerator into a trash bag. We could dispose of it in New Orleans. When I opened the sliding glass door, the wind almost knocked me off my feet. I'd only thought it was powerful an hour before.

The wild sound of a horse neighing was blown to me, and I rushed outside to see if I could spot the animal. The gusts could have blown a tree down on a fence, freeing livestock. If so, I would have to catch the animal and contact Snill. He would likely know to whom a wandering horse belonged. As the former postmaster, he knew everyone on the island.

I scanned the high dunes around the cottage and thought I was hallucinating. Below me, two horses reared and pawed the wind. They were harnessed to a chariot.

Somewhere between Tinkie in the kitchen and the third floor, I had lost my mind.

"The Romans flogged me in the street and then raped my daughters."

I whirled to confront a tall woman with long tawny curls that hung below her waist. She wore a multicolored tunic and cloak held with a big broach. "Who the hell are you?" I knew it was Jitty, but I didn't know who she was pretending to be.

"Boudicca, queen of the Iceni. I bested legions of Roman soldiers and burned London to the ground."

"Obviously a warrior-queen. Thank goodness you've given up the widow routine. You were about to send me into a terminal depression." This was history I hadn't a clue about. "Why are you here?"

"When my husband, King Prasutagus, died, he left the kingdom to be shared between Rome and me and our daughters. There was no male heir, and we had willingly joined the Roman Empire. Yet we were treated as a conquered nation. Not the smartest move. I am not a woman to accept a public flogging nor the abuse of my daughters. I fought back."

"Jitty, just tell me why you're here as a warrior-queen. Please. I'm too tired to try to figure this out."

"Some say I died by my own hand rather than be taken as a slave. Others believe I died of illness or wounds sustained in battle." She shrugged. "Does it matter? I never lived a day as a slave to any man or to Rome."

"I'm not a slave to Graf. I don't want to go to war. I want to go home to Zinnia. I want to teach our children to ride and to plant the land and to dance the twist." My voice held a spark of anger. "I don't want to drive off and leave Graf, but I won't stay and fight. Waging war won't make him love me."

I gripped the balcony railing and gazed out at the tumultuous Gulf. The chariot and horses were gone. Jitty stood beside me.

"Listen to me, missy. This ain't over 'til the fat lady sings, and I don't hear no music. Get yourself together and drag that man to New Orleans. Don't look back. That's not the word from the Great Beyond; that's the word from me, Jitty the haint."

She lifted her hand, and I thought I felt the sensation of warmth on my cheek. "Fight for him, Sarah Booth. The only thing I can tell you for certain is that if you don't fight with everything in you, regret will be your companion for the rest of your days."

Her words exhausted me, and I closed my eyes for five seconds. When I opened them, Jitty was gone.

Footsteps thudded on the stairs, and I prayed that Graf had returned. It wasn't him, though. It was my partner.

"Sarah Booth, let's go." Tinkie signaled me from the doorway. "The weather is only getting worse. I left a note on the counter for Graf telling him we're stopping by the marina on our way off the island and to New Orleans. He can come or not. At this point, if he wants to shack up with his honey and blow out to sea, it's his choice."

"I know." I took my cell phone charger and the few cosmetics I'd left in the bathroom. "My dress!" I pulled the carefully wrapped ball gown from the closet. I'd almost forgotten about it. I grabbed Graf's tux, too. "I'm ready now."

With Sweetie and Pluto at my heels, we scurried down the stairs and into the car.

22

Arley McCain's navy slicker immediately caught my eye when we pulled up at the marina. Angela, looking like a bedraggled, drowned rat, struggled beside him as the two of them hauled at thick ropes, trying valiantly to tie the *Miss Adventure* from three angles in the hopes of keeping her from crashing into the dock.

"Pull the slack out and tighten the ropes," Arley instructed.

"I'm trying." Angela's jaw was clenched with the effort as she threw her slight weight against the lurching ship.

Tinkie and I jumped out to help. I left the car door wide, allowing Sweetie and Pluto on the dock to watch. The clouds hovered low in the sky, making me think of the Delta when a thunderstorm covered the horizon. As a child, I used to think that God was angry with us when gray overwhelmed the horizon. I knew better now, but the building mass of gray still seemed filled with celestial wrath.

"Lend a hand," Tinkie said, shaking me out of my inertia.

I assisted Angela while Tinkie grabbed the end of Arley's rope that he'd wrapped around the docking post for leverage. The boat was like a bucking bronco, one that weighed several tons. Whenever we made a foot of progress, the sea would pitch the vessel against us and snatch back the ground we'd gained. The boat's hull thrashed, only inches from the solid pilings.

"This is never going to work," I said.

"If we don't secure this boat, she'll batter herself to death against the dock pilings." Arley was grim in his prediction.

"We need more muscle." I was strong, but I wasn't freaking Hercules.

"Well, conjure it up, little missy," he grunted.

If only I had that power. I felt a tug on the rope behind me and turned to find Sweetie Pie holding the rope in her teeth. She threw all eighty pounds of her weight into the fight.

"Well, I'll be," Arley said, a little in awe of my hound. "I've never seen anything like it. It's almost as if the dog knew what you were saying."

"Almost as if," I said, giving Sweetie a wink. When I glanced at Pluto, he was cleaning one back leg. It stuck high in the air as if he hadn't a care in the world. Pluto, too, understood what we were doing, but he simply wasn't going to trouble himself about helping. Typical cat.

The wind calmed, and Arley and I managed to take up the slack on our line and tie it off. Then we rushed around the dock to help Angela and Tinkie.

"Do you think it will hold her?" Angela asked

Arley as she looked at her hands, where the rope had torn blisters and flesh.

"Margene is down to a Cat One. It just depends on the tide, which side the wind comes from. I won't lie to you; this ship should have gone inland or to the west. She's a valuable boat, Angela. You could have sold her and made a nice profit. But no one will want her if she's broken up or at the bottom of the marina."

I thought he was being a little hard on Angela, especially in light of the fact she'd been abducted and drugged, or at least whacked on the head. I started to say so, but Tinkie frowned and shook her head.

"Let's just hope she survives," Angela said.

We all stopped as a car pulled into the parking lot. Phyllis Norris jumped out and hurried over to us. "Angela, I've been worried sick! Where have you been? Why didn't you return my calls? I was afraid something terrible had happened."

"Angela was detained, and not by her own choice." I had to speak up.

"I never wanted to push you, Angela, but if the boat survives the storm, you should sell her." Arley wiped his palms on his jeans, and I realized his hands were shaking. "I'm too old to endure this stress."

Angela lifted her chin. "I'm sorry, Arley. And I'm sorry I worried you, Phyllis. When this storm is over, I'll list Dad's boat. I want to take her out one more time after Margene has blown through."

"You haven't taken her out in I can't remember when," Phyllis said. "What's going on?"

"Just a farewell sail." Angela bent to tie her shoe. "I realize I don't have the skill or the wherewithal to keep her in tip-top shape. She should belong to someone who will love her as much as Dad did."

"At last you're talking like someone with good sense." Phyllis had calmed down a bit, and the color receded from her cheeks. "Why don't we all go grab a bite to eat over at Bobo's? He always cooks a great gumbo when storms threaten. We can get over the bridge and be there before the winds pick up for the duration. Behind these feeder bands, there's a constant seventy-five-mile-an-hour blow. After we eat, we can move on to our various destinations."

I looked at Tinkie and shrugged.

"I need to pack a few mementos," Angela said. "Maybe I'll meet you later."

I started to point out that we'd left her at her house to do exactly that, but I kept my mouth shut. If Angela wanted Phyllis to think she was packing, she had a reason.

"Make it quick, Angela. The east end of the island is usually safe, but you don't want to be stranded." Phyllis gave her a hug. "Maybe after the storm has passed through, we'll get together to share a meal and some wine."

"I would love that, Phyllis."

"Anther time, then." Phyllis started to leave and then turned back. "Has anyone seen Randy Chavis? I've been calling him all day and can't get an answer."

Arley thought for a moment. "Last I saw him, he was going to Angela's house. Did you talk with him?"

"No," Angela said, glancing at me and Tinkie to be sure we'd back her up. "I didn't. What did he want with me?"

"Well, he was all fired up about talking to you. Said he'd figured something out and needed to tell you." Arley pulled his slicker down as the wind caught it. "He sure sounded like it was life-or-death. Bunch of drama queens. I'm tired of all of it." He stalked off toward the marina office.

Phyllis followed him to her car. In a moment, they were both gone.

"What are you hanging around here for?" Tinkie asked Angela.

"I won't leave without the telescope, and I couldn't very well get it with everyone standing out here."

"It's on the boat?" I asked.

"In a very safe place. My father had a lot of hidey-holes on the *Miss Adventure*."

"If that spyglass is on the boat, get it now. It could end up at the bottom of the ocean." Tinkie was shocked.

"I didn't say it was there." Angela looked all around. "I don't want to pull you two any deeper into this. By the way, I have tried to call Randy. He's not answering."

"Missing or hiding?" I asked.

Angela shrugged. "Go on to New Orleans. Please. You need to be off the island before the roads get too congested."

Angela was certainly edgy about something. "I wouldn't think there would be mass evacuation for this storm. Just folks in low-lying areas and along the coast."

"You never know. You need to hit the road. Really, ladies, you've done so much for me. Leave before you get hurt."

Tinkie and I exchanged a look. Angela wasn't worried about the storm. Something else had greatly unsettled her.

"Sure, we're gone. We'll talk tomorrow or Sunday." Tinkie gave Angela a hug, and I followed suit.

A loud clap of thunder made us all jump. The hiss of hard rain hitting the Gulf could be heard, and it was coming our way fast. We all ran for cover, including Sweetie Pie and Pluto, who streaked by me as if water would melt his fat little kitty self. He sure could move when he wanted to.

Tinkie and I made it into the car with only a second to spare. The rain came down so hard I had the sense a tidal wave had swamped the car. The din effectively silenced all attempts at conversation. Visibility was zero.

When the rain slackened, Tinkie started the car. "We have to follow Angela. She's in some kind of trouble, and she's trying to protect us."

"I concur."

But Angela had vanished.

"Well, sheet slitter!" Tinkie slammed the wheel with the butt of her hand. "She knew we'd try to follow."

"Indeed, she did." So what was our clever client up to?

Before I could pose my question, my cell phone rang. Cece Dee Falcon was calling. I put it on speaker so Tinkie could hear.

"I have some information, but I don't know how much it's going to help."

"Thank you, Cece," Tinkie said. "How are preparations for the ball?"

"The storm should blow through, and everything will be fine. They're predicting good weather for New Orleans tomorrow. Are you two on your way?"

"Just about." I shook a finger at Tinkie when she rolled her eyes. I wasn't lying. We were ready to clear out; we just hadn't made it off the island. It wasn't our fault we had to save a sailboat.

"You're still at Dauphin Island!" Cece wasn't pleased.

"We're loaded up and ready to go."

"Where's Graf?"

The silence said it all. Finally, Tinkie said, "We don't know. We left him a note and the SUV. He can leave if he wants to. We have Sweetie and Pluto and Sarah Booth's dress for the ball."

"When this ball is over, we'll find Graf and tar and feather him." Cece didn't take kindly to men who mistreated her friends.

"Not to worry." My voice cracked. I'd successfully failed to think about Graf while we were wrestling with the boat. Now my predicament crashed down on my head.

"Is that Marion Silber still on the island?" Cece asked. "The nerve of her tracking Graf down and following him on his vacation."

"She is." Tinkie answered for me. "Or she was. I don't know now. Surely with a child she's taken the necessary precautions."

"Did you find anything about the map and the French inscription?" I had to change the subject. I appreciated my friends' support and loyalty, but talking about Graf and the screenwriter only made it more real in my mind.

"I did. That's why I called. Sorry, I got off-track."

"No apologies. I'm glad you've got my back."

"Always, dah-link! Now here's the scoop. The map is a rough depiction of a coastline. Most

333

likely, Dauphin Island. It's impossible to say for positive because storms have changed the island so drastically. Those barrier islands walk. They literally move east and west, depending on the currents and winds churned up by hurricanes."

I couldn't hide my disappointment. I'd hoped for a definitive answer. Something we could use to pinpoint a specific location. "And the writing?"

"I have a rough translation. One of my journalist friends knows the head of foreign languages at Tulane University. So based on the time period, etcetera, etcetera, this is as close as we could get." She cleared her throat. "The rising sun intersects with the shadow of a wall. There lies the crossing of destiny and fortune."

"Say that again," Tinkie requested.

Cece obliged, and this time I grabbed a pen from the glove box and wrote it down on a napkin.

"Any idea what it means?" Tinkie asked.

"Not me," Cece said. "It's obviously a clue, but it's a code or something."

"Thank you, Cece. You have more to do than anyone I know, yet you made time to help us with this."

"I wish I'd been more successful." Her laughter filled the car. "We can worry this knot when you're in New Orleans. Once the ball is over, we'll figure it out."

"Of course we will," Tinkie said stoutly.

"Yes, of course. Thank you again." I said good-bye and clicked off the phone. "Let's go."

"Want to check on Graf one more time?" Tinkie asked.

"No."

Tinkie angled the car toward the road that would take us off Dauphin Island just as a red Jaguar turned toward us. Marion Silber was at the wheel, her daughter in the passenger seat. They were laughing as they passed.

Not fifty yards behind them was Graf in the SUV. He swung into the marina parking lot and walked over to the Cadillac.

"I've booked some hotel rooms in Mobile," he said. "Sarah Booth, we need to talk."

Do we really? I wanted to ask. Judging by his tone and the way he failed to look me or Tinkie in the eye, I wasn't certain there was anything left to say. "About what?"

"I have to tell you something important. And I want to do it before we leave the area. There's someone I want you to meet."

Tinkie reached out the window and grabbed his forearm. "If you're going to hurt Sarah Booth, just be a man and do it now. Stop dragging this out."

"There's been a terrible wreck of a tractor trailer and logging truck. I-10 West is closed," Graf said softly. "We can't get to New Orleans right now. It's foolish to head east or north. The storm will hit here and then hook to the northeast. Let's stay at the hotel for one night. Give me a chance to tell Sarah Booth some things I've just discovered. It's important. We'll be off the island in case the storm is worse than it appears."

"Okay." I agreed before Tinkie could tell him no. The look she threw me said I was being too easy, too willing to be stepped on. But I knew Graf. He wasn't the kind of man who took pleasure in cruelty. He had something to say, and whatever it was, he deserved the chance to say it.

He gave us the address of a hotel on the beltway, miles inland from the water. "The forecasters issued a new alert. Margene has picked up speed. She's barreling toward the coast. The good part is that if she maintains this pace, she'll make landfall and move inland quickly. Once Margene moves over land, she'll deteriorate rapidly into a tropical storm. We should be fine."

"They predicted landfall tomorrow morning. What's the new time frame?" The weather had changed that quickly.

"Sometime this afternoon. We'll be safe in Mobile."

"We would be safer in New Orleans." Tinkie's jaw clenched with anger. "Why can't you have your talk with Sarah Booth there? Or do it now. I'll go visit Arley so you can have some privacy."

"There's something Sarah Booth has to see." Graf swallowed, and I realized he was fighting to keep control of his emotions. "I want her to really understand."

I put a hand on Tinkie's shoulder. "I want a chance to talk with Graf." My voice was steady and clear, though I felt like a giant's hand was squeezing my heart.

"If that's what you want." Tinkie stared out the windshield.

"I'm going on to the hotel," Graf said. "Are you coming?"

"Yes." I answered when Tinkie didn't.

A moment later, he was driving off the island. The clouds opened. The rain was so loud, we didn't attempt to talk. When it finally passed, Tinkie put her hand on the key but didn't start the car.

"Is this what you really want? You should tell him to kiss your ass, and we should go to New Orleans. They'll have the interstate cleared in no time, or we can take the back roads."

"I have to talk to him. At least he's willing to tell me what's happening. I don't want any regrets because I was too much of a coward to hear him out."

A tear slipped down Tinkie's cheek. "I don't know why this is happening, but just for the record, it's wrong. And once the talking is done, the ass kicking is going to begin."

"Once you drop me and the critters at the hotel, you should go to New Orleans."

"And leave you possibly stranded here. Not on your life."

Striving for a shred of humor, I said, "And the moral of this story is, never, ever, leave your set of wheels at home."

We didn't go straight to the hotel but instead stopped at a store to pick up flashlights and batteries. The supply was meager, but we found two heavy-duty lights. Good for hurricanes and future endeavors of snooping in the dark.

"Do you think we'll lose power?" I asked.

Tinkie evaluated the people in the big box store. They had shopping carts loaded with beer and wine, chips and bread, bottled water and candy.

"These folks are preparing for the Second Coming. Only problem is, if they eat all that crap, they won't get airborne during the Rapture."

It was a relief to laugh. "How about some chips? Just in case."

Tinkie snared a bag of vinegar and salt chips.

"If I was certain we had a freezer in the room, I'd get some mocha-almond-chip ice cream since I never tasted the ice cream you bought before we had to toss it."

Tinkie pulled me down the aisle to the checkout. "Eat yourself into a coma. Right, that'll make you feel loads better."

"It will." I sounded like I was five. I snatched a

box of Krispy Kreme donuts on the way out, but Tinkie slapped my hands until I dropped them.

"Giving yourself dough belly won't help a bit. You eat all of this junk food, and you won't fit into your gown for the ball."

"I don't care."

Tinkie put her hands on her hips. "Well, I care. A lot. Whatever happens here in Mobile, we are leaving for New Orleans in the morning. You and me and Sweetie Pie and Pluto. Graf is welcome if he wants to come and treat you like the love of his life."

I ripped open the potato chips and stuffed a handful into my mouth.

"Sarah Booth!" Tinkie was shocked.

"You know he's not coming." I had to say it twice for her to comprehend me as I crunched the chips down.

She reached for the chip bag, but I snatched it away. I shoved another huge handful into my mouth. "Makes me feel better." Little pieces of chip flew from my lips. "Makes me feel a lot better." I ate more.

Tinkie patted my shoulder. "Okay. Let's pay for them before they think we're stealing."

I nodded. My cheeks bulged, and the vinegar was tart. I needed a Diet Coke. Or at least a Jack and water. Now there was a thought. "Liquor." I pantomimed mixing and swilling a drink.

Tinkie stepped very close to me and pinched my waist so hard I was paralyzed. "Stop acting like a very bad two-year-old."

Because my mouth was too full to speak, I nodded with great passion.

She let me loose and snared my wrist. "We're leaving."

And so we did.

We stopped at a liquor store and bought some Grey Goose and Jack Daniels, and, at my request, we drove downtown. I wanted to see the old oaks and the antebellum homes. In many ways, Mobile reminded me of Greenwood, Mississippi, because of the number of stately homes.

At last we pulled into the motel. I almost changed my mind when I saw the red Jaguar in the parking lot. I felt gut-kicked. This, I hadn't anticipated.

"I can't believe Graf." Tinkie pulled in beside the Jaguar. She immediately began rooting in her purse. "I have a Swiss knife. I'm going to stab her tires."

"Don't. Besides, the proper term is slash. Not stab. Slash." My stomach was a little queasy from the assault of fried potato chips, vinegar, and loads of salt.

"This is too much. You're worried about semantics while the woman who is wrecking your future is in the same hotel as we are. I knew Graf had lost his mind, but this is way over the top. To bring you here to see that she's here, too. I won't stand for it."

I looked around at the rain-swept parking lot. We were just off I-65, and northbound traffic slogged by at a slow clip. Evacuees. That wasn't a term I'd expected to use in America. My lack of experience had given me a certain naiveté. No wildfires in my life. No plagues or famines. I'd led a privileged American life.

Hurricane Margene was mild compared to many natural disasters—not to mention manmade ones such as prejudice, poverty, and pestilence. I'd had my vaccinations, my well-rounded menus, my education. While I knew the taste of personal tragedy, I'd been spared the big enchilada of disaster. Such a thing had never truly touched my world.

"I'm not prepared for hurricane devastation." I spoke softly and counted the steady stream of traffic that passed in the northbound lane of I-65. "Hey, there aren't any cars heading south." A real Sherlockian deduction.

"I know." Tinkie started to say something else but fell silent.

"I have to do this."

"I know." She cleared her throat. "I know you do. I would spare you this if I could."

I gave her a smile. "So, now that we understand the situation, I want to go in and talk to Graf, and then I'll be over to spend the night with you.

Tomorrow we can decide whatever is left to decide."

"Will you do me one favor?" Tinkie asked.

"Name it."

"How did that woman know to show up at Dauphin Island? Has he been seeing her for a while? I want the date he first betrayed you."

"Why do you care about that?"

"Specifics make a difference, at least to me. If this has been long-term and he let you beat yourself up again and again over his gunshot, I'll shoot him in the other leg. That's a promise."

The rain was a steady downpour now. No more intermittent deluges. Hurricane Margene was coming across the Gulf in a direct line.

A door opened on the second floor of the motel, and raucous party sounds spilled out. Loud music, people laughing. Someone cursing. A young man, drunk, judging by the way he stumbled, rushed out to the rail, and for one scary moment I thought he would fall—or jump.

"Hurricane party," Tinkie said. "I didn't think people did that after Camille in nineteen sixty-nine. No one took that hurricane seriously, and she killed over two hundred people. Some were so drunk they weren't aware the storm had turned deadly."

Accounts of Camille and Katrina were part of the oral history of the state. Written, too, but many folks could remember exactly what they were doing when those two storms hit the coastline. Camille and Katrina divided lives into before and after, an event when life was radically altered.

"I suspect those kids will survive Margene, unless they flip over the rail." I was procrastinating, and Tinkie was too kind to tell me to evacuate her car and face the music.

Not so true for Sweetie Pie. She yodeled softly in the backseat, reminding me that while I might enjoy sitting in a car in the rain, she wasn't thrilled with the activity. Pluto, too, weighed in with a kitty love nip on my ear and a tug of my hair.

"Okay, okay." I gripped the handle. All I had to do was open the door and walk to the room.

My cell phone rang, and relief buzzed through me. If anyone had ever been saved by the bell, this was it. I answered without looking. I didn't care who was calling. It was a delay, a reprieve.

"Hello!"

"Sarah Booth, it's Angela." She was so breathless I almost couldn't understand what she was saying. "The storm turned. It's coming right at us, and someone dumped Randy Chavis in my boat. He's unconscious, and I don't know what's wrong with him. If he dies, I'll be blamed."

23

I tuned the radio as Tinkie drove. Sure enough, Hurricane Margene had picked up speed and wind. Her barometric pressure was falling, which indicated she could grow into a stronger storm.

"Shit." Tinkie was worried.

The voice of an excited newscaster made us both lean forward. "Hurricane Margene, once sauntering through the warm Gulf waters, is making a direct run at Mobile Bay. Landfall on Dauphin Island should occur within the next three hours. Sheriff Osage Benson and Governor Betty Miller have strongly urged evacuation of the island. All residents are asked to be off the island in the next half hour."

"Will they even let us back on Dauphin Island?" Tinkie asked as she drove south like a bat out of hell.

"I don't know." I turned to the backseat. Sweetie was staring out the window at the gray sky, her eyes mournful. Pluto was curled in a ball. His attitude was to ignore anything he didn't like, and he didn't like the weather. He didn't like the tension, and he didn't like being confined in a car. He was a little black cloud of kitty disdain and discontent.

"Shouldn't you call Graf and let him know

what's going on?" Tinkie was pissed at him, but she was also the only adult in the vehicle.

"No."

"I'll say this once. You should call him. He doesn't deserve it, but you should do it anyway."

I opted for a text. "Emergency with Angela. Headed to D.I."

Tinkie nodded. "Okay, so we should call an ambulance, too. If Chavis is injured, he'll need medical attention. We'd better get it there now, before the storm isolates everyone still on Dauphin Island. Snill told me some people never evacuate and never will."

"Snill is a source of endless information. As to Chavis, if he's dead, Angela is correct. She'll be framed for this. We can't afford to call the cops until we see the crime scene." Someone in Mobile County had manipulated events for a second time to frame an innocent person.

"Jameson Barr isn't behind Angela's troubles," Tinkie said. "And neither is Commissioner Roundtree. The mastermind for these events has a very personal agenda."

"It has to be the treasure, but the entire tale sounds like local folklore, a story to entice the tourists. Finding that map on the wall of Fort Gaines, though, I'm beginning to believe John Trotter had accomplished his dream."

Tinkie and I had grown up on tales of treasures lost in the Mississippi River, or at old plantations where the silver and jewels were buried on the property to keep them from Yankee invaders. Most of them were romanticized family yarns with no basis in fact. Beloved, but ultimately untrue. Pirate treasure seemed to fall in the same category.

"True or not, someone *believes* the treasure exists." Tinkie swerved to a stop to avoid a tree that had blown over. It blocked the road, and two local men with chain saws were already at work clearing it away. "I think we're nuts to be driving into this storm."

My world was collapsing, but Tinkie and Oscar had a wonderful life. She shouldn't be doing this. I signaled for her to pull over at an abandoned roadside fruit stand. It marked the turnoff to Remy Renault's rental. "You're right. Turn around. I need to get you and the animals to safety. I have no right to endanger your life. Or theirs."

Tinkie's response was a soft snort. "You have no right to treat me like a child who has to be protected from her own choices. Think about this, Sarah Booth. You aren't responsible for what I do or the consequences that attach. You're always willing to take the blame and never the credit. If it's true that we create the reality we project with our thoughts and emotions, what kind of life are you building based on blame and guilt and unnatural responsibility?"

"Are you working with Jitty?" The question popped out before I could stop it.

"Who is this Jitty?" Tinkie had the scent of a hot trail. "You've said the name before. You think I don't pay attention, but I do. Who is she?"

"No one."

"You are such an awful liar. I know who she is. She was your great-great-great-grandmother Alice's nanny." She dared me to deny it.

When I didn't say anything, she huffed. "Well, aren't you going to make up another lie?"

"No." I was done lying. If she asked, I'd even tell her about dognapping her courageous little Yorkie, Chablis, way back in the first month I was home at Zinnia. That act of desperation had resulted in Delaney Detective Agency, but it would also be the one thing Tinkie would never forgive. Maybe that's what I wanted—punishment. Maybe she was right about me and my penchant for self-flagellation.

"How does Jitty figure into your life today? She's been dead for over a century."

"It's complicated."

"I'm not driving another foot until you tell me."

The urge to unburden myself overwhelmed me. I wanted to tell her everything. But I couldn't. Not the total truth. My relationship with the dead was my cross to carry. "Sometimes I talk to Jitty. It's like she watches over me. She's my guardian angel."

"Do you see her?"

"Yes." I would confess to visualization, but I would never tell her about Jitty's getups or her penchant for humor and harangues via her wardrobe.

"You're pulling my leg, aren't you?"

I only smiled. It wasn't a lie or a confirmation.

"Why do you talk to the spirit of a dead nanny from Civil War times?"

Sweetie's soft yodel underscored my answer. "Why not?"

"I worry about you, Sarah Booth."

"Don't, Tinkie. I'm fine. Maybe a little eccentric, but completely fine. Jitty keeps me company and makes me think about an action before I take it. Most of the time."

She put the car in drive.

"Take a right."

"Are you nuts? That looks like a wagon rut, and Angela is waiting for us."

"I think she was held captive there. Remy Renault's place. We're almost there, and we can check it out and be done by the time they clear the road."

She whipped down Heron Bay Road, which really was a rain-slicked rut. "I won't tell anyone about Jitty if you promise to stop pretending you're personally responsible for my welfare and happiness."

"What if I don't care if you tell?" I was playing with fire, but I couldn't stop.

"Oh, for heaven's sake, Sarah Booth. I don't care if you're a little nuts and talk to dead people. Fine by me. Maybe they have more gumption than you do. Maybe you ought to channel your aunt Loulane, though. She had a lot of common sense. But please, please stop trying to make my life perfect for me."

"You're my friend. I want you to be safe and happy."

"And you're my friend, and I would prefer it if you were sane." She wasn't completely teasing. "But you aren't. And you can't control the forces of my life. Let's both just let it go."

"Okay." I was all out of gas for an argument. Besides, we were at our destination.

"What do you hope to find?" Tinkie asked as we both ran from the parked car to the rental.

"Evidence."

"Of what?"

"That Angela was held captive here." I knocked on the door, but there was no answer. I tried the knob. It wasn't locked.

"We can't just break in." Tinkie kept looking toward the main house and the boat, as if she expected someone to materialize.

"We aren't breaking in; we're walking in an

open door." And I did just that. "While there's a break in the weather, why don't you check the boat?"

"Aye, aye, captain. I hope it's not as filthy as this place."

The place was cluttered squalor: plates with old food, roaches, and the smell of something dead.

"What is that?" Tinkie pinched her nose.

"I'll check the kitchen and work my way to the back of the house."

"I'll be on the sailboat." She took off across the yard.

The power was out and the daylight dim, but I found nothing in the kitchen and made my way to a bedroom. There was a smudge of dried blood on a pillow that could have come from Angela's head wound. I was careful not to touch anything. When the storm was over, I'd call the Alabama Bureau of Investigation. To hell with Sheriff Benson and his deputies. I'd get a nonbiased team of lawmen on the scene. But for right now—I stopped at a colorful painting tucked behind a chair. It was definitely the work of John Trotter. The missing painting from his boat.

I picked it up and moved to the light of the window. With rain cascading down outside, it gave the blues and greens a watery look. I realized then what I held in my hand. It was a shoreline. The varying shades of light aqua and darker blue-green indicated water depth. It was the coastline of Dauphin Island, and it was meant to be used as an overlay on top of another map.

"Tinkie!" I whispered her name and turned to run to show her. Before I cleared the front door, I heard her scream.

"Sarah Booth!" She was on the deck, waving. "Come here, quick!"

I tucked the painting in the front seat of her car and rushed to the boat. She didn't wait but rushed belowdecks. "What is it?" I asked as she threw open the door to a stateroom.

A blond woman sat on the floor at the foot of the bed. A small round hole in her forehead and her glazed eyes told me she was dead. Had been for a while.

"It's Lydia Clampett, I'll bet." I walked around the body.

"We need to get out of here."

I agreed and put words to action. We scampered to the deck, jumped to the dock, and raced to the Caddy.

"Where's her brother, Remy?" Tinkie asked as she pushed her wet hair out of her face and started the car.

There wasn't an answer for that, and I didn't want to wait around in case he showed up.

The elusive Lydia Renault Clampett had met a cruel fate. I dug in my pocket for a cell phone to call Coleman, only to discover the damned thing had no service. Perfect. Tinkie's cell phone was as useless as mine. And there was nothing we could do for the dead woman. And no way to find Remy Renault. We had to pack it in and retrieve Angela. Getting off the island was the priority. When we found a working phone, we could call the law and let someone know about Lydia Clampett.

The road was clear, and Tinkie drove as fast as the wind and rain allowed.

"Look, there's the bridge."

Rain was coming down in buckets, but the gray concrete outline of the Dauphin Island bridge loomed in front of us. We were crawling along, and I noticed an alligator on the side of the road. When we drew closer, it slipped into the water and marsh grass. Not a good idea to wade in those waters on a hot summer day.

"We haven't passed a single car coming or going."

"Because people with good sense are secure somewhere. They're tucked into homes and safe places, not out in the middle of an approaching hurricane." Tinkie flipped on the radio for the latest weather report.

"With sustained wind at seventy-five miles an hour, Dauphin Island should be feeling the brunt of the storm in half an hour. Hurricane Margene has picked up speed at an alarming pace. We're lucky with the daytime approach of the minimal hurricane. For those who haven't evacuated, batten down the hatches. It's going to be a wild ride."

I snapped off the radio. It didn't help to realize how foolish we were behaving.

My cell phone buzzed an alert that a text message had come in. I checked it. *Why are you going to the island?* Graf had sent the message.

I clicked past it. He'd lost the right to question me or my decisions.

Moving inch by inch, we made it over the hump of the bridge. As we descended, I was keenly aware of the pitching surf. Dauphin Island was normally a place of small waves where swimmers loved to body surf. Children often played in the tide under the eye of watchful parents. Today, the waters were pewter colored, ugly, and very dangerous. The deserted white-sand beaches stretched to the angry Gulf. I wondered how the turtles had fared. The storm would likely kill them.

Jitty would tell me that nature is cruel. Or something else equally true but useless that would include what a fool I was for driving into a hurricane instead of away from it.

At last we turned into the marina. Tinkie gripped the wheel even though she'd killed the engine. There was no sign of Angela or anyone else. The marina was desolate and dangerous. Only one boat remained, the *Miss Adventure*, which pitched up and down and side to side. The ropes were being put to the test.

"Is she on board?" Tinkie sounded doubtful.

"I presume so." I tried to call, but no answer. The only avenue open was to board the boat and see.

"We should have called the law or at least the paramedics."

I didn't disagree. "We would have, if our phones had service. The bigger question is how Chavis got on that boat." I'd searched the *Miss Adventure*. Chavis hadn't been there. So where had he come from? And how had he gotten there?

"Who do you think hurt Chavis?" Tinkie asked.

"I don't know. I had assumed he was the primary villain."

"Let's go. We won't have a better chance."

I cracked the window to give Sweetie and Pluto some fresh air and dashed behind my partner to the dock as rain pelted me like pebbles. Tinkie had foregone her stilettos for a pair of deck shoes, a wise choice under the circumstances. The dock was slick and difficult.

To my amazement, Tinkie leaped onto the deck of the *Miss Adventure* with the grace of a mountain goat. I lurched aboard like a drunk.

"Angela!" Tinkie cried, but the wind tore the word from her mouth. "Angela!"

"The master bedroom!" I signaled belowdecks. That's where Chavis would be. Whoever had attacked him would surely use the chance to reenact John Trotter's murder. The person or persons behind this were masters at manipulating events to paint a certain picture. This one would put Angela as the person who'd attacked and grievously injured—or killed—a lawman in the same place her father was killed.

Tinkie led the way down the narrow galley that was pitch-black. I couldn't see her in front of me, but I kept a hand on her shoulder. It was the only way not to bulldoze over her in the dark.

"We forgot the damn flashlights in the car," Tinkie whispered.

A sigh was my response.

At the door of the master bedroom, Tinkie slid it open as soundlessly as possible. Lightning flashed outside, and for one instant we could see the room as clearly as if the lights were on. Randy Chavis lay on the floor in the exact spot John Trotter had been killed, in an identical pose.

I only caught a glimpse of him, but his pasty skin color and stillness made me think he was dead. We were too late. The worst had been done. But why? And where in the hell was Angela? She'd called and said she was on the boat. So far, nada, and not even the sound of another living soul.

Tinkie, always the more compassionate, rushed forward. The lightning flash vanished, and so did my vision.

"He's alive!" Tinkie said. "He's unconscious. I can't tell how badly he's hurt."

I recalled a hurricane lantern that hung from

the wall, an ancient relic of days when oil lamps were used or when the ship's generator failed. I felt along the paneled wood until I found it. Once the chimney was removed, I flicked my Bic and fired the wick. Smoking did have some benefits.

Warm light illuminated the room.

"Good work," Tinkie said. "Now help me examine him."

The light swung as the boat pitched, but we could see well enough to determine the lack of open wounds on Randy Chavis. He was out of uniform and wearing gym shorts and a sleeveless sweatshirt emblazoned with a tequila brand. There was a small cut in his forehead. It should have been stitched, but it didn't appear life threatening. Head wounds had a tendency to bleed a lot, which might explain the blood in Angela's kitchen. Except for his pasty color and the pose of a dead man, Chavis looked mostly unharmed.

At Tinkie's behest, I helped her roll him over. No injuries to his back. At least no stab wounds or gunshots. Something was wrong with him, though. No man slept that soundly.

"Look!" Tinkie pointed to a tiny red mark on his neck. It was hard to see in the shifting lantern light, but it looked like a puncture wound of some kind. Just about where his artery might be.

"Angela was drugged. She said she felt a pinch at her neck."

"Exactly what I was thinking," Tinkie said.

"Randy!" I lightly slapped his face. "Randy! Wake up!"

He moaned and turned his head away.

"I think he's okay." Relief made my shoulders sag. I didn't care for Randy Chavis, but I didn't want him to die.

"Randy!" Tinkie shook him.

He came to bucking and thrashing, sending Tinkie sprawling into me. We both tumbled along the cabin floor.

"What? Where am . . . Where's Angela?"

"Good question." I gained my feet and pulled Tinkie to hers. "How did you get on this boat?"

He looked around. "I have no idea. Last I remember, I was at Angela's cottage. I went to warn her."

"About what?"

The boat lurched hard, and both Tinkie and I lost our footing. The lantern swung dangerously, and I heard a thump that sounded like flesh and bone meeting solid resistance.

When we'd righted ourselves again, we found Chavis in a corner of the cabin beneath several books and a large sailing trophy. Randy was again unconscious, and the trophy was etched with blood. This time, the lawman was bleeding from a knock on the side of his head.

"Dammit it all to hell." I wanted to scream. "He was about to tell us something important."

"Help! Please help me!" Angela's voice was small and faraway sounding.

"She's on deck," I said.

The boat lurched again and sent me and Tinkie reeling out the door and toward the stairs leading to the deck. Despite her cultured upbringing, Tinkie went up the ladder like a monkey, and I was right behind her.

We emerged into driving rain, gale-force winds, and the sight of Angela clinging to one of the ropes that tied the *Miss Adventure* to the pier. The line was inching out of her hands as the sailboat began to swing broadside into the waves. If that happened, we would be swamped and sink.

"Holy shit," I jumped forward to help her.

"How did the boat come untied?" I yelled at Angela. I'd been there when Arley tied it off. The knot had been solid.

The first wave washed over the side of the *Miss Adventure*, all but knocking me and Angela off our feet.

"Tinkie!" I dropped the rope and grabbed my partner's arm just as the water tried to suck her over the side.

"If we can't get the boat turned into the waves, she's going to founder and sink." Angela was eerily calm. "We have to bring Randy from below deck. We can't leave him there. If the boat goes down, he'll be trapped."

"He came to, but then a trophy hit him in the head." I had to fight to spit the words out loud enough for them to hear. "Tinkie, do you think you can revive him?"

"You need me up here." We were all holding the rope. When the boat shifted a little into the wind, we tightened the rope and fought to hold the small ground we'd gained. Tinkie was right. It would take all three of us to merely hang on.

"We can't hold her through the whole storm." Angela looked around frantically. "How did this happen? The ropes were tight."

The singing sound of rope against wood made us look at the second tie-line. It was slipping from the post on the dock.

"This can't be." Angela fought disbelief. "Those lines were properly tied. I knotted that one myself. And Arley knows how to secure a boat. Someone had to loosen them while I was below deck."

She was right, but it didn't stop the rope from slipping another few inches.

Tinkie hauled on the rope with all her weight. If we lost the center tie-line, we'd have only the one on the bow. We were holding the stern line, which had also been untied. The waves and wind would swing us around and smash us into the pier. While the boat would definitely be destroyed, it was also likely we would drown. Thrown into the water with the boat battering against the pilings, we'd probably be crushed.

The low and mournful cry of my hound made me look at the pier. Sweetie Pie and Pluto stood in the rain watching. I don't know how they'd managed to open the car door and escape, but there they were. Neither made an effort to seek shelter. They knew we were in grave danger.

"Get Arley!" I tried to shout at Sweetie and urge her to get help, but the wind and rain drowned my efforts.

"Grab the rope, Sweetie!" Tinkie had a more practical plan, but her words were lost in the storm's vortex.

"She can't hear us." My voice cracked as I yelled at Sweetie. "Get in the car!"

Debris was flying everywhere in the wind. Shingles from the marina roof ripped past my face, missing my nose by an inch. A plastic bag slammed into Tinkie, wrapping around her face as if it intended to suffocate her.

Sweetie gave a yelp as something struck her. "Go back to the car!" I wanted to tell her how much I loved her and that she would be fine. Harold Erkwell, a friend who'd taken the devilishly evil bearded dog Roscoe, would take her in. It had all been arranged. Another friend would take the three horses. And Pluto could go back to his owner, the eccentric Marjorie Littlefield, if Graf didn't take him to Los Angeles.

Lost in my thoughts, I didn't hear the crack of the figurehead against one of the pilings. I didn't see the chunk of wood that flew through the air and smacked my head. My knees folded, and I felt myself going down on the rolling deck, but I still couldn't comprehend what had happened to me.

I was simply sucked into a whirling black hole, and I didn't even fight against it.

I came to my senses with a burst of pain in my head, and a tunnel of bright, luminescent light. At the end of the tunnel, a trim woman in a black dress stood perfectly still. The skirt of her dress belled out around her ankles. When she realized I was awake, she approached. A great dread took hold of me. Her widow's weeds rustled, the taffeta in her skirt an indication of the time period.

Another Civil War–era visitation.

But this wasn't Jitty. This was a woman thinned by sorrow and loss. Was it my great-great-great-grandmother Alice?

Was I dead?

The series of Jitty's warnings came to mind—widows all, both real and fictional. Had she been trying to prepare me for the ultimate good-bye? But I wasn't ready to die. Not yet. I had much to accomplish.

The image of Graf and Marion Silber, together on the beach, filled my mind's eye in crisp detail. Had she been sent to help him after I was gone? The universe stepping up to the plate to be sure he wasn't left alone and injured? Instead of the woman who broke up my relationship, was she going to be the woman who saved the man I loved from desperate depression?

I wanted to weep, but my body failed to respond to any emotion or command. I floated on a cloud of white as the past whipped by me.

I held my father's hand as we walked down the driveway at Dahlia House. He sang an old western song about a horse, "Old Faithful." And I sang with him at the chorus. "When your roundup days are over, there'll be pastures white with clover, for you, old faithful pal of mine."

Dusk settled over us and bathed Dahlia House in a golden glow that made me think of heaven. The bright-green spring leaves of the sycamore trees that lined the drive shimmied like naughty dancing girls. "Why did you leave me?" I asked. "I needed you. I was just a kid."

"It's okay," Daddy told me. "We're with you, Sarah Booth. You will never be alone."

He was gone, replaced with another scene. I played in the dirt beneath a grove of old oaks behind Dahlia House. My mother sat on an oak branch that dipped low to the ground. It was the perfect seat, and she read a novel.

Wind ruffled the leaves, and the tall grass with golden tassels whispered to me, teasing me with promises of fairies. My mother had told me that the oaks were magical and that anything could happen in the shade of the trees if only I believed. Sometimes I caught a glimpse of the fairies and elves as they played in the shade.

Mama lowered her book and motioned me to her. I abandoned my Meyers horse collection and ran into her arms. My face pressed to her shoulder, I inhaled the lemony scent of magnolias. "I love you." I pressed the words into her skin.

"Love can never be broken or destroyed," she said. "Remember that always, Sarah Booth. Love replenishes itself once given, so never hold back."

She stood up.

"Don't go!" She was leaving. I knew it. The light that had surrounded us both was dimming, and a cold mist pushed in from the horizon.

"You can't stay here in memories. We're a nice place to visit, but not to linger. You know this is true. Jitty will tell you."

"I don't want to leave. I want to stay. With you. I won't go back."

Her hand brushed the tears from my cheeks. "No, that's not really what you want. You want to live and love."

"No. No, I don't."

"You have much to accomplish."

"I don't want any of it. Please." Her touch had grown cooler, and she was fading.

"You have to return, Sarah Booth. You've visited here too long as it is."

"Please. Stay with me." I couldn't face the future without her and Daddy. It wasn't a fair thing to ask. I'd been without them most of my life. Now that I had them back, I couldn't let go. Not again. This place was childhood, safe, filled with love. I would not go back to the present, a place of loss and struggle.

"Your mother is right. Go on, shoo!" Lawrence Ambrose, a wonderful writer whose murder I'd helped solve, stepped out of the shadows. I'd always felt he was a magical man, a writer whose wit and humanity had left a hole in my life when he was murdered. "Now vamoose!" He flicked his fingers at me.

"I'm not a chicken. You can't chase me away."

He swept a bow so low his shock of white hair almost touched the ground. "Touché, Sarah Booth. You are not a chicken. So jump back into life. This is no place for the living. You've been granted a wonderful gift. A moment of time with the people who love you. Take it back to the land of the living."

His clear gray eyes held another message. One of peace and contentment.

"I want to stay with y'all."

"A trifle on the stubborn side, aren't you?" He executed a spin and slide. "We're always here. Your time will be up before you know it. But not today."

He was simply gone. In his place the widow had

returned. She came toward me, and I knew she meant to take me back. I tried to run, but my legs refused all of my orders.

Her hair was marcelled in waves, parted in the center and held in a bun at the nape of her neck. Her eyes were sad—and empty.

"They killed him, you know. One last train robbery. That's what he said. Then he'd be with me and the children and lead an ordinary life. He wasn't a bad man. Not in the way of some men. He didn't beat me or the children. But he could be brutal. He could. They said he killed men when he robbed the trains."

She wandered around me, talking to herself.

"He called me Zee. I share my name with his mother. Peculiar, isn't it? Like we were destined to be together. But not so peculiar when you realize his mother was my aunt. We were first cousins, but we fell in love. Our engagement lasted nine years."

"Who are you?" I couldn't place her. I'd guessed her time period as post–Civil War. That was as definite as I could get.

"He rode with the James-Younger Gang for a while. For a man who robbed trains, he never had a lot of money for his family. I couldn't figure that. Whatever he stole never made it in our front door."

"Mrs. James?"

She faced me. "You can call me Zerelda. Or

Zee. There was no cause for the Ford brothers to kill him, you know. Just for fame. And a ten-thousand-dollar reward. But it never did them a lick of good. Not a lick. That Bob Ford shot Jesse in the head, and they were supposed to be friends. They put Jesse's body on ice and exhibited it. Our son never even knew who his daddy was until Jesse was murdered. Then he had to face the truth. It broke me."

"Jitty!" I couldn't take any more of this sad, sad woman. "Jitty! Drop the act. We need to talk."

Slowly the woman morphed into the mocha shades of my beautiful haint. "I thought the widow of Jesse James was a brilliant choice." She sighed. "After her husband's death, she spent the rest of her life in a debilitating depression. Not exactly the place I'd choose to hang out. Thanks for calling on me."

"You never appear when I call you."

She shrugged and moved on. "You know you've been on the border of death. I thought for a little while you were goin' to check out without leavin' a Delaney heir behind."

"What are you saying?" She was talking gibberish.

She tapped her skull. "Whacked in the head by a piece of flying debris. Under other circumstances, you might have died. And if you don't get up off your ass and help your friends, you gonna be deader than a flitter."

"What debris? How was I injured?" She wasn't making any more sense in her natural state than she had as Mrs. James.

"Think, Sarah Booth, but be quick about it. You're 'bout to join the dead in Davy Jones's locker if you don't wake up and help your partner. Things are going to hell in a handbasket fast!"

I couldn't deny her sense of urgency, but I hadn't a clue what she was talking about. "What's the message from Zee James?"

"You can't let loss break you." She tapped her foot. "Is that clear enough? Wake up, Sarah Booth. You're hidin' out. Tinkie and Angela are in real trouble. Wake up, stand up, and stop wallowin' in loss."

Jitty was enigmatic but never harsh. "What bee buzzed your bonnet?"

"Wake up!"

I drew back from the ferocity of her command and felt wet wood beneath my face. I opened my eyes and saw Tinkie's deck shoes slipping on the rain-soaked deck of a boat. It took a few seconds for reality to return, but when it did, I sat up.

"Sarah Booth, thank God!" Tinkie burst into tears. "I thought you were dying. That piece of wood struck you right in the forehead. Frontal lobe damage and all that." She crouched down and grasped my chin. "You haven't been lobotomized, have you?"

"No." I snatched my chin away.

"Then get up and help us."

With the boat thrashing, I had no choice. Jitty had put it before me, in no uncertain terms. It was fight and survive or give up and die. Not a Delaney born had ever been a quitter. I would analyze Jitty's appearance as Zerelda Mimms James, wife of the notorious outlaw, when I had some quiet time alone.

24

For the next half hour, Angela, Tinkie, and I fought the rising winds. We'd gain several inches on the rope, and then the wind would shift and pull harder against us. Ultimately, we were losing ground.

When Randy Chavis stumbled up from below deck, I was actually glad to see him.

"What the hell?" He shielded his face with his arm, covering a big gash on his left forehead that matched a smaller wound on the right side. The rain washed the blood from his face and chest. "What happened?"

"You were brained by a trophy," Tinkie said, not wasting any words on niceties. "You and Sarah Booth have matching noggins."

I rubbed the goose egg on my forehead. "Thanks."

Randy took in our predicament and grabbed an extra coil of rope. Tying them together, he was able to use the main mast as leverage. The four of us pulling with everything we had in us were able to stabilize the *Miss Adventure*.

"If the water gets any rougher, she'll break free," he said. "Why is she still berthed here?"

"Let's go below deck," Angela said. "We need some answers."

With the boat securely tied, at least for the moment, we trooped below. Getting out of the rain and wind was an immense relief. My body felt as if it had been battered all over by tiny fists. I slumped into a chair, and Angela tilted my face up to examine my damaged forehead.

"You need to see a doctor."

No doubt. If I told her about Zee James's visitation and my haint Jitty, she'd think I needed more than an M.D. More like a psychiatric facility.

Tinkie shifted her attention to Chavis. "You should have stitches."

"Pull out a needle and thread. We aren't going to find a doctor for the next twenty-four hours." Chavis wasn't kidding.

"I'll try taping it," Tinkie said. She was a lot better with wounds than I was, but sewing a forehead was more than she could take on. She turned his head so she could examine his neck. "Bring that lantern."

We all moved in close to look at the clear puncture wound in his neck. When we were done with him, we went to Angela, who had an identical mark on her neck.

"So what happened?" Tinkie demanded. "The two of you were in Angela's cottage and something obviously went down."

"I'd come to warn her," Randy said. His eyes widened. "Shit, I forgot about this in all the furor of securing the boat."

"What?" We were a Greek chorus.

"Someone in the sheriff's department is out to get you, Angela. And"—he frowned and looked down at his feet—"and I think you're right about Larry Wofford. I think he's innocent. I was duped."

His stunning confession froze us for the space of a few seconds. "What changed your mind?" I had to know. Call me cynical, but I considered the possibility that Randy's abrupt about-face was calculated to lull us into trusting him.

"It was what the museum owner, Prevatt, said to me when I called to update him about the stolen telescope."

"What did he say?" Angela put her hands on her hips.

"Something about how he'd been double-crossed for the last time by men in uniform."

Tinkie was puzzled. "And how does that clear Wofford?"

"It's the context of the comment." Chavis spoke directly to Angela. "I told Prevatt we'd searched the cottage the private investigators were renting and we'd searched your place and the ship and come up with nothing. No trace of the missing spyglass. He said he wouldn't trust Mobile County deputies as far as he could throw them, that he knew how they could change evidence to convict an innocent man."

"Did he mention Wofford by name?" I asked.

"No." Randy looked less certain. "I'm sure that's who he meant, though. And he seemed to think I was involved in framing Wofford. When I asked him what evidence, he changed the subject quickly. Like he realized he'd made a mistake."

"What evidence might that be?" Angela asked.

I knew. "The security cameras." I'd never understood why the cameras failed that night.

Randy looked miserable. "I took the CDs from the recorder into the station, but it was the next day before I looked at them. They were blank."

"Wiped by someone."

He took a deep breath. "The recordings from the night before the murder were perfect. Arley couldn't find anything wrong with the cameras or recorder. We chalked it up to the rain."

"Would you testify to that?" Angela asked.

"I will. I know you don't believe me, Angela, but I like Wofford. I didn't want him to be guilty. That's the way the evidence laid out. I did my job, even when I didn't like it. The evidence said Larry was the killer."

"Except the evidence was tampered with." Angela's face was pale. "He's been in prison over a year."

"I realize that." Randy held out a hand to her. "I'll do everything I can to make sure his conviction is overturned. We'll need more than Prevatt hinting Larry Wofford was set up and blank surveillance cameras, though."

He wasn't wrong about that.

"Arley's testimony hurt Wofford, and I know Arley only told the truth as he saw it." Randy pressed the heel of his palm to his forehead. I didn't doubt he had a whopper of a headache. "Sheriff Benson was positive Larry killed John Trotter. I let his attitude compromise my own. I shouldn't have rushed to charge Larry. Maybe if I'd held off, the investigation would have been more thorough."

"Why *did* you rush to charge Larry?" Tinkie asked.

"Sheriff Benson said it would be best for Angela if we could close the door on the investigation quickly. He said Wofford did it, and the best thing we could do for Angela was put him behind bars and hold the trial as soon as possible."

"The sheriff." Awareness dawned. "And now that Tinkie and I are poking into the past, who should end up abducted, drugged, and left to die on a boat freed from its moorings in a hurricane?"

"Me." Randy's voice was dead. "He used me, didn't he?"

"I think he intends to frame you for killing Angela and Angela for killing Lydia Renault Clampett," I added. I turned to Tinkie. "I'll bet Randy's and Angela's fingerprints and blood are at each scene."

"I wonder if Renault was in on the frame?" Tinkie asked.

The wind caught the boat, and we all lost our footing. The lantern swung, creating crazy shadows. We regained our balance, and the conversation continued.

I thought back to my encounter with Sheriff Benson. He'd been annoyed and helpful in just the right quantities. Antagonistic and gracious—hitting exactly the right notes. And he'd been very careful to control the situation. I'd been so focused on Randy Chavis as the bad guy I hadn't considered Benson.

"But why?" Randy asked. "What does the sheriff or any of the detectives have to gain by sending an innocent man to prison?"

"The person who finds the treasure stands to gain a fortune. Wofford was collateral damage. A scapegoat to take the blame."

Tinkie picked up the explanation. "They were getting rid of Randy, the same way they eliminated John Trotter. Two birds with one stone. Randy is the weak link in the case against Wofford. Once he realized Larry was innocent, they knew he'd fight to free Larry. They had to kill Randy or set him up for murder. They would take care of two big problems. It's just a miracle Angela came to her senses and got out of that apartment before they went back to question her and then kill her. It's all about the timeline."

Another wave slammed into the boat. I had one more thing to reveal.

"I found something at Renault's place, something I think he stole from John Trotter." I told them about the painting in the car. "It was always the treasure. The painting depicts the coastline of Dauphin Island." I went to the bookcase and selected a slender tube pushed into the back. "If my guess is right, this will be a nautical map of Dauphin Island today." I unrolled the paper in the tube, revealing a map with figures, depths, reefs, shallows, and debris, all clearly marked.

"Anyone can order that map or even print it off the Internet," Angela said.

"The painting your father did is the coastline of Dauphin Island as it was during the time of Armand Couteau. He's researched it. That's why he painted on a translucent surface. It's meant to be put over this!"

"My father found the treasure," Angela whispered. "He did it."

A large wave hit the boat hard, and Tinkie fell to her knees. I landed on top of her. "I've had enough. We can finish this on land." Tinkie signaled everyone to follow her on deck. "Let's get off the boat while we can."

"I'll be right behind you," Angela called.

I figured she was retrieving the spyglass, but I saw no reason to point that out to Randy Chavis. While he might not be the bad guy I'd assumed, he was still a deputy and Angela had broken the law. We could sort through the legalities of her actions once the storm passed.

When we reached topside, the wind was relentless. I was worried sick about Sweetie and Pluto. They weren't on the dock, and I hoped they'd taken shelter back in the Cadillac. Which would be soaked. Funny, but I didn't recall leaving a window open wide enough for Sweetie to get out. Or even Pluto, for that matter. For a fat kitty, he could slink through some mighty small openings, but I'd left only a crack in the window.

A very bad feeling hit me.

Someone else was on the dock. Someone who had let my animals out of a safe car in a hurricane. Someone who was watching us, and likely waiting for us to get back to the dock.

I searched the rain and windswept pier and the surrounding parking lot. Tinkie's red Caddy was a blur in the savage weather. I couldn't see anyone or anything else. Still, my heart raced, telling me that my gut knew what my eyes couldn't see.

Someone was there.

Angela joined us, and I shifted close to her. "Do you have the spyglass?"

She nodded.

"Someone is waiting for us, and I think they mean us harm."

Angela lifted the glass to her eye and swept the parking lot. "There's a dark car parked near the roadway. Black sedan."

"Who does it belong to?" Like the car that had tried to run me and Tink down, and also the one drifting through Angela's neighborhood when shots were fired. We knew it wasn't Randy Chavis, since he was with us.

"I don't know." She scanned the horizon much as a sailor would. "I don't see any movement."

Tinkie and Randy joined us, and to his credit, he didn't say a word about the stolen spyglass. "What's up?" he asked. He took a look through the telescope. "That's Sheriff Benson's car."

I motioned them down the steps again. We were safer out of the wind and rain and also out of sight. "Someone let Sweetie and Pluto out of Tinkie's car. I'm afraid they're waiting for us to get on the dock." I'd finally put it together. "They want the spyglass. That's what they've been after the whole time. It's the key to the treasure."

"What good will it do them? They could've had it anytime. It's been in the museum for two years," Randy said.

"But they didn't have the other parts. The way John's painting fits into the location of the treasure, the map on the wall at Fort Gaines. The rising sun intersects with the shadow of a wall. There lies the crossing of destiny and fortune." Tinkie repeated the words written by Armand Couteau.

"What does that mean?" Randy asked.

"We need to be at the old fort at sunrise with

the telescope." I wasn't certain what that would yield, but I had no doubt the words of the prisoner Armand Couteau had been left for LuAnn. He knew she would understand. He'd wanted her to claim the treasure, except she was as much a prisoner as he was.

"Do you think we'll find the treasure?" Tinkie asked. "Is there really a treasure?"

"I think someone is afraid we'll find it. Angela, who else knew you'd taken the telescope?"

"I didn't tell anyone, but the assumption by all involved was that I stole it."

"The correct assumption." Randy was slightly peeved. "Dammit, Angela. I can't just ignore this. I never took you for a lawbreaker."

"And I never took you for a toadie." Angela was hot.

"Stop it, you two. We'll worry about the telescope when the storm is over and we're safe. So who else knew about the theft?"

"Prevatt," Angela said.

"He's a skunk," Tinkie said. "He's probably in this up to his eyebrows.

I didn't disagree, but while he was a skunk, he wasn't a brainy skunk. There was a partner—one who was diabolical enough to plot a devious crime.

"Who else?"

"Snill, Phyllis—"

"And the sheriff," Randy interrupted. "He knew,

and he sent me to check it out. Mobile isn't even my beat."

That was the final straw. Benson had set Randy up by saddling him with a murder investigation when he wasn't a detective, and he'd sent the patrolman to investigate robberies outside his beat. "Benson is involved. Which means we may be confronting law enforcement officials any minute. And there's no way to tell how they'll react to whatever Benson told them."

"The sheriff fooled me. I'm sure he has others duped." Randy was glum. "If they're waiting for us to disembark, they'll swarm us as soon as we're on the dock. That's our weakest point. We'll all be huddled together. They don't know if we're armed or not."

"Which means they might shoot us." Tinkie wasn't kidding.

"She's right." Randy rubbed his chin. "If the sheriff has made them believe we're armed and dangerous . . ."

He didn't have to finish the sentence. And I had to get to the dock. What had they done to Sweetie and Pluto? I knew the consensus was going to be against me, but I had to take action. "I'm going to jump to the dock."

"No, Sarah Booth!" Tinkie had her stubborn face on. "You are doing no such thing. Let Randy go. He's a sheriff's deputy. He stands a better chance than any of us."

Randy started toward the door. "I'll do it. She's right."

"And if they shoot you dead, they'll figure out how to frame us for it." With the highest law official in the county involved, he could make almost anything happen and report it as he saw fit. We were in a definite pickle.

The boat made a radical shift. We grabbed at whatever we could to keep from being pitched to the floor.

"Shit," Angela said. "We don't have a choice. We have to get off this boat."

"Then we'll all go." Tinkie intended to stop me from trying it on my own.

We crept up to the deck and stopped dead. In the short space of time we'd been belowdecks, we'd been swallowed by wind and rain.

25

The howl of the wind obliterated all other noises, and the rain lashed my face so harshly I had to throw up an arm to protect my eyes. The boat rose at least eight feet on a swell and then plunged to the bottom. My stomach flipped a dozen times. I stumbled across the deck and grabbed a rope circling the mast. We were all going to be pitched over the side of the boat.

Before anyone could stop him, Chavis leaped over the boat railing. To my utter amazement, he made it to the dock, which was vaguely visible as a darker outline in the storm. Wind-driven rain blasted into our faces with the force of nails. We had to turn away.

"Dammit it all to hell!" There was no way to see if he'd made it safely up the dock or been swept away by the waves crashing over the slick boards. Or predict what he would do once he made it to the marina. Randy Chavis was a wild card. He'd seemed to be on Angela's side at the end, but there were no guarantees he'd shown his true colors.

And no way to calculate how badly he could damage us.

He could tell Benson we were all on board

the boat without weapons. Sitting ducks for what-ever plot the sheriff decided to unfold.

And I still didn't know if my dog and cat were safe. Worry for my pets made me anxious. I didn't feel so self-satisfied and smug about failing to tell Graf what I was doing on Dauphin Island. He was the only person who might come looking for us, but I'd pretty much kiboshed that possibility.

A tug on my sleeve made me duck below as I followed Tinkie. While I hated being imprisoned in the dark boat, she was right. Rain was coming down like the sky had no bottom.

Angela slammed the hatch shut, and the noise of the storm lessened, though the swaying of the boat made me queasy. To top it off, my teeth were chattering so hard they sounded like castanets. I was soaked, freezing, and nauseated. My equilibrium was taking a beating as the boat lurched again. My stomach roiled, and I fought seasickness.

"Just think, if we had some tequila, some cosmetics, and some light, maybe a little calm weather, and some gourmet snacks, we could play beautician. Sarah Booth desperately needs a makeover, and, Angela, I could update your drowned-rat look."

Tinkie's silly comment snapped the tension and gave us all a chance to catch a second wind.

"We need a gun." Angela was far from defeated.

"If they're out there with the intention of killing us, I'd like to get a few shots off first."

"Do you have a gun?" I was a good shot, but Tinkie was Dead-Eye Pete.

Angela shook her head. "Dad never believed in guns. I urged him to get one out here in the marina, but he never would. He said he drank too much, and he was afraid he'd shoot himself. Ironic, right?"

"Yeah, ironic." I felt like a rat in a tunnel with a big hungry cat waiting for me to poke my head out.

Tinkie stepped up to raise our flagging spirits. "Sarah Booth and I have been in much worse places. I concede, we've seldom looked this bad, but we've been in more danger. Tell me, though, do you think Randy will betray us?" It was the question on all of our minds.

"I don't know." Angela pushed her damp hair from her face. "I misread Randy. I never even gave him the shadow of a doubt. I don't know what he'll do. I only wish I could get you two off the island and safely away. People have been hurt because of me. Now you two are in this mess and your dog and cat are wandering out in a hurricane."

"Don't hog all the credit. Sarah Booth and I are capable of getting into trouble a lot deeper than this on our own." Tinkie's words held no sting. "How much longer can this storm last?"

"Maybe two hours. It was moving at a really fast clip. When it gets calm, that's the eye. Once that passes, it will rain and blow again. That's the tail of the storm."

Angela spoke as if she'd weathered more than a few hurricanes. "So it won't get any worse than this?" I asked.

"If we're lucky."

There was enough doubt in her voice to keep me from getting too hopeful. "Can Sweetie and Pluto survive this out in the open?"

"They'll find shelter. There are plenty of places around the marina for them to duck into cover, and this is going to be a really small storm."

That made me feel a little better. Maybe it was my imagination, but the storm did seem to be lessening. And I'd always heard that the back end wasn't as fierce as the leading edge. Maybe the worst was behind us.

"Do you think Renault is in collusion with the sheriff?" I told Angela about the motorboat Arley had heard the night her father was shot. "I think Renault may be the killer. I know he stole that painting. The question is, did he steal it after he killed your dad or before."

"He was always jealous of Dad. Jealous and lazy. He would sneak over here when Dad was gone to the store and poke around. Dad caught him a couple of times and warned him, but Remy would sneak back."

"There's something I don't understand. What did John's death accomplish?" Tinkie asked. "No one has been able to recover the treasure."

I saw where Tinkie was coming from. "Maybe they weren't after the treasure. Maybe they were determined to stop John from finding it."

"It was after the telescope went missing that my latest troubles started," Angela said. "Maybe you're onto something."

"Actually, it was after you talked to me about looking into your dad's murder."

The wind picked up again, and I thought I felt a small shift. But that wasn't possible. We were tightly strung between heavy-duty pilings. We should ride out the storm in relative safety.

"So is it the investigation into your father's murder or the possibility of finding the treasure that's at the root of these attacks against Angela, and how does that tie into framing Wofford for a murder he didn't commit?" I asked.

"We don't have enough evidence to support any of the theories exclusively." Tinkie was better at adding up the facts than anyone I knew.

"How do we get more evidence?" I asked.

"We could catch Benson and torture him until he talks." Tinkie was only half-kidding. After the week we'd had, she was game for using the Taser a bit or possibly waxing sensitive body areas. Nothing that would permanently maim a body, yet something that would be certain to elicit a wagging tongue and a bit of screaming.

"As soon as the storm is over, we can confront Prevatt and make him squeal." Tinkie was looking forward to that possibility. The snippy little museum curator had gotten under her skin. "He knows more than he's telling. He had the telescope all of those years and kept it locked away in a case. Not until—"

I put it together. "Not until I found that map at the old fort. I sent a photo to Cece."

"Can the sheriff intercept phone messages?" Tinkie asked Angela.

"They can tap your cell phone. Or get to your phone records. I suppose a text with an image attached would be easy to get."

"Shit." Tinkie was grim. "That's how they knew. The map. When you stole the telescope, they figured you knew how to find the treasure." Tinkie paced the narrow hall.

At last I was keeping up. "So the map at Fort Gaines does show how to locate the treasure."

"It's part of how we'll find it."

"The map, painting of Dad's, and the spyglass of Armand Couteau. It's just like I thought. Armand could see the beach from the window of his prison before he died."

"You believe the treasure is real?" Angela asked.

"I believe at one time it was. And I think your father figured this out. He believed it was real, and whoever killed him did, too."

"Then whoever killed him likely took the treasure already." Tinkie was the pragmatist in the group.

"I don't think so," I said. "If that were the case, no one would be messing with Angela now. She wouldn't be a threat. There would have been no need to send Wofford to prison or kill your father."

"You really believe there is a treasure and we might find it?" Angela asked.

"I do." I dared a look at Tinkie.

"Me too," she said. "At first I thought it was a bunch of malarkey, but after all of this, there has to be a solid motivation behind the actions. Money is always a good place to start."

"Dad wasn't the kind of man people wanted to hurt. It has to be money." Angela slumped down onto the steps. "I would give all of it away for a week with my father."

Tinkie sat beside her and patted her back. She was always the first one to offer sympathy or comfort, but Angela's words pierced my heart. I knew exactly how she felt.

As we sat in the galley, a strange calm settled over the boat.

"It's the eye. Let's get on land." Angela reached up and opened the hatch. For the first time in what seemed an eternity, there was no rain. And no wind. We inched up onto the deck.

The sky was leaden, and the clouds roiled, but

we were in the midst of an eerie calm. No sea-gulls cried for scraps, and the normal sounds of motorboats pulling in and taking off were gone. It was as if all living creatures had been wiped from the planet.

"How long will the eye be over us?" Tinkie was the last out of the hatch, and she looked around with distrust.

"The eye was very small. It's not a big window of time. Let's jump to the dock and get out of here."

"Good plan." I scanned the dock. Tinkie's red car was easy to spot now that the torrential rains had stopped. There was no sign of my dog and cat, though.

"I'll jump first and pull the boat closer to the pier," Angela offered.

She was about to act on her words when we saw two people coming down the pier toward us. It took a moment to recognize Arley and the sheriff. I clutched Tinkie's shoulder. We both grabbed Angela before she could make the jump.

"Where's the spyglass?" Benson called out to us. "I think you'll want to give it to me."

"Why should we?" I had a lot of bravado, which vaporized when he pulled the gun from Arley's back and pointed it at us.

"Because if you don't, I'll shoot Arley first and then you. Maybe in the leg, if my aim is good. Maybe in the heart. I only need one of you alive to tell me where to find that damn telescope. I've spent way too much effort trying to recover it."

"There's no treasure," Tinkie said. "It was a story John Trotter told everyone. It isn't true."

"I'll say one thing for you ladies. You don't give up easily. There is a treasure. John knew it, and I know it. John couldn't keep his mouth shut, and he told too many people how he had found the treasure and was on the verge of bringing it up. He'd made arrangements with a salvage company to haul it from the bottom. All he needed to find the exact location was that damn telescope. Now where is it? I'm not going to ask again. I'm just going to start shooting. Arley here will be the first."

"Angela, give it to him. He will hurt you." Arley didn't attempt to move as he spoke. "Benson, you'll never get by with this. Why are you even doing it? Everyone on the island knows this was John's treasure. If you try to claim it, folks are going to start asking a lot of questions you don't want to answer."

"Shut up." Benson struck the side of Arley's head with the gun barrel and sent him sprawling to the pier. "I don't need you interfering and I don't have time to play. Chavis is trying to get off the island on foot and I need to round him up." He pointed the weapon at Tinkie. "The stolen item. Now."

Angela slowly withdrew the spyglass from beneath her jacket. "You mean this?"

"Bring it over here." Benson cocked the gun. "Stop clowning around, Angela. I'll shoot these women and claim self-defense. Everyone believes me. I'm the sheriff."

"I don't care about the treasure. You can have the telescope. Just free Larry Wofford. He didn't kill anyone."

"Beyond my control." Benson's patience was about to snap. "You're not in a position to bargain, Angela. You're a smart woman. Smarter than your father, I hope."

His words cut through me. "You killed John Trotter." I walked toward the deck railing, putting myself between Benson and Tinkie. "Why?"

"John found the treasure."

"And he wouldn't share?"

Benson looked at me as if I'd grown a second head. "John wouldn't let it go. He simply couldn't understand how finding the treasure would be the worst thing that ever happened."

"What in the world are you saying?" Tinkie stepped out from behind me. "You don't want the treasure, but you killed a man over it?"

The sound of a motorboat made us all pause. Phyllis Norris cut through the rough water as she aimed the powerful sea-lab craft toward us. "Turn back! Turn back!" I tried to signal her away, but she didn't understand what I was doing. She kept heading straight for us.

"Phyllis! Turn away!" Angela waved her arms frantically, but the biologist kept coming.

Phyllis angled the boat alongside the pier and tossed a line to the sheriff. He caught it and deftly tied off her boat. She nimbly jumped to the wooden dock. If she noticed the gun in Benson's hand, it didn't register.

"Let her go," Angela said. She turned to Phyllis. "You need to take your boat and get out of here. The eye will pass shortly, and the weather will be too rough. You shouldn't be out on the water."

Arley saw an opportunity and jumped to his feet. He took a swing at Benson and caught the sheriff on the jaw, but it was a glancing blow. Benson used the gun as a club. The blow he struck on Arley's head took him to the deck. He crumpled in a heap, and this time there was no doubt he was out cold.

Almost as if the sky rebelled, thunder ripped, and a jagged fork of lightning shattered the gray horizon.

Phyllis stared at Angela as if she spoke a foreign language. She turned to the sheriff. "I told you she hadn't figured it out." Anger colored her words. "Now we have a confrontation for no good reason. We could have stolen the spyglass back. But no, you had to muck everything up.

And I didn't see a sign of Chavis. He's still on the island somewhere."

She stepped behind him. "Get the spyglass and kill them."

"What?" Angela started to jump from the boat to the pier, but the sheriff waved the gun.

"Stay back," he ordered. With his free hand, he grabbed Norris's shoulder. "We don't have to kill them."

"Of course we do. I told you Angela would never give up. Never. Once she believed Larry was innocent, she wasn't going to rest until her father's killer was put away." She turned to us. "Well, here I am. And it's too late. You won't be around to exact revenge."

"You killed Dad? Why?" Angela asked.

"He found the treasure. He left me no choice."

Angela was like a deflated balloon. "Why did you kill him? He loved you. He talked about you all the time and how much he wanted to provide for you, what he would do when he found the treasure. Why?"

"The worst thing that could happen to me and this island would be for the treasure to be found. The ecosystem is strained to the breaking point. Can you imagine the hordes that would show up if a pirate's treasure was truly found? The development, the treasure hunts in the Gulf, the carnival rides, the restaurants, the nasty, polluting humans who would be here year-round clutching for some scrap of pirate's gold with their greedy hands? This was John's vision of the future. He wanted to bring tourism to the island. He thought it would afford a better lifestyle for some people."

We were in serious trouble. She was crazy as a betsy bug on hot asphalt.

"Shoot them, Osage. Then untie the boat and let the storm take it. We'll destroy that damn spyglass and be free of the Esmeralda treasure forever. You and I will save paradise." She shook free of him and started to walk away, but he grasped her hand.

"Phyllis, let's think this through. If the bodies are recovered with bullet wounds, folks won't let this go. We got lucky with Trotter and Wofford. Two private investigators and Angela on top of that greedy bastard Renault and his conniving sister. It's too much."

Phyllis stopped and reversed. She looked at the three of us on the deck of the *Miss Adventure*. "Untie the boat. The eye is passing. Let the storm take them out. They'll drown."

"We tried that once and—"

"We'll make sure they aren't rescued this time." Phyllis pointed to one of the ropes. "Hurry. If Arley wasn't so big, we'd put him on the boat, too. We'll have to figure another means of disposal for him. We'll put him on the boat with that stupid bitch Lydia. We can make it look like they shot each other."

The sheriff bent to free the boat from the dock ties we'd worked so hard to establish.

"Don't do this," I said to him. "She's making you a murderer."

"We've gone too far down a long road for me to turn back now." Benson had one line free and moved to the next one. "This island is everything to her, and she's everything to me. I never had a chance when John was alive. Now, though, she needs me. I can't stop. We have to protect the environment."

"This is crazy." Tinkie leaned over the rail. "You'll get caught. So far, you haven't done anything. Sheriff, you've been in office twenty years. You're going to throw that away and end up in prison."

"That won't happen. As primary law enforcement official of this area, I'll make sure your deaths are listed as a tragic accident. Victims of the storm. Three foolish women who failed to heed warnings, take precautions, and who attempted to sail a vessel into the teeth of a hurricane. You thought you could get to the nonexistent pirate's treasure before the hurricane struck. Tragic, but no one's fault."

He could sell fireballs in hell.

"Don't you want the spyglass?" Angela held it out, bait for a hungry shark.

Phyllis stepped forward. "Good try, Angela. We never wanted the telescope. Don't you get it?

We don't want the treasure to be found. It was never about *taking* the treasure, it was about *keeping* it from being discovered."

Tinkie leaned over to me. "That woman is bat-shit crazy. And the sheriff isn't far behind her."

I only nodded. But Benson was a crazy man with a gun in one hand and the rope that tied us off to the safety of the dock in the other.

"Phyllis!" I yelled after the biologist. "Phyllis, we can work this out. Angela doesn't care about the treasure. She only wants to free Wofford."

"And how would she manage that without sending me to prison? Not really an option from where I'm standing." She put a hand on the sheriff's arm and squeezed. "Set them adrift. We've got about five minutes before the eye wall passes over us and the back end of the storm kicks in."

"Sheriff, if you set us adrift, that's tantamount to murder." Benson was guilty of a dozen legal infractions, but he hadn't killed John Trotter. Now he was colluding in a triple homicide. "Retrieve the treasure in secrecy. No one has to know about it. We know where it is, and if you let us live, we'll tell you. Millions in Spanish gold and jewels. You can have all of it. It can be recovered without fanfare, and you can use the money to protect the island."

The wind gusted and swung the bow of the boat toward the dock. Benson had freed one tie-line. We only had two left—and those not for long.

The winds picked up, and lightning fractured the heavy sky. Any minute, the clouds would open up and visibility would be cut to zero. If the *Miss Adventure* was freed from her mooring, we would either be smashed against the pier or pulled out into the vortex of the storm. I didn't have much sailing experience, but I had enough to be terrified.

"You don't get it." Phyllis loosened another mooring. "Forget about trying to bribe Osage with the treasure. Take that damned spyglass to the deepest part of the ocean where it belongs. And you go with it." She cast the line free.

The *Miss Adventure* swung broadside into the growing swells. We were in serious, serious trouble.

"This is not looking good for the ladies of detection," Tinkie said softly.

"You are a brilliant master of the understatement."

"We should jump in the water and swim for shore." Angela walked to the rail and leaned over.

A bullet exploded only inches from her hand. When I looked back at the pier, Phyllis had the sheriff's gun. "Don't try it. If you jump, we'll shoot you in the water. Chances are better than fifty percent that the storm will pull you out for shark chum, and I'm willing to risk it to be rid of you all. Your best chance is to ride the storm out in open water."

And that was no chance at all. "She wants the storm to kill us. That way she and the sheriff can pass off our deaths as accidental or any way they wish."

The first pattering of a gentle rain began. Our window of time was closing fast. Phyllis aimed for the final tie-line.

"When I get back on dry land, I'm going to snatch that bitch bald-headed," Tinkie said, and she wasn't understating her intentions. She was petite, but she was scrappy.

"That makes two of us. I was a fool not to realize how precious the environment was to her. She said it over and over again. I never considered she'd kill the man she was seeing."

"You think you're feeling like a patsy. She fed me information to stop Roundtree's development," Angela said. "I should have known. She killed my father because he finally realized his dream."

Tinkie put her hands on her hips. "She'll pay."

"Right. We can haunt her from our watery grave." Angela was exhausted.

"Phyllis! Don't do this." I tried one more time.

Her response was to bend to the task of freeing the last line. The knot defied her, and she began to tear at it. Thunder roared, and a blur of red, gray, and white zoomed down the pier and knocked Phyllis flat. She gave a tiny cry as the wind was knocked from her lungs.

With a deep growl, Sweetie Pie grabbed her raincoat and dragged her to the edge of the pier. Just as my dog was about to push her off, Benson regained his wits and went after Sweetie.

Never in a rush, Pluto arrived on the scene. He jumped on Benson's ass and dug in with all four claws. Watching Benson buck and whirl was amusing, but my focus was on the tie-line. Inch by inch it came unwound from the dock. With every swell the *Miss Adventure* rode, she slowly freed herself, moving away from land and into the open water and the rapidly approaching storm.

The rain increased.

"What should we do?" Tinkie asked. She, too, saw the inevitable.

"What can we do?" I asked.

With a splash, Sweetie nudged Phyllis off the pier and into the water.

"Phyllis! Wait!" Benson plunged in after her. Pluto leaped to safety just in time.

"Sweetie, get the rope!" I feared she wouldn't understand, but once again I underestimated my dog. She grabbed the end of the rope, which was thankfully still wrapped around the piling, and braced herself to hold the boat from slipping free of all moorings.

"Let's jump in the water before it gets any

rougher," Tinkie said. "We can make it to shore."

"If the boat shifts in the wind and current, we could be crushed."

"If we stay on board this boat, we could end up in the Bermuda Triangle. How does that work out for ships?" Tinkie was fed up with inaction.

I ignored Tinkie's sarcasm and focused on the more immediate problem. "Sweetie can't hold us much longer." She fought with every fiber of strength, but the tide and wind were pulling her down the pier.

"You should have taught her how to tie knots," Tinkie said. "As soon as we're back in Zinnia, I'm going to start a class for her and Chablis. Tying and untying knots is a good thing for a PI dog to know."

She was rambling because she was as scared as I was.

Sweetie was at the end of her rope, literally, and the distance from deck to dock had increased by twenty feet. The storm was sucking us out.

"I'm going to start the motor, and we can set the sails and try to run parallel to the coast. Since this is the back end, the winds may assist us." Angela had finally settled on a plan. "We'll head west, out of the storm. Let's get busy."

She disappeared into the wheelhouse. I looked at Tinkie. "Do you know how to set the sails?"

"No, but we better learn quickly." She went to

the mast and began to untie the sail. "If we angle into the wind wrong, we're dead."

Even as she spoke, the boat was snatched by wind and water, and Sweetie was pulled to the edge of the pier.

"Let go!" I had to make her give it up. She couldn't save us. She was just an eighty-pound dog trying to hold a sailboat. But she would die trying. "Sweetie! Let go!"

And then the rain unleashed. The back end of the storm hit us hard.

"Shit." Tinkie stumbled into me, blinded by the onslaught of water. "I've ruined my freaking manicure. Not to mention my hairdo. I'm going to look like crap for the Black and Orange Ball."

My friend was not shallow. She was brave. She was not worried about a stupid ball, but if she pretended hard enough that the ball was our biggest future concern, maybe we wouldn't turn into gibbering idiots from terror.

"Don't give up yet," I said to her. "Don't quit." Words to live by. Or die by.

We struggled with the sail, and I prayed Sweetie had let us go. The rain eased a bit, and I looked to see if Sweetie and Pluto had left the pier. To my surprise, a dark-haired man ran toward my dog.

"Tinkie! Look!"

She swung around to the pier, and her breath escaped in a gasp. "It's Graf."

"Graf?" I was incredulous. He'd come. Even when I thought he wouldn't, he found me. Somehow he realized I was in trouble, and he came to save me.

He grabbed the tie-line from Sweetie and was using the rocking of the swells to pull the sailboat close enough to the pier that he could retie us. To my amazement, a very unstable Arley forced himself to his feet and assisted Graf.

"Grab the other tie-line." I began to pull one from the water. If we could throw it to Graf, he could retie us. We might be able to get off the ship before it either wrecked or broke free.

Tinkie, Angela, and I watched as Graf and Arley fought against the elements in a valiant effort to save us. We were helpless to act. Two men and a dog struggled to hold a sailboat as the back end of Hurricane Margene rushed to shore.

Pluto, because he was a cat and disdained physical exertion, watched attentively. He'd done his part to send the sheriff into the deep, and now his work was complete.

"They're doing it!" Tinkie hadn't forgiven Graf for his conduct, but she was certainly willing to appreciate his courage and help. "Sarah Booth, they're going to save us!"

"Oh, shit." Angela pointed to the south.

A wave at least eight feet high was headed straight at us. The boat was positioned to cut through the wave. We wouldn't be swamped, but the surge would be treacherous.

The water took us high and then dropped us into a trough. It was the sensation of a roller coaster as we plunged down, down, down. And when I turned back to the pier, Graf and Sweetie stood, defeated. The *Miss Adventure* had broken free.

26

"Get the main sail unfurled!"

Angela snapped orders as she engaged the boat's motor, which might give us clearance out of the marina and into open water. Then what? I didn't want to think. And I didn't want to stare back at Graf, who was standing on the marina as forlorn as my dog.

The waves came at us hard, lifting us up and dropping us as rain lashed so hard my hands slipped on the coils of the rope that held the sail. Frantic to release the canvas, I struggled for all I was worth. Tinkie, too, worked the knots.

The roar of the wind increased, and to the west I saw a waterspout form. The aquatic tornado wavered like a top, then rushed toward land. They often played out as soon as they touched land, but it was a fearsome sight.

A sudden shift in the boat sent Tinkie sprawling, and she managed to grab hold of a tarp and hang on until I could get to her. When I had her on her feet, I looked back to land.

Graf lifted a hand. A signal of what? Thanks. Remorse. Good-bye?

"He tried. He did everything he could. That wave was just too much." Tinkie put a hand on my shoulder. "He came back to save you, Sarah Booth. He still loves you."

"Yeah." I didn't know what I thought or felt. Staring at Graf in the rain and wind, I knew I loved him. Despite the betrayal and the pain, I loved him. If the water didn't get me, then heartbreak surely would. "I think I'll make a perfect mermaid."

"Oh, Sarah Booth." Tinkie put her arm around my waist and squeezed. "We aren't going to die, but I have no doubt your heart is broken. Help me set the sail. I can't do it by myself."

As I turned to go to the mast, I stopped. "No!" I shouted the word at Graf, but it was too late. He dove into the water and began swimming toward the boat.

"Angela, cut the motor! Graf is swimming toward us."

"Has he lost his mind?" Angela left the wheelhouse and ran to the rail. "Get a line. He's going to have to climb up."

The boat rose and fell, lumbering into one wave sideways so that it washed over us and nearly took us all overboard. Graf seemed to make progress and then fall back. After ten minutes, I could see he was tiring. Tinkie appeared beside me with a flotation ring. Before she could swing it, Angela hefted it from her and gave a mighty heave. Her aim was good, and Graf hooked it with one arm.

"Pull, ladies! Pull!" Angela ordered. And we obliged.

"When he gets on deck, I'm going to kill him," Tinkie huffed. "Of all the damn fool things to do, jumping into the ocean in the middle of a hurricane takes the cake."

She was absolutely correct, but I couldn't stop grinning. Graf had chosen me. He'd come to save me. The storm brewed around me, but the emotional oppression that had flattened me was gone. Sure, we had a lot to talk through, but at least he would be around to talk with. After that, I might have to kill him for scaring me so.

It took all of us hauling on the life-preserver rope, but we got Graf to the boat, and he climbed aboard.

Events blurred as we fought the wind and seas to keep the boat from capsizing. Angela and Graf were able to angle the *Miss Adventure* so that she rode the waves rather than plowed through or wallowed in them. Graf had more experience as a sailor than the rest of us, and his split-second decisions and knowledge saved us time and again. Even with his expertise, it was a long two-hour ride in freezing rain and gales.

By late afternoon, the storm had passed. On the southern horizon, the sun came out with the promise of a perfect fall day.

"I have a sense of what Noah went through," Tinkie said as she came to stand beside me at the bow. Our palms and fingers were rope-burned and covered with popped blisters. "If men judge a woman by the softness of her hands, à la Scarlett O'Hara, I'm doomed."

"We're pretty much a mess." The pain would kick in soon enough, but at least we were alive to feel it.

Graf came out of the wheelhouse and walked toward us. He put an arm around each of us. "That was a close call."

"Yeah." I found my throat had closed with emotion.

"How'd you end up untied and loose in the storm?" he asked.

I cast a glance at Tinkie. She nodded and told him the sequence of events.

"You could have been killed," Graf said. "All three of you." It was a statement of fact, not an accusation.

My heart faltered. "Yes, we could have been murdered, but you came to help us."

"Tinkie, could I have a word with Sarah Booth?"

Graf had come to save us, but not to stay. I knew it the moment our eyes connected. Tinkie left us, and we were alone in the Gulf, now returned to a beautiful blue. A few seagulls had even found the boat to circle and beg for food. The natural world was returning to order. My world—it was about to change.

"Who is she?" I asked. It was pointless to dance around the matter and pretend.

"Her name is Marion Silber. She's a screenwriter and an old friend."

"Friend?" I couldn't stop myself.

"She was more than a friend several years ago. We were close."

I had a few bitter remarks, but I couldn't say them. If I spoke, I'd break down. So I let him continue.

"It was before I came back to Mississippi to find you. Several years before that. When I left New York and went to Hollywood, I met Marion. She's a talented writer, and she wrote several scripts for me to star in."

"Quite the team. A double threat." I meant to sound light, but I was far off the mark.

"She has a child, a daughter. Katlyn. She's mine."

That stopped me. An overwhelming tide of anger, pain, bitterness, sadness—a thousand emotions swept over me. Graf had a child, a daughter. A beautiful girl with flowing dark-blond curls who danced at the edge of the water, just as I'd imagined our child would. We'd planned to have children together, but that future had been washed away with the storm.

I felt his hand on me, and I knew I'd staggered. "You never said a word about a child." The betrayal was almost too much.

"I didn't know." He turned my face so that I had to look at him. "I love you, Sarah Booth. I will never love anyone with the depth I love you."

"Why couldn't you tell me?"

"Once Marion told me about Katlyn, I had to think things through. Just to be certain, I ran a DNA test. There's no doubt. When I had the results, I was going to tell you. While I was waiting, though, I felt as if I'd betrayed you, even though I've never been unfaithful. Never wanted to be. I'm in love with you, but I was eaten up with guilt. I had to figure out what I owe my daughter."

The curse of my life would be the men I fell in love with were men of honor. "I thought you didn't want me anymore."

"I could never stop wanting you." His fingers curled in my hair, and he pulled me against his chest. "But I couldn't be close to you until I had an understanding of my obligation to Katlyn and how I intended to act on it."

"And Marion? She should have told you about your child."

"She should have. When we parted, it was with anger. When she found out she was pregnant, she was too angry to tell me. And up until recently, she and Katlyn have been the perfect family unit."

"You had a right to know about your child."

He nodded. "I agree. But there are extenuating circumstances. Marion fell in love with someone else. For a long time, he was Katlyn's father. It seemed the perfect solution. But that relationship ended, and as Katlyn grew up, Marion realized that it was wrong not to tell me. Hollywood is a very small world, and she looked me up, meaning to introduce me to Katlyn. She discovered that I was in love with you. Deeply in love. And she knew that telling me about Katlyn would change my life. So she never contacted me. She didn't want to interfere. She and Katlyn were happy. It wasn't until recently that Katlyn began asking about her father. She turned seven, and Marion didn't want to lie to her."

"Does she know you're her father?"

"Yes. I told her. And I had to tell you."

From the center, I'd been suddenly pushed to the periphery of Graf's life. "What are you going to do?"

"I want to be part of her life."

I nodded, because that was the only correct answer. "And what does that mean for us?"

"I don't know. Can you accept this? Can we work through it?"

I wanted to say yes, but I couldn't until I had more answers. "How does Marion fit into your life?"

"I don't know. She's Katlyn's mother. I haven't figured out the hard parts. I'm not even certain who I am after the shooting. It wasn't the pain that worked on me; it was the idea that everything I believed about me, my future, my place in the world was destroyed in a moment. I couldn't grasp that, and I didn't know how to handle it. I did a poor job of adjusting."

"I understand. To be injured so seriously, perhaps crippled. That's impossible to get hold of all at once. But you're going to be fine. You're a hundred percent now."

He nodded. "I will fully recover. I believe it now. I didn't at first. I should have had more faith, but for a while I was lost." His dark hair fluttered in the wind. "I also know I can't expose my daughter to danger, to people trying to kill you or me or her."

I'd thought this through, and I had been ready to give up my career as a private investigator. What had happened to him wasn't just or fair. I had brought it down on him because of my work. "I can change careers."

"Oh, Sarah Booth, I don't think anyone will ever offer me more, but I came to another truth in all of this time I've spent searching for answers. To ask you to do that is to change who you are. That's not something I want on my conscience. I've talked about this with Oscar, and he's as scared for Tinkie as I am for you. But somehow he's able to step aside and let her work. Maybe he has more faith than I do or is less afraid. Maybe his heart is stronger. I just know I can't ask you to change who you are, and I can't change who I am."

"If you want to live with Marion and Katlyn, just say so. Don't put it off on me or my career." He'd made me angry. I couldn't change the past, but I was willing to reshape the future. Now, suddenly, that wasn't enough.

"I'm not involved with Marion. That time has passed. I have no romantic feelings for her, though she had hoped differently. And I want you to know I wasn't aware she would be here on Dauphin Island. My agent told her I was here, recuperating, and she came without my knowledge. But I am deeply involved with my daughter. I always wanted children. Just watching the expressions on Katlyn's face or listening to the things she says—it's a love I never anticipated."

I turned away. "I could love her as my own daughter."

"I don't doubt that for an instant." He folded me into his arms. "I need some time, Sarah Booth. I'm going back to Hollywood and work. Once I've settled into a routine with Katlyn and my job, I want you to come out. We'll see how we fit then. I need to get my feet under me, to learn how to be Katlyn's dad. And you need to honestly assess how much you can change without harming yourself."

Whether Graf could see it or not, I realized he was crafting a life that didn't include me. "If that's what you need."

"Give things a chance to settle."

"Yes," I said. "Things will become clearer." But I didn't need Jitty to predict the future. I could feel it in my bones. "I love you, Graf. More than I ever realized." I turned in his arms and kissed him long and deeply.

And then I walked to the wheelhouse. Angela and Tinkie were pointedly looking out at the calming Gulf waters, where a Coast Guard cutter had appeared on the horizon.

"We have to find Sweetie and Pluto at the marina. And make certain Benson and Phyllis get their just dues," I said, surprised at the steadiness in my voce.

Tinkie held out her cell phone. "We called it in, but Randy Chavis beat us to the punch. He hid out until Benson took Arley to the pier. Then he broke into Arley's office and kept trying until he raised the Coast Guard and the ABI. He managed to haul the sheriff and Phyllis out of the drink. The Coast Guard has them. They were pretty battered by the pier pilings, but they're alive. Randy filled the authorities in on what had transpired, and they're both under arrest. They're holding them at the marina. And Sweetie and Pluto are just fine."

"Good work," I said.

"Thank you, Sarah Booth and Tinkie," Angela said. "You figured out who killed my father, and I'll be able to get Larry out of prison."

But it wasn't a happy ending. Not in the least. Not for a single one of us.

27

When we arrived at the old fort, stars still spattered the night sky, but the herald of dawn was lightening the east. Any moment, the sun would peek over the horizon.

"Ready?" I asked Angela. She held the stolen spyglass, ready to sweep the horizon at first light. We'd placed John's aquatic painting over the nautical map and found the placement of the shoreline of Dauphin Island when Couteau was alive. We were ready for sunrise. Ready to prove our hypothesis that the angle of the sun and the mark on the spyglass would yield the watery grave of the treasure.

The sun began to chase the night away, and Saturday morning dawned clear and calm. Hurricane Margene had defied all predictions, rushed to make landfall hours earlier then predicted, and finally cleared out leaving minimal damage. Now, fall was in the air. Angela swept the horizon with the telescope while Tinkie and I watched. Our job was over. Phyllis Norris was behind bars. Benson, too. Remy's body was discovered tied to the anchor of his own sailboat and sunk underwater. He'd thrown in with Phyllis and Benson to rob John Trotter, and they'd killed him and his sister in an elaborate frame to put Angela and Randy behind bars. Now Randy and other officers were working to dismantle the corrupt law-enforcement machine the sheriff had built up over two decades.

Once Angela went back to work as a journalist, I felt sure other heads would roll. There would be a clean house, at least in Mobile County. At least until a new crop of crooks could organize and move in.

"What do you see?" Tinkie was almost jumping up and down, a perfect imitation of Chablis, who had a tendency to hide her intelligence by acting hyper.

"Wait a minute. The sun has to have the correct angle." Angela was surprisingly calm as she fiddled with nautical implements. She'd taken a crash course from her friend and former postman, Terrance Snill.

"What will you do with the treasure, if there is one?" I asked.

"I'm going to help Larry pay his debts and compensate his attorney and donate the rest to Project Innocence. That organization takes on cases where people have been falsely convicted."

"Nothing for yourself?"

The masculine voice made my heart drop—Graf was gone, but I still hadn't accepted it—but it was only Snill, come to help us with the last of the treasure hunt.

"I have everything I need. Or I will when Larry

is released." Angela's grin changed her whole personality. "It should be soon. And they'll clear his record. You know, he isn't bitter at all. He said going to prison saved him from drinking his life away."

"Larry's a wise man to take all of this as an opportunity," Tinkie said. "*I* took it as an opportunity to increase my valuable antique collection, thanks to Mr. Snill." She looped her arm through his. "What's in your hand? A love letter to me?"

My partner was full of herself—an obvious overcompensation because I was suffering the loss of Graf. She frisked and flaunted to keep the atmosphere lively as we waited for Angela to discover whatever she would find.

"It's some research for Sarah Booth. About that slave girl, LuAnn." He handed the paper to me, though it was too dark inside the fort to read it.

"She was sold to Alabama and later sold again to a plantation in Mississippi. She had a little girl, who I believe ended up being sold to a Delaney of Sunflower County."

A chill swept through the little dark room. Each of us felt it, and we all reacted. "What was that?" Angela asked.

I knew exactly who had graced us, but I couldn't say. "What happened to LuAnn?" I asked.

"She died in childbirth. The little girl, her name was—"

"Jitty." I could feel her in the room. So this was what she'd wanted me to find out. History. The daughter of a stolen princess. The daughter of a pirate. A child who lost her parents much earlier than I had lost mine. No wonder Jitty and I had such a strong bond.

"How did you know that, Sarah Booth?" Tinkie shot me one long, suspicious look.

"I don't know." I feigned innocence. "Maybe Madame Tomeeka isn't the only psychic in Zinnia."

"So does Jitty tell you secrets when you talk to her?"

I had to improvise and quickly. Once my partner was on a scent, she didn't let go. "I read about the little girl in some of Alice's letters in the attic. When I was researching the whole history of the Richmonds and Falcons. Jitty was bought from another plantation to be a playmate for Alice's older sister, who later died of rheumatic fever."

"Isn't that a strange coincidence? It's almost as if you were led here to Dauphin Island," Angela mused.

I didn't mention the fact that when I was looking for a place for Graf to recuperate, I'd walked away from my computer, only to find the Dauphin Island Web site had been pulled up when I returned. Jitty had no corporeal powers—at least I didn't think so.

"Everything happens for a reason," Snill said. "Now the bad guys and gal are behind bars, Randy Chavis is going to be acting chief deputy until the governor can appoint a sheriff, and I have found a buyer for the *Miss Adventure*. Let's see if we can find the treasure before life blows up again."

"Look!" Angela focused out the window with the spyglass. "I see where it would be. That's where Dad indicated the shore used to be back in the day of Couteau."

Snill took the glass from her. "By damn, that would have been the perfect place to bring a treasure almost to shore and sink it, except for the damage done by hurricanes in recent years. Katrina cut the westernmost tip off the island, and Isaac came close to severing another part. Couteau couldn't possibly have foreseen the damage that man and nature could do to his paradise. So he sneaked the treasure close to the shore. I'm sure he meant to retrieve it. And he marked the spyglass so that it could be matched with the message. What a brilliant man!"

"Let's take the *Miss Adventure*," Angela said. "I'm a certified diver. I can see if there's anything hidden. If there is, we can make the necessary plans to bring it up."

"What fun!" Tinkie all but clapped her hands. She was ready for another adventure at sea. You could knock my partner down, but you couldn't

417

keep her on the floor. I was a different kettle of fish.

"Y'all treasure hunt as much as you want. I'll stay here with Sweetie and Pluto." I'd had enough sailboats to last me the rest of my life. I had no intention of ever putting foot on another one.

"Are you sure?" Tinkie asked. "She shouldn't be alone." She spoke to the group.

"Oh, for heaven's sake, I'm fine. I'm not going to hurl myself off the parapets of the fort. Even if I did, it's not much of a drop." My efforts brought forth some smiles. "I really don't want to climb aboard a boat for a long, long time."

"I understand that." Angela patted my arm. "We'll be back in an hour."

"I'm walking to town," I said. Graf had taken the SUV when he left, but I had a ride to New Orleans with Tinkie, who would take me back to Dahlia House after the ball.

For now, I wanted solitude so that I could tell the island—and many of my dreams—good-bye. It was going to be a crystal-clear October morning. The last of the month. The beginning of a new life for me. "I need to be alone, and walking helps me think."

"Meet us at the marina," Tinkie said.

"Will do."

They hurried away from the old fort, and I took

one last walk around the fortress that had seen so much heartbreak and conflict.

Hurricane Margene had blown through without much damage. The power was already restored. No lives and little property were lost. The rhythm of normal island life resumed. Not so true for me.

Sweetie fell in beside me as I walked. We rounded a corner, and she began to bark. I wasn't surprised when I came upon the figure of a slender woman in a black tasseled cowgirl outfit, complete with black shiny boots and a black cowboy hat with a veil. Cowgirl widow.

"Dale? Dale Evans, is that you?" The woman looked just like the wife of my favorite childhood cowboy, Roy Rogers.

"Not Dale Evans, but another singin' widow."

My brain was in no condition for Jitty's high jinks. "Spill it. Who are you?"

"I'm a faux widow." She spoke with a Southern drawl. "I wasn't really married to Hank when he died. Fact is, he'd married that Billie Jean Jones. I paid her thirty thousand dollars, which was a right smart amount of money at the time, for her to quit callin' herself his widow. That title was rightfully mine."

"Another hint, please." I could almost place her.

"Nicknamed my son Bocephus."

"Miss Audrey!" I had her. Wife of Hank Williams Sr.

"If we'd stayed married, I might have kept him from the bottle."

Given what I knew of her life, I didn't think that was an accurate prediction, but who was I to question a ghost. "It must've been fun, traveling and singing with the Drifting Cowboys."

"We didn't have air-conditioned tour buses and fancy hotel rooms. Hank loved the music. That's what kept us on tour."

"Why are you here, Jitty? I know who you are. I know your history."

"I'm here for you, Sarah Booth. Married, divorced—it doesn't matter if you love a man. You'll grieve for him when he's gone."

I couldn't discuss Graf with her. Not yet. I'd rather she goad and torment me than offer widow's weeds and condolences. "We're each set upon a path. For a time, Graf's and mine ran parallel. Now they don't." I fought to maintain my calm. "Thank you for letting me see your past, your royal highness." If I teased her, I wouldn't cry.

"In another country, at another time, I would have had a very different life."

"Instead, you worked and fought for survival at the side of a woman whose family paid cash for you. I'm sorry, Jitty."

"Truth is, Sarah Booth, the Delaney family gave me a childhood. And my best friend, Miss Alice. That wasn't true for a lot of slaves, but for me, I had a real family. My mama and daddy were dead and gone. Wasn't no bringin' them back. But having Miss Alice and her family, and later Coker, that was a good life."

"Did you know you were a pirate's daughter?"

"Not for many years. Alice told me one day when we were in the field digging for potatoes. We were about to starve, and she took my mind off my growling stomach by telling me the story of Armand and LuAnn. Of course, she spiced it up and made it a lot more romantic. Accordin' to Miss Alice, their love woulda overcome all obstacles, had Armand lived."

"And maybe it would have."

"Yes, maybe it would." Jitty was so sad. We were both missing things that could never be returned to us. "So what will you do now, Sarah Booth?"

It was a question I dreaded. "Go to New Orleans and attend the Black and Orange Ball. I owe Cece that much. And Tinkie. She would miss it for me, but I won't ask that. Then I'll go home to Dahlia House. After that . . ." I shrugged. "I don't know."

"Can you forgive Graf?"

"What's to forgive? He has a child. We both agree Katlyn is his first priority. It's strange how life changes so drastically in one moment. The split second my parents died, that shift in consciousness when Graf learned he was a father. It's like the twist of a kaleidoscope. A completely different picture from one moment to the next."

"Some women wouldn't be so philosophical about it."

I knew what she meant, but what was the point of anger? It wouldn't change the facts or the way I'd learned about them. "This wasn't some trap Graf set or some scheme he cooked up. He was sandbagged as much as I was. I only wish he'd told me sooner."

"Speaking the hard truth has never been a man's strong suit." She laughed. "He did come to save you. I know he loves you."

I thought about Coleman Peters, who had also loved me. "Sometimes love isn't enough."

"And sometimes it's just the right amount." She laughed. "Let's stroll into town. You done good on this case. Freed an innocent man and put two criminals behind bars."

"Lost a fiancé and gained a royal haint." I patted my leg, and Sweetie fell into step. Pluto, always an aristocrat, sashayed in front of us. "I have to call the wedding officiant and cancel the wedding."

"Probably a good thing to do." Jitty fell into step beside me. "I'll walk a ways with you, Sarah Booth. Just for the company."

For those who couldn't see Jitty, I was just another crazy cat/dog lady ambling along the beach. Maybe, in my heart, that was who I needed to be for the moment.

• • •

"You look absolutely marvelous, dah-link!" Cece walked around me, pulling at the beautiful black and orange gown that Graf had found for me on Rodeo Drive. She tugged a strap and tucked a stray curl into place, straightening the black opal necklace that she insisted I wear "for luck."

We were in the lovely hotel suite Cece had arranged for us. The Black and Orange Ball was almost upon us. My most personal wish was to be left alone so I could have a good crying fit, but that would have to wait.

"You do look stunning," Tinkie said. Even with her five-inch stilettos, she only came to my chest.

"And both of you are gorgeous." They were. Cece had imported a gown from a chic New York designer, and Tinkie's dress was made by Sunflower County's finest seamstress, a woman whose creations rivaled any designer in the world.

"Now tell me again what Angela found at the bottom of the ocean?" Cece was like a child when it came to pirate's treasure.

"Spanish gold, diamonds, emeralds, rubies, sapphires, and silver. Estimated at approximately ten million. She's a wealthy woman." Tinkie checked it off on her fingers. "Can you believe it? Her father was right all along."

"And she managed to bring the treasure up, with Snill's and Commissioner Roundtree's help, without a big hullabaloo. The delicate ecology of Dauphin Island is safe, at least for now." That was the part I was proud of. Angela had done the impossible and kept a low profile about the treasure.

"Can you say ironic," Tinkie said. "Phyllis killed to keep the treasure secret, and Angela managed to bring it up without a single person catching on. She'll never tell where she found it."

"Is she really donating it to the legal fund to help people falsely accused?" Cece was itching to cover the story.

"Most of it. She has a few other charities. And she promised Delaney Detective Agency a very hefty fee." Tinkie gave me a high five. "We can invest in some needed equipment and have a nest egg for the lean times."

"Does Oscar know about the whole boat and near-death-in-a-hurricane episode?" Cece asked.

"No, and I don't see a reason to tell him." Tinkie bounced onto the bed. "No point stirring up hornets with a short stick, as Aunt Loulane would say. Now enough shoptalk—let's focus on the ball. This is so exciting, Cece! You've done a marvelous job yet again."

"And Sarah Booth's surprise still awaits." Cece and Tinkie giggled like schoolgirls.

"I've ordered room service for Sweetie, Pluto, and Chablis." Tinkie always took care of the small details.

"Pluto hasn't eaten since Graf . . . left." The damned cat was making me crazy.

"Yes, he's down in the dumps." Tinkie scratched him under the chin. "It's a good thing Chablis was here to rouse Sweetie's spirits."

"And the case is wrapped up?" Cece was impressed.

"Benson confessed to everything and identified Phyllis Norris as John's killer. He also gave a statement that she shot Lydia Clampett and her brother Remy Renault. There are a lot of legal twists and turns Wofford will have to take, but his name will be cleared. That's what Angela wanted more than any treasure." Angela had saved the man of her dreams, and I had lost mine.

"A case wrapped up in minimal time. We are celebrating tonight. Remember, Cece has promised you a surprise."

"I can't wait." I forced out the words with a smile, which earned me a hug from my two best friends.

"Always game," Cece said. "But I promise, this will lift your spirits. In fact, Madame Tomeeka and Millie are in charge of your surprise. They're making sure . . . all needs are met."

Despite the fact that my heart was dragging behind me, they'd piqued my curiosity. "I believe it's showtime. Let's get downstairs so I can find out what you've been holding out on me."

The clock on the dressing table of the elegant room chimed the hour. It was ten o'clock on Halloween. The Black and Orange Ball had officially begun.

"I have to receive my guests." Cece fluttered out the door.

"Ready?" Tinkie asked.

I really wasn't. "Let me use the lady's room. You go ahead. Oscar is waiting for you."

Tinkie was far too smart for me, but she was also compassionate. "You'll come down, won't you?"

"I promise. I just don't want to walk in right this minute. There's always such a procession." And I had expected to do this as Graf's bride.

"I know. The high-society ladies like to be seen." She kissed my cheek. "If you aren't down in half an hour, I'm going to drag you, and I promise I will make a huge scene."

"I wouldn't disappoint my friends. I just need a moment to gather myself."

"Thirty minutes." She walked out the door, her gown trailing behind her.

Sweetie gave a low moan, and I went to the bed and stroked her silky ears. Pluto rubbed against me, and I gave him the black portion of my gown to hide any kitty hairs he might leave behind. "We'll be okay," I promised them. "It's hard, but we can survive."

Sweetie licked my hand, her eyes sadder than I could ever remember.

"Survival isn't an option. It's a command performance."

I recognized the voice from *National Velvet, Butterfield Eight, Cleopatra*, and a host of other movies. Liz Taylor stood in the center of the room. She looked as if she'd stepped off the 1958 film set of Tennessee Williams's wonderful play *Cat on a Hot Tin Roof*. Except she wore black.

She was in mourning. Another widow.

"You can give it a rest," I told her. "Graf isn't dead, but he might as well be. He's just as gone."

"I'm dead, and I'm not gone."

She had a point. "Why did I have to go through all of this? I could have walked away from Graf back in the beginning. I could have spared myself all of this pain. What's the point of loving someone only to lose them?"

Liz's beautiful violet eyes shone with tears. "Widowed at twenty-six."

"And married eight times." I knew my scandal stats, but I also had deep compassion for the glamorous movie star. She'd loved—and lost— more than once, yet she'd never stopped trying. "Why is it so hard to love someone?"

"Love requires vulnerability. That's an uncomfortable place for most of us. We end up there, and then we begin to fight it."

"You make it sound so hopeless."

"Humans are complex." Her long eyelashes fluttered against her cheek. When she looked at me again, the sadness was palpable. "Never forget that he loves you, Sarah Booth. He does. But he can't hold on to you and himself at the same time. Not right now."

"He has a child." That hurt. I couldn't deny it. At last I'd admitted that I wanted a child with Graf. Now that we weren't together, it wouldn't happen. Yet he had a daughter.

"A child with another woman." Liz put it on the line. "Hard to forget that."

"I could love Katlyn. I told him I could, and I meant it."

"Yes, that's true." She turned her profile to me. "You have a generous heart. But there was a time when you couldn't open it for Graf."

"In the beginning—"

"Everything in life is timing, Sarah Booth. Whether it's a great movie role or a love affair. Seems to me you've had your share of crossroads where you picked one path over another. Just like me."

"That may be true, but it doesn't make this any easier."

"Everything ends. Even the most remarkable childhood." The first hint of Jitty began to peek through the Liz disguise. "A great heart can't stop loving."

I tried to pinpoint which play or film her line

was from, but I had to concede that it was strictly from Jitty's heart.

Liz morphed into my wonderful haint. "Now get your butt down to that party. There's a surprise waitin' for you if you'd only be smart enough to enjoy it."

"But—"

It was too late. Jitty disappeared just as the door of the hotel room opened. A tall, handsome man stood in the doorway, his blond hair cut to perfection. There was something familiar about him. And then I saw his electric-blue eyes. He hadn't touched me, but the riff of a blues tune raced up my spine.

"Sarah Booth, Tinkie said I would find you here."

"Scott?" I couldn't believe it. Scott Hampton was a phenomenal blues musician and a man I'd fallen hard for—and walked away from—in my past. "What are you doing here?"

"Playing the ball. Cece hired me."

"How did she find you? Last I heard, you were touring in Europe."

His grin reminded me of all the reasons I'd fallen for him. "I bought that blues club in Zinnia. Playin' the Bones. I'm tired of the road. Tired of living like a nomad. That time we spent together was the closest to feeling at home I've ever come. I figured I'd give Sunflower County a chance, see if my roots would grow there."

He could have knocked me over with a feather. "I'm glad." And I was.

"Cece and Tinkie filled me in on the pirate's booty. You're building up quite the successful career as a private investigator."

And I was sure they'd filled him in on plenty of other things as well. "Yes, I've been busy."

He indicated the bottle of Jack Daniels beside the ice bucket. "Let me make you a drink, and then we should repair to the ballroom. Cece will skin me if I'm not there to perform on time. And you too. They sent me to fetch you."

Bless their little hearts.

Sweetie saved me from responding. She went to Scott and licked his hand. She remembered him. Even Pluto checked him out and gave him a pass. Chablis slept on. Her reunion with Sweetie and Pluto had exhausted her.

Scott made a stiff Jack on the rocks for each of us. "To good times in Sunflower County."

We clinked glasses, and I drank. The burn went all the way to my toes.

"Now let's show these New Orleanians how to party." He offered his arm.

Together, we left the hotel room and arrived at the ball. My friends crowded close, and Scott left us to set up for his performance.

I looked at Cece, Harold, Millie, Tinkie, Doc, Madame Tomeeka, and Oscar. My friends clustered around me, protective and loving. My heart was broken, but I wasn't going to die. That much was clear. I would survive, as Jitty had pointed out. And maybe, sometime in the future, I would love again.

Center Point Large Print
600 Brooks Road / PO Box 1
Thorndike ME 04986-0001 USA

(207) 568-3717

US & Canada:
1 800 929-9108
www.centerpointlargeprint.com